VICTORIAN RELIGIOUS DISCOURSE

VICTORIAN RELIGIOUS DISCOURSE
NEW DIRECTIONS IN CRITICISM

Edited By

Jude V. Nixon

VICTORIAN RELIGIOUS DISCOURSE
© Jude V. Nixon, 2004

First published 2004 by
PALGRAVE MACMILLAN™
175 Fifth Avenue, New York, N.Y. 10010 and
Houndmills, Basingstoke, Hampshire, England RG21 6XS
Companies and representatives throughout the world

PALGRAVE MACMILLAN is the global academic imprint of the Palgrave Macmillan division of St. Martin's Press, LLC and of Palgrave Macmillan Ltd. Macmillan® is a registered trademark in the United States, United Kingdom and other countries. Palgrave is a registered trademark in the European Union and other countries.

ISBN 1–4039–6522–6 hardback

Library of Congress Cataloging-in-Publication Data
    Victorian religious discourse : new directions in criticism / edited by Jude V. Nixon.
       p. cm.
    Includes bibliographical references and index.
    ISBN 1–4039–6522–6 (alk. paper)
    1. English literature—19th century—History and criticism. 2. Christianity and literature—Great Britain—History—19th century. 3. Religion and literature—Great Britain—History—19th century. 4. Christian literature, English—History and criticism. 5. Religious literature, English—History and criticism. I. Nixon, Jude V., 1953–

PR468.R44.V53 2004
820.9'3823—dc22   2004040007

A catalogue record for this book is available from the British Library.

Design by Newgen Imaging Systems (P) Ltd., Chennai, India.

First edition: August 2004
10 9 8 7 6 5 4 3 2 1

Printed in the United States of America.

For Jennifer

CONTENTS

Contributors   ix
Acknowledgments   xi

Framing Victorian Religious Discourse: An Introduction   1
   Jude V. Nixon

PART I
THE HIGHER-CRITICAL DEBATE

1 The Victorian Radicals: Time, Typology, and Ontology in
    Hopkins, Pusey, and Müller   27
    Jerome Bump

2 "Kill[ing] Our Souls with Literalism": Reading *Essays
    and Reviews*   51
    Jude V. Nixon

3 *Skeptical Women v. Honest Men v. Good Old Boys*: Gender
    Conflict in the High Victorian Religion Wars   83
    Janet L. Larson

4 "Decomposing" Texts: Browning's Poetics and
    Higher-Critical Parody   117
    Suzanne Bailey

5 "Our King Back, Oh, Upon English Souls!": Swinburne,
    Hopkins, and the Politics of Religion   131
    Renée V. Overholser

PART II
RELIGION AND THE AESTHETIC IMAGINATION

6 Hearing Adventure: Giuseppe Caponsacchi,
    Browning's "Hollow Rock"   157
    Joseph A. Dupras

7 Faith, Romance, and Imagination: Newman the Storyteller   175
    Bernadette Waterman Ward

8   A "Thousand Solaces" for the Modern Spirit: Walter Pater's
    Religious Discourse   189
    Lesley Higgins

9   "Amen in a Wrong Place": Charles Dickens Imagines the
    Victorian Church   205
    Natalie Bell Cole

10 "Poetry is Where God is": The Importance of Christian Faith
    and Theology in Elizabeth Barrett Browning's
    Life and Work   235
    Alexandra M. B. Wörn

References   253
Index   273

CONTRIBUTORS

SUZANNE BAILEY teaches in the Department of English Literature at Trent University, Ontario, Canada. She has published in *Victorian Poetry, Women's Writing, Victorian Studies, Canadian Literature*, and other journals.

JEROME BUMP is Professor of English at the University of Texas at Austin, where he has taught since 1970. He has held fellowships from the National Endowment for the Humanities and the Woodrow Wilson foundation. Professor Bump is the author of *Gerard Manley Hopkins* (1982) and fifty articles and chapters, primarily on Victorian literature. He edited *Gerard Manley Hopkins: A Centenary Celebration* (1989) and *Texas Studies in Language and Literature* (1986–92), and serves on the advisory boards of *Victorian Poetry* and *The Hopkins Quarterly*.

NATALIE BELL COLE is Associate Professor of English at Oakland University. She is the author of articles on George Meredith, Charles Dickens, and Nathaniel Hawthorne.

JOSEPH A. DUPRAS is Professor of English at the University of Alaska Fairbanks, where he has taught for twenty-five years. His specialty is nineteenth-century British literature, and he has published in various journals, including *Victorian Poetry, Papers on Language and Literature*, and *Victorian Literature and Culture*. He is currently working on a book on Robert Browning's audiovisual poetics.

LESLEY HIGGINS is Associate Professor of English at York University, Ontario, Canada. She is the author of *The Modernist Cult of Ugliness: Aesthetic and Gender Politics* (2000) and coeditor of *Walter Pater: Transparencies of Desire* (2002). Her essays can be found in *Victorian Poetry, Victorian Studies, Southern Review, Rethinking Marxism, English Literature in Transition*, and *Journal of Pre-Raphaelite Studies*. Professor Higgins is currently completing an edition of Gerard Manley Hopkins's Oxford essays and notebooks.

JANET LARSON is Associate Professor of English and Director of the English Graduate Program at Rutgers University in Newark, New Jersey. She is the author of *Dickens and the Broken Scripture* (1985) and numerous articles on topics in Victorian religion and literature, nineteenth- and twentieth-century women writers, film, and drama. Her book in progress, *The Victorian Woman's Bible: Interpretation and Cultural Discourse in Anglo-American Women's Letters*, examines junctures of social and scriptural interpretation in a spectrum of women's texts and places these practices into histories of ideas, biblical hermeneutics, various nineteenth-century discourses, and movements for reform. Before coming to Rutgers, she worked as a writer and associate editor for *The Christian Century*.

JUDE V. NIXON is Professor of English at Oakland University, and director of The Honors College. The author of *Gerard Manley Hopkins and His Contemporaries: Liddon, Newman, Darwin, and Pater* (1994) and numerous book chapters, Professor Nixon has published in journals such as *Renascence*, *The Hopkins Quarterly*, *Carlyle Studies Annual*, *Modern Philology*, *Victorian Poetry*, *Victorian Studies*, *Dickens Studies Annual*, *Modern Philology*, *Nineteenth-Century Literature*, and *Texas Studies in Literature and Language*. He is currently at work on *Race and the Victorians: Representing Blackness*. Professor Nixon serves on the editorial boards of *Victorian Poetry* and *The Hopkins Quarterly*.

RENÉE V. OVERHOLSER is Adjunct Assistant Professor of English at Hunter College, City University of New York. She has published on Hopkins, Swinburne, and Anna Jameson, and is currently working on a study of the Victorian discourse of miracles as part of her focus on Victorian religion.

BERNADETTE WATERMAN WARD is Associate Professor of English at the University of Dallas. The author of *World as Word: Philosophical Theology in Gerard Manley Hopkins* (2002) and many shorter works on Victorian writers, she has presented lectures yearly for the Venerable John Henry Newman Association since 1996, as well as lecturing on Newman at Notre Dame and the Pittsburgh Oratory. Professor Ward is a member of the Association of Literary Scholars and Critics. Her current work in progress is on Scotist aesthetics and the question of suffering in Hopkins.

ALEXANDRA M. B. WÖRN is currently finishing a doctorate in the Faculty of Divinity, University of Cambridge, on Elizabeth Barrett Browning's faith and theology. She studied English Literature and Theology at the University of Tübingen in Germany and holds an M.Phil. in Divinity (2000) from the University of Cambridge. In 2001 she cofounded and organized the Inter-Disciplinary Seminar in the Faculty of Divinity at Cambridge for the encouragement of interdisciplinary dialogue between theology and other disciplines.

ACKNOWLEDGMENTS

A collection of essays owes much to those colleagues whose work comprises the volume. To them I owe an immense debt of gratitude. I am also grateful to Oakland University, to my colleagues in the Department of English, especially Natalie Cole, Brian Connery, and Mary Papasian, to my staff in The Honors College, Brian Murphy, Karen Conn, and Dawn Deitsch, Kresge Library at Oakland University, especially the staff in the inter-library loan office, and the staff at the University of Michigan libraries. I wish to thank other colleagues, among them Donald Rackin, David DeLaura, George Tennyson, Janet Larson, Dennis Taylor, Mariaconcetta Constantini, Stéphanie Bérard, and Marjorie Stone, and friends who routinely inquire about my undertakings and thus provide quiet support, among them Kathy Hayes, Carol Kaiser, and Bryna Frank. I wish to thank the staff at Palgrave, especially Farideh Koohi-Kamali and Melissa Nosal. As always, my great source of support has come from relatives, especially my mother Berna and uncles Hayes and Byron, and family, Jackie, Jason, Jeremy, and my wife Jennifer, to whom the book is dedicated.

Earlier versions of Jude V. Nixon's "Framing Victorian Religious Discourse: An Introduction," Jerome Bump's essay "The Victorian Radicals: Time and Multivalence in Hopkins, Pusey, and Müller," Jude V. Nixon's " 'Kill[ing] Our Souls with Literalism': Reading *Essays and Reviews*," Suzanne Bailey's " 'Decomposing Texts': Browning's Poetics and Higher Critical Parody," Renée V. Overholser's " 'Our King Back, Oh, upon English Souls': Swinburne, Hopkins, and the Politics of Religion," and Joseph A. Dupras's "Hearing Adventure: Giuseppe Caponsacchi, Browning's 'Hollow Rock' " appeared in a special double issue of the journal *Religion and the Arts* 5.1–2 (2001). Permission to reuse material from these essays had been granted by the editor of Brill Academic Publishers. A version of Lesley Higgins's essay, "A 'Thousand Solaces' for the Modern Spirit: Walter Pater's Religious Discourse," appeared in an earlier form in the journal *English Literature in Transition* 38.3 (1995): 285–303. Permission to reuse material from that essay has been granted by the editor of *ELT*.

FRAMING VICTORIAN RELIGIOUS DISCOURSE: AN INTRODUCTION

Jude V. Nixon

Religion and religious discourse contributed meaningfully to the formation and definition of British national identity in the nineteenth century. "The center of Victorian discourse, in which all questions were implicated and to which all road led, was religion."[1] Important to that ideology of Englishness was the cultivation of "Distrust, even hatred, of papist and the papacy," according to Richard Helmstadter. "In the nineteenth-century, anti-Catholicism was closely bound up with the Irish question, as well as with the tendency of Protestant Britons of all political parties and all denominations to identify their anti-Catholic venom with a self-satisfied celebration of British liberty."[2] England's sense of itself—England's Englishness—involved the way religion, and especially Protestantism, factored into nationness. "Protestantism was," Linda Colley writes, "the foundation that made the invention of Great Britain possible," forging "an unquestioned equation," according to Gauri Viswanathan, "of Englishness with mainstream Anglicanism."[3] Not surprisingly, Colley commences her seminal study *Britons* with Protestantism, noticing that what cemented the nation was neither geography nor racial identity but religion, essentially Protestantism: "it was this shared religious allegiance...that permitted a sense of British national identity. ...English Francophobia," for example, had much to do with the sense that France was a Catholic country.[4] According to Frank Turner,

> Anglican culture first and foremost rested upon a religious definition of cultural identification and political outlook. From the Restoration through the battles over Catholic Emancipation and after, spokesmen for the Anglican monopoly had defined their character and that of the political and social culture that they defended in terms of the dual opposition to Roman Catholics and Protestant Nonconformists. Roman Catholicism was identified with tyranny, potential domination by a foreign prince, superstition, idolatry, and Ireland.[5]

Much of the literature of the nineteenth century reflects "this play of Protestant against Roman Catholic."[6] Englishness simply constituted Anglicanism. Thus, when Jane Eyre was considered an interloper, as someone estranged from an essentialized English family, she had to be troped as something entirely Other; and but for a racialized outsider, such as Eliot's gypsy or Thackeray's Sambo, what better assignation than Catholic, an "infantine Guy Fawkes."[7] Englishness comprises a particular kind of character (istics) and characters. British national identity, like Victorian discourse, is constituted through exclusion, enacted largely around religion.

Because a sense of Englishness meant familiarity with a canon, a set of particular English religious texts, those outside the fold are naturally drawn to heretical or heterodoxical texts; for female prodigals, this also includes a preference for biblical texts thought to be unsuited for their gender. Jane Eyre is vilified by Reverend Brocklehurst for her canonical preferences—her fondness of the Revelation, Daniel, Genesis, Samuel, parts of Exodus, the Kings, Chronicles, Job, and Jonah—and for her aversion to the Psalms, which she finds "not interesting" (*JE*, 26–28). The goal of organized religion, as in putting down social upheavals and all threats to the patriarchal management at Lowood, likened to quelling "the Babel clamour of tongues" (*JE*, 39), was to secure the status of women as social subalterns. This means recommending for Jane a " 'Child's Guide' . . . containing 'an account of the awfully sudden death of Martha G—, a naughty child addicted to falsehood and deceit' " (*JE*, 30). Clearly, Jane's canonical preference, in the words of Dorothy Mermin, was a way to "wrench Christianity out of its male-centeredness."[8] In *The Mill on the Floss* (1860), Maggie Tulliver, similarly, frequents religious texts considered by men morally unbecoming for women, especially prepubescent girls: Defoe's *The History of the Devil* and Jeremy Taylor's *Holy Living and Dying*. To "vindicate the variety of her reading" and to convince her male detractors that she is interested in "prettier books," books that make her appear less of a witch, Maggie cites her familiarity with the Protestant classic, Bunyan's *The Pilgrim's Progress*, which, as only the precocious Maggie would have observed, also contains "a great deal about the devil."[9] In fact, it was this interpretive privilege sponsored and endorsed by *Essays and Reviews* that allowed for different discursive readings of the Bible, including opportunities for women to read the same text more broadly and completely and from a female, if not feminist, perspective. Eliot's other heroine, Dorothea Brooke, as A. D. Nuttall observers, "reads Protestant Jeremy Taylor far into the night, and Anglican Richard Hooker also figures in her misguided girlish dreams of an ideal husband," and "at the same time she reads Catholic Pascal." Dorothea, he concludes, "is a personality stretched, in a rich awareness, between Protestant and Catholic worlds."[10]

The Pilgrim's Progress, and especially the episode of the battle between the devil (a representation of Dante's Charon) and Christian, also features centrally in Maggie Tulliver's early religious education. The subsequent Tulliver estate sale, viewed from the loss of *The Pilgrim's Progress*, was for Maggie lamentable, something resembling a kind of familial death: "everything is going away from us—the end of our lives will have nothing in it like the beginning!" (*MF*, 197). Eliot, we know, was fascinated by the prophetic tradition, especially by the early Patricians and Scholastics. *The Mill on the*

Floss contains numerous references and allusions to the Great Deluge and Jonah, and Maggie is extremely familiar with the Bunyan text and attracted to sages and poets:

> If she had been taught "real learning and wisdom, such as men knew," she thought she should have held the secrets of life; if she had only books, that she might learn for herself what wise men knew! Saints and martyrs had never interested Maggie so much as sages and poets. She knew little of saints and martyrs, and had gathered, as general result of her teaching, that they were a temporary provision against the spread of Catholicism, and had all died at Smithfield. (*MF*, 234)

Later in the novel when she experiences a crisis of faith, Maggie promptly laid aside Virgil, Euclid, and Aldrich, all "wrinkled fruit of the tree of knowledge," and took up the Bible, Thomas à Kempis's *Imitation of Christ*, and John Keble's *The Christian Year*, which "filled her mind with a continual stream of rhythmic memories" and taught her "to see all nature and life in the light of her new faith" (*MF*, 239). In *Great Expectations* (1860), Pip's return to the marshes, getting lost along the way,[11] is troped as an infernal journey meant to analogize "Christian's pilgrimage through the Valley of the Shadow of Death" where Pip would later encounter the Apollyon, Orlick. "The reliance on recollections of *The Pilgrim's Progress* and the recognition of Orlick as performing the part of Apollyon in this scene," say F. R. Leavis and Q. D. Leavis, "are so obvious when one sees it so that one wonders that this is not a commonplace." To stage Pip's resolve during the trial scene and after Magwitch's death, Dickens returned to *The Pilgrim's Progress* and the trial of Faithful with Christian in attendance.[12]

Victorian religious discourse, then, locates England's sense of itself tied inextricably to masculinity, race, and imperialism.[13] In *The Making of Victorian England*, Kitson Clark claims that in "no other century," save perhaps the twelfth and seventeenth, "did the claims of religion occupy so large a part in the nation's life."[14] More recently, Cynthia Scheinberg has argued that the "engagement with religion has been seen as a central organizing principle for constructing a canon of male English Christian writers."[15] There is clearly a religious sensibility at work in the literature and culture of the nineteenth century, which necessitates critical consideration. The seriousness, deliberateness, and purpose accorded Victorian science, Turner believes, ought to be directed to Victorian religion, especially its relationship to Victorian secular society. Turner is particularly attentive to the problematics of the nineteenth-century crisis of faith, which superseded intellectual and/or theological factors. "Victorian faith entered crisis not in the midst of any attack on religion but rather during the period of the most fervent religious crusade that the British nation had known…indeed during the last great effort on the part of all denominations to Christianize Britain."[16]

Without some acquaintance, then, with nineteenth-century religion and religious discourse, much of Tennyson, Browning, Arnold, the Rossettis,

Hopkins, and Swinburne remains inaccessible; so too the essayists (Carlyle, Newman, Ruskin, Arnold, and Pater) and novelists, especially the Brontës, Elizabeth Gaskell, and George Eliot, whose entire corpus interacts meaningfully with nineteenth-century religion and religious discourse. Victorian autobiography, the genre of the crisis of faith, and arguably the most representative nineteenth-century literary form, employs structurally plots of religious conversion modeled either after Augustine (Hopkins's "lingering-out sweet skill") or Paul (Hopkins's "át ónce, as once at a crash").[17] In other words, the Victorian *bildungsroman* is structured around a conversion plot— "God's active transformation of the passive Christian. ...Transformation into the perfect unity of God turns into the development of one's unique self."[18] Dickens's wonderful opening to *David Copperfield*, "I Am Born," discloses his subtle workings with the Genesis narrative of beginnings: "To begin my life with the beginning of my life."[19] Here as elsewhere in Dickens can be seen a veiled use of biblical allusions, at times for satiric purposes, evidence of a tentativeness toward evangelical Christianity. Just why and how religion and religious discourse matters to Dickens has remained largely elusive, especially for someone who did not ardently embrace Christianity yet whose *Life of Our Lord* (1848), as Zemka has observed, not only participates in "the larger cultural trend of the period" but also "testifies to the strength of the author's belief in the religiosity of childhood."[20] And what if any influence Dickens's *David Copperfield* (1850) had on Holman Hunt's *The Light of the World* (1854) and it on Dickens's own *Little Dorrit* (1855–57) remains intriguing. John Stuart Mill's acknowledged skepticism, Ruskin's systematic rejection of his formative evangelicalism ("From John Bunyan and Isaac Ambrose, I had received the religion by which I still myself lived, as far as I had spiritual life at all"), Newman's religious war with the so-called liberals and subsequent spiritual rebirth, Carlyle's wrestle with the specter of unbelief, Swinburne's religio-politics, and Pater's religious aestheticism all cannot be appreciated unless viewed within the compass of institutional Christianity and its authenticating texts.[21]

The role of George Eliot in lending shape and definition to all that constitutes religious discourse in the nineteenth century cannot be overestimated. Strauss's and Feuerbach's Higher Criticism exerted a powerful influence on her fiction, especially on the legendary and apocalyptic *Romola* (1863) and *Middlemarch* (1872). Additionally, her novels reflect the belief that inherent in this life is the belief that all humans suffer, and some remarkable ones suffer for the sins of others (a belief Dickens shared), dramatize the emerging evangelicalism on England's provincial stage, and biblical or religious chapter titles structure her texts, as *The Mill on the Floss* (1860): "The Valley of Humiliation" (Bunyan's *Pilgrim's Progress*), "Wheat and Tares" (Matthew 13), and "The Great Temptation" (Milton's *Paradise Lost*). Thomas à Kempis's *The Imitation of Christ* becomes for a disillusioned Maggie an ascetic or pietistic model of spirituality, both Maggie and Dorothea are made to undergo the same spiritual pilgrimage Bunyan's Christian experienced, and the apocalyptic flood imagery informs *Romola* and *The Mill on the Floss*. In the Tulliver household, the Bible, a reject from the estate sale, still occupies a critical place, albeit an archival one, a repository of the family's history containing a disastrous fall and an unforgiving spirit; religion fails to play an active or meaningful role in the Tullivers' daily life, a life marked by "no active, self-renouncing faith," "little trace of religion," and "still less of a distinctly Christian creed" (*MF*, 214, 219–22). In an intriguing study, *George Eliot and the Landscape of Time*, Mary Wilson Carpenter believes that understanding "traditionally Protestant interpretation of Biblical prophecy" helps us "to better understand George Eliot's 'creation' as a historian." Reading *Adam Bede* (1859) in accord with the Anglican lectionary, and *The Mill on the Floss* as apocalyptic history, Carpenter explores Eliot's formative education in the "School of the Prophets," her interest, that is, in biblical prophecy, especially the millenarian view of prophecy as continuous—"an inspired map of time"—that "reached new heights of scholarly development, as well as popular interest, during the Victorian era."[22]

Adam Bede, Eliot's highly religious, dissenter novel, opens with Thomas Carlyle's religion of work, followed by Dinah Morris's Sermon on the Mount, and ends with an upper-room discourse and last supper between Adam, the Man of Sorrows, and Bartle Massey. The novel attempts to marry Anglicanism with a culturally progressive Methodism, a political alliance crucial to an emergent middle class. The third chapter of *Adam Bede*, "After the Preaching," concerns English domesticity and the family. Eliot's coquettish vixen and autoerotic, the lovely material girl Hetty Sorrel, "a perfect Hebe," cared little for "what was meant by the pictures in the Pilgrim's Progress, or in the old folio Bible," "[r]eligious doctrines had taken no hold on Hetty's mind," and she had "never appropriated a single Christian idea or Christian feeling."[23] Conversely, Eliot's exemplar of English industry, provincialism, and manfulness, the eponymous Adam Bede "knew no better lyrics than he could find in the Old and New Version and an occasional hymn," and "had read his Bible, including the apocryphal books, *Poor Richard's Almanac*, Taylor's *Holy Living and Dying*, *The Pilgrim's Progress*, with Bunyan's *Life and Holy War*," books neglected by the mainstream religious establishment against which the novel writes (*AB*, 211–12). The respectable Reverend Irwine, representative of the secular Established Church and model for Eliot of a different kind of spirituality (established order as opposed to evangelical sloppiness), was attracted to the paganism of Sophocles, Theocritus, and Aeschylus, the "savouriness" of which was "quite absent from any text in Isaiah or Amos": "Mr Irwine's recollections of young enthusiasm and ambition were all associated with poetry and ethics that lay aloof from the Bible" (*AB*, 69).

Charlotte Brontë's *Shirley* (1849), considered by Ruth Y. Jenkins a "revisionist feminist parable" and the "fullest articulation" of a "woman's search for her place in a patriarchal culture,"[24] deals profoundly with many of the prevailing questions of nineteenth-century religion, even anticipating the (gender) bias readers bring to biblical interpretation. As Gianni Vattimo has recently observed, "Beginning with St Augustine and his reflections on the Trinity, Christian theology is in its deepest foundations a hermeneutic theology: the interpretive structure, transmission, mediation and, perhaps, the fallenness do not concern only the enunciation, the communication of God with man; they characterize the intimate life of God itself, which therefore cannot be conceived in terms of an immutable metaphysical plenitude."[25] In the novel, Caroline Helstone observes:

> ...if I could read the original Greek, I should find that many of the words have been wrongly translated, perhaps misapprehended altogether. It would be possible, I doubt not, with a little ingenuity, to give the passage quite a contrary turn: to make it say, "Let the woman speak out whenever she sees fit to make an objection";—"it is permitted to a woman to teach and to exercise authority as much as may be. Man, meantime, cannot do better than hold his peace," and so on. (*Shirley*, 323)

Like Caroline Helstone, George Eliot's provincial Lisbeth Bede challenges patriarchal readings of the Bible and calls into question the whole matter of multiple readings of the Bible and perhaps also what has been included and excluded in the formation of the canon. As far as Lisbeth is concerned, "Take no thought for the morrow" could well be applied to Seth's indolence and irresponsibility, causing his brother Adam to assume the bulk of the family duties: "Why, as Adam has to take thought for thee." Lisbeth rejects any reading that restricts the passage to the mere sense that it means "we shouldn't be over-anxious and worreting ourselves about what'll happen tomorrow":

> Ay, ay, that's the way wi' thee: thee allays makes a peck o' thy own words out o' a pint [point] o' the Bible's. I donna see how thee't to know as "take no thought for morrow" means all that. An' when the Bible's such a big book, an' thee canst read all thro't, an' ha' the pick o' the texes, I canna think why thee dostna pick better words as donna mean so much more nor they say. (*AB*, 46)

Employing a clerical plot and making full use of the range of biblical parables, *Shirley* is decidedly religious. It features such chapter titles as "Levitical," "Noah and Moses," "Valley of the Shadow of Death," "Phoebe," and "Case of Domestic Persecution." "Brontë's grafting of Christian imagery onto her secular narrative," says Jenkins, "signals the larger, Christian context in which *Shirley* must be read."[26] Indeed, the Victorian novel, Valentine Cunningham has observed, is a novel about Dissenters, about separating oneself from the trait group to form new groups.[27] In *Darwin's Cathedral: Evolution, Religion, and the Nature of Society*, David Sloan Wilson studies religious group identity in relationship to Darwinian thought, a factor crucial to the development of the nineteenth-century novel, which evolved in consort with the emerging Darwinian science.[28] That the nineteenth century manifested arguably the most volatile restructuring of religious groups and formation of new ones, all concurrent with the rise of evolutionary biology and the configuration of new scientific subdisciplines, is hardly coincidental, something Wilson's groundbreaking study only begins to explore. Victorian religious discourse cuts across the entire spectra of mainstream nineteenth-century literature and culture, whether by tacit reference or total engagement. It could be argued that central as it is to the literature, religious discourse in effect legitimized Victorian literature.

The ubiquitous Bible and other standard Protestant apocryphal texts pervade the fictional Victorian home. "In seeking to understand the ahistorical approach to Victorian culture," says Turner, "it is also important not to underestimate the impact made on later generations by the large, well-bound sets of collected works of major Victorian writers."[29] So formative is a particular religious tradition to English identity that Aurora Leigh's patrimonial Englishness, forcing her "to speak his tongue," constitutes familiarity with "the collects and the catechism, / The creeds, from Athanasius back to Nice, / The Articles." But to intimate how outdated, in part because they elide the woman question and exclude women from the dominant discourse, Barrett Browning through Aurora considers these supposedly progressive doctrinal positionings "Tracts *against* the times."[30] Catherine Earnshaw's library of "antique volumes" (in *Wuthering Heights*) includes a Testament and the printed sermons of the Reverend Jabes Branderham, redactions of Old and New Testament passages, works whose antiquarian effects are of a piece with the wuthering trope in the novel. To Emily Brontë, daughter of an Anglo-English clergyman, institutional religion remains haunting and sepulchral.[31] And as in her sister's novel, *Shirley*, "[t]he Church does not fare well."[32]

In *Olive* (1850), Dinah Craik's clergyman, the secular Harold Gwynne, has a copy of Newton's Sermons covered in dust, and a "large unopened packet—marked 'Religious Society's Tracts'" served as prop for his telescope, testament to Harold's curiosity for science and neglect of his clerical commitment. Relegated to the anachronistic, religion succumbs to a kind of antiquarianism when it, like Edward Casaubon's conservationist and mummified *Key to All Mythologies*, refuses to engage emerging seminal questions.[33] Harold Rothesay's Bible, retired to "the farther shelf" of his library, lacks pride of place, spatially displaced by texts of "all [heterodoxical] faiths," all "variations of sects." Harold Gwynne's secularism, with sermons modeled after Locke or Bacon, "more suited to the professor's chair than the pulpit," along with his peculiar Sunday strictures on his daughter, so concerned his mother that Mrs. Gwynne felt they might imperil Ailie's juvenile faith. She therefore intervened, taking precaution that Ailie "keeps Sunday properly and reverently" by removing "her playthings and her baby-books" and teaching her "a few of Dr. Watts's moral hymns."[34] And so too the young Ruskin, whose evangelical mother ensured that his regular diet of Sunday reading avoided most everything but *Robinson Crusoe, The Pilgrim's Progress, Holy War,* and *Foxe's Book of Martyrs.* Similarly, Gabriel Oak's library (in *Far From the Madding Crowd*) contains copies of *Paradise Lost* and *The Pilgrim's Progress*, which, along with *Foxe's Book of Martyrs*, David

Hempton sees as "Britain's most widely circulating works of popular piety."[35] Hardy's pious evangelical and provincial voice, Joseph Poorgrass recalled that it was an infirmity that caused him to take up *The Pilgrim's Progress:* " 'Twas a bad leg allowed me to read the *Pilgrim's Progress.*"[36] The strictly evangelical, instead of habituating themselves on Sundays with "light reading and secular entertainment," often took up *Pilgrim's Progress* and *Paradise Lost.*[37]

Much earlier than Hardy and other Victorian half-believers, Caroline Bowles Southey (1786–1854), wife to the Poet Laureate, had her poetic persona in her verse autobiography *The Birth-day* (1836) recall how central, foundational, and vital orthodox religion was to that English family. On the "old walnut-tree bureau" in the library of her character Ephraim were books belonging to his intellectually acquisitive wife Priscilla, which on her death were bequeath to the child visitor/poet:

> The Holy Bible, cased in green shaloon,
> And Book of Common Prayer (a fine black type)
> Were laid conspicuous on the central spot,
> As first in honour: flanked on either side
> By Taylor's Golden Grove, The Pilgrim's Progress,
> And Fox's Book of Martyrs. How I loved
> To ransack those old tawny, well-thumbed leaves,
> Supplying my fill of horrors! Sermons too— . . .
> And fifth other rarities and treasures. (2768–851)[38]

The prevalence of seminal Christian religious texts constituting the fabric, if not plot, of Victorian literature—the novel no exception—underscores the centrality of religion to the dominant ideology. In arguing the importance of poetry to Victorian religious discourse, especially the contributions of women, Scheinberg underestimates the profound though subtle ways the nineteenth-century novel informs the prevailing religious discourse. Scheinberg insists that "the novel has never claimed the deep relationship to religion that poetry has in the English literary tradition."[39] While poetry might well be the site where institutional religion is contested, the nineteenth-century novel, including, and especially, the novels written by women, enacts the complex and shifting role of religion in Victorian culture. In fact, the novel is where religion is most problematically staged.

Indeed, religion was "an inextricable part of the cultural fabric" of the nineteenth century.[40] As Hillis Miller puts it, "God is, in one way or another, a starting place and presupposition,"[41] even for a religious skeptic, hedonist, and profligate as Arthur Huntington, in Anne Brontë's *The Tenant of Wildfell Hall* (1847), who "with a puritanical air of mock solemnity" holds "his prayerbook upside down, or open at any place but the right."[42] Any failure, therefore, to recognize religious typology or typological symbolism causes us to "under-read and misread many works" and "deprive many Victorian works of a large part of their context."[43] To Hardy's Jude Fawley, "the most real" of the Anglican divines were "the founders of the religious school called Tractarians," and especially "the well-known three, the enthusiast, the poet, and the formularist"—Newman, Keble, and Pusey, respectively—"whose teaching had influenced him even in his obscure home." In Jude's later agnosticism, they would become "Tractarian Shades": "I seem to see them, and almost hear them rustling. But I don't revere all of them as I did then. The theologian, the apologists and their kin the metaphysicians, the high-handed statesmen, and others, no longer interest me. All that has been spoilt for me by the grind of stern reality!" At Oxford, Jude caught sight of Newman and cited in detail passages from the *Apologia*. Hardy's Christminster is Tractarian Oxford "in whose history such men as Newman, Pusey, Ward, and Keble, loom so large." Jude's Artizan's Mutual Improvement Society at Aldbrickham comprises young men "of all creeds and denominations, including Churchmen, Congregationalists, Baptists, Unitarians, Positivists, and others."[44] Everywhere in Hardy, institutional religion is in decline, and its new fabric cannot replace the spontaneity and vitality of its old forms. A restorer of old religious edifices, Hardy stages this decline using architectural tropes:

> Above all, the original church, hump-backed, wood-turreted, and quaintly hipped, had been taken down, and either cracked up into heaps of road-metal in the lane, or utilized as pig-sty walls, garden seats, guard-stones to fences, and rockeries in the flower-beds of the neighbourhood. In place of it a tall new building of modern Gothic design, unfamiliar to English eyes, had been erected on a new piece of ground by a certain obliterator of historic records who had run down from London and back in a day. The site whereon so long had stood the ancient temple to the Christian divinities was not even recorded on the green and level grass-plot that had immemorially been the churchyard, the obliterated graves being commemorated by eighteenth-century cast-iron crosses warranted to last five years. (*Jude*, 16)

Yet another Hardy novel, *Far From the Madding Crowd* (1874), discourses meaningfully on religion. In fact, so important is religious discourse in Hardy that his use of the Bible and biblical names, as well as references to Dante's *Inferno*, is frequent and heavy-handed, even clumsy. Hardy's religion virtually assaults the reader. Hardy's heroine, Bathsheba, frequents the Old Testament book Ruth, and even plays the role of kinsman redeemer, a Boaz to Sergeant Troy as Ruth; and religious decay—"worn-out religious creed"—is everywhere in the novel. The new hymn sung by Garbriel's choir is Newman's "Lead, kindly Light," which revives spiritual feelings Bathsheba thought long "dead within her." Hardy even ridicules the "two religions going on in the nation now—High Church and High Chapel," the one in which "they pray singing, and worship all the colours of the rainbow," and the other in which "they pray preaching, and worship drab and whitewash only" (*FMC*, 114, 298, 173).[45]

Similarly, Mary (Mrs. Humphry) Ward's amiable clergyman, Robert Elsmere, routinely turns to Dante, Virgil, and Milton for spiritual sustenance

and to become intimate with his wife Catherine, the two of them "lost in love
and faith—Christ near them—Eternity, warm with God, enwrapping them."
Robert's Greek New Testament performs a similar relational function. But
this confidence is later tested when in his crisis of faith Robert begins to question the authenticity of the Bible. Even John Keble's otherwise reliable
Christian Year, given its broad spiritual appeal and popularity, provides assurance only to Catherine.[46] Protestant religious tomes, chiefly the Bible, the
Articles, the lectionary, *Tracts for the Times, The Pilgrim's Progress, The
Christian Year*, and *Holy Living and Dying*, are important intertextual sites in
Victorian literature, which alter the texts themselves. Lifted out of their host
context, reinscribed, and reinterpreted, these sacred texts perform a quite different role and are assigned a differential value. This is especially so in the
writings of Victorian women who employ the same religious discourse to
query, expand, revise, and/or reject the existing tradition, using the same discourse "in a very different fashion and even appropriating its cultural authority for feminist purposes"; for them, the "patriarchal domination of that
discourse does not amount to monolithic control."[47] "Through reading or
hearing others read Protestant publications like Bunyan and Foxe, through
studying the Bible, or listening to sermons, or leafing through the dog-eared
pages of almanacs and homily books," as Colley points out, "Protestant
Britons learnt that particular kinds of trials, at the hands of particular kinds of
enemies, were the necessary fate and the eventual salvation of a chosen people."[48] These tomes served to legitimize a people and authorize their ideology and practices, including the export of Christianity abroad, "the
translation of Evangelical faith into a dialect of international commercial capitalism."[49] Religion quite often found itself inextricably connected to capitalism, imperialism, and militarism. These "Victorian 'prophets' had begun to
identify the divine scheme with their own party politics," wherein "England
was specifically commissioned to carry Protestantism to the rest of the
world."[50] Consequently, "religious questions were necessarily political ones;
and political ones...were saturated with religious significance."[51] Through
its countless missionary societies, English religion went hand in hand with the
nation's industrial and imperial project, the two inextricable and seamless.
The goal was as much to get rich as it was to save souls. "The Bible Society
contributed to nineteenth-century imperial ideology by textualizing the
world as a Protestant and British totality. The histories that it produced were
books [chiefly poetry, the novel, and the essay] that tried to write an empire
inspired by, structured by, and composed of the Bible."[52] In the "double stratum or the double root" of the word "religion"—"*religio*, scrupulous attention, respect, patience, even modesty, shame or piety"; and "*religare*...linking
religion to the *link*, precisely, to obligation, ligament and hence to obligation,
to debt"—Jacques Derrida sees an "internal splitting...peculiar or 'proper'
to religion, appropriating religion for the 'proper' (inasmuch as it is also the
unscathed: *heilig*, holy, sacred, saved, immune and so on), appropriating religious indemnification to all forms of property, from the linguistic idiom in its
'letter,' to blood and soil, to the family and to the nation."[53]

Attempts to frame Victorian religious discourse must draw from the disparate ways religion, both as subject and practice, mattered in the nineteenth century. No single critical text, no poetics, really, formulates Victorian religious discourse. "A great critical need of our time," Dennis Taylor has observed, "is for ways of discussing religious or spiritual dimensions in works of literature," and especially, I might add, discussions that situate the religious not as something separate from but connected to an overall interpretation and understanding of the text. In other words, feminist, Marxist, and postcolonial approaches to Victorian literature—to instance but three—are incomplete exclusive of critical considerations of a religious, patriarchal economy. Absent this understanding, and it has largely been absent, "an important part of the literature we read goes untouched by our discourses," says Taylor. "There is a need in our time for religious interpretations that are substantial enough to enter into a productive and competitive relation with the reigning critical discourses."[54] The absence of a religious literary criticism leaves seismic interpretive gaps in literary works, of the kind Jonathan Culler notices. Missing in the critique of comparative literature, says Culler, is the place of religion, which "cries out for attention, not least because religion provides an ideological legitimation" so much more consequential than "the ideological positions comparatists do spend their time attacking." Seldom has anyone produced "even the mildest critique of religion," which Culler is convinced is the "proudest heritage of comparative literary studies," one threatened to be made defunct through critical neglect. What is especially missing and needed, says Culler, is a legitimate critique rather than a tacit acceptance of religion and religious discourse, "far more important than the popular question of whether deconstruction is politically progressive or regressive," and so should be "as much a subject of debate and critique as other ideological formations and discourses."[55]

> Now if, today, the "question of religion" actually appears in a new and different light, if there is an unprecedented resurgence, both global and planetary, of this ageless thing, then what is at stake is language, certainly—and more precisely the idiom, literality, writing, that forms the element of all revelation and of all belief, an element that ultimately is irreducible and untranslatable—but an idiom that above all is inseparable from the social nexus, from the political, familial, ethnic, communitarian nexus, from the nation and from the people: from autochthony, blood and soil, and from the ever more problematic relation to citizenship and to the state. In these times [as in all times, really], language and nation form the historical body of all religious passion.[56]

Terry Eagleton expresses the same view—the glaring absence of critical attention to religion—even more succinctly: "Religion has been for most of human history one of the most precious components of popular life, even though almost all theorists of popular culture embarrassedly ignore it."[57]

Indeed, many works of criticism have attended to the influence of the Bible and of religion in general on Victorian writers and texts, and an equal number has addressed sage discourse in Victorian literature. A valuable and much more recent addition has been studies examining the ways Victorian women writers enter only to rewrite and reauthorize the hegemonic patriarchal discourse, such as Lynda Palazzo's *Christina Rossetti's Feminist Theology* (2002). Palazzo's work undertakes an examination of Rossetti's writings, looking in particular at "the damage inflicted on women by a patriarchal religious system" and how Rossetti attempts "to reconstruct a feminist God-language, by using metaphors, preferably scriptural ones, with which to debate woman's relationship with God." Palazzo finds Rossetti "interpreting the Bible primarily, although not exclusively, for women," and "attempting to formulate a method of interpretation that is distinctly feminine . . . reading consciously for gender" and "developing a way of studying the scriptures which is available exclusively to women." The "historical roots of modern feminist approaches to the problem of gender in Christianity, and in particular of feminist christological inquiry," according to Palazzo, "lie in the nineteenth century."[58] Largely occluded from that discourse, but for George Eliot, who received " 'sage' status . . . largely on the basis of interpretations which reconcile her novels with the values of male-dominated tradition and ignore her female precursors," are the Victorian female preachers, according to Christine L. Krueger, in *The Reader's Repentance* (1992). "Eighteenth-century evangelicalism fostered the emergence of female orators and writers of remarkable authority," says Krueger, "whose legacy shaped social discourse throughout the Victorian period and enabled female novelists . . . to be recognized as social critics." Focusing specifically on Elizabeth Gaskell and George Eliot, Krueger's study examines the empowerment of women in the evangelical tradition and "reconsiders the history of women's social writing in terms of female preaching tradition" calling "on males to repent."[59]

J. Hillis Miller's well-worn *The Disappearance of God* (1963) studies five Victorians as "a set of people living without God in the world." Miller is convinced that the condition of a disappearing God, the sense that "God himself has slipped away from the place where he used to be," a "*Deus absconditus*, hidden somewhere behind the silence of infinite spaces," is a crisis so significant that it simply "must not be misunderstood."[60] In yet another important work, George Landow's *Victorian Types Victorian Shadows* (1980) observes the prevalence of biblical typology and typological structures in Victorian literature, arts, and culture. Drawing from John Holloway's *The Victorian Sage* (1953) and George P. Landow's *Elegant Jeremiahs* (1986), Thaïs E. Morgan's *Victorian Sages and Cultural Discourse* (1990) examines the Victorian sage and its gender relationships—"the power of gender and the gender of power"—the way, for example, "new historicism, reader reception, psychoanalysis, Marxism, semiotics, and deconstruction" can be applied to the mixture of genres that is discourse. "Because of the commanding position it held within the Victorian hierarchy of genres, sage writing provides an exemplary site for analyzing the strategies used by both women and men in the establishment and contestation of cultural power during the 1800s."[61]

Similarly, Ruth Y. Jenkins's *Reclaiming Myths of Power* (1995) examines "the conflict between four Victorian women [Florence Nightingale, Charlotte Brontë, Elizabeth Gaskell, and George Eliot] and their culture, their ethical beliefs, and the limited opportunities to enact their faith." Jenkins believes that the consort of "secular and spiritual ideologies—both exploiting women—limited women's access to power and, subsequently, the requisite authority necessary to evoke substantive change." By "omitting women writers (and consequently female experience) from this inquiry, and thereby assuming a singular perspective, scholars have misconstrued the full scope of Victorian spirituality." In so doing, they have failed to recognize that "many women's spiritual crises and their related writings attribute humanity's apparent falling away from God to a patriarchal appropriation of the sacred, forcing women to become Christian martyrs under androcentric hegemony." All four women, and many of their female contemporaries, "reappropriated the substance and the language of the Judeo-Christian narrative to authorize their subversion of patriarchal institutions."[62]

George Tennyson's *Victorian Devotional Poetry* (1981) traces the Tractarian heritage in nineteenth-century devotional poetry, and John Maynard's *Victorian Discourses on Sexuality and Religion* (1993) looks at the ways sexuality was negotiated by Victorians, specifically Clough, Kingsley, Patmore, and Hardy; "sexual discourse," Maynard concludes, is "anything but free from religious issues and traces."[63] Also negotiating religion and gender, *Masculinity and Spirituality in Victorian Culture* (2000), edited by Andrew Bradstock and others, examines "the complex interrelationship between religion and gender which existed in Victorian society." Social historians, they believe, have failed "to give sufficient weight to the influences of either traditional religion or less orthodox forms of spirituality on men's lives."[64] In *Word Crimes* (1998), Joss Marsh exposes blasphemy in Victorian literary satire, humor, and culture, and Gauri Viswanathan's *Outside the Fold* (1998) argues that conversion is central to Englishness: "With the departure of members from the fold, the cohesion of a community is under threat just as forcefully as if its beliefs had been turned into heresy." As Viswanathan sees it, in an increasingly secular and pluralistic society, England struggled to install minority religious groups into an ideal of nationhood: "Dissent, as much as assimilation, is the necessary disruptive mechanism for the exercise of tolerance by the state."[65] Anne Hogan's and Andrew Bradstock's *Women of Faith in Victorian Culture* (1998) investigates the complex cultic image of the domesticated Victorian Angel in the House, especially as that image becomes empowering or debilitating. Additionally, the collection looks at women's missionary activities, women hymn-writers, and the generally neglected obituaries of nonconformist women.[66] More singular in focus, Michael Wheeler's *Ruskin's God* (1999) pursues the impact of Christianity on Ruskin, whose "remarkable knowledge of the Bible," Wheeler finds, "equipped him with critical tools which...were now applied to religious art."[67] In an even more generic way, two early authorized texts, Northrop Frye's *Anatomy of Criticism* (1957) and Frank Kermode's *The Sense of an*

Ending (1966), explore the apocalyptic impulse and myth in literature, particularly relevant to Victorian literature, where, as Peter Lineham points out, "Popular apocalypticism" became "a very important factor in the social character of religion in the period."[68] Both Thaïs E. Morgan and Mary Wilson Carpenter pursue similar apocalyptic traces, especially as they relate to women.

The essays represented in this collection, vastly different as they are from each other, "a spectrum of variations within a single tradition" (Hillis Miller), find points of intersection as they address whole or in part issues dealing centrally with nineteenth-century religious forms of expression. In fact, their very difference reveals the protean ways religion was negotiated in the nineteenth century. The goal of this collection, then, is not to re-present Victorian religious discourse as singular but as varied, informing and informed by culture. But the volume does not pretend to tell the whole story, confining Victorian religious discourse largely to Christian and Jewish utterances and expressions, exclusive of other mythologies.[69] The Volume also ignores the occult in Victorian literature, which, as Gauri Viswanathan observed in the 2003 Modern Language Association conference, not only problematizes belief and unbelief but also demonstrated how colonialism erased only to reappropriate ancient religions. The slight exception to all of this is Nixon's treatment of *Essays and Reviews*, wherein three of its writers— Williams, Goodwin, and Jowett—insist on the centrality of non-Judaic textual and cultural considerations to any understanding of the biblical canon. There is, in other words, an inescapably racial dimension to religion in the construction of Empire, a point touched on in *Essays and Reviews* in Frederick Temple's evangelistic appeal for the education of the world, Roland William's demand that we raise the same degree of critical suspicion about the "Hebrew annals" as we do "Gentile histories," Baden Powell's celebration of aboriginal ingenuity, and Benjamin Jowett's endorsement of Buddhism as a legitimate and comparable religion. Still, readers especially interested in the impress of Judaism on Victorian literature and culture should consider Suzanne Bailey's treatment of Robert Browning's "Jochanan Hakkadosh" (1883), an example of Browning's Orientalism. The poem, says Bailey, is "notable for its foregrounding of the materiality of language through Browning's use of Hebrew script and supplementary notes, which both mimic the dialogism of Talmudic commentary yet bear an important relationship to the poem's concern with the nature of knowledge and the role of the scholar." Readers might also wish to turn elsewhere, to Cynthia Scheinberg's *Women's Poetry and Religion in Victorian England* (2002), which examines the way Jewish and Christian women employ "the discourse of the Judaic, Hebraic, and Jewishness in their poetry," including "the often implicit dialogue about Jewishness that pervades Victorian women's poets."[70] The turn to religious poetry, Scheinberg believes, authorized Victorian women poets. Generally ignored, then, is the Victorian fascination with the other (except with the other as Papist), its obsession, that is, with the exotic, non-Western and non-Judaic cultures, as in Edward

FitzGerald's *Rubáiyát of Omar Khayyám*. This topic would have been unavoidable in this collection had Max Müller undertaken for *Essays and Reviews* an exposé of Eastern religions. Nor is much attention paid here to sexuality on the borders, practiced by "the other Victorians" (Steven Marcus's term). Attitudes toward racial, religious, and sexual differences have common axes, and crisscross in particularly traceable trajectories—the "playing off of religion against sexuality."[71]

There is also a more complex aesthetic dimension to Victorian religious discourse not entirely explored in the collection, but for the quite limited ways Ward explores it in her study on Newman and Higgins in her essay on Pater. Little, for example, but for Bump's passing comments on the Pre-Raphaelites, is said on how Victorian religious discourse is represented in art, Pre-Raphaelite art, such as Hunt's *The Light of the World* (including Carlyle's critique of it), *The Shadow of Death*, *The Hireling Shepherd*, *The Scapegoat*, *Melchizedek, and The Finding of Christ in the Temple*, Millais's *The Vale of Rest*, Rossetti's *Ecce Ancilla Domini (The Annunciation)*, *The Girlhood of Mary*, and *Christ in the House of His Parents*, Seddon's *Jerusalem and the Valley of Jehosophat*, and Madox Brown's *Christ Washing Peter's Feet*. Pre-Raphaelites' typological symbolism acknowledges Ruskin as its foremost theorizer. In *William Holman Hunt and Typological Symbolism* (1979), George P. Landow shows how the Pre-Raphaelites employed typological symbolism, in which art is at once presentational, representational, and symbolic. Put differently, Pre-Raphaelite religious typology is both metaphoric and metonymic. As problematic is the extent to which Pre-Raphaelite art is religious, satiric, and/or social commentary. "Countless sermons, tracts, and hymns," according to Landow, "taught Victorian worshippers of all sects to read the Bible in search of types."[72] Also ignored in the volume, but for its brief treatment by Renée V. Overholser in the context of Hopkins's Marian poems, is the iconography of the Virgin Mary in Victorian literature, "too foreign and Catholic, as well as too wholly maternal, for most English to use."[73] Yet, images of Mary persist, "symbolically charged and highly visible in Victorian England,"[74] and especially the way the Victorian idealized woman was frequently troped as a Madonna or Pieta, often better off dead. One can observe this in Charlotte Brontë's *Shirley* (1849), Craik's *Olive* (1850), Gaskell's *Ruth* (1853), Browning's *The Ring and the Book* (1868–69), and Eliot's *Romola* and *The Mill on the Floss*. The Victorian idealized woman was frequently troped as a Madonna or Pieta, often better off dead.

Finally, I am using the term "discourse" as Hayden White understands it—as a way, that is, of speaking literally and tropically about a specific field and how through that discourse one comes to terms with the things constitutive of the entire cultural milieu. Discourse, says White, engages "problematical domains of experience" and functions as "a model of the metalogical operations by which consciousness, in general cultural praxis, effects such comings to terms with its milieux."[75] Any treatment, then, of the "relationship between religion and the arts" is bound to be a "promising area of study."[76] These essays, then, addressing the disparate ways religion informs nineteenth-century England, attempt to locate the religious discourse operative in Victorian literature, art, and culture, seek to make available new understandings of Victorian literature, and elucidate the extent to which religious discourse is vested in Victorian cultural thought and practice. But there is a sense too in which these essays are not only about Victorian religious discursive practice, but also about what Vattimo sees as "the robust presence in our popular culture of the return of the religious... motivated above all by the sense of impending global threats [need I invoke here the apocalyptic, the sense of an ending?] that appear quite new and without precedent in the history of humanity": "We therefore want to follow this trace of the trace, to take as constitutive for a renewed reflection on religion the very fact of its return, its re-presentation, its calling to us with a voice that we are sure we have heard before."[77]

The essays are evenly divided. Part I, "The Higher-Critical Debate," deals largely with historical, critical, and literary responses to nineteenth-century biblical higher criticism. Looking at Hopkins, Pusey, and Müller, Jerome Bump examines the "historical particulars" that "constituted meaning in Victorian England," locating them largely in "palimpsest," texts "written over," "the inscribed surface of events," as Michel Foucault might say. All the layers, "whether we are conscious of them or not," Bump insists, "contribute to our experience of reading Victorian religious discourse." In fact, the essays in the collection, whether dealing with Hopkins, Pusey, Browning, or Pater, focus on the idea of the palimpsest and polyvocality, texts and voices, multiple speaking selves. The history of ideas might well be about things written-over or things over-heard. According to Bump, "the Old Testament is not the only text of the ancient world 'over which' or 'against which' Christianity has been inscribed. To understand that reading experience we need, at times, to be a geologist of discourses." Jude V. Nixon offers a reading of the English higher-critical *magnus opus, Essays and Reviews*, an archive more disruptive to Victorian culture than its precursor *The Origin of Species* in that it fomented suspicion about authorship, authority, and canonicity that in turn contributed to a plethora of critical theories of reading. Higher Criticism is the precursor to deconstruction and any number of post-critical textual approaches.

Going beyond received histories of "the Victorian Church" as well as "current masculinity studies," Janet L. Larson examines the "wider discursive battleground of popular biblical and theological debate as a displaced arena of conflict between the sexes and over gender in the writing of women as well as men" at times "breaking into open hostilities, more often carried on unconsciously or in code...Besides fending off such threats as the Darwinian view of 'man' (*The Origin of Species*, 1859)," Larson argues, "the Essayists' manly self-idealizations registered anxieties about new challenges to men's authority being raised by mid-Victorian lady preachers and novelists as well as the organized women's movement, which emerged just ahead of *Essays and Reviews*." Larson finds it "striking how often the language of gender appears in the writing of the High Victorian religion wars," and so considers a number of individual cases of women's religious criticism: Sarah Lewis's *Woman's Mission* (1839); Frances Power Cobbe's *Broken Lights* (1864) and *Dawning Lights* (1867); Florence Nightingale's *Cassandra* (1860, privately published in *Suggestions for Thought*) and her epistolary debates with Benjamin Jowett; Charlotte Brontë's reinterpretation of Eve in *Shirley* (1849); and, finally, how the widely read novel by Mary Ward, *Robert Elsmere* (1888), reflects the impact of biblical criticism on domestic life and relations. In her essay on Robert Browning, Suzanne Bailey focuses on the poet's obsession with and poeticizing of higher criticism, his preoccupation, that is, both with "text and testimony." Bailey also examines nineteenth- and early-twentieth-century parodies, the "mock-confusion rife in satiric treatments, of higher criticism," whereby, for example, "one humorist uses the higher criticism as a pretext for re-writing Shakespeare, and produces a textual monster, in which Ophelia marries Romeo and Juliet runs off with Hamlet." Such parodies of higher criticism, she argues, "map the contested terrain of a nineteenth-century battle over the nature of fact, evidence, and historical knowledge, pitting the advocates of literal readings of texts against a nineteenth-century version of postmodernist textuality." Of particular importance to Bailey is the way Browning anticipates his " 'postmodern successors,' particularly in his sense of the limitations of textual evidence and the possibility of multiple points of view on factual events." Renée V. Overholser undertakes a historical and critical examination of how the poetry of Swinburne and Hopkins represents "radically opposing alternatives to the Protestant narratives," the one, Swinburne, summoning an all-out assault on Romanism, and the other, Hopkins, dramatizing England's need to return to its formative roots in Roman Catholicism. Overholser elucidates Hopkins's attempts to rewrite Swinburne, that in "framing his own call, Hopkins appropriated...elements of Swinburne's texts to the uses of his own religion," and shows how both poets respond to seminal nineteenth-century Catholic manifestos.

Part II, "Religion and The Aesthetic Imagination," pursues the dialogic trace between religion and aesthetics in the nineteenth century and the cultivation of a particular religious aesthetic, one in which aestheticism manifests a religious sensibility. In other words, for a vast majority of Victorians aestheticism became if not a wholesale substitute for at least an essential part of the new religion. Delving into "overhearing," the way Browning's dramatic monologues generate meaning from "listening and deaf spots," Joseph A. Dupras explores the prominence of the "Aural dimension of creativity and religion" ("acoustic markers") in *The Ring and the Book*. Lacking Pompilia's keen sense of hearing, her "experienced ear"—this woman who "carries not only pictorial significance but also acoustic markers"—Caponsacchi (Browning's "Hollow Rock") remains "earthbound and enervated." According to Dupras, "The way Caponsacchi valorizes, or re-peals, his life's most telling experiences can test whether readers are keen enough to learn from Browning's refinement of a psychological branch of otoscopy practiced in numerous poems throughout his career." And it is left to alert reader "to distinguish acoustical signs of a corrupt Church mimicking Christian values." Bernadette Waterman Ward, in her essay, shows the transformative effects of storytelling in Newman, how—that is, Newman's "understanding of the place of story in the spiritual life—'real' life—challenges us to confront the narrow, blunting, scorched-earth lovelessness." Newman, Ward contends, "encouraged the writing of English saints' lives, just as his hero St. Philip Neri 'substituted, for the chivalry or the hurtful novels of the day, the true romances and the celestial poetry of the lives of the saints.' ... The stories of saints must be told to keep alive the very capacity for understanding virtue: single-hearted chastity, noble humility, firm resolve, joyous endurance, gentle gift, heroic charity." Looking at the largely unexamined manuscripts of Pater—"Art and Religion," "The Aesthetic Life," "The History of Philosophy," "Thistle," and "Moral Philosophy"—Lesley Higgins believes that "critical nervousness about the possible role of religious dogma in Pater's life and texts has occluded the pivotal place of religious discourse throughout his writings." Most importantly, "such an oversight has obscured the extent to which these discursive practices provided an important response to 'the conditions of modern life' as Pater encountered them in the late nineteenth century." Pater "rethinks and re-imagines religious discourse," Higgins finds, "similar to the way Foucault, meditating on Nietzsche's writings, rethinks history." The fragment "Art and Religion," for example, "identifies religious discourse as an important site of resistance to the encroaching and often 'sterile' scientism of the age," and "The Writings of Cardinal Newman" remains central to Pater's own understanding of doctrinal development and the syntax of assent. Pater's entire career, Higgins insists, discloses a continual "engagement with religious discourse."

Dickens's readers catch glimpses of the materiality of religion in his novels, particularly the materiality of the Victorian church. Both Dennis Walder and Janet Larson, says Natalie Cole in her essay, "locate Dickens in relation to Victorian currents and cross-currents of faith, Larson explaining that Dickens 'deplored the acrimonious religious debates of his day,' but was well aware of them, and Walder emphasizing Dickens's Unitarian-inflected, liberal Christianity: '[Dickens] strongly supports the basic intention of the liberal Christian manifesto, *Essays and Reviews* (1860), to reconcile Christianity with the intellectual tendencies of the age and so save religion and the Church.'" But no Dickens critic, Cole contends, has meaningfully mapped the contours of Dickens's faith by considering the fiction in relation to the essays. The essays from *The Uncommercial Traveller* series from the last decade of Dickens's life particularly demonstrate "the tension that Dickens felt between 'a nostalgia for the security of knowing' and his conviction that nineteenth-century churches and the landscapes that contain them had no permanence except in memory." Finally, in her chapter, Alexandra M. B. Wörn notices a decided link between poetry and theological discourse in Barrett Browning: "Poetry is where God is." Wörn's concern in exploring Barrett Browning's corpus, in particular *Aurora Leigh* and *A Drama of Exile*, is whether and in what manner doctrine and literature can be brought into a creative dialogue;

"for Barrett Browning poetry, nature, and God were interlinked. She understood poetry to be a response to nature, which was created by God. ... Her poetry reflects the tension between the religious ideas she inherited, particularly from her father, and those she would later hold in more or less conscious opposition to what she had been instructed." Dorothy Mermin has reminded us that in *The Seraphim and A Drama of Exile*, the latter "a sequel to *Paradise Lost* that centers on Eve's self-sacrifice, suffering, and love," Barrett Browning, "more boldly, used Christianity to authorize her entry into poetry at the highest level."[78] Women's religious poetry evidences their "creative and original engagements with religious texts and theology"; and it is in the poetry that "the urgency of linking theological analysis and Victorian women's texts rises considerably."[79] In closing, I return to Culler, who faults critics of comparative literature for working to legitimate rather than criticize and situate religious discourse, demanding that we "turn some of our analytical energies on our reaction to religious discourse and ideology."[80] It is my hope that this volume in some small way answers this call, demonstrating that religious discourse, hardly a subdiscipline or an ancillary critical stance, occupies a prominent place in Victorian literature.

NOTES

1. Dorothy Mermin, *Godiva's Ride: Women of Letters in England, 1830–1880* (Bloomington: Indiana University Press, 1993), 107.
2. Richard J. Helmstadter, "Orthodox Nonconformity," in *Nineteenth-Century English Religious Traditions: Retrospect and Prospect*, ed. D. G. Paz (Westport, Connecticut: Greenwood Press, 1995), 73. See the exchanges between Carlyle and John Forster on Roman Catholicism in Jude V. Nixon's " 'Return Alphias': The Carlyle/Forster Unpublished Letters and Re-tailoring the Sage," *Carlyle Studies Annual* 18 (1998): 83–122.
3. Linda Colley, *Britons: Forging the Nation, 1707–1837* (New Haven: Yale University Press, 1992), 54; Gauri Viswanathan, *Outside the Fold: Conversion, Modernity, and Belief* (New Jersey: Princeton University Press, 1998), 9.
4. Colley, *Britons*, 18, 25.
5. Frank Turner, *Contesting Cultural Authority: Essays in Victorian Intellectual Life* (New York: Cambridge University Press, 1993), 46.
6. A. D. Nuttall, *Dead From the Waist Down: Scholars and Scholarship in Literature and Popular Imagination* (New Haven: Yale University Press, 2003), 36.
7. Charlotte Brontë, *Jane Eyre* (New York: W. W. Norton, 1987), 21.
8. Mermin, *Godiva's Ride*, 118.
9. George Eliot, *The Mill on the Floss* (New York: W. W. Norton, 1994), 16–19. In *The Secular Pilgrims of Victorian Fiction* (Cambridge: Cambridge University Press, 1982), Barry V. Qualls traces the impress of *Pilgrim's Progress* on Victorian fiction, arguing that Bunyan and Francis Quarles provided "the significant context in which Carlyle and the novelists of this study [Charlotte Brontë, Dickens, and Eliot]—and indeed most Victorian writers—worked. ... Lacking Bunyan's assurance, readers and writers held all the more tenaciously to his language. They were determined to shape the facts of this world into a religious topography, making a path towards the Celestial City" (ix, 12).

10. Nuttall, *Dead from the Waist Down*, 40–41.

11. Charles Dickens, *Great Expectations* (New York: Penguin, 1996).

12. F. R. Leavis and Q. D. Leavis, *Dickens: The Novelist* (London: Chatto & Windus, 1970), 320–23.

13. See, for example, John Maynard's *Victorian Discourses on Sexuality and Religion* (New York: Cambridge University Press, 1993), and David Alderson's *Mansex Fine: Religion, Manliness, and Imperialism in Nineteenth-Century British Culture* (Manchester: Manchester University Press, 1998).

14. Qtd. in Richard D. Altick, *Victorian People and Ideas* (New York: W. W. Norton, 1973), 203.

15. Cynthia Scheinberg, *Women's Poetry and Religion in Victorian England: Jewish Identity and Christian Culture* (New York: Cambridge University Press, 2002), 2.

16. Turner, *Contesting Cultural Authority*, 75.

17. See especially Avrom Fleishman, *Figures of Autobiography: The Language of Self-Writing* (Berkeley: University of California Press, 1983); George P. Landow, ed., *Approaches to Victorian Autobiography* (Athens: Ohio University Press, 1979); Heather Henderson, *The Victorian Self: Autobiography and Biblical Narrative* (Ithaca: Cornell University Press, 1989); and Linda H. Peterson, *Traditions of Victorian Women's Autobiography: The Poetics and Politics of Life Writing* (Charlottesville: University Press of Virginia, 1999).

18. Todd Kontje, *The German Bildungsroman: History of a National Genre* (Columbia, South Carolina: Camden House, 1993), 1–2.

19. Charles Dickens, *David Copperfield*, ed. Jerome H. Buckley (New York: W. W. Norton, 1990), 9.

20. Sue Zemka, *Victorian Testaments: The Bible, Christology, and Literary Authority in Early-Nineteenth-Century British Culture* (California: Stanford University Press, 1997), 120.

21. John Ruskin, *Praeterita* (New York: Oxford University Press, 1989), 455. The novel *Romola*, according to Mermin, "shows how women came literally to be worshipped: how legends of the Madonna...were formed. ...Romola is [Anna] Jameson's Madonna: heroic and tender, intellectual and maternal" (121–22).

22. Mary Wilson Carpenter, *George Eliot and the Landscape of Time: Narrative Form and Protestant Apocalyptic History* (Chapel Hill: University of North Carolina Press, 1986), ix, 3–4.

23. George Eliot, *Adam Bede*, Oxford World's Classic (New York: Oxford University Press, 1996), 101, 142, 384. For additional samples of Victorian religious readings, see George P. Landow, *Victorian Types Victorian Shadows: Biblical Typology in Victorian Literature, Art, and Thought* (Boston: Routledge, 1980), 22–23.

24. Ruth Y. Jenkins, *Reclaiming Myths of Power: Women Writers and the Victorian Spiritual Crisis* (Lewisburg, Pennsylvania: Bucknell University Press, 1995), 72, 89.

25. Gianni Vattimo, "The Trace of the Trace," in *Religion: Cultural Memory in the Present*, ed. Jacques Derrida and Gianni Vattimo (California: Stanford University Press, 1998), 88.

26. Ibid., 91.

27. Valentine Cunningham, *Everywhere Spoken Against: Dissent in the Victorian Novel* (Oxford: Clarendon Press, 1975).

28. David Sloan Wilson, *Darwin's Cathedral: Evolution, Religion, and the Nature of Society* (Chicago: The University of Chicago Press, 2002). For more on the impact of Darwinian science on the nineteenth century, see Gillian Beer, *Darwin's Plots: Evolutionary Narrative in Darwin, George Eliot, and Nineteenth-Century Fiction* (London: Ark Paperbacks, 1985); *Open Fields: Science in Cultural Encounter* (New York: Oxford University Press, 1996); George Levine, ed., *One Culture: Essays in Science and Literature* (Madison: The University of Wisconsin Press, 1987); *Darwin and the Novelists: Patterns of Science in Victorian Fiction* (Chicago: The University of Chicago Press, 1991); Tess Cosslett, *The "Scientific Movement" and Victorian Literature* (New York: St. Martin's Press, 1982); Bernard Lightman, ed., *Victorian Science in Context* (Chicago: The University Press of Chicago, 1997); Peter Allan Dale, *In Pursuit of a Scientific Culture: Science, Art, and Society in the Victorian Age* (Madison: The University of Wisconsin Press, 1989); and David Cahan, ed., *From Natural Philosophy to the Sciences: Writing the History of Nineteenth-Century Science* (Chicago: The University of Chicago Press, 2003).
29. Turner, *Contesting Cultural Authority*, 41.
30. Elizabeth Barrett Browning, *Aurora Leigh* (New York: W. W. Norton, 1996), 1: 391–94.
31. Emily Brontë, *Wuthering Heights* (New York: W. W. Norton, 1990), 16, 18.
32. Jenkins, *Reclaiming Myths of Power*, 91.
33. Eliot's Edward Casaubon is thought to be a parody of the seventeenth-century French classical scholar, Isaac Casaubon (1559–1614). In 1854, Eliot succeeded Mark Pattison as book review editor of the *Westminster Review*. She was obviously aware of Pattison's interest in Isaac Casaubon, of whom Pattison published an 1875 biography, *Isaac Casaubon, 1559–1614*, "concealed autobiography," says Hugh Lloyd-Jones (qtd. in Nuttall, *Dead from the Waist Down*, 2), three years after Eliot's *Middlemarch*. Eliot, it is popularly believed, used Pattison as model for Casaubon and his wife Emilia Frances Strong as model for Dorothea. "Even today there is no better single study of Casaubon available" (123). Nuttall's recent work, which takes its title from Browning's "A Grammarian Funeral," examines all three Casaubon figures—Edward, Pattison, and Isaac.
34. Dinah Craik, *Olive*, Oxford World's Classic (New York: Oxford University Press, 1996), 89, 170–72.
35. David Hempton, *Religion and Political Culture in Britain and Ireland* (New York: Cambridge University Press, 1996), 146.
36. Thomas Hardy, *Far From the Madding Crowd* (New York: W. W. Norton, 1986), 59, 169.
37. Landow, *Victorian Types*, 21.
38. In *Caroline Bowles Southey, 1786–1854: The Making of Woman Writer*, ed. Virginia Blain (Aldershot: Ashgate, 1998), 193.
39. Scheinberg, *Women's Poetry*, 4.
40. Altick, *Victorian People*, 203.
41. J. Hillis Miller, *The Disappearance of God: Five Nineteenth-Century Writers* (Cambridge, Massachusetts: Harvard University Press, 1981), 15.
42. Anne Brontë, *The Tenant of Wildfell Hall*, Oxford World's Classic (New York: Oxford University Press, 1992), 167.
43. Landow, *Victorian Types*, 3.

44. Thomas Hardy, *Jude the Obscure*, Oxford World's Classics (New York: Signet, 1961), 82–83, 387, 85, 105, 300.

45. Hardy's rustics, as well as Housman's poetic characters, as Carol Efrati has noted, quote routinely from the Bible "to demonstrate that the habit of applying biblical quotations to the events of daily life, as well as the propensity for debating the significance of various passages, was pervasive in Victorian England" ("A. E. Housman's Use of Biblical Narrative," in *A. E. Housman: A Reassessment*, ed. Alan W. Holden and J. Roy Birch [New York: Macmillan, 2000], 188). As meaningful are the numerous and often deliberate readings and misreadings of actual biblical narratives (for example, Browning's Fra Lippo Lippi's confusing Herodias with Salome, and the interpretive latitudes Housman took in "The Carpenter's Son" and "Easter Hymn") and what those might constitute in Victorian literature.

46. Mary (Mrs. Humphry) Ward, *Robert Elsmere*, Oxford World's Classic (New York: Oxford University Press, 1987), 269, 315–17. Hardy's Sue Bridehead's landlady, Miss Fontover, with "a dab at Ritual," knew "the Christian Year by heart" (*Jude*, 97).

47. Christine L. Krueger, *The Reader's Repentance: Women Preachers, Women Writers, and Nineteenth-Century Social Discourse* (Chicago: The University of Chicago Press, 1992), 6.

48. Colley, *Britons*, 28.

49. Zemka, *Victorian Testaments*, 190.

50. Carpenter, *George Eliot*, 62.

51. Mermin, *Godiva's Ride*, 107.

52. Zemka, *Victorian Testaments*, 221.

53. Jacques Derrida, "Faith and Knowledge: The Two Sources of 'Religion' at the Limits of Reason Alone," in *Religion: Cultural Memory in the Present*, ed. Jacques Derrida and Gianni Vattimo (California: Stanford University Press, 1998), 34–41, 46.

54. Dennis Taylor, "The Need for a Religious Literary Criticism," in *Seeing Into the Life of Things: Essays on Literature and Religious Experience*, ed. John L. Mahoney (New York: Fordham University Press, 1998), 3. As important as religion and the discourse are to Victorian literature, Herbert F. Tucker's *A Companion to Victorian Literature and Culture* (Oxford: Blackwell, 1999) does not grant the topic a section unto itself. But for the very useful "Clerical" section, the topic is largely ignored, even in places where one might ordinarily expect it to be addressed, as in the section "Passing On: Death." Not even a glancing reference is made to Newman's *The Dream of Gerontius*, the metatext, really, of Victorian "Passing On." For more on this, see Geoffrey Rowell's *Hell and the Victorians* (Oxford: Clarendon Press, 1974); Michael Wheeler's *Death and the Future Life in Victorian Literature and Theology* (New York: Cambridge University Press, 1990); and Alison Milbank's chapter, "Life After Death," in *Dante and the Victorians* (Manchester: Manchester University Press, 1998).

55. Jonathan Culler, "Comparative Literature and the Pieties," *Profession* (1986): 30–32. I owe this source to Dennis Taylor.

56. Derrida, "Faith and Knowledge," 4.

57. Terry Eagleton, *After Theory* (New York: Basic Books, 2003), 99.

58. Lynda Palazzo, *Christina Rossetti's Feminist Theology* (New York: Palgrave, 2002), xii, 21, 119, xii.

59. Krueger, *The Reader's Repentance*, 3–6.

60. Miller, *The Disappearance of God*, 1–2, 6.

61. Thaïs E. Morgan, "Victorian Sage Discourse and the Feminine: *An Introduction*," in *Victorian Sages and Cultural Discourse: Renegotiating Gender and Power*, ed. Thaïs E Morgan (New Brunswick: Rutgers University Press, 1990), 18, 2.

62. Jenkins, *Reclaiming Myths of Power*, 18–19, 25.

63. George B. Tennyson, *Victorian Devotional Poetry: The Tractarian Mode* (Cambridge, Massachusetts: Harvard University Press, 1981); Maynard, *Victorian Discourses*, 3.

64. Andrew Bradstock, Sean Gill, Anne Hogan, and Sue Morgan, eds., *Masculinity and Spirituality in Victorian Culture* (New York: St. Martin's Press, 2000), 1–2.

65. Joss Marsh, *Word Crimes: Blasphemy, Culture, and Literature in Nineteenth-Century England* (Chicago: The University of Chicago Press, 1998); Viswanathan, *Outside the Fold*, xi, 17.

66. Anne Hogan and Andrew Bradstock, eds., *Women of Faith in Victorian Culture* (New York: St. Martin's Press, 1998).

67. Michael Wheeler, *Ruskin's God* (New York: Cambridge University Press, 1999), 71–72.

68. Northrop Frye, *Anatomy of Criticism: Four Essays* (New York: Athenaeum, 1969); Frank Kermode, *The Sense of an Ending: Studies in the Theory of Fiction* (London: Oxford University Press, 1967); Peter J Lineham, "The Protestant 'Sects,'" in *Nineteenth-Century English Religious Traditions: Retrospect and Prospect*, ed. D. G. Paz (Westport, Connecticut: Greenwood Press, 1995), 154.

69. None of the essays as such explores the role of Judaism in Victorian literature, which, we know, concerned Victorians, interested as they were in prophetic/sage discourse and in a culture intolerant to the very religion informing sage discourse. See, for example, Eliot's representation of Judaism in *Daniel Deronda*. Carlyle, for another, invents for his fictional autobiographical self a history connected to Talmudic and Rabbinical lore, to say nothing of Teufelsdröckh's obsession with the Hebraic, whether the slough of Despair in Bunyan's *The Pilgrim's Progress*, his connection to Melchizedek, a young Ishmael, Moses's appearing in a basket, his Pisgah speech, and the Pillar of Cloud and the Pillar of Fire. Carlyle's *Sartor Resartus* is a more Hebraic than Hellenic text. And for all of this, Carlyle's anti-Semitic remarks are well chronicled. For useful observations on Victorian reactions to Judaism, see Stephen Prickett, "Purging Christianity of its Semitic Origins: Kingsley, Arnold and the Bible," in *Rethinking Victorian Culture*, eds. Juliet John and Alice Jenkins (New York: St. Martin's Press, 2000), 63–79. See also David J. De Laura, *Hebrew and Hellene in Victorian England* (Austin: University of Texas Press, 1969); and Scheinberg's *Women's Poetry*, and "Victorian Poetry and Religious Diversity," in *The Cambridge Companion to Victorian Poetry*, ed. Joseph Bristow (New York: Cambridge University Press, 2000), 159–79.

70. Scheinberg, *Women's Poetry*, 3, 5.

71. Nuttall, *Dead from the Waist Down*, 42.

72. George P. Landow, *William Holman Hunt and Typological Symbolism* (New Haven: Yale University Press, 1979), 7.

73. Mermin, *Godiva's Ride*, 123.

74. Carol Marie Engelhardt, "The Paradigmatic Angel in the House: The Virgin Mary and Victorian Anglicans," in *Women of Faith in Victorian Culture: Reassessing the Angel in the House*, eds. Anne Hogan and Andrew Bradstock (New York: St. Martin's Press, 1998), 159.

75. Hayden White, *Tropics of Discourse: Essays in Cultural Criticism* (Baltimore: The Johns Hopkins University Press, 1978), 2–10.

76. D. G. Paz, "Introduction," in *Nineteenth-Century English Religious Traditions: Retrospect and Prospect* (Westport, Connecticut: Greenwood Press, 1995), ii.

77. Vattimo, "The Trace of the Trace," 80.

78. Mermin, *Godiva's Ride*, 113.

79. Scheinberg, *Womens's Poetry*, 3, 15.

80. Culler, "Comparative Literature," 31.

PART I

THE HIGHER-CRITICAL DEBATE

CHAPTER 1

THE VICTORIAN RADICALS:
TIME, TYPOLOGY, AND ONTOLOGY IN
HOPKINS, PUSEY, AND MÜLLER

Jerome Bump

Our experience and understanding of Victorian religious discourse would be greatly enhanced by increasing our awareness of the complexity of their sense of time. Like us, they inherited a faith in "progress," reinforced by the advance of science and technology, and thus a perception of time as homogenous, linear, and unrepeatable. In Victorian religious discourse, this sense of linear time is most striking in "popular apocalypticism."[1] However, instead of placing their faith in this movement toward a better future, many Victorians in the humanities, arts, and religion, whom we shall call the "Radicals," thought they could reach their goals by going backward rather than forward in time. For some the goal was to break through linear time into a cyclical, reactualizable time and/or into an eternal presence.

Because we are so biased toward linear time and the idea of progress, our language tends to prevent fair description of the Victorian Radicals. The obvious exception is the term "classic," reserved for Hellenism, that is, the values of Greek and Roman civilization. Linguistically, Hebraism did not fare as well in Victorian culture. In general, our synonyms for "regress" are "go back," "lose headway," "lose ground," "retreat," "revert," "relapse," while "backward" invokes "backward-looking" and "backwater." Those who choose this direction sometimes argue that they are "conserving" the basic truths of civilization. The term "conservative" can suggest simply "traditional" but it too often has the negative connotations of "conventional," "old-fashioned," "old school," and "unadventurous." "Reactionary" is most consistently negative in its connotations: "intransigent," "backward-looking," "die-hard," and "dyed in the wool." Both "conservative" and "reactionary" also have misleading political associations with the rich or with capitalism. One example will suffice to suggest how deceptive these connotations are. A truly conservative or reactionary Christian may be one who wishes to return to the life style of the apostles. That, however, was the opposite of capitalism and materialism: "and all that believed were together and had all things in common; and sold their possessions and goods" (Acts 2:44–45, Jerusalem Bible). "Return" is perhaps the best word for our purposes because, while it can mean simply "go back," it also has the connotation of "homecoming" or "return to the origin." "Radical" might be a good substitute for "reactionary" because, although it retains the connotations of extremism, it simply means "return to the roots" and thus invokes the synonyms "fundamental," "essential," "deep-seated," "thorough," "far-reaching."

Whatever the terms, if linear time was to be experienced, often the direction the Victorian Radicals chose was toward home, a return to origin. From their point of view, outside of science and technology, the odds are very heavy that what is accepted at the moment as a new truth of human experience will not survive the scrutiny of centuries. More than likely the novel truths of the day will become the silt of tomorrow. Many Radicals rejected the idea of striking progress in the humanities and religion because they believed that in their fields there was nothing *really* new under the sun. Friedrich Max Müller, for instance, wrote, "Of religion, too, as of language, it may be said that in it everything new is old, and everything old is new, and that there has been no entirely new religion since the beginning of the world."[2]

In the nineteenth century the equivalent of scientific experiment in the humanities and religion was trying out different ways of thinking and feeling in one's own personal life experience.[3] The basic assumption was that one would discover that the fundamental truths of the human life experience (unlike those of science and technology) had been discovered thousands of years ago, and the project of the humanities or religion was to translate them into terms accessible to the current population. As Holloway and others have shown, the goal was to discover a new language rather than a new truth,[4] though of course a new language changed the truth in minor if not major ways.

In nineteenth-century art and religion, one example of the impulse to return was medievalism, a subterranean current in English life that flowed in a direction opposite to that of the mainstream linear narrative. In this movement, radicalism, ironically, became an *avant garde* stance, in the sense of going back to the "roots," as in the Pre-Raphaelite movement in art and literature. No doubt inspired in part by their rivalry with the Royal Academy, in his essay in the Pre-Raphaelite manifesto, *The Germ*, Frederic Stephens asserts that one contemporary school is better than another when it is combined with and/or closer to the creative wellspring or inspiration of a prior school. He asserted that contemporary art is in a state of winter, characterized by a "Poverty of Invention."[5] His solution to this crisis of creativity is a return to what he regarded as the springtime of art in the Middle Age. Stephens emphasizes that the "modern school" (the PRB) rebels against established authority and traditional landmarks (presumably those of the Royal Academy) because it models itself on "the earliest Italian school" which was ostensibly the most original of all schools and cannot be surpassed by any.[6]

Eventually their aim was "to achieve freshness of response through radical innovation ... this avant-garde artistic role and strategy ... once established by the Brotherhood, is continued by their followers ... reversing stylistic expectations" and justifying them by "seeing themselves as the continuers of the single true tradition of western religious art cut off by the Renaissance."[7] If one goes back far enough, as Müller made abundantly clear, one goes back to nature. Hence movements such as the Pre-Raphaelites combined a return to medieval sources with a return to nature. According to William Rossetti, Stephens's aim in his essay in *The Germ* is to enforce "close study of nature, and to illustrate like qualities shown in the earlier school of art."[8]

Another sign of this desire to go backward rather than forward in nineteenth-century literature was the popularity of the figure of metalepsis. Harold Bloom, the foremost expert on competition between writers and their precursors, called this trope "aphophrades, or the return of the precursors," and emphasized that it was based on the ratio of "early and late," an over-coming of "temporality by a substitution of earliness for lateness."[9] He was apparently inspired by the more specific meaning defined by Hugh Blair, among others: "when the Trope is founded on the relation between ante-cedent and consequent, or what goes before, and immediately follows, it is then called a Metalepsis."[10] Bloom argues that the substitution of late for early is the "major mode of allusion" from the Renaissance to the present.[11] The popularity of this figure has been ascribed to an increasing sense of the ennui of belatedness, a pervasive entropy (W. J. Bate, Bloom), suggested in Stephens's critique of "Poverty of Invention" in the art of his day, but it can also be related to one of the cures for this entropy: return to the roots of the creative imagination.

For example, metalepsis became Gerard Manley Hopkins's characteristic defense against influence: reversing his subservient status as a successor by establishing closer access to the precursor's own wellsprings of imagination, thus figuratively becoming the precursor's precursor. As we have seen, the avante-garde stance of radicalism, "once established by the Brotherhood, is continued by their followers," and thus we should not be surprised to learn that one of Hopkins's primary modes of response to the Brotherhood was to surpass their return to the "root" or origin. Indeed, spurred on by various competitive impulses, his reaction became an attempt to be more radical, more true to ancient roots and sources of creativity than the Pre-Raphaelites were themselves. Many of Hopkins's allusions became metalepses or tran-sumptions, attempts to subsume and "leap over" them as it were, and go directly to the source, that is, attempts to make his late commitment surpass their early allegiance to exemplars such as Dante, Savonarola, and Jesus.

Metalepsis is related to a figure very popular not just in the nineteenth century but in two thousand years of Christianity: biblical typology, the ten-dency to move back from the New Testament to the Old. At times, as in the gospel of John, the direction is clearly reversed: Christ precedes all creation ("In the beginning was the Word"). More often, the goal was to demonstrate "progress." Because Christian apologists did not want the new dispensation to be perceived as merely a belated imitation of the old, they stressed the mechanical meaning of the term "type" as merely a rough draught, or less accurate model, from which a more perfect image is made. The Old Testament type was represented as but a shadowy foreshadowing, anticipation, or prefiguration of the fully developed New Testament anti-type, as in Newman's sermon, "Moses the Type of Christ": "Christ, then, is a second Moses, and greater than he, inasmuch as Christ leads from hell to heaven, as Moses led the Israelites from Egypt to Canaan."[12] As in metalepsis, the goal is to demonstrate that a more recent hero better fulfills ancient prophecies than the older one.

However, when the typologist turned to liturgy, the focus was on the traditional function of authentication by parallels with the past. The goal of the typology of the Eucharist, for example, was not to demonstrate superiority of the current ritual to the Last Supper, but to establish perfect correspondence with it. Hopkins's use of typology[13] draws on this as well as more familiar traditions. Take, for example, his words, "And the azurous hung hills are his world-wielding shoulder / Majestic—as a stallion stalwart" ("Hurrahing in Harvest"). We know that his comparison of the majesty of the hills to a stallion is a simile, the kind of comparison in which "like" or "as" reminds us of the separation between the sign and the thing signified. However, Hopkins makes sure we do not confuse the shoulder image with a metaphor (in which the "like" or "as" is merely implied) by stating explicitly that the hills "are" the shoulder of God. Some poets create metaphors in this way, but Hopkins does not usually use "is" or "are" simply to equate one noun with another unless he intends a more or less literal meaning.

For most Victorian readers, Hopkins's phrase "the azurous hung hills are his world wielding shoulder" is "written over" Jesus's statement in the New Testament, "This is my body," when he held up the bread at Passover. These words instituted the most extraordinary symbol in the Western world, one that is literally consumed by hundreds of millions of people every week. The usual explanation for his remarkable imagery is that Hopkins converted to Roman Catholicism because of its doctrine of transubstantiation, but to assert that the bread, before a priest consecrated it, the wheat from which it was made (and the "azurous hung hills"), were already the body of God was usually considered a heresy, a label a devout priest like Hopkins would never have accepted. So what kind of religious discourse, what kind of spiritual figure of speech, is this?

As George Landow reminded us, to understand the surface layers of such imagery we need, first of all, to recover a way of interpreting language and nature that has almost completely disappeared, a way of thinking that is the key to many literary works published in the nineteenth century and before, biblical typology:

> Although it is a commonplace that we have lost the intimate knowledge of the Bible that characterized literate people of the last century, we have yet to perceive the full implications of our loss. In the Victorian age—to go back no farther—any

person who could read, whether or not a believer, was likely to recognize scriptural allusions. Equally important, he was also likely to recognize allusions to typological interpretations of the scriptures. Typology is a Christian form of scriptural interpretation that claims to discover divinely intended anticipations of Christ and His dispensation in the laws, events, and people of the Old Testament. When we modern readers fail to recognize allusions to such typology, we deprive many Victorian works of a large part of their context. Having thus impoverished them, we then find ourselves in a situation comparable to that of the reader trying to understand a poem in a foreign language after someone has gone through his dictionary deleting important words. Ignorant of typology, we under-read and misread many works, and the danger is that the greater the work, the more our ignorance will distort and inevitably reduce it. . . . The persistent inability of critics to perceive how deeply Hopkins is rooted in his Victorian environment appears nowhere more clearly than in their failure to perceive the genesis of his most characteristic poems in typology.[14]

Of course, biblical types pervade English literature, both secular and religious, from the earliest times to 1900, and typological symbolism appears in secular Romantic poems, such as those of Wordsworth, as well as Victorian religious poems such as those of Hopkins.

However, the particular form of typology that inspired Hopkins involved many more layers of discourse than the Evangelical typology described by Landow. We are advancing in our understanding of Protestant typology, especially as it relates to apocalyptic theology,[15] but neither Roman nor Anglo Catholics necessarily shared that theology and typology. We need to remember that the Catholic Emancipation Bill was seen by the Evangelical apocalyptics as one of "the seven vials, whose outpourings of disaster heralded" the Second Coming.[16] They identified Roman Catholicism as the "reign of the beast" and the Pope as "the beast" or Antichrist.[17] From this point of view, "Puseyites" were also the Antichrist and "Tractarianism is the smoke from the bottomless pit."[18] Obviously such a theology would not attract those who, like Hopkins, felt the lure of the Oxford Movement.

Nor was such vitriolic language acceptable at Balliol College, Oxford, when Hopkins matriculated in 1863. Hopkins entered an intellectual milieu full of many other competing worldviews. The air of Balliol was filled with the reverberations of *Essays and Reviews*, published just three years before. This critique of biblical criticism was dominated by the master of Balliol, Benjamin Jowett. "Located at the head of Oxford's Broad Street, Jowett's Balliol was thought 'the focus or center' of Broad-Church liberalism, around which 'currents and counter-currents formed a kind of vortex.' "[19] However, it would be a mistake to assume that this vortext generated "hatred" of others and "venom" toward opposing points of view, such as that generated by anti-Catholicism.[20] Hopkins's classmate, Martin Geldart, describes the atmosphere of Oxford (Bosphorus) in 1863:

Never was I in an intellectual atmosphere so fearless and so free. I never knew what true tolerance without indifference was till I came to Bosphorus. It was a new experience to me altogether—to me who had been brought up to regard Ritualism and Rationalism as the two right arms of the devil, to find myself suddenly launched among a lot of men who were some of them Ritualists of the deepest dye, some of them Rationalists, some of them Positivists, some of them Materialists, all eager in advancing their respective views, and yet all ready to listen with courtesy to their opponents. Nobody was shocked or offended by anything; everyone was open to argument; and here was I (the almost solitary Evangelical of the crew, who had been taught to regard any deviation from the doctrine of justification by faith in the "all-sufficient sacrifice" as something wicked and monstrous; who had never before, or scarcely ever before, seen a heretic or High Churchman, in the flesh) quite taken aback to find how earnest, how serious, nay how good, how much better than myself (to say nothing of how much cleverer—for that I was prepared), these High Churchmen, and above all, these heretics were. What was more, they were quite ready to listen to me as I to them. I found none of that pride of intellect among them against which I had been warned; but, on the contrary, a candid, straightforward way of looking at things, which, ignore it as I would, I could not but feel I had too often missed among my former associates.[21]

In such an atmosphere, Ritualists, such as Hopkins and Pusey, devoted to reviving the religion of the Middle Age, at times could find common ground with Liberals like Müller and Jowett.

A better known source of our impressions of that atmosphere is Hardy's *Jude the Obscure*.[22] His "hero" Jude became a "heretic"[22] eventually, but when he sought entrance into Balliol he was a "Radical," in our sense of the word. We need to remember that Balliol was not the only Oxford college to which Jude applied, just the only one that sent a reply. There is nothing in the novel to suggest that Jude was drawn to Jowett or the rationalism of *Essays and Reviews*. Indeed, when he was first attracted to "Christminster," what drew him there was the Oxford Movement, the opposite of Jowett's Liberalism, and the chance of becoming a priest.

To understand Oxford in 1863, we have to allow for motivations other than reason: "the ultimate impulse to come had a curious origin—one more nearly related to the emotional side of him than the intellectual."[23] When Jude gets to Oxford he encounters ghosts: "among whom the most real to Jude Fawley were the founders of the religious school called Tractarianism; the well known three, the enthusiast [Newman?], the poet [Keble], and the formularist [Pusey?], the echoes of whose teachings had influenced him even in his obscure home" (*Jude*, 65). Hearing similar echoes, Hopkins entered Balliol primarily because he won a scholarship there, and looked beyond its walls for spiritual guidance, to Pusey, to Pusey's disciple Liddon, and finally to Newman.

Hence, if we are to begin to uncover the strata of meaning in the work of Hopkins, a good place to begin is *Lectures on Types and Prophecies of the Old Testament*, by Edward Bouverie Pusey, Regius Professor of Hebrew at Oxford and Canon of Christ Church. In them we will a find fuller exposition of the theory of the biblical symbol briefly suggested by Coleridge. In

The Statesman's Manual Coleridge uses the biblical "types and prophecies" approach primarily for political purposes, but lists among "the miseries of the present age" that "it recognizes no medium between Literal and Metaphorical"; the Bible, on the other hand, he believed, "gives birth to a system of symbols, harmonious in themselves, and consubstantial with the truths, of which they are the conductors": in the Bible a symbol "is characterized...above all by the translucence of the eternal through and in the temporal. It always partakes of the reality which it renders intelligible, abides itself as a living part in that unity of which it is the representative."[24] Inspired by Coleridge, and by the Church Fathers who he believed "fearlessly blend the sign and the thing signified,"[25] Pusey restored what he argued was the ancient Hebrew symbolism which guaranteed that God was not just like a burning bush but actually in it. Hopkins attended lectures on the Old Testament by Pusey, and is but one of many writers influenced by him and by the Oxford Movement.

The latter, also known as Tractarianism, was an important nineteenth-century religious activity, and Pusey is acknowledged as one of the primary leaders, but he is conspicuous by his absence in books on the literary influence of the movement[26] as well as books on the impact of biblical typology, not only Landow's book on Evangelical Protestant typology, but even G. B. Tennyson's *Victorian Devotional Poetry: The Tractarian Mode.* Tennyson does establish that the biblical types advocated in the Oxford Movement, inspired more by Church Fathers than Evangelical preachers, are fundamentally different in kind from the usual types: "Protestant-minded interpreters will hold to a fairly narrow typological reading that is concerned for the most part with finding prefigurements of Christ in the Old Testament. Catholic-minded, including Orthodox, interpreters will indulge in broader readings, finding also in the Scriptures types and shadows of Church practices. Not surprisingly, the Tractarians are in the second camp."[27]

To understand the Tractarian approach to the Bible, it is helpful to consult Pusey's sermons and his *Lectures on Types and Prophecies of the Old Testament.* As George Tennyson pointed out, "Catholic-minded interpreters found also in the Scriptures types and shadows of Church practices. Not surprisingly, the Tractarians are in the second camp.... Beyond that, the Tractarians held typology to be a warrant for various kinds of non-Scriptural symbolism, where it merges with Analogy."[28]

In his influential *The Disappearance of God* J. Hillis Miller also emphasizes analogy:

> In the Presocratic philosophers, in the earliest books of the Old Testament,...our culture, at its beginnings, experienced the divine power as immediately present in nature, in society, and in each man's heart....The Reformation...meant a weakening of belief in the sacrament of communion....Instead of being a sharing in the immediate presence of Christ, the communion service becomes the expression of an absence....As Claude Vigée has suggested, the Protestant reinterpretation of the Eucharist parallels exactly a similar transformation in literature. The old

symbolism of analogical participation is gradually replaced by the modern poetic symbolism of reference at a distance....[L]iterary symbols can only make the most distant allusions to [God], or to the natural world which used to be has abiding place and home. [Therefore,] for Gerard Manley Hopkins, in the middle nineteenth century, the chief attraction of Catholicism is the doctrine of the Real Presence.[29]

Yet that was also a central contribution of Anglicanism, as interpreted by Pusey, and his view of it may well be why Hopkins revered him "most of all men in the world."[30]

However, the words "analogy" and "analogical participation" may not be sufficiently inclusive to describe Tractarian typology or Hopkins's religious discourse. The word "consubstantial"—in Coleridge's statement that the Bible "gives birth to a system of symbols, harmonious in themselves, and consubstantial with the truths, of which they are the conductors"—suggests other terms. It is most familiar to us in the context of interpretations of the Eucharist. In that regard it is useful to recall that in a famous sermon, arguing from types and prophecies of the Old Testament, Pusey insisted on the "Real Objective Presence" of God in the Eucharist, but was censured and suspended by his Oxford superiors. Some answers to our question about Hopkins's figure of speech emerge when Pusey's *Lectures on the Types and Prophecies of the Old Testament* is supplemented with his 1843 sermon on the Eucharist. Together, these works define, explain, and document the use of an unusual literary symbol—distinguished from other figures of speech, including "analogy" and other uses of the word "type"—that helps us define his radicalism and challenges accepted opinion about the disappearance of spiritual modes of understanding in modern culture.

Hopkins encountered Coleridge's ideal symbol that "abides itself as a living part in that unity of which it is the representative" in Pusey's lectures, before he converted to Catholicism. The root meaning of "analogy" seems too limited: "likeness between things in some circumstances or effects, when the things are otherwise entirely different."[31] The basic concept of an analogy is that the compared objects are parallel, but of course parallel lines never meet. Aware that the word "analogy" was inadequate, Wordsworth tries to redefine it: "He bids us seek for real and not fanciful analogies.... The symbolic value of natural objects is not that they remind us of something that they are not, but that they help us to understand something that they in part are."[32] The Tractarians carried the Romantic project further, stating explicitly that their concept of the typological symbol meant more than mere similitude. Even Keble, whose own poetry is oriented to similes, insisted that "type" in the Tractarian context was something quite different:

We know not how much there may be, far beyond mere metaphor and similitude, in His using the name of any of His creatures, in a translated sense, to shadow out something invisible. But thus far we may seem to understand, that the object thus spoken of by Him is so far taken out of the number of ordinary figures of speech, and resources of language, and partakes thenceforth of the nature of a Type.... Poetry lends Religion her wealth of symbols and similes: Religion restores these again to Poetry clothed with so splendid a radiance that they appear to be no longer merely symbols, but to partake (I might almost say) of the nature of sacraments.[33]

George Tennyson focuses on Baptism as a sacrament especially dear to the Tractarians, but the Tractarian type could be an "instrument" not just of grace (as in Baptism) but also of the Real Presence, as in the Eucharist. If the Calvinist model of the Eucharist was basically a simile, the Tractarian model was a symbol that participates in the reality it names: an instrument as well as a type. To Newman, "material phenomena are both the types and the instruments of real things unseen."[34] As we have seen, in Hopkins the hills are not just like God's body: they are part of it and thus present the reader of the Book of Nature not only with grace but with the real presence of that which they represent. Yet this is not the heresy of pantheism because nature is only a part, not the whole, of God.

Hopkins's focus on hills is no accident. Pusey found more types in nature than in history: "the typical character of nature we understand beyond that of ordinary history because the emblems of the physical world chiefly have been adopted into the language of Holy Scripture, and so their nature individually discovered, whereas of profane history we have no direct use but only judge according to the analogy furnished by sacred" (*Lectures on Types*, 25). Pusey cites "a philosophic German, 'Whoso feels his call to seek out order in the confusion of Fable, let him gaze on the book of Nature, and in its holy characters read of Poetry, of Metaphysics, of commentary, and of revelation? He will find there most excellent harmonizing" (*Lectures on Types*, 17).

The stress on something inside the object corresponding to something inside the observer is very strong:

The book of God's works and the book of God's word correspond because they are emanations of His Word. . . . Nor indeed would external nature convey [its message] unless it had in it somewhat of God for it acts upon us not by reflection or by understanding but by direct impression, . . . by immediate influence so that nothing exercises so congenial an influence on man's soul, is so harmonized with it, as the visible works of God, except His words or his works in other human souls. Whence it seems that there is something more akin in external nature to that part of man which is from God than in anything else except what is more directly from God. . . . A proof that this expressiveness really lies in the object and is not the work of imagination (otherwise than as imagination is employed in tracing out the mutual correspondences of images with reality or with each other) is furnished by this, that when religious poets (as Wordsworth or the author of *The Christian Year*) have traced out such correspondence, the mind instantly recognizes as true not as beautiful only and so not belonging to their minds subjectively, but as actually and really existing (objective). As the Christian poet just alluded to has well said:

Every leaf in every nook
Every wave in every brook
Chanting with a solemn voice
Minds us of our better choice,

nor out of sculpture could one learn better to read the book of God's work than in him. (*Lectures on Types*, 17)

Pusey cites Richard Hooker's *Ecclesiastical Polity*: "All things have partaken of God.... They are his offspring and so being such must (in so far as they have not been marred and deformed by sin) bear a certain impress and image of Himself... So that all things which god hath made are in that respect the offspring of God (Acts 17, 20, 29). They are *in Him* as effects in their highest cause, He likewise actually is in them the... influence of His Deity being their life."[35] Pusey underlines Hooker's words "in them" to make sure that his listeners understand that God's creatures are not only like God in the sense of bearing his impress and image, but also that God actually indwells in them. The basic image is obviously not parallel but intersecting lines.

Inspired by Eucharistic theology, Pusey focused on how this symbol is different from conventional analogy: it is a figure mediating between the worldly and the unworldly that avoids both pantheist heresies (that God is pure soul outside the world and that God and the world are one):

> The pseudo-spiritualist and the carnal man alike see in the water, the bread, and the wine nothing but the bare element, and thereby each alike deprives himself of the benefit intended for him. The carnal will live on bread alone. The pseudo-spiritualist without it. The carnal mistakes the clouds and darkness for Him who is enshrined within it; the pseudospiritualist would behold Him Whom "man cannot see and live"... the Light inapproachable, whom no man hath ever or can see.... The carnal neglects the revelation; the pseudospiritual would know the unrevealed God. The danger of an age which thinks itself enlightened is of course this last, only it shall be borne in mind that a pseudospiritual mind is also unspiritual, that in a different way incapable of seeing things spiritual. This whole system of religion, contemplative and practical, is one of God's condescension: God cometh down to us, not we mount up to God. Its cornerstone and characteristic is "God manifest in the flesh." And with this, as God appointed it, all is in keeping. Neither the letter without the spirit, nor the spirit without the letter. (*Lectures on Types*, 23)

Hence Pusey is as opposed to abstraction as he is to pseudospiritualism: "When moderns then attempt to translate into plain terms the figurative language of Holy Scripture and substitute abstract and, as they would have it, clearer terms for the types and typical language of the OT they uniformly by this transmutate and evaporate much of their meaning" (*Lectures on Types*, 24). (Like Pusey, Luther felt that the "important thing is the real presence of Christ in the Eucharist, and not the theory that by this presence is explained."[36]) Pusey, therefore, along with Duns Scotus and Müller (as we shall see), inspired the radical theology of immediate sensory apprehension of God that apparently alienated Hopkins from his superiors at St. Beuno's. (Like most Jesuits, Hopkins's superiors preferred Suarez's more abstract Aristotelianism.)

Pusey's model, as we see in the discussion of pseudospiritualism, is not analogy but the Eucharist, specifically the representation of it in John 6, which he frequently cites. The focus on John 6 is typical of his radicalism, his return to the first millenium. The text usually selected to defend the Eucharist was 1 Corinthians 11, but before the twelfth century it was John 6.[37] Pusey's radical version of John 6 forces us to confront what is extraordinary about the most remarkable symbol in the Western world. Imagine yourself a Jew in the synagogue at Capernaum when these words were first pronounced:

"I am the living bread which came down from heaven: if any man eat of this bread, he shall live for ever: and the bread that I will give is my flesh, which I will give for the life of the world." The Jews therefore strove among themselves, saying, "How can this man give us his flesh to eat?" Then Jesus said unto them, "Verily, verily, I say unto you, Except ye eat the flesh of the Son of man, and drink his blood ye have no life in you. Whoso eateth my flesh, and drinketh my blood, hath eternal life; and I will raise him up at the last day. For my flesh is meat indeed, and my blood is drink indeed. He that eateth my flesh and drinketh my blood dwelleth in me, and I in him. As the living Father hath sent me, and I live by the Father, so he that eateth me, even he shall live by me. This is that bread which came down from heaven: not as your fathers did eat manna, and are dead: he that eateth of this bread shall live forever." These things said he in the synagogue, as he taught in Capernaum. Many therefore of his disciples, when they had heard this, said, "This is an hard saying; who can hear it?" When Jesus knew in himself that his disciples murmured at it, he said unto them, "Doth this offend you? . . . there are some of you that believe not." . . . From that time many of his disciples went back, and walked no more with him. Then said Jesus unto the twelve, Will ye also go away? (*Lectures on Types*, 111)

Had we been there, who among us would not have been offended and left with the disciples who went back? Yet this is apparently one of the primary texts "over which" Hopkins's line "And the azurous hung hills are his world wielding shoulder" is inscribed.

A large section of *Lectures on Types* is devoted to Old Testament precedents for this view of the Eucharist. Pusey's best precedent is a description of the Holy of Holies as not only the ark of the covenant but "the golden pot that had manna." The source, however, is not the Old Testament but Paul's letter to the Hebrews (9:4). Pusey admits that "this aspect of manna was indeed, it appears, lost at a comparatively early period at least [by the] building of Solomon's temple (1K 8, 9): There was nothing in the ark save the two tables of stone" (*Lectures on Types*, 112).

Pusey was clearly a "Radical," seeking the root of force and creativity in the past. Obviously, he moved far past Zwingli in his Eucharistic typology. His stress on the Real Presence, derived from the first centuries of Christianity, is the key to understanding Hopkins's words "And the azurous hung hills are his world wielding shoulder." If this sentence were based on the Catholic understanding of the Eucharist of the last thousand years the verb would be not "are" but some equivalent of "become," for the doctrine of transubstantiation asserts that the bread becomes, is changed into, the body of God by the words of the consecration. That doctrine endows the priest with godlike powers and no doubt appealed to many poets in the nineteenth century.

Hopkins was obviously attracted to the Romantic preoccupation with the individual personality, especially in his poems about God and the self, but the medievalism represented by Keble, Pusey, and Newman became for him a counterpoise to the romantic obsession with individual talent. Instead of being a God-like Romantic creator, a religious medievalist was expected merely to identify connections he did not invent and suggest how they pointed to a reality infinitely greater than his own. As in T. S. Eliot's "Tradition and the Individual Talent" he was asked for "a continual surrender of himself as he is at the moment to something which is more valuable," a "continual self-sacrifice, a continual extinction of personality."[38] Hopkins was trying to make this kind of sacrifice when he joined the Society of Jesus, and he often tried to surrender to the more valuable tradition in his art as well.

Hopkins's use of "are" in "The azurous hung hills are his world-wielding shoulder" suggests that for him as for Pusey the more valuable tradition in typology and liturgy was that of the Fathers. The difference is perhaps most obvious when we put the archaic text of the fourth-century *De sacramentis*[39] next to that of the Roman Canon. In the latter God is asked to accept the offering "*ut nobis corpus et sanguis fiat dilectissimi filii tui Domini nostri Iesu Christi*" ("so that it may become for us the body and blood of your son, our Lord Jesus Christ"), but in the former God is asked to approve the offering "*quod est figura corporis et sanguinis Domini nostri Iesu Christi*" ("because it is the figure of the body and blood of our Lord Jesus Christ").[40] There is a world of difference between "fiat" and "est," and Hopkins's "are" is clearly in the tradition of "est." We are not suddenly brought into the world of the eternal present, but reminded that we *are* already there. In terms of imagery, the key is the word "figura," in this case meaning "antitype," with the power of the sacrament deriving from "an antitypical correspondence with the elements of the Last Supper."[41] After the fourth century this typological sacramentality was weakened by allegorism and naive realism in the Middle Age and finally gave way to the doctrine of transubstantiation in the Renaissance. With the Reformation it seemed to be lost altogether, until it was revived by Pusey, Hopkins and other Radicals.

*   *   *

Pusey saw types everywhere, even in "pagan" cultures: "it seemed important to show how deeply and widely types were in the whole constitution of things and the hold which they have taken upon man's nature might have been illustrated much more largely by reference to the extensive use of symbols, or artificial types, throughout all Heathen antiquity . . . this way of looking on things as in themselves significant adds much to the vividness and force of typical language" (*Lectures on Types*, 21). By acknowledging the existence of types in earlier cultures, Pusey draws our attention to many more layers of meaning in the palimpsest of Victorian religious discourse.

Another clue to that discourse is Hopkins's diary entry of 1864: "Mem. To read ... Max Müller."[42] A few entries later he makes notes remarkably like those of Müller as he attempts to trace the origin of the word "goblin" through Slavonic, Gothic, Latin, and Sanskrit. Humphry House notes that when Hopkins was at Oxford, "Friedrich Max Müller (1823–1900) was already one of the chief living authorities on comparative philology as well as an outstanding Sanskrit scholar. At the time of this note (Summer 1864), he held the Taylorian Chair of Modern European Languages in Oxford. He had already published ... 'An Essay on Comparative Mythology' (1856) ... and *The Science of Language* .... GMH certainly read *The Science of Language* .... Manley Hopkins sent Max Müller a copy of his *Hawaii* (1862): they corresponded about the chapter on language and later met in Oxford" (*Journals*, 317).

Most readers who have written about Hopkins and Müller have focused on *The Science of Language*[43] or Müller's debate with Darwin.[44] But Hopkins was also interested in Müller's pioneering work in comparative mythology and religion, including non-Western and non-Judaic cultures. In 1886, for example, Hopkins wrote to a friend about "a mythical being in the Veda" and "a heavenly greyhound, hound of dawn (I have, in spite of Lang, a considerable belief in the Solar myth and especially in these 'hounds of dawn,' which are really very widespread and found in Greek, Irish, Egyptian—? The 'divine jackals'—as well as Indian mythology"; Hopkins also speculates on the origin of a Greek word coming most likely "from Aten or Athen the disk of the sun as from Ahana the pretended dawn goddess. We do know the one was worshipped (furiously) and we do not the other" (*Further Letters*, 262–63).

Our experience and understanding of the religious discourse of the Victorian Radicals would be greatly enhanced by recovering this cast of mind. Müller often used the metaphor of "strata"; his Rede Lecture of 1868, for example, was titled "On the Stratification of Language." In his 1867 preface to his *Chips from a German Workshop* he wrote:

> There is to my mind no subject more absorbing than the tracing the origin and first growth of human thought. ... Language still bears the impress of the earliest thoughts of man, obliterated, it may be, buried under new thoughts, yet here and there still recoverable in their sharp original outline. The growth of language is continuous, and by continuing our researches backward from the most modern to the most ancient strata, the very elements and roots of human speech have been reached, and with them the elements and roots of human thought. ... But more surprising than the continuity in the growth of language, is the continuity in the growth of religion. Of religion, too, as of language, it may be said that in it everything new is old, and everything old is new, and that there has been no entirely new religion since the beginning of the world.[45]

Though he does not use the word, Müller uses the basic model of religious discourse as "palimpsest." Deriving from the example of a text on a manuscript written over previous, still somewhat legible, texts (exemplified

more often now in chalkboards only partially erased), the word has come
to mean any object or image that includes layers of meaning beneath its
surface meanings. Perhaps the most felicitous definition for our purposes
is from a dictionary of mining terms: "a structure or texture of metamor-
phic rocks in which remnants of some pre-existing structure or texture are
preserved."[46]

In our culture the most obvious example is the New Testament, which is
often "written over" the Old Testament. Traditional readings of this
palimpsest were challenged by Müller's research and that collected in *Essays
and Reviews*. One of Müller's key allies in England was Baron von Bunsen;
Rowland Williams's essay, "Bunsen's Biblical Researches," in *Essays and
Reviews*, was identified by Basil Willey as "the head and front of the book's
offending."[47] Yet, as we shall see, Hopkins's spirituality seems at times an
example of Bunsen's ideally esemplastic Christianity that "assimilated the
relics of Gentile form and usage."[48] As Bunsen, Müller, and Pusey point out,
the Old Testament is not the only text of the ancient world "over which" or
"against which" Christianity has been inscribed. All the layers of meaning,
whether we are conscious of them or not, contribute to our experience of
reading Victorian religious discourse. Hence, to understand that reading
experience we need, at times, to be a geologist of discourses.

For example, Pusey cites many of the Fathers who, when they first articulated the theology of the Eucharist, were responding to the demand of the
mystery religions for a concrete, material expression of the real presence of
the divinity in this world, a mode of access to an eternal present tense, a time
out of (linear) time. Hopkins revered Pusey "most of all men in the world"
partly because he could tap this ancient nonbiblical strata of symbolism so
well in his lectures.

In his 1867 preface Müller insisted that "in order to understand fully the
position of Christianity in the history of the world, and its true place among
the religions of mankind, we must compare it, not with Judaism only, but
with the religious aspirations of the whole world, with all, in fact, that
Christianity came either to destroy or to fulfill" (*Chips*, xxvii). Müller
stressed that he was merely repeating the arguments of the Fathers of the
Church, the authorities to whom Pusey and the Tractarians usually appealed:

> The Fathers of the Church, though living in much more dangerous proximity
> to the ancient religions of the Gentiles, admitted freely that a comparison of
> Christianity and other religions was useful. "If there is any agreement," Basilius
> remarked, "between their (the Greeks') doctrines and our own, it may benefit
> us to know them. . . . To the missionary, more particularly, a comparative study
> of the religions of mankind will be, I believe, of the greatest assistance. . . .
> [M]issionaries, instead of looking only for points of difference, will look out
> more anxiously for any common ground, any spark of the true light that may
> still be revived, any altar that may be dedicated afresh to the true God. . . . Every
> religion, even the most imperfect and degraded, has something that ought to
> be sacred to us, for there is in all religions a secret yearning after the true,
> though unknown God." (*Chips*, xix, xxi, xxx)

Like the Fathers, Müller's goal was to discover what Pusey might call "types" among the "pagans":

> If we once understand this clearly, the words of St. Augustine, which have seemed startling to many of his admirers, become perfectly clear and intelligible, when he says: "What is now called the Christian religion, has existed among the ancients, and was not absent from the beginning of the human race, until Christ came in the flesh: from which time the true religion, which existed already, began to be called Christian."... Justin Martyr, in his "Apology" (A. D. 139), has this memorable passage ("Apol." i.46)... those who live according to the Logos are Christians, notwithstanding they may pass with you for Atheists.... Clement (A. D. 200).... "It is clear that same God to whom we owe the Old and New Testaments, gave also to the Greeks their Greek philosophy, by which the Almighty is glorified among the Greeks." (*Chips*, x–xi, xxviii, xxix)

These remarks direct us to the non-Hebraic strata of John 6 and "And the azurous hung hills are his world wielding shoulder." We can look for relevant "types" even in the mystery religions so popular in the Roman world when Christianity began to spread rapidly, especially after Constantine. One of the striking features of "Roman" Catholicism that no doubt attracted Hopkins is that it, like the Roman empire before it, assimilated so many of the features of the cultures it converted. In this case, the types and precedents seem to have influenced not only the liturgy but also the "catholicity" of the Fathers, especially the Greek Fathers, upon whom Pusey and Müller relied so heavily.

Many Fathers who first articulated the theology of the Eucharist were responding to the popular demand for a concrete, material expression of the Real Presence. Many of the first converts no doubt recalled the sacred cup of the Eleusinian mysteries, the Bacchanalian emphasis on ingestion of the life of the divinity, Eucharistic precedents in the Mithraic cult, and the eating and drinking of the worshippers of Attis. While these were apparently very different from the Christian liturgy, they reveal the hunger for communion with the divine in the first centuries of Christianity. The popularity of Attis, Osiris, and Adonis (all men who died and returned as gods) paved the way for the communion rites of Christianity.

Hence one reason why Hopkins revered Pusey "most of all men in the world" may well be that he could tap these ancient nonbiblical strata of symbolism not only in his lectures but also in his sermons. As we have seen, in Hopkins the hills are not just like God's body: they are part of it and thus present the reader of the Book of Nature not only with grace but with the real presence of that which they represent. Pusey articulated this idea better than his Tractarian colleagues, Newman and Keble. For example, in his famous sermon, "The Holy Eucharist a Comfort to the Penitent," preached before the university in Christ Church Cathedral in Oxford in 1843, Pusey invoked the power not only of typological sacramentality but also of the mystery religions. He stressed the present tense in all the variations of the phrase "This is my Body.... This is My Blood" as in " 'Whoso eateth My Flesh and drinketh My Blood' (He Himself says the amazing words) 'eateth Me,' and so receiveth into Himself in an ineffable manner, his Lord Himself, 'dwelleth' (our Lord says) 'in Me and I in Him' and having Christ within him, not only shall he have but he 'hath' already 'eternal Life.'" The Greek strata are obvious in Pusey's footnote:

> For here it is especially to be observed, that Christ saith that He shall be in us, not by a certain relation only as entertained through the affection, but also by a natural participation. For, if one entwineth wax with other wax and melteth them by the fire, there resulteth of both one.... For in no other way could that which is by nature corruptible be made alive unless it were bodily entwined with the Body of That Which is by nature Life.... This is (if we may reverently so speak) the order of the mystery of the Incarnation, that the Eternal Word so took our flesh into Himself, as to impart to it His own inherent life; so then we, partaking of It, that life is transmitted to us also, and not to our souls only, but our bodies also since we become flesh of His flesh, and bone of His bone and He Who is wholly life is imparted to us wholly.[49]

To support this argument he cites Cyril of Alexandria,[50] but the appeal of the mystery religions is clear.

What no doubt especially endeared Pusey to Hopkins was that this sermon made Pusey a martyr to the cause of this remarkable symbolism. If the Liberals had their martyr in Rowland Williams, who was indicted for heresy after his article on Bunsen appeared, the Tractarians had theirs in Pusey. After Pusey delivered his sermon, the Board of Heresy was summoned, and the vice chancellor requested a copy of the sermon. The Provost of Oriel wrote that he believed Pusey's problem was the "indiscreet adoption, in its literal sense of the highly figurative, mystical, and incautious language of certain of the old Fathers" (*Nine Sermons*, 317). Pusey was denied the usual chance to defend himself in person. The Board of Heresy did offer Pusey a chance to recant his stress on the "carnal and corporal presence of Christ" in the Eucharist, his stress on the continuation into the present moment of the Great Sacrifice, and his focus on "the body and blood of Christ as present with the consecrated elements by virtue of their consecration before they are received by the communicant and independently of his faith" (*Nine Sermons*, 323). However, Pusey's recantations were not accepted and the most severe possible penalty was assessed: suspension from preaching for two years. Pusey wrote a letter of protest to the vice chancellor and made a public protest to no avail.

Ten years later he repeated the same doctrines in a sermon on the Eucharist and escaped censure. However, in 1854 Archdeacon Denison's sermons on the Eucharist came under similar attack, and Pusey was moved to write his book on the Real Presence distinguishing between his position and that of the Roman Catholics' "transubstantiation" and the Lutherans' "consubstantiation." Pusey insisted that "This is my Body" cannot be understood figuratively in the usual sense and that the natural substance persists after the consecration. Nevertheless, Denison's belief that "worship is due to the Real though Invisible and Supernatural Presence of the Body and Blood of Christ" was condemned by a high church court, and he was cut off from all his preferments. Denison refused to recant. Again Pusey mounted a public protest. Keble joined in with a treatise titled "Eucharistical Adoration," but it too came under attack in Scotland when six bishops met to condemn the Bishop of Brechin, an ally of Keble's and Pusey's, who was censured and admonished in 1860. So when Hopkins entered Oxford in 1861, Pusey was clearly the famous champion of the Real Presence, the person most fully identified with the theology and the literary theory, as it were, behind a statement such as "and the azurous hung hills are his world wielding shoulder."

At the same time at Oxford, Müller was promulgating the model of what we have been calling the palimpsest of religious discourse. In the context of his research, we have only begun to explore the strata of meaning of Hopkins's sentence. Müller focused on Teutonic, Slavonic, and Celtic as well as Greek, Roman, and Sankrit mythology. Hence another layer of meaning of "and the azurous hung hills are his world wielding shoulder" and Hopkins's other poems composed in Wales is that of Celtic mythology, but that is a strata we do not have space to excavate here.

Particularly important to Hopkins, Pusey and Müller demonstrated that the oldest and most significant layer of meaning in many of those texts, underneath Celtic mythology and the mystery religions, was the primal religious feeling inspired by nature that directly conveyed a sense of an eternal present/ce.[51] As we have seen, Hopkins had "a considerable belief in the Solar myth and especially in these 'hounds of dawn,' which are really very widespread" (*Further Letters*, 263). Exploring this myth in his 1856 essay, "Comparative Mythology," Müller cited Wordsworth:

> "Not unrejoiced, I see thee climb the sky / In naked splendor, clear from mist and haze." Antiquity spoke of the naked Sun, and of the chaste Dawn hiding her face when she had seen her husband. Yet she says she will come again. And after the Sun has travelled through the world in search of his beloved, when he comes to the threshold of death, and is going to end his solitary life, she appears again in the gloaming, the same as the dawn,...and she carries him away to the golden seats of the immortals. I have selected this myth chiefly in order to show how ancient poetry is only the faint echo of ancient language, and how it was the simple story of nature which inspired the early poet, and held before his mind that deep mirror in which he might see reflected the passions of his own soul....[T]he ancient poet had still the heart of nature to commune with, and in her silent suffering he saw a noble likeness of what he felt and suffered within himself....[H]e would remember his own fate and yet forget it, while telling in measured words the love and loss of the Sun. Such was the origin of poetry.[52]

While "Hurrahing In Harvest" does not tap the solar myth directly, like so many of the poems Hopkins composed in Wales in 1877 it is focused on the sky. It was preceded that year by "God's Grandeur," which begins, "The world is charged with the grandeur of God. / It will flame out, like shining from shook foil," and ends with the central event of the solar myth, the dawn, now given a Christian interpretation:

> And though the last lights off the black West went
>   Oh, morning at the brown brink eastward, springs—
> Because the Holy Ghost over the bent
>   World broods with warm breast and with ah! bright wings![53]

The next poem Hopkins composed that year ("The Starlight Night") also focused on the skies, beginning with the injunction, "look, look up at the skies!" And then, of course, he composed the great poem of this great year, this time beginning with the dawn and its embodiment: "I caught this morning morning's minion, kingdom of daylight's dauphin, dapple-dawn-drawn Falcon." Again the grandeur of God flames out ("the fire that breaks from thee") and the poem ends with colors of the dawn: "gold-vermilion." In the ensuing "Hurrahing in Harvest" the speaker looks up, at clouds that mold and melt "across skies": "I walk, I lift up, I lift up heart, eyes, / Down all the glory in the heavens to glean our Saviour." As the speaker's eyes move down to the horizon he feels the ecstasy he ascribed to the windhover:

> And the azurous hung hills are his world-wielding shoulder
> Majestic—as a stallion stalwart, very-violet-sweet!—
> These things, these things were here and but the beholder
> Wanting; which two when they once meet,
> The heart rears wings bold and bolder
> And hurls for him, O half hurls earth for him off under his feet.

For Hopkins it is no accident that nature brings the speaker close to the infinite, for that is the essence of the aboriginal spirituality of nature uncovered by Müller. In his lectures on natural religion, looking back on his career, Müller, like Pusey, Scotus, and Hopkins, emphasized that God is apprehended better through the senses, especially sensations of nature, than through abstractions: "It has been my chief endeavour to show that religion did not begin with abstract concepts and a belief in purely extra-mundane beings, but that its deepest roots can be traced back to the universal stratum of sensuous perception. . . . I spoke of the sensuous pressure of the infinite which is contained in the simplest perceptions of our senses."[54] He speaks of what Pusey would call natural "types" of the infinite, of objects that can embody spirituality: "A stone is not infinite, nor a shell, nor an apple, nor a dog, and hence they have no theogonic capacity. But a river or a mountain, and still more the sky and the dawn, possess theogonic capacity, because they have in themselves from the beginning something going beyond the limits of sensuous perception, something which, for want of a better word I must continue to call infinite" (Müller, *Natural*, 148). Like Coleridge, Pusey, and the Tractarians, Müller finds himself describing something more than a metaphor, something between the mortal and the immortal: "The human mind in discovering the infinite behind the finite, does not separate the two. We can never draw a line where the finite ends and the infinite begins. The sky, for instance, was perceived as blue or grey, it had its horizon, and so far it was perceived as finite; but it was at the same time the infinite sky, because it was felt that beyond what is seen of the sky there is and must be an infinite complement which no eye could see. The infinite per se, as a mere negative, would have had no interest for primitive man; but as the background, as the support, as the subject or the cause of the finite in its many manifestations, it came in from the earliest period of human thought" (Müller, *Natural*, 149). Müller then provides us perhaps the ultimate layer of meaning for "And the azurous hung hills are his world wielding shoulder":

> The early settlers of this earth, when standing at the foot of a mountain and looking up to where its head vanishes in the clouds, could not help feeling overawed by these stupendous giants. We take all these things for granted, and we have learnt to know what is beyond these mountains; nay, how they were made, and how they can be unmade. But to early people a mountain-range marked the end of their little world. They saw the dawn, the sun, the moon and the stars rising above the mountaintops, the very sky seemed to rest on them; but what was beyond or beneath or above, no one could guess. In later times the highest mountains were often believed to be the seats of the gods, and the highest points were often chosen as the most appropriate for building temples to the gods. . . . When from some high mountain peak our eye travels as far as it can, watching the clouds, and the sky, and the setting sun and the rising stars, it is not by any process of conscious reasoning that we conclude that there is something infinite beyond the sky, beyond the sun, beyond the stars. It might truly be said that we are actually brought in sensuous contact with it; we see and feel it. In feeling the limit, we cannot help feeling also what is beyond the limit; we are in the actual presence of a visible infinite. (Müller, *Natural*, 151–54)

Is it appropriate to cite Müller in this way to explicate Hopkins, to hear echoes of the old nature religions in the poetry of an acolyte of the Oxford Movement? One answer may be still be heard and seen in the spiritual heart of Oxford, Christ Church Cathedral. To this day, a bust of Pusey looks on there as the Eucharist is celebrated, often in Latin, with a strong emphasis on the Real Presence. To the north of the altar the old shrine to St. Frideswide (650–735), destroyed by Protestants, has been reconstructed. On its side are stone carvings of the traditional "green men,"[55] though in this case they have become "green women," merging with images of St. Frideswide. They are only the most obvious relics of the old nature religions. The presence of the past is seen and felt in the light streaming through the deep green leaves of the stained glass windows all around the cathedral designed by Hopkins's fellow medievalists, Morris and Burne-Jones. This and many other stone and glass palimpsests were read and understood by Victorian Radicals of all persuasions, Müller as well as Pusey, and, if we are to understand Anglo and Roman Catholic religious discourse, we would be well advised to acknowledge their point of view as well as that of mainstream Protestantism.

Moreover importantly, for some people, to step into the Oxford cathedral is to step not only farther and farther into the past, but finally into a time out of time, an eternal present. This sense of an eternal present/ce is "radically" different from the modern sense of the present moment as the only time there is. For example, there is little sense of an eternal presence in the new intertextuality, one concerned with a " 'structural or synchronic model of literature as a sign system' replacing an older 'evolutionary model of literary history.' "[56] This synchronic model of literature is more akin to the sense of time of that more and more dominant figure of our time, computer man, who

> is less aware of history than his predecessor and is not likely to see the historical currents in which he is caught. He tends to project the present indefinitely in both directions . . . progress in computers and in the rest of our current technology is so rapid that it tends to negate history. In the past, technological progress was a matter of years and decades; even the engineer had to take a somewhat longer view of his subject. Today engineers, like the Red Queen in *Though the Looking Glass*, must run as fast as they can to remain in one place. . . . We must find ways to bring history into the computer world. At the very least, we must make sure that the record of history and culture is preserved in the coming age.[57]

To preserve that record we need to maintain historical literary criticism. The New Historicism, like the old, shares with Reception Theory an emphasis on formulating what Hans Robert Jauss calls " 'questions that the text gave an answer to' at the time of its production and thereby discovering 'how the contemporary reader could have viewed and understood the work' " and the significance " 'Of the historical particulars that partially constituted its 'meaning' upon composition or first publication.' "[58] When we understand the historical particulars of the sacramental typology of the Victorian Radicals we access dimensions of time lost to our contemporaries.

NOTES

Versions of this essay, on Hopkins and Pusey, were presented at the National University of Ireland at Maynooth on July 25, 1999, and at the University of Sydney on August 25, 1999. An early draft of the section on Müller was presented at the University of Caen, December 13, 2001. I would like to express my gratitude to the International Hopkins Conference, Sydney Society for Literature and Aesthetics, and Professor Rene' Gallet for these opportunities and their helpful feedback, and to the librarian of Pusey House, Oxford, the Rev. William Davage, for access to Pusey's *Lectures on Types and Prophecies of the Old Testament*.

1. Jude V. Nixon, "Framing Victorian Discourse."
2. Friedrich Max Müller, *Chips from A German Workshop. Vol. I: Essays on The Science of Religion* (New York: Charles Scribner's Sons, 1887), x.
3. See Robert Langbaum, *The Poetry of Experience; The Dramatic Monologue in Modern Literary Tradition* (New York: Norton, 1963).
4. See the discussion of the Victorian sage in Nixon, "Framing."

5. Frederic Stephens, "The Purpose and Tendency of Early Italian Art," in *The Germ: A Pre-Raphaelite Little Magazine*, ed. Robert Stahr Hosmon (Coral Gables: University of Miami Press, 1970), 58–64, 63.

6. Ibid., 58–64.

7. Herbert Sussman, *Fact into Figure: Typology in Carlyle, Ruskin, and the Pre-Raphaelite Brotherhood* (Columbus: Ohio State University Press, 1979), 8–9.

8. William Michael Rossetti, "Introduction," *The Germ*, appendix 1, in *The Germ*, 247–58, 253.

9. Harold Bloom, *A Map of Misreading* (New York: Oxford University Press, 1975), 73, 84, 95.

10. Hugh Blair, *Lectures on Rhetoric and Belles Lettres*, 2 vols. (Brooklyn: Thomas Kirk, 1812), 1: 339.

11. Bloom, *Map*, 103; cf. 73, 84, 95, 125–43.

12. John Henry Newman, *Parochial and Plain Sermons*, 8 vols. (London: Rivington, 1875), 7, 121–22.

13. See Jerome Bump, *Gerard Manley Hopkins* (Boston: Twayne, 1982), 80–92, 98–100, 117–18, 129–31, 136–44.

14. George P. Landow, *Victorian Types, Victorian Shadows: Biblical Typology in Victorian Literature, Art, and Thought* (Boston: Routledge, 1980), 3, 7.

15. Nixon, "Framing."

16. Mary Wilson Carpenter, *George Eliot and the Landscape of Time: Narrative Form and Protestant Apocalyptic History* (Chapel Hill: University of North Carolina Press, 1986), 3, cf. 13.

17. Ibid., 8–9.

18. Ibid., 19.

19. Qtd. in Nixon, "Kill[ing]," note 71.

20. Nixon, "Framing."

21. Nitram Tradleg (Martin Geldart), *A Son of Belial. Autobiographical Sketches by Nitram Tradleg* (London: Trubner and Co., 1882), 138–39.

22. Nixon, "Framing."

23. Thomas Hardy, *Jude the Obscure* (New York: W. W. Norton, 1978), 63.

24. Samuel Taylor Coleridge, "The Statesman's Manual or The Bible the Best Guide to Political Skill and Foresight: A Lay Sermon," in *Collected Works of Samuel Taylor Coleridge*, ed. R. J. White, vol. 6 (1816; reprint, New Jersey: Princeton University Press, 1972), 29–30.

25. Edward B. Pusey, *Lectures on Types and Prophecies of the Old Testament*, ms. Pusey House, Oxford, 107.

26. Jerome Bump, review of *Gerard Manley Hopkins and Tractarian Poetry*, by Margaret Johnson, *English Literature in Transition* 41, no. 4 (1998): 232–36.

27. G. B. Tennyson, *Victorian Devotional Poetry: The Tractarian Mode* (Cambridge, Massachusetts: Harvard University Press, 1981), 147.

28. Ibid., 147.

29. J. Hillis Miller, *The Disappearance of God: Five Nineteenth-Century Writers* (Cambridge, Massachusetts: Harvard University Press, 1981), 2, 6.

30. Gerard Manley Hopkins, *Further Letters of Gerard Manley Hopkins*, ed. Claude Colleer Abbott (Oxford: Oxford University Press, 1956), 98.

31. *Webster's International Dictionary of the English Language*, second ed., s.v. "analogy."

32. W. R. Inge, *Christian Mysticism*, fourth ed. (London, 1918), 309.

33. John Keble, *Keble's Lectures on Poetry*, trans. E. Francis, 2 vols. (Oxford: Clarendon Press, 1912), 2:481.

34. John Henry Newman, *Apologia Pro Vita Sua*, ed. David J. DeLaura (New York: W. W. Norton, 1968), 27–28.

35. *Lectures on Types*, 15. Admittedly, at times Pusey talks in terms of analogy, but he is referring to what Wordsworth might call "real analogy"; Pusey writes, "the province of the true poet has been not to invent likenesses, but to trace out the analogies which are actually impressed upon the creation"(*Lectures on Types*, 15). Pusey emphasizes that these connections are actually in nature, not merely comparisons made up by poets: "these religious meanings were not arbitrarily affixed by their own minds but...they arose out of, and existed in, the things themselves....[T]his expressiveness really lies in the object and is not the work of imagination." (*Lectures on Types*, 16–17).

36. Ernico Mazza, *The Celebration of the Eucharist: The Origin of the Rite and the Development of Its Interpretation*, trans. Matthew J. O'Connell (Collegeville, Minnesota: The Liturgical Press, 1999), 236.

37. Ibid., 200.

38. T. S. Eliot, "Tradition and the Individual Talent," in *Selected Prose of T. S. Eliot*, ed. F. Kermode (New York: Harcourt, Brace, Jovanovich, 1975), 38.

39. The redaction preserved by Ambrose of Milan: Mazza, 141.

40. Mazza, 142–43.

41. Mazza, 140.

42. Gerard Manley Hopkins, *Journals and Papers of Gerard Manley Hopkins*, ed. Humphry House (Oxford: Oxford University Press, 1959), 36.

43. James Milroy, *The Language of Gerard Manley Hopkins* (London: Andre Deutsch, 1977); Cary Plotkin, *The Tenth Muse: Victorian Philology and the Genesis of the Poetic Language of Gerard Manley Hopkins* (Carbondale: Southern Illinois University Press, 1989).

44. Jude V. Nixon, *Gerard Manley Hopkins and His Contemporaries: Liddon, Newman, Darwin, and Pater* (New York: Garland, 1994).

45. Max Müller, *Chips from A German Workshop*. Vol. I: ix–x.

46. *Dictionary of Mining, Mineral, and Related Terms*, U.S. Bureau of Mines, http://imcg.wr.usgs.gov/dmmrt/.

47. Nixon, "Framing."

48. Nixon, "Framing."

49. Edward B. Pusey, *Nine Sermons Preached Before the University of Oxford and Printed Chiefly Between 1843–1855* (Oxford: James Parker and Co., 1879), 11–12.

50. He could also have cited Augustine. "Especially when commenting on passages of John, Augustine sees the Eucharist as life, to the point of remarking that Christians who speak the Punic dialect usually call the Eucharist simply 'life.'" Mazza, 158.

51. Bump, *Gerard*, 141–45.

52. Friedrich Max Müller, *Chips from A German Workshop. Vol. II: Essays on Mythology, Traditions, and Customs* (New York: Charles Scribner's Sons, 1890), 104–07.

53. All citations of Hopkins's poetry are from *The Poems of Gerard Manley Hopkins*, ed. W. H. Gardner and N. H. MacKenzie, fourth ed. (London: Oxford University press, 1967).

54. Friedrich Max Müller, *Natural Religion: The Gifford Lectures, 1888* (London: Longmans, Green and Co., 1889), 141.

55. See William Anderson, *Green Man: The Archetype of Our Oneness with the Earth* (London: Harper Collins, 1990; Compassbooks, 2002).

56. Thaïs E. Morgan, "Is there an Intertext in this Text? Literary and Interdisciplinary Approaches to Intertextuality," *The American Journal of Semiotics* 3 (1985): 1–40, 2.

57. J. David Bolter, *Turing's Man: Western Culture in the Computer Age* (Chapel Hill: University of North Carolina Press, 1984), 225–26, 229.

58. Antony H. Harrison, *Victorian Poets and Romantic Poems: Intertextuality and Ideology* (Charlottesville: University Press of Virginia, 1990), 12, 14.

CHAPTER 2

"KILL[ING] OUR SOULS WITH LITERALISM": READING *ESSAYS AND REVIEWS*

Jude V. Nixon

> *The old teachings, believed for a thousand years, are on the point of collapsing.*
> *There is less wood in the beams of these structures than in the supports which*
> *are supposed to hold them up. But the new knowledge is a new building of*
> *which only the scaffolding is there.... What is written in the old books does*
> *not satisfy mankind any more.... [T]he universe lost its center overnight*
> *and in the morning it had a countless number of centers.*
>
> —Bertolt Brecht, *Galileo I*

If Charles Darwin's *The Origin of Species* (1859) swept across England like a cataclysmic flood, as Charles Kingsley presciently observed, then the pseudonymous *Essays and Reviews* (1860) was the storm.[1] From this blast "troubling the stagnant waters of orthodoxy," English orthodoxy became "convulsed with indignation and panic." Constituting "a landmark in the history of English theology," *Essays and Reviews* was even "more alarming— a conspiracy of clergymen to blow up the Church from within."[2] This was precisely what the architects of the Oxford Movement of 1833 had dreaded and wanted to preempt: the theological and biblical skepticism of German higher criticism. With its "guerilla warfare of essays," where "hundreds of points are touched, none completed," *Essays and Reviews* was viewed as an act of what we now call bio-terrorism, "the scattering of poison in the wells of a city," a metaphor based on the familiar nineteenth-century practice of dumping raw, untreated sewage into the streets, which then contaminated the water supplies.[3] In a related metaphor, the most recent editors of *Essays and Reviews* likened its effect to an illness and an epidemic: "the rising temperature of the established church as fears of heretical fever . . . gripped the nation" (*E&R*, 30). In the language of another favorite metaphor, *Essays and Reviews* virtually "set a torch to what proved to be dry timber."[4] No fewer than "400 pamphlets, tracts, lectures, sermons, and charges were published as attacks on *Essays and Reviews*" (*E&R*, 42).

Sales of these two Victorian archives were remarkable. *The Origin of Species* sold all 1,250 printed copies on the day of publication. Three months later, 1,200 new copies were printed. In contrast, from March 1860, when *Essays and Reviews* appeared, to March 1861, its nine editions saw sales totaling well over 20,000 copies, and 24,250 copies by its thirteenth edition of 1869. At the end of seventeen years, *The Origin of Species* has sold 17,000 copies.[5] Had *Essays and Reviews* seen publication in 1859, as was planned (its delay due to Jowett's tardiness), it would have waged an impressive argument for its own monumentalism, to say nothing of how it may have shaped the reception of Darwinism, its favorite point of comparison.[6] George Moberly observes the volume's frequent intimations of doubt regarding "the descent of mankind from a single pair," and Ieuan Ellis is convinced that to understand the cultural context of *Essays and Reviews* is "to see it as a religious counterpart of those historically-dominated studies . . . which proposed to explain society and its institutions by their historical origins, an evolutionary process from lower to higher, from simpler to more complex forms."[7] Science wedded to higher criticism offered new ways of examining the archive: "the possibility for interpretation at variance with the received orthodoxies of the Christian Establishment was greatly expanded in the nineteenth century, first with the advances in the sciences, especially astronomy, geology, and biology, and secondly in the fields of biblical interpretation, especially the historical and higher critical study of the Bible" (*E&R*, 71).

The essayists, because of their historicist turn—relating the past to the historical present—admit an epistemological link to Darwinism, a discursive field accommodating entire systems of thought. Baden Powell, who along with Jowett explicitly referred to Darwin, predicted that Darwinism would soon commence "an entire revolution of opinion in favour of the grand principle of the self-evolving powers of nature" (*E&R*, 258). And Temple, arguing the "advance" of culture and the "evolutionary" development of man, assumes a Darwinian ideology.[8] The essayists intended to present their views as developmental and to show that the biblical canon reveals the same unstable features as the history of doctrinal development. Stephen Prickett puts it best, insisting that science, and Darwinian science in particular, "provided not so much a new metanarrative as a methodology for reconstructing and rehabilitating a religion whose cultural roots penetrated so deeply into their own sense of identity and purpose as to make it almost indispensable."[9] But whereas *Essays and Reviews*, at least on the surface, appears to have had a residual impact on Western culture, in comparison to *The Origin of Species*, and while the consternation it provoked seems today little more than an annoyance, to Victorians it was seismic: it so undermined the received assumptions about canonicity and consensus on matters of authority/authorship that orthodoxy would never again reconstitute itself with the same degree of coherence, confidence, and conviction. The essays in the collection engaged "the relations between religious faith and mid-Victorian discussion about education, theology, science, history, literature, biblical studies, politics, and philosophy," and did so in such profound ways that "For a decade after its publication it provoked intense controversy in the church, the university, the press, the government, and the courts, both ecclesiastical and secular" (*E&R*, 3). In fact, while *Essays and Reviews*, says Linda Rozmovits, "may have been directed...as a reassessment of the status of the Bible, its effects in the sphere of secular literature were no less powerfully felt." It served as a way to "bridge the traditional gap between sacred and secular texts."[10]

Critics of *Essays and Reviews* note this very connection between the secular and sacred, combining even, as Gladstone discovered, Homer with Dante.[11] Elinor S. Shaffer observes the same: "The men who were prepared to apply the methods of secular literary criticism to the Bible were naturally quick to carry the results of their Biblical criticism back into secular literature," an "intricate relationship between *critica sacra* and *critica profana*" largely ignored. "Yet, its overwhelming importance for nineteenth-century literature has never ceased to be proclaimed."[12] One reviewer saw *Essays and Reviews* "in direct antagonism to the whole system of popular belief," a feeling shared by the Balliol undergraduate Martin Geldart who, regarding Jowett's essay, remarked: "I had always, it seemed, held the same, only without knowing. But at the end of the essay where was my orthodox faith? Overturned in irretrievable ruin, never to be rebuilt upon the old foundations."[13] "For writers the most auspicious of the prevailing winds of doubt," says Dorothy Mermin, "was the movement in biblical interpretation known as Higher Criticism, which read the Bible not as a direct revelation from God but as a myth that had developed in history and could be interpreted by the same methods as, say, the Homeric epics, of which the tradition of single authorship was also in dispute.... To most pious people the Higher Criticism seemed just another rationalist attack on faith; but to others the idea that religion is the product of the human imagination offered the exhilarating hope both of reinterpreting the Judeo-Christian myths and of making new ones."[14]

The essayists are a fairly homogeneous lot—all English, all male, and almost all Oxonians and clergymen, fashioning what Sue Zemka calls "the internal constructions of their own legitimacy."[15] And while the essays comprise a residual dissimilarity, they are really "homogeneous fields of enunciated regularities" that "characterize a discursive formation," presenting the male body as archive of England's intellectual and religious life, very much in the tradition of the Oxford Movement with its conservative ideology and "program of masculine self-fashioning."[16] Thomas Carlyle, for example, committed to preserving the established hierarchies—whether gender, political, or racial—as something divinely ordained and sanctioned, had pronounced in *Sartor Resartus* great Englishmen as sacred texts, placing cultural authority squarely in the heroic patriarchal character. "Even in its 'Germanism,' *Essays and Reviews* is a very English book," investing much in a particular English personality and character.[17] Like the very monument it seeks to demythologize, *Essays and Reviews* claims even as it obliterates canonical authority, turning the tables, says one critic, on "the old ortho-doxy," while simultaneously establishing "a new, Critical orthodoxy."[18] The essayists wanted to re-place or dis-place the interpretive hegemony by providing alternative models of reading, effecting, as Fredric Jameson puts it, "the forcible or imperceptible transformation of a given text into an allegory of its particular master code or 'transcendental signified.'"[19] They were concerned with a particular hermeneutic strategy and the character of evidence, with a school built around a "verifying faculty." And they intended to wrest the argument away from verbalness and to place Christianity, as A. P. Stanley has suggested, "beyond the reach of accidents."[20] All of the essayists seem committed to questioning themes of convergence and culmi-nation, remaining dubious about the derivative totalities. And however much they acknowledged points of intersection, juxtaposition, and overlap-ping, their method remained individualistic. Jowett, in particular, wanted to push back "further and further the line of antecedents to reconstituting tra-ditions . . . disassociating the reassuring form of the identical."[21] Trafficking freely in the domain of the forbidden, *Essays and Reviews* is clearly a discourse of desire.

Many observers saw *Essays and Reviews* as doctrinally bankrupt, offering little more than moral instructions on how best to achieve what Jowett has called "an ideal of life." The essayists, neologians as they were called and their apologetic a "negative theology" (Moberly), often dismissed as the philoso-phy of the nineteenth century or a new school of English theology, wanted to establish biblical interpretation on an entirely new trajectory of thought by removing it from its historical foundation, all the while invoking the past, the major strategy of theories of discontinuity. Repeated declarations of historical continuity are themselves credible indicators of rupture. *Essays and Reviews* should be regarded as one of those "phenomena of rupture," for "most rad-ical discontinuities," as Michel Foucault has observed, are "the breaks effected by a work of theoretical transformation" dislodged from the ideology of the past under the assumption that the past was in fact ideological.[22]

Wanting to disavow the tyranny of institutional fiat, *Essays and Reviews* asserts no single authorial claim. Instead, nontraditional in method, uncon-ventional in language, and unconcerted in character, it veils itself in the murkiness of multiple authorship, deferrals, and refusals. It asserts separate, sometimes even contradictory, histories of the volume's genesis as a way to dispense with the trace of editorial identity, accountability, and ownership. On the contrary, "most Victorian social narrative and cultural interpreta-tion," Zemka finds, "establish a network of references, quotations, and voices that connect their authority to social and historical externalities."[23] *Essays and Reviews* concerns itself with a discursive object, but admits no nexus of regularities governing the dispersion of the essays. What we have is a "manifestation of the subjectivity of the absent author,"[24] an attenuation or fading of the human voice in time. Temple's lead essay and reputation as successor to Arnold and Tait at Rugby might single him out as editor; Jowett's magnetism filled the void following Newman's Oxford exile, and his essay perhaps more than any of the others seems to define the volume. But in fact it was Wilson who initiated the collection, including crafting the preface. Indeed, we have "authorities of formulation" but no "enunciating subject" (Foucault). Authorial accountability is dispersed, concealed, if not altogether voided. But the authorial disclaimer does not tell the whole story or the truth of it. The prefatory address "To the Reader," hardly spontaneously generated, had to have been composed either by one of the essayists (Wilson), through a collaborative act, or by the publisher J. W. Parker. Peter Hinchliff finds it "a little disingenuous in the suggestion that the whole thing was simply an innocent mistake."[25]

Thus, the very attempt to suppress or displace authorship and with it authority—Scripture being synonymous to authority—all the more proclaim it. As important—and this the main site of skirmish—the disclaimer implies a maverick production, a direct assault on Victorian accountability and reserve. Moberly enumerates the ways in which this "ocean of speculation and free-thinking" weakened the faith of those "imperfectly grounded in Christian truth" and assaulted what had been "authoritatively taught." He castigates the essayists' "claim of freedom from mutual responsibility," asking, "If the seven stars be, as they say, wholly separate and unconnected with one another, by whose doing is it that they appear to us in the form of a constellation of no good omen to the cause of Christian truth?" Moberly notices "a distinct harmony" among the essays, "set as they are in one key, and taking different notes in the same chord." For example, he finds Temple's introductory essay bearing "unintended resemblance" and set within a "neighbourhood where it seems to bear so close a relation to all that follows it." A *Westminster Review* article Moberly cites recognized the "virtual unity in the purpose of the whole," and felt that "each writer received a weight and an authority from all the rest of his associates."[26]

In offering a reading of *Essays and Reviews,* I am concerned with its theological character, politics of legitimacy, and desire to replace the received canonical hermeneutic (essentially literalism) with new interpretive hegemonies armed to combat what Jowett has called an "abominable system of terrorism."[27] I wish to explore the archaeology of the text, its *schemata*, its orderings and enunciations, to read for alternative and/or competing discourses, metatexts, which threaten to disrupt the narratives from within. I also wish to observe the ways in which "the 'world' of the text," as Paul Ricoeur would say, shatters "the world of the author."[28] Finally, I intend to trace the rhetorical relations among the essays, examining the ways in which the essayists deploy new contours of reading, having obliterated the established literary maps. The essayists intended to rid orthodoxy of its interpretive hegemony and to open the biblical text to new interpretive strategies, new frontiers of scholarship. In Ricoeurian language, they wanted to see the Bible as "a work of art, a literary work, which transcends it own psycho-sociological conditioning and thus becomes open to an indefinite range of readers and readings within different sociocultural contexts." As such, "The text must be able to be de-contextualized, from both a sociological and a psychological point of view, in order to be able to be re-contextualized in fresh situations."[29] For while the canon as a totalizing body might well be closed and fixed once and for all times, literary criticism, rather than historicism or rhetoricism, loosens up the text from within and re-presents it as open and evolving, releasing the vitality of the archive. To the essayists, language is "a ceaseless activity—an energeïa."[30] "A genuine higher criticism of the Bible," Northrop Frye has observed, "would be a synthesizing process which would start with the assumption that the Bible is a definitive myth, a single archetypal structure extending from creation to apocalypse."[31] The goal of the essayists, then, was to make the Scripture speak again, to make the rocks cry out, attempting a *positivity* (and the volume as a whole was viewed in Comtean terms) whereby the archive is understood not as a "closed, plethoric totality of a meaning" but as an "incomplete, fragmented figure." The essayists wanted to characterize "a group of statements, in order to rediscover not the moment or the trace of their origin, but the specific forms of an accumulation," to locate the *positivity* of revelation and its meaning in "their event-sequence or narrative character."[32]

To begin with, the essayists were conservationists and not chaoticists, attracted as they were to the myth of repeatable materiality, what Pattison himself calls "the law of continuity." Mindful, perhaps, of Carlyle's understanding of history as the past, present, and future preserved in the moment, and attracted to the law of conservation ("The universe would eternally repeat the same changes in a fixed order or recurrence, though each cycle might be many millions of years in length"), a repeatability Nietzsche later calls "eternal recurrence," Temple asserts that nothing from the past is altogether lost but merely converted into the present. Rowland Williams, similarly, demonstrating his awareness of the prevailing vitalism, the theologically informed assumption that energy conservation relates to the Divine effluence, envisions the "Divine energy as continuous and omnipresent," with "the stream...never varied in its flow" (*E&R*, 181). And Powell, following in a long line of nineteenth-century energeticists such as Hermann von Helmholtz and James Prescott Joule, entertains a non-dissipative structure, an infinite reservoir of energy: "universal self-sustaining and self-evolving powers which pervade all nature" (*E&R*, 256). Employing, liberally, tropes of the first law in their discourse (salvation, for example, is a "commercial transfer"), the essayists wanted their claims to be perceived not disruptive of but in accord with the natural flow of ideas, as a "living, continuous open history."[33] They wanted their neologistic assumptions, viewed as a *devenir*, connected seamlessly to the very tradition their strategies sought to dismantle.[34]

The opening essay, Frederick Temple's revised university sermon, "The Education of the World," takes its title from Lessing ("The Education of the Human Race") and employs loosely Butler's analogy principle.[35] The essay argues the "perpetual development" of an individual from birth to death, progressing sequentially through childhood, youth, and manhood. Mary Wilson Carpenter sees this method in accord with Daniel's Four Empires (Babylon, Persia, Greece, and Rome) of Protestant biblical prophecy, reduced by Temple to "tutors" or "Educators" of the world. "Temple converted the Four Empires to an educational scheme and daringly considered the Hebrews as merely one of those educators."[36] For him, cultural systems, texts really, are similarly open, fluid, and developmental. Temple's model presents a childlike dependence on law to a point of maturation along a continuum when law mutates into personal habits. The education of the world was set in motion when diverse races, while introducing a regressive instability, infused the system with revitalizing energy. But Temple's sense of the contributions of non-Hebraic races and acknowledgment of the impress of hybrid cultures on Western Christianity, all "united into one stream," is decidedly masculine: it transforms "the human race into a colossal man." The Early Church, an effete body, a feminized ideal, was "not meant for our model" because she exhibited "disorders, violent quarrels, licentious recklessness of opinion," behavior endemic to the artfulness of a Victorian hussy. Temple's mature church, on the contrary, is by disposition and character male not female, a "full-grown man" (*E&R*, 153, 155), ascribing health, and here spiritual health, to the religious patriarchy, the male body.

Most disturbing to Victorians was Temple's views on incomplete revelation and toleration, the latter the antithesis not to dogma but to dogmatism. One of the earliest to censure *Essays and Reviews*, the Anglo-Catholic Henry Parry Liddon saw Temple's essay as part of "the creed of Positivism."[37] According to Temple, the Church is incapable, "any more than a man is capable, of extracting, at once, all the truth and wisdom contained in the teaching of the early periods" (*E&R*, 160). Simply put, biblical revelation does not contain a totality of truth, for truth is contingent and changeable, a relativity that calls us "to modify and soften the hardness and severity" of principles that have become "immutable statements." Temple questions the received assumptions about the canon as an agreed upon body of texts, sacred and authoritative, and argues, instead, an open canon, from the very fact that its truths are contingent on "the progress of knowledge or growth of the human mind." Revelation, then, constitutes the developing nature of knowledge, an organicity that delimits its "supreme authority." Nigel Cameron sees a relationship between development and education, but does not formulate any direct links to Temple's essay, responsible in the main for "the marriage of a developmental theory and literary analysis" and for the rationale for the progress of Critical thinking after the 1870s.[38]

Rowland Williams's "Bunsen's Biblical Researches," called by Basil Willey the "head and front of the book's offending," attracted some of the fiercest criticism, in part because the review elides the impress of British national character on which, as Sue Zemka has observed, "the claims of English linguistic and theological purity" had historically been grounded.[39] Williams makes no attempt to accommodate Bunsen's speculations to Victorian cultural thought, connected as Bunsen was to England social and political life.[40]

Williams even fails to separate himself dispassionately from his subject, disclosing, instead, a relationship in which "sympathy" becomes "entire agreement." Many observers felt that acting both as Bunsen's "reporter" (Moberly) and expert ventriloquist, Williams was employing Bunsen to broadcast his own heterodoxy. Relying on progressive revelation, "the law of growth, traceable throughout the Bible as in the world," and convinced that we cannot deploy criticism of "Gentile histories" and then exempt the "Hebrew annals" from similar critical scrutiny, Williams reviews Bunsen's several treatises to explore the Bible from a comparative religionist perspective. He denounces the supernaturalism on which traditional biblical interpretation is based, and pronounces literalism and revelation fictions, the disease of the age.[41] The history of the Church is one of "turbulent growth," manifesting the character of a "democracy" and of "poetry."

Bunsen attempts an examination of the Bible from non-Hebraic sources, "the relics of Gentile form and usage" (E&R, 198), in light of the antiquity of other non-Hebraic cultures. He wants to "unroll tangled records, tracing frankly the Spirit of God elsewhere" (E&R, 181–82), convinced that not only was there a bible antedating the Judeo-Christian canon, but that the Jewish religion is neither the only sacred one nor the only one in which divine providence has acted. There has been, as Williams puts it, "divine footsteps in the Gentile world." Esemplastic, Christianity "assimilates the relics of Gentile form and usage" (E&R, 195, 198). Bunsen employs the Egyptian record to expand the narrow biblical chronology and to accommodate the development of commerce, civil government, language, and racial types. To derive the "unity of mankind" requires, Williams believes, a "cradle of larger dimensions." It was this insistence on an extended chronology for linguistic as well as geological shifts that led to Williams's indictment for heresy.

Bunsen's biblical criticism attempts not so much to de-historicize Scripture as to re-historicize it. Concerned about the quality, character, and integrity of biblical evidence, Bunsen naturalizes the Great Deluge, reads Genesis as an incomplete history of origins, finds the biblical chronology unreliable, and interprets the narrative of the Red Sea crossing as "the latitude of poetry." Mosaic only in character and sensibility, the Pentateuch is neither of one age nor of single authorship, but a product of "gradual growth" and a "composition out of older material," analogized as "a tree rooted in the varying thoughts of successive generations," an aggregate of fragmented genealogy, history, and song, all "embedded in a crust of later narratives." Venerating Bunsen's Germanism—a "pathway streaming with light"—Williams faults the early Church Fathers for deriving no clear interpretive method of symbolizing and literalizing, and for failing to appreciate "the force of analogy." The Messiah of Isaiah 52 and 53, an unstable signifier in Talmudic literature, but ossified into a type during Jewish persecution, is probably Jeremiah, perhaps his editor or biographer Baruch, or some suffering prophet or remnant. Conversely, the historical Jesus, a prophet to all humanity, a high priest to all religions, the embodiment of his own aspirations, and whose oracles transcend time, races, and nationality, is more of a diffusive moral agent than a spiritual savior.

Williams vindicates the exercise of reason, "a verifying faculty" he calls it, attempting to "make rationality the *telos* of mankind" and investing the history of thought to its preservation.[42] He finds it disingenuous to posit the least rational view of the Gospel as the "truest," to suggest that "faith should have no human element, and its records be exempt from historical law," that "traditional fictions about our canon" should be accepted uncritically, and that a "fabric of mingled faith" should be maintained by suppressing reason. Inspiration, determined by consensus ("the written voice of the congregation," the sense in which the text has been read by the community), must be understood "consistently with the facts of Scripture, and of human nature." As such, inspiration cannot be safeguarded by "disparaging the instruments which His wisdom chose for it." Williams's sense of history involves both the divine and human: "the more Divine the germ, the more human must be the development" (*E&R*, 194–99). The review concludes with a poetic tribute to Bunsen, a benediction, really, to human achievement (Linnæus's systematics): "Even like Linnæus kneeling on the sod, / For faith from falsehood severed, thank I God." Rhyming "sod" with "God" intimates the Incarnation, involving the human and Divine in the interpretive process. The couplet also implies that Darwin's primordial germ ("sod") can transcend to the Godlike: "not dead my soul to giant reach." Like his fellow essayists, Williams is not after a "doxology" nor does he wish "to draw up a list of founding saints"; instead, he wants to "uncover the regularity of a discursive practice."[43]

Baden Powell's "On the Study of the Evidences of Christianity" seeks to differentiate Christianity's "*essential doctrines*" from its "*eternal accessories*," the one fixed, the other developing. His argument follows Coleridge's *Aids to Reflection* (1825), which requires the rational faculty to "make good every sentence of the Bible to a rational inquirer."[44] Coleridge emerges a seminal voice, an "innovator" whose "religious thought" must be understood in relationship to higher criticism.[45] His "Confessions of an Inquiring Spirit" (1840), containing "scattered commentary on the issues of Higher Criticism" in that it "celebrates the sympathetic reader of the Bible as the most credible witness to is sacred intentions" and grants "priority to questions of personal literary interpretation,"[46] likewise examines the relationship between faith and the evidentiary. It finds those who argue infallibility in conflict with what precisely the term means, and insists that a theory of inspiration must engage the language of sense, science, and philosophy. While Scripture might well have been supernaturally delivered, once written it forfeits its supernatural character. In this sense, says Ricoeur, Christianity is "from its very beginning an exegesis," for speech now in the medium of writing "touches us through its 'meaning' and its 'issues' . . . although no longer the 'voice' of its proclaimer."[47]

"[C]ontemplative and theoretical," Powell's essay wants evidence interacting with feelings and reason, conscience and the intellect, the moral and the religious. Although jettisoning orthodox beliefs (among them, narratives of the miraculous and closed revelation), Powell foregrounds his argument against evidentialism in a hermeneutics of character: English empiricists and divines (Butler, Douglas, Warburton, Whately); religious statesmen (Coleridge, Paley, the Newmans); and national icons (Johnson). Wanting to avoid the usual "polemical acrimony" in favor of a "calm and unprejudiced" survey of the evidentiary argument, Powell welcomes a debate characterized by reserve ("calm" rather than "hasty and captious"). He separates "matters of *external fact*" from "moral or religious doctrine," insisting that while the former appeals to "reason and intellect," the latter, tied to faith, requires "other and higher grounds of judgment and conviction" (*E&R*, 234–35). To make historicist claims for Christianity while attempting to safeguard it from criticism compromises its essential historicity. The moral argument, it must be said, is no small matter, for the arguments against higher criticism, at least the way John Henry Newman saw it, concerned the preference for intellectual to moral arguments, which he perceived as a drift toward the liberalism of the day. This explains why Newman, so often in the *Apologia Pro Vita Sua*, attempts to dispense with logic, preferring, instead, conscience.

Most Protestants, Powell reasons, regard "narratives of the marvelous" as closed, fixed, sacralized, and once and for all canonized. Powell's positivism rejects the evidentiality of miracles in favor of "sensible facts"; we simply cannot have "a *Deity working miracles*," restricting the evidentiary to Miracles. Hardly "the *sole certificate* of Divine communication," miracles become "invested with the character of articles of faith." Belief, conversely, is the "*result*" of faith and not "*antecedent*" to it: "the Gospel miracles are always *objects*, not *evidences* of faith" (*E&R*, 259–60). English divines who reject the primacy of miracles do so because it confines faith and moral truth to the external and sensible rather than to the internal and spiritually informed, "*preliminary* moral convictions." In fact, the stronger one's belief in miracles, the less miraculous miracles become. Like Temple and Williams, Powell capitulates the received tradition to the claims of "advanced physical knowledge" (*E&R*, 251, 261). Making what one reviewer calls "an armistice with science,"[48] Powell wants science addressing things "properly belonging to the world of *matter*," and suspended when it comes to "*spiritual* truth" (*E&R*, 251). Thus, "miraculous narratives become invested with the character of faith" (*E&R*, 259–60). The need for evidence subjects miracles to scientific inquiry, placing them beyond the purview of the miraculous. Evidence and faith engage altogether different epistemics, the one "matters of knowledge," the other "the mysterious things of the unseen world" (*E&R*, 252).

The most Coleridgean of the essays, Henry Bristow Wilson's "The National Church," wanting to employ "the best method of adjusting old things to new conditions," derives a foundation of the Church based either on Individualism, the deliberate bifurcation of ecclesiastical and political powers, or on Multitudism, the wedding of Church and State. And in fact concerns about a National Church cannot be separated from the discursive context of disestablishment and the relationship between Church and State. Wilson sees the National Church an essential "organ of the national life." Because citizenship within a nation implies membership within a spiritual community, contemporary religious models should seek not merely to accept the received tradition but to repair "ancient paths," raise "fresh structures," and "transmit something better" (*E&R*, 276–77). In his apology for the essayists accused of having a "disease contracted by means of German inoculation,"[49] Wilson wants to devise a uniquely English biblical criticism, skeptical at the moment of "observation and thought" (*E&R*, 180–82) but able in the long run to accommodate science and literature. He is convinced that within a National Church, Christianity would exert a diffusive spiritual influence on contemporary, secular culture. That Church, however, should neither expect nor require complete assent on narrow doctrinal points, and must be eclectic rather than exclusive, multivalent rather than uniform. Wilson finds it untenable to demand either "unanimity in speculative doctrine" or "uniformity of historical belief," which did not exist even in Apostolic times. Christianity has historically selected from Scripture aspects relevant to the "circumstances of [its] own existence" (*E&R*, 284–85).

Home to religious fanatics as well as empiricists, a National Church should aspire "to raise each according to his capacities" and not "provoke the individualist element into separatism" (*E&R*, 291). A true National Church, which "must be the model for the contemporary faithful,"[50] accommodates both literalists and idealists, each holding different assumptions about the Scriptures—one the verbal accuracy of its history, the other its spiritual, allegorical essence. For Coleridge, as it is for Wilson, "God's eternal Word is expressed and later re-expressed through commentary, gloss, and interpretation by particular people at different times according to their different lights."[51] But when in a "scientific and literary age" a Church becomes exclusive in matters of doctrine, it forfeits its national character and alienates adherents impressed by literature and science and unperturbed by narrative discrepancies, scientific difficulties, and evidentiary defects. The Church of Christ, Wilson believes, is more anthropocentric than theocentric, founded on "the manifestation of a divine life in man" than in "an abstractly true and supernaturally communicated speculation concerning God" (*E&R*, 302–07). Wilson wants to expand the nationalistic configurations of Christianity, forcing it "against its will" to abandon tendencies to exclusivity. Thus, his "bright centre of spiritual truth" is not some constellation of dogma and the dogmatic, but ideology and morality, which the evolutionist sympathizer, Samuel Butler's young Ernest Pontifex, in his crisis of faith also embraced: "he no longer believed in the supernatural element of Christianity, but the Christian morality at any rate was indisputable."[52]

Wilson's assumptions clearly troubled Victorians. Most vexing, though, was his desacralizing of Scripture, desire for greater openness to new knowledge and an ever-evolving canon, expansive definition of inspiration, accommodation on disparate doctrinal positions, and rejection of Christianity's specialness. Like Coleridge, he believed that Scripture is "a living and progressive organism, one that comes into existence in human time and continues to develop in that 'fallible' and limited sphere."[53] In its formularies, Protestantism in general and Anglicanism in particular assert a foundation in "the 'Word of God,'" a claim by no means coeval to "Holy Scripture," "Canonical Books," and "Old and New Testaments." The term "canonical," as Wilson reads Article VI, could mean "regulative" or "determined" books, those ratified by the Church, while the non-canonical are non-regulative books. The authorship and dates of the canonical books, he argues, were "not determined by any authority," for even as these books evolved ("grew") and contested their own canonical positions, questions remained regarding their authorship and authority. Thus "the Word of God," while not "co-extensive" with Scripture, is yet "contained" in it. An "emblematic force" pervades Scripture as convincingly as "literal truth," not unlike the way parable, fable, or proverb, all fabular narratives, articulate truth claims, even if the events they describe actually "did not happen."[54] The real specialness of the Scripture, Wilson believes, resides in the "supernatural property" of words that "address themselves intelligibly to the unlearned and learned alike" (*E&R*, 293). Though "agreeable to the Word of God," the Articles are not "co-extensive with the Bible, much less of equal authority with it as a whole." Lutheran or Calvinist in tone, the Articles have been subject to "affixing different signification" to terms "by reason of different interpretations of Scriptural passages" (*E&R*, 296–98). Wilson's doxology celebrates an environment conducive to spiritual growth, greenhouses "where the undeveloped may grow up under new conditions—the stunted may become strong, and the perverted be restored." His National Church is a "Universal Parent" in whose "nurseries" and "bosom" infants find safety, sustenance, vitality, and repose.

C. W. Goodwin, like Baden Powell, explores the presumed conflict between Christianity and the natural sciences, albeit dated, given Darwin's recent findings and corrections of Lyell. The "growth of geology," Goodwin observes, has challenged received assumptions about divine revelation, making attempts to reconcile the Mosaic narrative to emerging geological discoveries quite problematic. A well-known Egyptologist, Goodwin, in "On the Mosaic Cosmogony," offers a close reading of the Mosaic narrative of creation in light of new discoveries in geology and paleontology. He attacks theological geologists who attempt to fabricate a cosmogony, an originating theory of creation. While Goodwin desires a broader chronology than contemporary cosmogonists are unwilling to concede, he does not advocate an indefinite time-span for the creation event: "No blank chaotic gap of death and darkness separated the creation" (*E&R*, 357). Goodwin moves to retell the narrative of the Genesis creation, observing its scientific character but directing hard questions to its scientific claims. He reads the creation story as a Hebrew myth satisfying the "wants of man" and forming "a sufficient basis of theological teaching" (*E&R*, 370), a point John Tyndall, the noted physicist, would make, calling Genesis "a poem, not a scientific treatise."[55]

The real problem with the Mosaic narrative, according to Goodwin, is that unlike other cosmogonies it makes no pretense to poetic conventions: the mythical, the symbolic, the imaginative, and the vagaries of individual personality. Eric Auerbach's characterization conforms to Goodwin's: "more comprehensible in his presence," says Auerbach, Homer's Zeus is quite different from the God of the Bible. "Far from seeking, like Homer, merely to make us forget our own reality for a few hours, it seeks to overcome our reality: we are to fit our life into its world, feel ourselves to be elements in its structure of universal history."[56] In fact, comparisons to Homer would be employed routinely by higher critics, who make the same argument for Moses and the Pentateuch as they do about the identity of an actual Homer and the epics which they believed originated from a folk tradition—a point even Brecht's Galileo makes when he cites Homer and the Bible as his favorite texts. Goodwin himself is not averse to mythologizing science, personifying each star as a "self-luminous body" composed of the same material as the sun, the "whole tribe...at an incalculable" distance from the earth (*E&R*, 348). The passage evokes similar Victorian scientific allegorizing, whether Carlyle's famous Schwarzwald passage (in *Sartor Resartus*) on the blacksmith's little fire as the all-encompassing flame of divine, universal energy, Tyndall's "unbroken ocean of fiery fluid matter," or Hopkins's mythological stars (in "The Starlight Night") as "fire-folk sitting in the air," his image for the heavenly sanctum enclosing and disclosing "Christ and his mother and all his hallows."[57] Goodwin cites a cadre of English theological geologists for whom the Mosaic record validates "*appearances*," not "facts" nor "*physical realities*," a narrative, really, manifesting a unity of design that discloses divine presence. Not "designed to teach...natural philosophy," Scripture, rather, is meant to inform man of "his origin and fall, and to draw his mind to his Creator and Redeemer" (*E&R*, 360–61). In fact, Goodwin contends, the Bible's value as a tome of religious instruction is best preserved "not by striving to prove it scientifically exact...but by frank recognition of the erroneous views of nature which it contains." Knowledge of physical science, he reasons, is not what the writers of Scripture intended.

The bulk of Goodwin's essay treats uncritically the creation narrative as accepted by Jews and discussed by Hebrew scholars, even as Goodwin wants that narrative to accommodate modern astronomy and geology. In fact, his attempt to reconcile the two incompatible accounts was a last-ditch effort by biblical cosmogonists, fearful of the "shivering existence" of theological inquiry, to salvage some vestige of the scientific credibility of Scripture. As long as the simple creation myth has sustained human history and theological instruction, the developing scientific discourse need not displace it. Goodwin concedes that a certain amount of "violence" has been done to "the grand and simple words of the Hebrew writer," an account both human and Divine—the "utterance" human; the "knowledge" Divine (*E&R*, 356, 370). As a result, theological geologists, anxious to reconcile the Mosaic cosmogony to emerging scientific trends, are willing only to capitulate that the second three days of creation, if reclassified, can be "tolerably well assimilated" into the geological divisions; the real problems, they concede, are in the first three days. As Goodwin sees it, the problem is not with the Mosaic account, but with the assumptions made about divine revelation from the narrative: an *a priori* principle of interpretation, and the popular bias that the Bible, "bearing the stamp of Divine authority, must be complete, perfect, and unimpeachable in all its parts." From this postulate, "a thousand difficulties and incoherent doctrines have sprung out" (*E&R*, 368–69). Scripture, he reasons, was "not designed to teach us natural philosophy"; thus it is "vain to attempt to make a cosmogony out of its statements."

Goodwin's sense of the relations between science and revelation is one of exclusion and subtraction. His essay, which A. O. J. Cockshut calls the "clearest contemporary account of the great dispute over Genesis,"[58] shaped Victorian debate over plenarity, disrupting the already unstable ground of nineteenth-century theological inquiry. The "little scare about geology" and the "theological bugbear" it posed to Theobald Pontifex as he prepared his sermon, in Samuel Butler's famous parody, *The Way of all Flesh* ("an antiscriptural comedy soaked in scriptural idiom"[59]), would soon break out into national hysteria (*WF*, 71, 81). In this work by Butler, "the shrewd spokesman of relativity theory,"[60] gone was the will to believe:

> In those days people believed with a simple downrightness which I do not observe among educated men and women now. It had never so much as crossed Theobald's mind to doubt the literal accuracy of any syllable in the Bible. He had never seen any book in which this was disputed, nor met with anyone who doubted it. True, there was just a little scare about geology, but there was nothing in it. If it was said that God made the world in six days, why He did make it in six days, neither in more nor less; if it was said that He put Adam to sleep, took out one of his ribs and made a woman of it, why, it was so as a matter of course.... This was the average attitude of fairly educated young men and women towards the Mosaic cosmogony fifty, forty, or even twenty years ago. (*WF*, 81–82)

When young Ernest Pontifex matriculated at Cambridge, he began to question canonical authority, asserting that the Psalms "had probably never been written by David at all, but had got in among the others by mistake," an argument the post-1870s critical consensus on the Psalms would pursue. Butler recalls that

> Between 1844, when *Vestiges of Creation* appeared, and 1859 [*sic*], when *Essays and Reviews* marked the commencement of that storm which raged until many years afterwards, there was not a single book published in England that caused serious commotion within the bosom of the Church.... At no time probably since the beginning of the century could an ordinary observer have detected less sign of coming disturbance than at that of which I am writing.... Ernest had hardly been ordained before three works in quick succession arrested the attention even of those who paid least heed to theological controversy. I mean

Essays and Reviews, Charles Darwin's *Origin of Species*, and Bishop Colenso's *Criticisms on the Pentateuch*. (*WF*, 228–31)

To such Oxford educated, skeptical clergyman like Ernest's mentor, Pryer, "A more unreliable book [the Bible] was never put upon paper."[61] Thus, for Ernest, it was only a matter of time before the "Resurrection and Ascension of Jesus Christ, and hence his faith in all other Christian miracles, had dropped off him once and for ever." For "If there was no truth in the miraculous accounts of Christ's Death and Resurrection, the whole of the religion founded upon the historical truth of those events tumbled to the ground" (*WF*, 261, 302, 308). Ernest's crisis of faith is shared by any number of Victorian eponymous heroes, such as Hughes's Tom Brown, who, upon graduation from Oxford, was left with "perplexities, and doubts, and dreams, and struggles,"[62] or Mrs. Humphry Ward's amiable clergyman, Robert Elsmere, who believed that the solution to his religious angst can be found thorough an emotional engagement with the biblical text:

> During these three miserable months it cannot be said—poor Elsmere!—that he attempted any systematic study of Christian evidence. His mind was too much turn, his heart too sore. He pounced feverishly on one test point after another, on the Pentateuch, the Prophets, the relation of the New Testament to the thoughts and beliefs of its time, the Gospel of St. John, the evidence as to the Resurrection, the intellectual and moral conditions surrounding the formation of the Canon. His mind swayed hither and thither, driven from each resting-place in turn by the pressure of some new difficulty.[63]

To these Victorian half-believers, "The loss of his religious Belief was," Carlyle's Teufelsdröckh concludes, "the loss of everything," a "fever-paroxysms of Doubt" caused by "Inquiries concerning Miracles, and the Evidences of religious Faith."[64]

The sixth essay, Mark Pattison's "Tendencies of Religious Thought in England," and influenced no doubt by Pattison's 1857 *Westminster Review* essay, "The Present State of Theology in Germany," pursues a "continuity" of religious development, what he calls the "progress of theology." Chadwick considers Pattison's essay "the best single study in the book," so seminal that students turned to it "a hundred years after it was written."[65] Pioneering "the history of ideas," Pattison, deeply entrenched in eighteenth-century scholarship, equaled only to his eighteenth-century sensibility, moves to trace "the filiation of consecutive systems" without neglecting "any link in the chain."[66] The most conservative of the essayists and an early Tractarian, Pattison was remembered by Newman as one of the faithful friends who visited him at Littlemore on the eve of his Oxford exile and the only essayist of whom Newman felt "I may still call my friend."[67] Vestiges of Tractarianism persist when Pattison sees the movement breathing life into the sepulchral remains of Christian antiquity. While his sensibilities might well be Romish, Pattison fears the encrustation of doctrine, the fossilization of religion whereby "an unmeaning frostwork of dogma" becomes disassociated from "all relation to the actual history of man." He wants, instead, a faith kept vital through the spirit of free inquiry, not a canon of fossilized ideas that "locks up virtue in the cloister, and theology in the library" (*E&R*, 412–13).

Pattison rejects any move to exempt the Bible from critical scrutiny. To the degree that Christianity is a "historical phenomenon"—and Pattison's essay seeks a basis in historical objectivity, making it at times appear evasive— "it must be treated on the same terms as any other part of history." As in his 1857 *Westminster Review* article praising the "historico-critical" school of hermeneutics, Pattison's contribution to *Essays and Reviews* continued his "liberal programme" of emphasizing "the impartial and scientific investigation" of Christian revelation.[68] He identifies those "agencies" at the beginning of the eighteenth century shaping "the production of the present." Pattison charts the history of deistical thought, and "it is history that engages his intelligence,"[69] commencing with Locke's *Reasonableness of Christianity* and culminating with *Tracts for the Times*. The middle year, 1750, demarcated the two hemispheres of thought, internal from external evidentialism, both a residual theology. In the first, reason and revelation harmonized; in the second, "Old Bailey Theology," "Evidences" occupied center stage, giving rise to an "unwholesome state of theological feeling," whereby reason, not the Church, determined Scriptural intention. The goal, whether of essays, sermons, or philosophical treatises, was to "'prove the truth' of Christianity" through reason, for which "Evidences," no longer the basis of faith, became its substitute and "credibility" its watchword (*E&R*, 391–92).

First-phase tendencies, from 1688 to 1750, witnessed a rationalism more methodological than doctrinal, "an unconscious assumption rather than a principle." No longer "the devout condition of the entire inner man" but a form of "regulative truth," faith had become a matter of conduct, an "efflux" of character (*E&R*, 398–99). Were it not for Coleridge's magisterial *Aids to Reflection*, which silenced the "evidence-makers" and revived the "rationalist theology of England" in its "last stage of decay and dotage," theology would have expired altogether. Coleridge emerged an important critical voice in the historical argument:

> For Coleridge, the crucial importance of a work like the Bible lies in its continuous historical existence. Because it must be read through the mediation of its transmitters, that is, through the Church, readers cannot receive its words except through acts of faith or, as we should say, through tendentious interpretations, acts of conscious commitment to the received materials. The Bible comes to us bearing with it the history of its criticism; it is a writing which also contains its own readings and which generates the cumulative history of its own further retransmissions and reinterpretations.[70]

Pattison reads theology as "contemplative" and "speculative," unconcerned with evidence, whether internal or external. He maps the shift from the historical to the critical, and rejects the entire furniture of historical criticism, what he calls the "rein of pedantry" (*E&R*, 402–03). According to eighteenth-century thought, in which reason, and not ecclesiastical jurisprudence, determined Scriptural intentions, "The aids of history, the ordinary rules of grammar and logic, were applied to find out what the sacred writers actually said. *That* was the meaning of Scripture, the message supernaturally communicated." To consider any text apart from its context contravenes authorial intention: "Where each text of Scripture has but one sense, that sense in which the writer penned it, it can only be cited in that sense without doing it violence" (*E&R*, 401). Like his fellow essayists, and indeed like so many leading nineteenth-century intellectuals, Pattison does not grant biblical interpretation democratic consensus, by which we mean subjecting interpretation to individual taste. Resenting the popularizing of literary decorum, he advocates, instead, an elitist discourse of authority (though many have observed among the essayists a form of anti-intellectualism), "cloistered academic" conversing exclusively with a "learned educated class." Pattison wants to retain the "speculative reason of the few," not the "half-educated" "popular assembly," the "natural conscience of the many," whom he believed unfit to rule on essential doctrine. Because theology is by nature polemical, Pattison anticipates the rise of skepticism, the most perverse form of which is not "the hollowness of mankind," but excessive reflexivism, a kind of vampiric recoil of the self preying upon "its own vitals" (*E&R*, 404). This "new art of doubt"[71] is not so much skeptical unsteadiness as it is judicial caution. Critical as he is of extreme rationalism, Pattison is distressed by the "want of manliness in men" that favors unhealthy female gossip instead of open dissent.

The less-bourgeois second-phase tendencies, "*Rationalismus vulgaris*," from 1750 to 1833, divests itself of all but morals. The real "defect" in the theology of the eighteenth century, according to Pattison, is "not in having too much good sense, but in having nothing besides." A theology needs to emphasize more than just morals; it needs doctrine, which includes a scientific theology and transcendent objects of faith. Failing that, the result is a "utilitarian theology" emphasizing "virtue and religion," "life and manners," "improving the temper," and "making the heart better" (*E&R*, 409–12). Pattison wants a theology dislodged from philosophy, a supernaturalism in harmony with rational religion and with the requirements of verifiable evidences.[72] However, he resents a theology that, forfeiting the symbolic or analogical, becomes "petrified," experiencing as it were arterial blockage: "When it is stiffened into phrases, and these phrases are declared to be objects of reverence but not of intelligence, it is on the way to become a useless encumbrance, the rubbish of the past, blocking the road." In this condition, virtue becomes cloistered, theology and philosophy fossilized and antiquarian, and spirituality turns into a "caste sanctity.... The ideal of holiness...withdrawn from public life." All cease to exert any meaningful social influence (*E&R*, 412–13).

The last essay, Jowett's massive "On the Interpretation of Scripture" was meant originally for the republication of his Pauline Epistles. Chadwick singles it out for its "depth of penetration," Willey sees it as the volume's "centre of gravity," and Cameron calls it the "*Magna Carta* of Criticism in Britain."[73] The essay questions the resurrection, reinterprets the atonement, asserts the hybridity of Jewish and Christian historical narratives, and espouses the benefits of a comparative study of religions, exposing Jowett's liberal reputation and rejection of his early evangelicalism and attraction to Puseyism.[74] Interpretive disagreements, Jowett finds, are influenced by philosophical differences and "the growth or progress of the human mind." Like Wilson, he sees attempts to "pull the authority of Scripture in different directions" not all that unique; "the same phenomenon," he believes, can be found in "the past history of the Church." Differences in interpretation vary from age to age, informed as they are by the prevailing discursive fields and premise of taste. Every age has seen attempts by both pagans and Christians "to adapt the ideas of the past to the wants of the present," whether through allegory, logic, or rhetoric: "What men have brought to the text they have also found there." Jowett charts the shift from an "arbitrary and uncertain" rhetorical method to a more scientifically precise critical method. To the rhetorician committed to edification, the meaning of the text is never paramount. And without an effective critical method reconciling the warring factions of history, science, and revelation, Scripture, rather than being "a rule of life or faith," assumes the vagaries of religious opinion: "The unchangeable word of God . . . is changed by each age and each generation in accordance with its passing fancy. The book in which we believe all religious truth to be contained, is the most uncertain of all books, because interpreted by arbitrary and uncertain methods" (*E&R*, 501).

By what Jowett calls "refinements of signification," an emphasis on etymological nuances with little regard for the every-day parlance, words are made to mean more than what they actually do. Jowett wants to dissociate "interpretation" from "adaptation" and "application." To assert his own philological authority—that "knowledge of the original language is a necessary qualification of the Interpreter of Scripture"—Jowett accuses early scholastics of reading the Scripture "crosswise" by neglecting its grammatical features and overlooking its arbitrary verbal indicators. The result are "explanations of Scripture [that] are no longer tenable."[75] Rhetorical dinosaurs, these scholastics "belong to a way of thinking . . . once diffused over the world, but has now passed away" (*E&R*, 528). Difficulties in interpretation—emerging from partial knowledge of etymology, defective copies, and the want of key historical data elucidating how manuscripts in dead languages are preserved—are not unique to the Scripture; "they are found equally in sacred and profane literature." Though sacred literature is unique in style and subject, requiring "a vision and faculty divine," the real furniture of interpretation—"the meaning of words, the connexion of sentences, the settlement of the text, the evidence of facts"—coheres in all literature, sacred as well as secular. Jowett, however, wants the "liberal" study of Scripture to furnish an "ideal of life" absent for the most part in classical literature.

Jowett observes Victorian anxiety over disruptions of the accepted critical consensus, the kind that Carlyle, for one, expressed when he satirizes the

conflict over plenarity: "Neither," says Teufelsdröckh, "shall ye tear out one
another's eyes, struggling over 'Plenary Inspiration,'...try rather to get a
little even Partial Inspiration, each of you for himself."[76] Aids to interpretation—grammar, rhetoric, and logic—are deployed not to determine "the
true rendering" of the text but to facilitate "a received one." The history of
the Scripture, Jowett would argue, followed a process whereby *oral speech*
became *document*, then *monument*, an archival domain, a reservoir of totalities comprised of institutional fiats, fictions, and narrative accounts. The
goal of the interpreter, as Jowett sees it, is "to define within the documentary material itself unities, totalities, series, relations,"[77] to recover, in his
words, the meaning of the words "as they struck on the ears or flashed before
the eyes of those who first heard and read them" (*E&R*, 481). Jowett
intends to excavate the layers of interpretation, to reconstruct the foundational environment of the text, wanting, that is, to recover some real or
imagined beginning, some coherent point of origination. But "Historical
reactions," Willey astutely observes, "never go back to the originals"; rather,
"they are syntheses of thesis and antithesis; old affinities are revived, but in
the light of intervening experience." And as Christopher Herbert only
recently observed, "theories of origin or causality in intellectual history rarely
meet even minimal norms of scientific method, and that they rarely can claim
to be anything more than erudite legends."[78] Any Genesis, one could say, as
Carlyle did, is really a re-Genesis, even an Exodus, or T. S. Eliot, in the "East
Coker" section of *Four Quartets*, "In my beginning is my end."[79] Birth is
simultaneously a delivery, an expulsion. Wilson Harris, in *Jonestown*, puts it
this way: "To sail back into the past is to come upon 'pasts' that are 'futures'
to previous 'pasts' which are 'futures' in themselves to prior 'pasts' *ad infini-
tum*. There is no absolute beginning, for each 'beginning' comes after
an unwritten past that awaits a new language. What lies behind us in linked
incalculably to what lies ahead of us in that the future is a sliding scale
backwards into the unfathomable past within the Virgin womb of time...."[80]
The interpreter must, as it were, empty himself of all existing prejudices
and attempt to peal away layer by encrusted layer of interpretive assumptions in order to expose the textual fabric, "the real meaning, or kernel,"
which "seems to lie deeper, and to be more within" (*E&R*, 517–18).
Interpretation involves not remembering but disremembering, for the very
act of interpretation is itself erased in the process and the interpreter is left
"alone in company with the author," in "a world by itself." The real intent
of Scripture is "to be gathered from itself": "Scripture should be interpreted
in Scripture" (*E&R*, 508, 519–22).

   Jowett's hermeneutical model is essentially inductive, what he calls
"the exercise of manly sense and industry" (*E&R*, 504). Any other interpretive
model, like the literalist approach to the Bible as "*no* other book," is female,
impotent, and suspect, to say nothing of the diseased; "manly" becomes synonymous to "healthful." The interpreter's objective is "to read Scripture like
any other book," and to get to things "as they truly are": "*Interpret the
Scripture like any other book*" (*E&R*, 481–82, 504). The "Historical-critical

method" Jowett privileges "meant that putative claims of fact in the Bible were subjected to independent investigation to test their veracity," absent any guarantee from "the authority of the Bible itself."[81] The very phrase, "like any other book," as Cameron observes, leaves "Critical scholars who claimed to believe in the supernatural on the horns of a dilemma," for it seems to contest "the possibility of the supernatural in Scripture, including, presumably, the very idea of revelation."[82] Jowett desires a prolegomena, a history of interpretation, which would excavate or implode edifices of interpretive traditions. Inspiration, to begin with, has become something "incapable of being defined in an exact manner." Employed initially to capture the "prophetic spirit of Scripture," inspiration has metastasized into a "technical term." Driven by creedal and political agendas ("pressed into the service of the interpreter"), inspiration has occasioned the "practical abuse of Scripture," whereby "the book is made the sport of opinion and the instrument of perversion of life." A "symbol of fanaticism" and a "cloak of malice," Scripture assumes "an apologetic character," and has been further deployed to legitimize a host of egregious practices—slavery, polygamy, spurious philanthropy—which only a careful, systematic, and critical interpretive method could extirpate.

A relative neologism ("not found in the earlier confessions of the reformed faith"), "inspiration" ceases to mean anything because it has come to mean so many things. Neither the Gospel nor the Epistles declares "supernatural views of Inspiration." The Apostles deny "any inward gift," nor do they claim to have been influenced by "any power external to them different from that of preaching or teaching." And nowhere do they "lead us to suppose that they were free from error or infirmity." As Sue Zemka has pointed out, fallibility is crucial to the "structure by which these text replicate a Christian economy of salvation, where sin is fundamental as grace, where sin, in fact, is a prerequisite of grace."[83] Inspiration, then, according to Jowett, means "That idea of Scripture which we gather from the knowledge of it," with allowances made for "progressive revelation" and "well-ascertained facts" which "cannot be true in religion when seen by the light of faith, and untrue in science when looked at through the medium of evidence or experiment." Jowett and his fellow essayists were intent on redefining inspiration in the context of new revelation and its relationship to the existing archive. No mere "book of statutes" covering a "multitude of cases," the Bible is a complex system of doctrine or practice ("multiform diversity," says A. P. Stanely) manifesting different styles, written by authors from varied educational, social, and political backgrounds, and set across a broad expanse of time.

Still, the archive is often uncritically quarried, whereby words, "singled out and incorporated in systems, like stones taken out of an old building and put into a new one," are used to construct new edifices of thought and so "acquire a technical meaning more or less divergent from the original one" (E&R, 498). Jowett traces the evolution from orality to document, a tradition in which the first three Gospels commenced "orally" and were then "slowly put together and written" (E&R, 500). He thus subjectivizes the new criticism, situates the gospel in the "soul," and establishes the evangelistic agenda on "the expression of universal truths" and not on the beliefs of particular nations or churches (*E&R*, 531). Jowett argues a "rational" interpretation to dispel the "crude and dreamy vapours of religious excitement," "new sources of spiritual health" as antidote for the stagnant doctrinal disease, and a disengagement of theology from existing formulas. "The truths of Scripture again would have greater reality if divested of the scholastic form in which theology has cast them" (*E&R*, 534). Jowett's subjectivism is one removed from temporal restraints and cleared of the accretions built around "party politics," the political, propagandistic, and bureaucratic machine that drives theological traditions and their interpretive hegemonies.

Yet, despite Jowett's attempt to dismantle the received tradition of interpretation and to confront its tyranny, one should not overlook his decidedly elitist hermeneutics, meant not for "the multitude," the "half-educated," but for "the few," those who, like Darwin's cultivated man, possess "a finer perception of language, and a higher degree of cultivation" (*E&R*, 520). Like Coleridge, he defends "a specialized mode of scholarly, literary, and political analysis of the Bible as the exclusive capacity of an intellectual minority."[84] While Jowett concedes a complex structure, he also recognizes a quality of simplicity whereby those same truths are accessible to the common man who approaches the Bible without great intellectual dexterity and unimpeded by an epistemology held hostage by an interpretive tradition. As it stands, the current historical criticism reads the Bible as though it were a closed, static text whose every claim—scientific, historical, and religious—applies equally and with the same power of conviction in every age. But because Christianity is dynamic, it requires, Jowett insists, an interpretive model conducive to unchanging principles of the faith: love, justice, mercy, and peace. Whereas the Bible's canonical status might well be closed, the texts themselves contain instabilities, ruptures, gaps, all aspects of the volatility of life and energy. To make any claim for cultural relevance, the texts themselves must be dynamic rather than static. Jowett is after an interpretive theory of the "life of Christ in the soul, instead of a theory of Christ which is in a book or written down," a theory that conveys to heathens "universal truths" rather than one advocating "the tenets of particular men or churches." Scripture, Spinoza had argued when formulating the historical-critical hermeneutic Jowett and the essayists would later adopt, intends "not only to teach the right kind of religion but to move men's hearts to its practice."[85] So disengaged from theological formulas, Scripture would approach a condition of the heart, removing the boundary conditions separating Christianity along largely political lines (*E&R*, 531). As the editors of *Essays and Reviews* have noted, "The idea of interpreting texts according to the insight of the heart was a widespread notion in the nineteenth century," evident in writers such as Carlyle and Ruskin, who follow a Romantic poetics. "By bringing language 'near to the language of men' the hermeneutic possibility in Jowett's reading the Bible like any other book, as a book speaking directly to the heart, becomes possible" (*E&R*, 118–19).

Jowett desires a text that speaks with increasing relevance to a global community, a text that has more to do with the spirit and less with the letter, a text that concerns itself with the essence of Christianity than the accidents. A liberal approach to interpretation would reveal a truly multivalent text, lacking authorial, historical, and textual coherence. It will reveal the best of poetry, the noblest of history, the greatest of epics, and will differentiate itself from classical or other sacred writings by the very fact that it facilitates "the contemplation of man as he appears to God" (*E&R*, 533). Jowett's points here are precisely the ones Eric Auerbach argues in his brilliant comparison of the Homeric stories to the Elohistic (Old Testament) ones, finding the two "equally ancient and equally epic texts" congruent on many points. In Auerbach's more contemporary higher-critical reading of the Bible,

> the Biblical narrator, the Elohist [unlike the Homeric], had to believe in the objective truth of the story of Abraham's sacrifice....He had to believe it passionately; or else...he had to be a conscious liar—no harmless liar like Homer....Indeed, we must go even further. The Bible's claim to truth is not only far more urgent than Homer's, it is tyrannical—it excludes all other claims. The world of the Scripture stories is not satisfied with claiming to be a historically true reality—it insists that it is the only real world, is destined for autocracy....The Scripture stories do not, like Homer's, court our favor, they do not flatter us that they may please us and enchant us—they seek to subject us, and if we refuse to be subjected we are rebels.

But this subjugation, once so easy, says Auerbach, becomes more problematic the further removed in time we are from the actual historical narratives. If these Biblical stories are to exert "their claim to absolute authority, it is inevitable that they themselves be adapted through interpretive transformation." Because "when, through too great a change in environment and through the awakening of a critical consciousness, this becomes impossible, the Biblical claim to absolute authority is jeopardized; the method of interpretation is scorned and rejected, the Biblical stories become ancient legends, and the doctrine they had contained, now dissevered from them, becomes a disembodied image."[86] This is precisely the kind of fossilizing effect the essayists were seeking to preempt. The new criticism Jowett advocates recognizes Christianity's political alliance with nation and works to eradicate religious, class, and racial differences—"to look at all men as they are in the sight of God, not as they appear to human eye, separated and often interdicted from each other by lines of religious demarcation." Criticism, as such, is more theocentric than anthropocentric, for it looks not on the outward appearances but on the heart, not on the external forms of a received tradition but on the inner life of faith. Attracted to a truly fluid, dynamic, and protean text, Jowett is understandably fascinated by the parabolic nature of Scripture, given the nature of parables "to evoke the transcendental," to "penetrate where syllogisms fail to affect an entrance."[87]

As a literary trope, parables, because as stories they infuse "extraordinary themes with analogies drawn from workaday occurrences," and do so "in pithy, ordinary talk," present a powerful mimesis.[88] Concerned more with the figural than the literal, parables problematize reading and maintain the vitality of the canon by keeping it open to de-constructions and re-constructions. To remain relevant, Scripture must avoid the polemical and the rhetorical, the former reducing it to a particular and thus singular apologetic, often political, and the latter valorizing the sentimental and the appeal to the conscience. Ultimately, in as much as they were intent on excavating the layers of interpretation and interested in reconstructing the foundational environment of the text, to recover some real or imagined beginning, the essayists were after an archaeology, wanting, in the language of Foucault's *Archaeology*, to ascertain fixity and shifts, to describe the different "*species of dissension*," to explore and map discursive practices, and "to maintain discourse in all of its many irregularities; and consequently to suppress the theme of a contradiction uniformly lost and rediscovered, resolved and forever rising again, in the undifferentiated element of the Logos." Their range is "a tangle of interpositivities whose limits and points of intersection cannot be fixed in a single operation." In attempting to liberate culture from the terror of the continuous, to which all of culture becomes inextricably linked, archaeology proposes to reposition the continuous from its status of "original passivity" by inverting its arrangement and playing one off against the other "to show how the continuous is formed in accordance with the same conditions and the same rules as dispersion; and how it enters . . . the field of discursive practice."[89]

Like so many watershed events in Victorian England—the Darwinian controversy, the Condition-of-England Question, the Irish Question, the Negro Question, the Woman Question, the Indian Mutiny, and the Morant Bay Rebellion—the controversy over *Essays and Reviews* polarized public opinion. Most nineteenth-century reviews were quite simply horrified that this disreputable publication, with its heterodoxical assumptions and where the sense of an author virtually disappears, came not from religious skeptics but from prominent clergymen within the pale of Anglicanism. As a result, the evangelical organs—the *Christian Observer*, the *Record*, and the Scottish *North British Review*—demanded the essayists censured and the volume condemned. Non-sectarian journals such as *Fraser's* and the *Westminster Review* assumed a less partisan, sometimes even laudatory, tone. Perhaps the most intriguing essay on the controversy, Matthew Arnold's "The Bishop and the Philosopher" (1863) advocates limiting freedom of inquiry and religious speculation by the clergy and isolating literary criticism from theological criticism, the latter committed to preserving the integrity and sacredness of the canon.[90] Arnold wants to suppress religious inquiry in his agenda for "general culture." And as much as he valued "Openness of mind and flexibility of intelligence," he is nonetheless bothered by the assault on Victorian reserve by *Essays and Reviews* and *The Pentateuch Critically Examined* (1862).[91] The display of these two documents amounts to seminal spillage, uncontrollable discharge, and unmanageable flow. Arnold's model discourse is not Colenso's "weak trifling," his flaccid pen, but Spinoza's manly prowess, the "superior man," whose seminal material ("strong thought") is "cast into the huge caldron, out of which the new world is to be born" (*BP*, 53–55).[92]

Promoting his own brand of textual elitism, Arnold talks about the "respectable recognition of a superior ideal...in the intellectual sphere" ("LI," 236). For criticism to have merit, it must be contained and measured, not "flung broadcast, in the crudest shape, amidst the undisciplined, ignorant, captious multitude."[93] Addressing specifically the Colenso tract, Arnold, in "The Function of Criticism," is convinced that "criticism cannot follow this coarse and indiscriminate method."[94] Here Arnold, like Jowett, exhibits the same "megalomania" Zemka observes in Coleridge.[95] Nothing so unsettled Arnold as "the baneful notion that there is no such thing as a high correct standard in intellectual matters; that every one may as well take his own way." To Arnold, "there is a right and a wrong" (*LI*, 236, 243). And it is this refusal to entertain relativity positions that causes Herbert to see Arnold's politics as "marked by a distinct strain of authoritarianism"[96]—the "mirror-image" of nihilism.[97]

The affects of *Essays and Reviews* on doctrine, culture, and the Victorian collective imagination were incalculable, signaling, says Altholz, "the commencement of an era of religious doubt.... Seeking to lance the boils of error and deceit, the Essayists had touched the rawest nerves of Victorian orthodoxy."[98] No other publication has so shifted the ideological contours and the epistemological grounds upon which Victorians and their predecessors had so comfortably rested. And even today the aftershocks are still being felt—the war over literalism is still being fought on all fronts, especially the social and political, on whether, for example, biblical language prohibits the promotion to the bishopric of an openly gay Anglican clergyman with his out-of-the-closet partner. And, in a different but nonetheless related context, does the language of the American Constitution regarding the place of religion in public life and the Declaration of Independence support the placing of the Ten Commandments in a public space, the Alabama Judicial Building? These issues of literalism and interpretation continue to bedevil Western culture, and shape in no small way public policies. As Terry Eagleton only recently observes in his analysis of fundamentalism and its relationship to textuality, "Fundamentalism is a textual affair," it is "a kind of necrophilia, in love with the dead letter of a text."[99] *Essays and Reviews* contested the sacredness of the archive, its watertight authenticity on which authority has been inscribed and ascribed, and granted all sorts of legitimacies. It was indeed a document of disablement and disempowerment, for it presents truth not as a stable entity but as something developmental, multiple, communal, provisional, and contingent. The intent of the volume was to open up what the essayists felt was a fossilized canon, allowing in so doing new inquiry and explorations in order to vitalize the archive. For them, to borrow an expression from Browning's "Fra Lippo Lippi," God should still be seen in the Garden creating Eve; "sacred history" must be understood "as ongoing literary interpretation."[100] Resistant to all forms of literalism and essentialism, the Bible should be, as indeed it is, a dynamic, organic document containing principles relevant and applicable to all times—as myth, allegory, and poem in the truest sense—rather than a dogmatic, exclusionary text.

NOTES

1. Elizabeth Barrett Browning employed the same metaphor: "Do you hear of the storms in England about *Essays and Reviews?*" she wrote to Miss. E. F. Haworth in January 1861 (*The Letters of Elizabeth Barrett Browning*, ed. Frederic G. Kenyon, 2 vols. [New York: Macmillan, 1898], 2:426–27). All references to *Essays and Reviews* are from *The 1860 Text and Its Reading* (ed. Victor Shea and William Whitla [Charlottesville: University Press of Virginia, 2000]). Hereafter *E&R* followed by the page number. The essays appear in the following order: Frederick Temple, "The Education of the World" (137–80); Rowland Williams, "Bunsen's Biblical Researches" (181–232); Baden Powell, "On the Study of the Evidences of Christianity" (233–73); Henry Bristow Wilson, "Séances Historiques de Genève—The National Church" (275–344); C. W. Goodwin, "On the Mosaic Cosmogony" (345–86); Mark Pattison, "Tendencies of Religious Thought in England, 1688–1750" (387–476); and Benjamin Jowett, "On the Interpretation of Scripture" (477–593).
2. William O. Raymond, *The Infinite Moment and Other Essays in Robert Browning* (Toronto: University of Toronto Press, 1965), 23; Basil Willey, *More Nineteenth Century Studies* (New York: Columbia University Press, 1956), 137.
3. George Moberly, *Sermons on the Beatitude*, 3rd ed. (Oxford: James Parker, 1870), xxii, xxv. Newman employed the expression, "*to poison the wells,*" to describe Kingsley's attack on him, which John Henry Newman's *Apologia Pro Vita Sua* (ed. David J. DeLaura [New York: W. W. Norton, 1968]) sought to answer.
4. Nigel M. de S. Cameron, *Biblical Higher Criticism and the Defense of Infallibilism in 19th Century Britain* (Lewiston: The Edwin Mellen Press, 1987), 266.
5. For more on sales of the *Origin*, see Charles Darwin's *The Autobiography of Charles Darwin, 1809–82*, ed. Nora Barlow (New York: Norton, 1993), 122–26; for sales on *Essays and Reviews*, see *E&R*, 14–15, 24–26.
6. The way the "credibility of the Bible" was handled "(together with uneasiness over man's place in the universe) goes a long way toward explaining the storm which the publication of Darwin's *The Origin of Species* unleashed in England" (Hans W. Frei, *The Eclipse of Biblical Narrative: A Study in Eighteenth and Nineteenth Century Hermeneutics* [New Haven: Yale University Press, 1974], 54). Charles Darwin, *The Origin of Species* (New York: Penguin, 1958).
7. Moberly, *Sermons*, xii; Ieuan Ellis, *Seven Against Christ: A Study of Essays and Reviews* (Leiden: E. J. Brill, 1980), 92.
8. In a August 1, 1869 letter to Florence Nightingale, Jowett voiced the hope that Temple would turn out to be another Whewell (*Dear Miss Nightingale: A Selection of Benjamin Jowett's Letters to Florence Nightingale, 1860–93*, ed. Vincent Quinn and John Prest [Oxford: Clarendon Press, 1987], 175). Connecting the early (1855) version of the Temple's essay to Darwinism, Peter Hinchliff observes: "Though Darwin had not yet published his theory of evolution, it had already been argued, on the basis of geological evidence and the existence of fossils, that creation had not remained unchanged. But a

contrast between the static universe and a developing human race was Temple's main theme—the growth, the progress, and the *education* of the human race" (*Frederick Temple: Archbishop of Canterbury* [Oxford: Clarendon Press, 1998], 61).

9. Stephen Prickett, "Purging Christianity of Semitic Origins: Kingsley, Arnold and the Bible," *Rethinking Victorian Culture*, ed. Juliet John and Alice Jenkins (New York: St. Martin's Press, 2000), 65–66.

10. *Shakespeare and the Politics of Culture in Late Victorian England* (Baltimore: The Johns Hopkins University Press, 1998), 19.

11. Hinchliff, *Frederick Temple*, 67.

12. *"Kubla Khan" and the Fall of Jerusalem: The Mythological School in Biblical Criticism and Secular Literature 1770–1880* (Cambridge: Cambridge University Press, 1975), 63. I do not, of course, believe that the issues *Essays and Reviews* raised about myth, literalism, and the role of allegory had a comparatively limited impact than *The Origin of Species*. Interpretation and paradigms of reading, we know, profoundly affect all discourse, which in turn determine public policy and welfare. The distinctions between the literal and the figural, according to Andrew E. Benjamin et al., draw on a number of crucial analogous polarities, to name but a few: "grammar/trope, truth/poetry, science/rhetoric, discovery/justification, philosophy/literature" (*The Figural and the Literal: Problems of Language in the History of Science and Philosophy, 1630–1800* [Manchester: Manchester University Press, 1987], 2). Never an entirely innocent enterprise, to say nothing of the deliberate manipulation of language for certain political ends, reading is inseparable from political in-formation as it is from political formation. A particular theory of reading informs all politics.

13. Qtd. in Moberly, *Sermons* lxx; Martin Geldart, *A Son of Belial: Autobiographical Sketches* (London: Trubner & Co., 1882), 160. The title of Geldart's book, punning on Balliol College, comes more directly from John Milton's *Paradise Lost* (2nd ed., ed. Scott Elledge [New York: W. W. Norton, 1993]) and describes one of Satan's lieutenants (and his followers as "the sons of Belial" or "sons of darkness") whom Milton connects to perverse sexual practices and sexual immorality—fornication, homosexuality, and rape. Milton uses as his proof texts accounts of the deviant sons of the high priest Eli (1 Sam. 2:12–25), Sodom and Gomorra (Gen. 19), and Gibea (Jud. 19). See *PL*, 1.490–505; 2.109–16.

14. *Godiva's Ride: Women of Letters in England, 1830–1880* (Bloomington: Indiana University Press, 1993), 115–16. As A. D. Nuttall has observed, "the nineteenth-century historians of competing mythologies have their own overarching story to tell, and this overarching story has the status of a deep, explanatory myth" (*Dead from the Waist Down: Scholars and Scholarship in Literature and the Popular Imagination* [New Haven: Yale University Press, 2003], 58).

15. Sue Zemka, *Victorian Testaments: The Bible, Christology, and Literary Authority in Early-Nineteenth-Century British Culture* (California: Stanford University Press, 1997), 17.

16. Michel Foucault, *The Archaeology of Knowledge* (New York: Pantheon, 1972), 145; James Eli Adams, *Dandies and Desert Saints: Styles of Victorian Manhood* (Ithaca: Cornell University Press, 1995), 95.

17. Thomas Carlyle, *Sartor Resartus*, ed. Rodger L. Tarr and Mark Engel (Berkeley: University of California Press, 2000), 132; Josef L. Altholz, *Anatomy of a Controversy: The Debate over "Essays and Reviews"* (Hants,

England: Scholar Press, 1994), 32. According to Shaffer, "The history of Biblical criticism exhibits in a very well-defined way the relations between German and English thought" (*Fall of Jerusalem*, 5).

18. Cameron, *Biblical Higher Criticism*, 75.

19. *The Political Unconscious: Narrative as a Socially Symbolic Act* (Ithaca: Cornell University Press, 1981), 58.

20. Qtd. in Altholz, *Anatomy*, 47.

21. Foucault, *Archaeology*, 12.

22. Ibid., 4–5.

23. Zemka, *Victorian Testaments*, 11.

24. Patrocinio P. Schweickart, "Reading Ourselves: Toward a Feminist Theory of Reading," *Gender and Reading: Essays on Readers, Texts, and Contexts*, ed. Elizabeth A. Flynn and Patrocinio P. Schweickart (Baltimore: The Johns Hopkins University Press, 1986), 47.

25. Hinchliff, *Frederick Temple*, 65.

26. Moberly, *Sermons*, iv–vii, xxix, lxx.

27. Eric Auerbach reads the biblical narrative, or at least the agenda of its most conservative exponents, similarly. "The Bible's claim to truth is not only far more urgent than Homer's," he writes; "it is tyrannical—it excludes all other claims. The world of the Scripture stories is not satisfied with claiming to be a historically true reality—it insists that it is the only real world, is destined for autocracy.... The Scripture stories do not, like Homer's, court our favor, they do not flatter us that they may please us and enchant us—they seek to subject us, and if we refuse to be subjected we are rebels" (*Mimesis: The Representation of Reality in Western Literature* [New Jersey: Princeton University Press, 1953], 14–15).

28. "Philosophical Hermeneutics and Theological Hermeneutics," *Studies in Religion* 5, no. 1 (1975): 18.

29. Ibid., 18.

30. Humbolt; qtd. in Michel Foucault, *The Order of Things* (New York: Vintage, 1994), 290.

31. Northrop Frye, *Anatomy of Criticism: Four Essays* (New Jersey: Princeton University Press, 1957), 315.

32. Foucault, *Archaeology*, 125; Frei, *Eclipse*, 59; see Frei for more on positivity, "the affirmation of a direct or unmediated intervention of the Godhead in the finite realm," which means miracles not as "contranatural physical events" but as "miracles of character" (58).

33. Foucault, *Archaeology*, 14.

34. For a study of the history of higher criticism leading up to and following *Essays and Reviews*, see John Rogerson, *Old Testament Criticism in the Nineteenth Century* (London: SPCK, 1984).

35. Butler's analogy also influenced Newman, providing, among other things, the epistemology for the Oxford Movement. Newman felt that despite its strength, the Analogy argument posed a crucial problem: "The danger of this doctrine, in the case of many minds, is, its tendency to destroy in them absolute certainty, leading them to consider every conclusion as doubtful, and resolving truth into an opinion..." (see the *Apologia*, 28–31).

36. *George Eliot and the Landscape of Time: Narrative Form and Protestant Apocalyptic History* (Chapel Hill: University of North Carolina Press, 1986), 78–79.

37. Qtd. in Jude V. Nixon, *Gerard Manley Hopkins and His Contemporaries: Liddon, Newman, Darwin, and Pater* (New York: Garland, 1994), 23.
38. Cameron, *Biblical Higher Criticism*, 82.
39. Willey, *Nineteenth Century*, 142; Zemka, *Victorian Testaments*, 72–73.
40. Thomas Arnold named his fourth daughter, Frances Bunsen ("Bonze") after Baron von Bunsen. Stephen Prickett sees Bunsen attempting to use religion to forge an all Aryan alliance in which Christianity would be purged of its Semitic origins. Bunsen's ideas, Prickett finds, tapped into "a huge existing reservoir of pro-Teutonic sentiment" (63). In a December 25, 1867 letter to his mother, Arnold commented on Bunsen's agenda: "Bunsen used to say that our great business was to get rid of all that was purely Semitic in Christianity, and to make it Indo-germanic." Arnold saw his father Thomas working in the same religious tradition; not only was his father "the only deeply religious man who had the necessary culture for it," but he "was, perhaps, the only powerful Englishman of his day who did so" (*The Letters of Matthew Arnold*, ed. Cecil Y. Lang, 4 vols. [Charlottesville: The University Press of Virginia, 1996–2000], 3:207). Not surprisingly, Arnold exhibited an anti-Semitic strain, assuming a patronizing attitude toward Jewish women, the prominent Victorian socialites, the Rothchilds (Clementina and Alice), "the first exquisitely beautiful, the second with a most striking character. What women these Jewesses are! With *a force* which seems to triple that of the women of our Western & Northern races" (*Letters*, 2:238). On January 21, 1872, he told his mother of his reading Isaiah and concerns about whether the "*eternal*" and "*ancient*" are synonymous, which, were it not, would mean that the Jews were not the "*ancient*" and thus by implication not God's chosen people. He also remarked about his encounter with Disraeli: "I met that famous Jew, Dizzy, on Monday and he was very amiable" (*Letters*, 4:89). Arnold also refused any involvement in the slavery question; see his March 31, 1856 letter to Mary Carpenter (*Letters*, 1:334–35)
41. It is a touch ironic that it was from Bunsen that Newman and Hurrell Froude borrowed a copy of Homer's *Iliad*, employing the language of Achilles's return to battle as the battle cry of the Oxford Movement.
42. Foucault, *Archaeology*, 13.
43. Ibid., 139, 144–45.
44. Samuel Taylor Coleridge, *Aids to Reflection, The Collected Works of Samuel Taylor Coleridge*, ed. John Beer, vol. 9. (New Jersey: Princeton University Press, 1993), 46, 147–48. Coleridge sees understanding as "discursive" and reason as "fixed"; understanding appeals to another authority, reason to its own; understanding is the faculty of "*Reflection*," reason of "Contemplation." Reason has a closer affiliation to the Intelligible and Spiritual than understanding.
45. Shaffer, *Fall of Jerusalem*, 1.
46. Jerome J. McGann, *The Beauty of Inflections: Literary Investigations in Historical Method and Theory* (Oxford: Clarendon Press, 1985), 143; Zemka, *Victorian Testaments*, 15, 18; Samuel Taylor Coleridge, "Confessions of an Inquiring Spirit," *The Collected Works of Samuel Taylor Coleridge*, ed. H. L. Jackson and J. R. de J. Jackson, vol. 12 (New Jersey: Princeton University Press, 1995).
47. Ricoeur, "Hermeneutics," 20.
48. Qtd. in Moberly, *Sermons*, lxxxiv.
49. "German learning, German historiography were in the air" (Nuttall, *Dead from the Waist Down*, 118).

50. McGann, *Beauty*, 144.
51. Ibid., 144.
52. Samuel Butler, *The Way of All Flesh* (New York: Penguin, 1986), 337.
53. McGann, *Beauty*, 144.
54. Owen Chadwick, *The Victorian Church*, 2 vols. (New York: Oxford University Press, 1966), 2:7.
55. John Tyndall, *Fragments of Science*, 2 vols. (New York: P. F. Collier, 1900), 2:224. For a fascinating and early (October 1852) look at how Victorians such as William Makepeace Thackeray debated literalism, see *The Letters and Private Papers of William Makepeace Thackeray*, ed. Gordon N. Ray, vol. 3. (London: Oxford University Press, 1946), where Thackeray warned his daughter Anne against the dangers of evangelicalism, but still reminded her of the need to respect the wishes of her evangelical grandmother, Mrs. Carmichael-Smyth (3:93–96).
56. Auerbach, *Mimesis*, 12, 15.
57. John Tyndall, *Heat Considered as a Mode of Motion* (New York: D. Appleton, 1863), 439; Gerard Manley Hopkins, *The Poetical Works of Gerard Manley Hopkins*, ed. Norman H. MacKenzie (Oxford: Clarendon Press, 1990).
58. A. O. J. Cockshut, *Religious Controversies of the Nineteenth Century: Selected Documents* (London: Methuen, 1966), 136.
59. Joss Marsh, *Word Crimes: Blasphemy, Culture, and Literature in Nineteenth-Century England* (Chicago: The University of Chicago Press, 1998), 183–84.
60. Christopher Herbert, *Victorian Relativity: Radical Thought and Scientific Discovery* (Chicago: University Press of Chicago, 2001), 62.
61. "Butler's composition of the *Way of All Flesh*," Marsh notices, "spanned the course of Foote's 'Bible-smashing' campaign from inception to imprisonment, 1871–84." The novel as a whole "exploits the range of comic blasphemous possibility produced by such close engagement with the Bible as G. W. Foote criminally perfected" (*Word Crimes*, 183).
62. Qtd. in Walter Houghton, *The Victorian Frame of Mind*, 1830–1870 (New Haven: Yale University Press, 1957), 20.
63. Mrs. Humphry Ward, *Robert Elsmere*, Oxford World's Classics (New York: Oxford University Press, 1987), 315.
64. Carlyle, *Sartor Resartus*, 121, 88. Similarly, at the university Teufelsdröckh was exposed to the "Progress of the Species" and "Inquiries concerning Miracles, and the Evidences of religious Faith," books related both in title and temper to the very ones that would soon alarm Victorians, *The Origin of Species* and *Essays and Reviews*.
65. Chadwick, *The Victorian Church*, 2:76.
66. Willey, *Nineteenth Century*, 151. For more on Pattison's near conversion to Rome and subsequent break with the Tractarians, see Nuttall, *Dead from the Waist Down*, 98–100.
67. *Letters and Diaries of John Henry Newman*, ed. Charles Stephen Dessain, vol. 19 (New York: Thomas Nelson, 1973), 487.
68. Duncan Nimmo, "Learning against Religion; Learning as Religion: Mark Pattison and the 'Victorian Crisis of Faith,'" *Religion and Humanism*, ed. Keith Robbins (Oxford: Basil Blackwell, 1981), 318–19.
69. Nuttall, *Dead from the Waist Down*, 104.
70. McGann, *Beauty*, 159.
71. Bertolt Brecht, *Galileo*, ed. Eric Bentley (New York: Grove Press, 1966), 123.

72. Altholz, *Anatomy*, 28.
73. Chadwick, *Victorian Church*, 2:76; Willey, *Nineteenth Century*, 140; Cameron, *Higher Criticism*, 76.
74. By 1871, that reputation was fully earned. In a sermon entitled "Darwinism, and Faith in God," preached at Balliol College, Jowett celebrated Darwin as "one of the greatest living Englishmen," entertained an extended geological chronology, accepted the theory of the "survival of the fittest," and felt that the advance of the physical sciences is "likely to have considerable effects upon morality and religion." Jowett concluded that "no one does more harm to religion or tends more to undermine the Christian faith than he who appeals eloquently to our religious feelings on behalf of a scientific untruth, or a conclusion not warranted by facts" ("Darwinism, and Faith in God," *Sermons on Faith and Doctrine*, ed. W. H. Fremantle [London: John Murray, 1901], 5–9, 17). Located at the head of Oxford's Broad Street, Jowett's Balliol was thought "the focus or center" of Broad-Church liberalism, around which "currents and counter-currents formed a kind of vortex" (Geldart, *Son of Belial*, 154). Interesting too was the fact that *Essays and Reviews* was book-ended by two Balliol men, Temple and Jowett. In a April 16, 1865 letter, Jowett told Florence Nightingale: "This is Easter Sunday. I don't suppose that we either have, or could by any possibility have, sufficient evidence of the resurrection to justify us in resting religion upon that.... I sometimes think that the death, & not the resurrection of Christ, is the really strengthening & consoling fact—that human nature could have risen to that does show that it is divine" (*Dear Miss Nightingale*, 52). Jowett's skeptical stance on the Resurrection is proof of his disbelief in miracles, those of Elisha's, for instance. He believed that religion should not be based on them, and had planned to address this view in the aborted second volume of *Essays and Reviews*.
75. The birth of philology took place in the nineteenth century but "has remained much more hidden from Western consciousness than that of biology and that of economics—even though it was part of the same archaeological upheaval; and even though its consequences have extended much further in our culture" (Foucault, *Order*, 282). Edward Said sees the "philological critic" of the nineteenth century "who has the skill to separate Semitic languages from the language of Indo-European culture" replacing "divine authority" (46).
76. *Sartor Resartus*, 144. *Sartor Resartus* also explores the historical critical method, concerned as the work is with the life and opinions of Diogenes Teufelsdröckh.
77. Foucault, *Archaeology*, 7.
78. Willey, *Nineteenth Century*, 138–39; Herbert, *Victorian Relativity*, 32.
79. T. S. Eliot, *The Complete Poems and Plays, 1909–1950* (New York: Brace and Company, 1958).
80. Wilson Harris, *Jonestown* (London: Faber and Faber, 1996), 5.
81. Frei, *Eclipse*, 18.
82. Cameron, *Higher Criticism*, 87.
83. Zemka, *Victorian Testaments*, 11.
84. Ibid., 29.
85. Frei, *Eclipse*, 43.
86. Auerbach, *Mimesis*, 14–16.

87. Lynn M. Poland, *Literary Criticism and Biblical Hermeneutics: A Critique of Formalist Approaches* (Chico, California: Scholars Press, 1985), 118; Thomas Huxley, *Science and Culture* (New York: D. Appleton, 1888), 10.

88. Frei, *Eclipse*, 15.

89. Foucault, *Archaeology*, 148–75.

90. Matthew Arnold, "The Bishop and the Philosopher," *The Complete Prose Works of Matthew Arnold*, ed. R. H. Super, vol. 3. (Ann Arbor: The University of Michigan Press, 1973).

91. "The Literary Influence of Academies," *The Complete Prose Works of Matthew Arnold*, ed. R. H. Super, vol. 3. (Ann Arbor: The University of Michigan Press, 1973), 237.

92. Spinoza's *Tractatus*, "its rudiments the method of the nineteenth-century Critics," "directly and indirectly" influenced "the debates of the nineteenth century" (Cameron, *Higher Criticism*, 264). For more on Arnold's response to higher criticism, see Prickett. For a reading of how the essayists and Colenso are presumed different from Spinoza, see Arnold's "The Bishop and the Philosopher."

93. "LI," 243, 236. Much of Arnold's views on this is expressed later in *Literature and Dogma* (1873), where he maintains that the best criticism of the Bible must harmonize old as well as new methods (see *Letters*, 4:168–69). Arnold was clearly not a biblical literalist, nor did he accept a conservative view of inspiration, believing, for example, that while "we may suppose that we have pretty nearly the actual words of whoever did write the Epistle in question" (the Epistle to the Romans), still there is in the Bible a great deal of interpolations. For more of this see *Letters*, 4:256–57. But believing, as he claims, that the Bible is "the only means by which our people, naturally hard and brutal, gets any exercise of its soul and imagination," he looks therefore "with disquietude on all merely negative criticism of the Bible, which must certainly at first dispose them to throw the book aside" (*Letters*, 4:259). Arnold resented any association whatsoever to the German Biblical Criticism ("it rather makes me angry"), believing that "they would have drowned me if it had not been for the corks I had brought from the study of Spinoza. To him I owe more than I can say" (*Letters*, 4:290). What he really wanted, as I argued earlier, was a kind of reverential attitude to interpretation rather than the brash, irreverent Germanism he sees on display in contemporary biblical criticism. Prickett sees in Arnold's "Hebrew" and "Hellene" a "less picturesque balancing of terms than part of a long-term programme for hellenizing, or, better still, 'indo-europeanizing' established Christianity" (*Rethinking*, 66).

94. "The Function of Criticism at the Present Time," *The Complete Prose Works of Matthew Arnold*, ed. R. H. Super, vol. 3. (Ann Arbor: The University of Michigan Press, 1973), 277–78.

95. Zemka, *Victorian Testaments*, 4.

96. Herbert, *Victorian Relativity*, 88.

97. Terry Eagleton, *After Theory* (New York: Basic Books, 2003), 96.

98. Altholz, *Anatomy*, 1, 33.

99. Eagleton, *After Theory*, 202, 207.

100. Zemka, *Victorian Testaments*, 18.

CHAPTER 3

SKEPTICAL WOMEN V. HONEST MEN V. GOOD OLD BOYS: GENDER CONFLICT IN THE HIGH VICTORIAN RELIGION WARS

Janet L. Larson

Whoever comes in contact with these writers must feel that he is dealing with minds in a state of disease—that he has the pretence of great intellectuality in very feeble and effeminate persons—that their writing is hardly like that of men....morally, it has the same emasculation of tone—absence of all vigor; yet there is not wanting the animus of pride, who kisses as he betrays.

> —Must We Burn Our Bibles? A Few Honest Words About the "Essays and Reviews"; Addressed to Honest People, by an Honest Man (1861)

That characteristic of the school which has been jocosely termed "Muscular Christianity," appears liable at every turn to degenerate into most obnoxious qualities—bluster and dogmatism, and a perpetual talk *about manliness, which is as much the reverse of real manliness, as the talk about purity...is the reverse of real purity.*

> —*Frances Power Cobbe*, Broken Lights: An Inquiry into the Present Condition and Future Prospects of Religious Faith (1864)

In the last 300 years much has been gained politically, but what has been done for religion? We have retrenched a good deal, but we have put nothing in the place of it. It has been all denying and no constructing.

> —*Florence Nightingale*, Suggestions for Thought (1860)

TRACKING GENDER TALKING

The battle over the Bible has long been understood as a symbolic center for broader crises of cultural authority in nineteenth-century England. More recent work has drawn attention to the ways anxieties about male authority and masculine identity drove contentions in the "Victorian Church," prompting discursive contest over who spoke for true manliness or was basely betraying it.[1] Although disparaging one's opponents in feminine terms was well established in English theological polemic, and biblical studies operated from androcentric assumptions, it is striking how often the language of gender appears in the writing of the High Victorian religion wars. We can readily find it in standard places, such as defenses of Apostolic Succession as the unbroken chain of God's holiest men; interpretations of the heroic character of prophetic genius; accounts of the contentious early Church as a feminized body; charges of "effeminacy" against temporizing laditudinarians or conservative bishops who would not "look facts in the face"; and reconstructions of the "historical Jesus" featuring the tender Galilean preacher, thronged by adoring women in Ernest Renan's *Vie de Jésus* (1863), displaying his stern manly character, as in J. R. Seeley's *Ecce Homo* (1865), or recovering Jesus's masculine "courage" to overcome the "weakness" of a feminized Christianity, Thomas Hughes's project in *The Manliness of Christ* (1879).[2]

The "Muscular Christian" school of Charles Kingsley and F. D. Maurice, fleshed out in Hughes's Tom Brown novels, was most notorious for its "perpetual *talk* about manliness," as Frances Power Cobbe put it with singular candor for a Victorian woman writer in *Broken Lights* (1864), her book-length contribution to the *Essays and Reviews* debate.[3] But it was the "honest men" of *Essays and Reviews* (1860) and their allies who took the manly ethos and ran with it for decades as they wrested the game from the Establishment old boys on the playing field of Victorian biblical studies. In their volume, the Essayists build up a collective masculine credibility through a network of gender-coded tropes, idealizing narratives of coming-to-manhood, references to commonalities of men's experience and virtues like "manly sense and industry," and uses of the feminine as a template for male lack, such as the "want of manliness in men who please themselves with insinuating unpopular opinions which they dare not advocate openly."[4] Elaborating a common educational trope, Frederick Temple's lead essay figures the human race as "a colossal man" and raises up modern biblical criticism over "all other studies" as the leading academic method for "the manhood of the world."[5] Critics who disparaged the Essayists in feminine terms—such as the Judas/temptress who "kisses" the Bible "as he betrays" it—betray irritation with a rival masculinist discourse even as they are discursively "emasculati[ng]" it.[6]

If as Jude V. Nixon argues the disparate articles in *Essays and Reviews* constitute what Foucault called " 'homogeneous fields of enunciated regularities' that 'characterize a discursive formation,' "[7] the fact that it was only an emergent discourse to the British public in 1860 made it all the more necessary to hitch the Essayists' bid for the authority of historical continuity to established hegemonies of gender as well as class, race, and nation. While Cobbe disputed their claims, her praise for "the simple manliness natural to those who are striving to speak out unpopular truths, and believe that they have got reason and science on their side" (*BL*, 69; cf. 91), echoed a common characterization of these English critics that enrolled them, as in late Victorian histories of biblical interpretation, in the heroic line of the first "Reformers" as champions of "truth" against the doctrinal distortions of the Church.[8] For all its accomplishments, the writing of the party Cobbe called the "Second Broad Church" (*BL*, 73–92) would become the long-term carrier of gendered discourse in English biblical criticism, sustaining its problems for women as well as for men.

Donald Hall's observation that phallic figures in "muscular Christian" writing registered "both a reaction to and an intensification of a gender power struggle that was well underway by the mid-nineteenth century" helps us identify a form of dual warfare that was engaged more broadly in Victorian religious discourse than in Kingsley's writing or *Essays and Reviews*.[9] Going beyond standard histories of the Victorian Church as well as current masculinity studies, this essay explores the wider discursive battleground of popular biblical and theological debate as a displaced arena of conflict between the sexes and over gender in the writing of women as well as men. Sometimes breaking into open hostilities, more often carried on unconsciously or in code, these peculiarly Victorian contentions operated on a "higher" plane of discourse where the combatants could express and act out personal and social grievances, anxieties, and desires in exalted language that served both to mystify these other agendas and to articulate matters of real religious concern to themselves and their readers. Although theology was men's business, women's expected affinity for religious subjects made the Bible wars a relatively more acceptable arena in which they could exercise cultural power than in advocating "woman's rights." This wider social struggle, engaged openly on other fronts, flows into and out of these texts on biblical and theological subjects—a cultural dynamic little studied, if at all, in modern histories of the Victorian Church, or of the Cause.

Dispersed across a wide cultural terrain, engaging writers with very different views, gender-and-Bible conflict spilled over into many genres besides the academic treatise and the theological essay, including public and private letters, sermon and pamphlet wars, cheap tracts, fictionalized debates, and men's and women's commentaries on each other's books. Here I want to sample this literature by inspecting a series of discursive sites, chiefly from 1860 to the 1880s, for signs of this dual conflict between female "skeptics" (in several senses) and their male critics, wrestling partners, "friends of the sex," and more generalized objects of attack, especially higher criticism. Besides the main contenders in this discussion—Sarah Lewis, the author of *Woman's Mission* (1839), Catherine Booth, Frances Power Cobbe (and Francis W. Newman, Matthew Arnold), Florence Nightingale (and Benjamin Jowett), Charlotte Brontë, and Mary Ward (and W. E. Gladstone)—we need to look at less-known periodical writers who addressed the cultural problematic of women's relations with men's "doubt." In examining texts, I am as much interested in *how* religious warfare unfolds in gendered patterns of discourse and argument as in the specific points at issue and the grounds on which these Victorians argue. Further, sampling writing over more than two decades can help us track the growing sense that men's religious questioning was opening a "gulf between the sexes," even though feminist campaigns did more in this period to show that their interests were different, even opposed. But we must first glance back, for the interrelations of gender ideology and religion had deep historical roots in English culture, which had set up women and men to become antagonists in the "Battle of Belief" long before Bible questions troubled the general public.

ENTANGLED ROOTS OF WAR

Whatever their persuasion, female participants in the Victorian Bible wars were all fighting an uphill battle in a millennial gender conflict, for from the Greeks onward "hermeneutics" had excluded women from both reason and interpretation. During the Enlightenment, formal Scripture study had become if possible an even more distinctly androcentric endeavor as "the proper study of Man" was folded into its horizon. With the arrival of the English Age of Reason, traditional means of keeping the unreasonable feminine out of this high-stakes game were refined even as men battled over the Scriptures on strictly "rational" grounds. Two emergences in the 1730s mark a defining cultural moment in this story: middle-class domestic ideology in its recognizable modern form was now being aggressively propagated in conduct books and pulpits, and a foreign-sounding word with Greek roots came into the academic clerical lexicon. Although liberal "hermeneutics" would transform many orthodox beliefs, at a time of deist challenge this new term was freighted with Churchmen's obligations to secure the Bible from men who were taking "such liberties with Sacred Writ," as one writer put it in 1737, "as are by no means allowable upon any known rules of just and sober hermeneutics."[10] With the development of the ideology of separate spheres during the eighteenth century and the dominance of rationalism in Scripture studies came a sexual division of biblical-textual labor in which the cultural authority of the academically trained clergy was enhanced by new *technē;* whereas in taking woman's humbler part of explaining the Bible to children in plain English (no small task), it mattered little what mothers knew or fudged so long as their hearts were with the God of the Church.

Mark Pattison, looking back in *Essays and Reviews* at "Tendencies of Religious Thought in England, 1688–1750," gives a less flattering view of men's "just and sober hermeneutics" in the deist controversy, when all parties assumed the "supremacy of reason," whether it was wielded to prove, with Locke, "The Reasonableness of Christianity," the internal consistency of divine revelation, or its inconsistency and absurdity (*E&R*, 389). The dominance of "the rationalizing method" in theology meant that "Every one who had anything to say on sacred subjects drilled it into an array of argument against a supposed objector," while both sides kept up the "rationalistic fiction" that their "beliefs were determined by an impartial inquiry into the evidence" (*E&R*, 390, 414). This exaggerated trust, Pattison observes, ironically ensured the notorious unreasonableness of eighteenth-century religious debate, with its arrogant exaggeration, charges and counter-charges of infidelity and moral villainy, and unmanly *ad hominum* arguments (*E&R*, 413–14). Painting a picture with *ad hominum* touches of another sort, he represents the combatants "braining" each other with arguments and descending to the "vulgarity" of belligerent self-display, as "the cassocked divine assumes the airs of the 'roaring blade,' and ruffles it on the mall with a horse-whip under his arm," and "Warburton's stock argument is a threat to cudgel any one who disputes his opinion" (*E&R*, 418, 413). Pattison attributes this "blustering language" to an outmoded cultural norm, belonging to an eighteenth-century "habit of exaggerating both good and evil," the complement to an "appetite for flattery as insatiable" for Warburton's "burly intellect" as for "Miss Seward and her coterie" (*E&R*, 413, 414). Going further back, he traces the behavior of this whole "polemical tribe" to the "stamp of advocacy...impressed on English theology at the Reformation" (*E&R*, 417, 414). "[C]urrent phrases" like " 'the enemies of religion,' " and " 'the bulwarks of our faith' " are not signs of an ingrained masculine discursive behavior supported by English institutions and laws, but holdovers from an earlier era when theology was "the study of topics of defence," as Pattison regrets it still is (*E&R*, 414).

The more fundamental error he charges against these predecessors is their understanding of "reason," in Locke's terms, as "natural revelation, whereby the eternal Father of light and fountain of all knowledge communicates to mankind that portion of truth which he has laid within the reach of their natural faculties...."[11] This democratizing definition of reason was highly attractive to learned eighteenth-century women who assimilated it to Genesis 1:26–27 and, supplementing the biblical text with contemporary philosophical ideas, constructed a powerful *a priori* principle out of the *imago dei*, with which to argue for restoring the fullness of "the image of God" to "male and female" as equally endowed with reason.[12] Progressive women were still using this principle in Pattison's day; but to this Oxford Essayist the notion of a "natural discernment," "belonging to all men of sound mind and average capacity," was but " 'Rationalismus vulgaris,' " and no basis for sound theology, which required "the higher, or philosophic, reason" of the few (408, 409).[13]

When eighteenth- and nineteenth-century exegetes read Genesis chapter 1 as cosmogonic myth or "the serpent" with the aid of comparative mythology, they did not do so to undermine the doctrine of woman's subjection, which still—anchronistically—could be indexed to a Bible that was losing its authority for Christian doctrine. The modern rule that the critic, as a "disengaged rational subject," detached "interpretation," or exegesis, from "application," or preaching, methodologically supported a double standard by which a Bible text's facts could be fiction to the exegete and still be "true" to his everyday social character.[14] Given the affinity between ideology and allegory, moreover, conventional abstractions about male and female "nature" could readily be folded into the allegorical readings many liberals favored for material like the Genesis stories, as the "kernel" of truth left after their ancient "husks" were shucked. By such "methods," the Adam/Eve binary was hermeneutically preserved for Victorian understandings that God reserved intellect to males when He "created man in his own image" and made "Woman" incapable, from "the very inmost nature of [her] soul, ... of severely impartial and logical reasoning ... of convincing, or being convinced, by truth alone."[15]

By the time Pattison wrote his essay, the Angel of the House was well established as an imaginary cultural savior from religious warfare and doubt because this figure was innocent of biblical criticism, while the female paragon who discoursed on the latest tidings from Tübingen was cast outside the pale as "mannish" by both Angels and men. Nightingale observed that the Englishwoman of the conventional type was not "'by birth a Tory,'—[as] has been often said" but was educated so by the wedding of social regimes to religious disciplines for female desire.[16] One popular aid to this formation in middle-class families was the book of Bible selections for children that doubled as a conduct book and taught reading according to gender. The anonymous "Lady" author of a pair of such books, deeply imbued with Victorian notions of sex and mind, heads *The Girl's Own Text Book* (1858) with a hymn verse defining a feminine hermeneutic of pure receptiveness to the Word:

> Oh write upon my memory, Lord
> The texts and doctrines of Thy Word;
> That I may break Thy laws no more,
> But serve Thee better than before.[17]

These lines serve a concealed misogynist logic—that sinful woman must be disciplined—which has been purified for young Victorian females as the imperative of self-regulation by internalized "laws." To convey these rules, the Lady author need not include in her little volume any of the usual Bible "texts" on the "doctrine" of Womanhood because she pre-interprets all her selections, mostly generic in reference, in the "Address to Girls," a lengthy, repetitious preface that seamlessly mingles cultural with biblical instruction. Here she specially recommends memorizing texts to acquire matter for meditation, since "girls especially, are often at a loss for subjects of thought. In fact, they seldom *think*," a want that "leads to other evils" including "foolish, idle, frivolous talking and jesting ... " (*Girl's*, x–xi). Yet the biblical food for thought offered in this preface mainly warns against thoughts girls must avoid, which cannot be expressed by the Lady and so contribute to *not thinking*.

Dark references in this manual to Eve's particular temptations (without mention of Eve)—"'the lust of the flesh, and the lust of the eye, and the pride of life'" (*Girl's*, 221)—are absent from *The Boy's Own Text Book* (1857), which came out first. Placing boys' Bible wisdom within a discourse of cultural wisdom meant to attach the affectivity of young males, the Lady's preface here appeals to the pleasures of physical exercise and urges pride in intellectual accomplishment: the little scholar will get knowledge and wisdom "unto salvation" by studying his 730 "portions of Scripture," that he might "run the race, and wag[e] the warfare, and rea[p] the eternal harvest of [his] labours."[18] Arranging his texts in pairs to show the harmony of the Old and New Testaments also invites his sense of self-importance by challenging him to tease out the typological foundations of Christian theology—to "*think*" already like a "clergyboy" (to borrow a sarcasm from Josephine Butler).[19] The biblical textuality of the "Address to Boys" licenses an exciting field of masculine activity and projects the image of a young member of the master class who will one day carry "his" Bible into the thick of public life, where a pledge of God's heavenly promises can be expected as he reaps rewards of his labors on earth. For this progressive half of the race, the Lady offers a modern-sounding rhetoric, almost "Muscular Christian," as though preparing Young England for going to school with Tom Brown; whereas a Calvinist rhetoric left over from Puritan England naturally suits girls, a class of readers who will " 'spend [their] years as a tale that is told' " (*Girl's*, 2; Ps. 90:9).

The separate spheres of feeling, thinking, and interpreting in which these twin manuals install boy and girl seem designed to prevent conflict between them, as indeed was the Lady's part, while her orthodox treatment of Scripture ensures that "disputes [are] shut up in God's promises."[20] But trouble is already brewing when the sexes are addressed like two sects in different historical eras, one living into the future, the "other" looking back. Teaching Bible reading according to gender from youth up in segregated educational settings prepared the subjectivities of adult males and females to perceive the nature of their relationship with the objects of religion differently—and so nurtured the potential for discord between them on the theological problem posed to the Bible by modernity, once it became a problem to the general public. Ironically, then, a sex-gender system liberal Bible critics did not question assured them a vigorously hostile audience among women whose mental channels were cut to the pattern of an earlier era. However a critic like Jowett might try to write off female contemporaries who "are fed or feed themselves on Methodistical or Catholic fancies" as enemies of progress, contributing to "all the mischief in the world done by conservatism," what such women thought and felt mattered because "in Victorian Britain the fate of [biblical] scholarship was closely linked to the larger climate of religious opinion."[21] As press and pulpit whipped up furor against the Seven Against Christ, Angels were only performing their duty as the nation's spiritual guardians when they openly deplored what such men were doing with God's Word.

The Angel's counterpart was an ideal of manhood that served as a hedge—in body imagery, a poised defensive weapon—against "the unknown, the threatening, and the potentially disruptive" in Victorian culture.[22] Besides fending off such threats as the Darwinian view of "man" (*The Origin of Species*, 1859), the Essayists' manly self-idealizations registered anxieties about new challenges to men's authority being raised by mid-Victorian lady preachers and novelists as well as the organizing women's movement, which emerged just ahead of *Essays and Reviews* with the establishing of the Langham Place Circle and the *English Woman's Journal* in 1858, amid spirited debate over the Divorce and Matrimonial Causes Act and its supposed threats to the Order of Creation. In this charged atmosphere, with women seen as the foes of intellectual progress in religion or as only too progressive, the wrangling in the Church over who spoke for true manliness was not just a contest of men *versus* men but responded to perceived female threats from more than one direction. The Essayists' operative gender binarism defined womanliness of *any* kind as Other, even as their scientist scholarly enterprise for "the select few" (Pattison, *E&R*, 408) wrote out qualities of mind and feeling a good many Victorian women valued, their methods for finding out "truth," and their definitions of what that was. This marginalizing of the other sex in the discourse of English biblical critics, secured practically by barring female scholars from Oxford, did not go uncontested: it provoked resistance from women across the religious and political spectrum, unleashing their differing hermeneutics of suspicion toward men's criticism and theology. Through the writing of women's "criticism" in this vein runs a common conviction, cutting across differences of creed, intellectual influences, politics, social vision, and class, that the higher critics were missing something higher, which these female contemporaries felt they could and must supply.

For all the power of Victorian mechanisms for forming sexed religious subjects, Bible-and-gender conflict was nonetheless no simple case of *Woman v. Man* or *Faith v. Doubt*. Especially after 1860, only one of its manifestations was the standoff between the pious (or "deluded") female and the male heretic (or "honest man"), which J. W. Bengough represents in his satirical poem on "The Higher Criticism" (1895) by setting a son's testimony to his "dear old mother, dead and gone,...a Higher Critic, too," who loved and "knew [the Book] through and through" as literal truth "from God direct," against a male proponent of "the new Negation School."[23] This scenario, a well-worn polemical device by 1895, omits nuances like conservative women's *resentment* of the power of academics and clergymen in religion questions. It cannot accommodate at all less orthodox and more equivocal female dissenters to men's criticism such as Nightingale, whose mind had absorbed "the ideas of the nineteenth century" (*C*, 55), but who did not buy higher criticism wholesale and formulated her own religious social philosophy while the liberals were only "denying" or dropping the ball (*ST*, 114).

Nightingale, Cobbe, and other progressive women thinkers complicate the story because they were provisionally indebted to the new "discursivity" founded by *Essays and Reviews* that introduced, in Foucault's terms, "the possibilities and the rules for the formation of other texts" with "differences," marked by "something other than [their] discourse, yet...belonging to what they founded." The Essayists tended to see in their "founding act an eventually restricted number of propositions" that advanced by further studies, would ultimately re-ground Christianity "beyond the reach of accidents," as they hoped; while opponents sounded the alarm that *Essays and Reviews* would indeed be "heterogenous to its subsequent transformations" by setting off an "endless possibility of discourse" leading to fathomless Negation.[24] But transformations of higher criticism were also going forward in Victorian women's discourse that in some way belonged to, yet was other than, the new discursivity of the Essayists—or its English precursors such as Dr. Arnold's writings, or German criticism—and did not inevitably end in nihilism.

Even George Eliot and Mary Ward wrote in reservations, supplements, and corrections when propagating historical criticism in their periodical essays; in her novels Eliot transformed the new discursivity within the texture of her philosophical narrative voice. Nightingale, who had been tutored by Baron von Bunsen, the distinguished orientalist and subject of a "heretical" article in *Essays and Reviews*, and had been absorbing "the ideas of the nineteenth century" from many sources before its publication, was a more critical transformer of biblical criticism, sometimes starting a sentence in its terms and then running off with the ball down a playing field of her own imagining. More orthodox Bible-reading feminists, including the Evangelical Josephine Butler, raid men's scholarly arsenals from " 'behind the lines' in both a textual and military sense"[25] and turn their hermeneutics into nonlethal weapons for a Bible-and-gender war of their own, the struggle to overthrow scriptural arguments for woman's nature and place. Free to obey the new rules selectively as non-members of the guild, reform-minded interpreters as diverse as Charlotte Brontë, Butler, Nightingale, and Cobbe simply "se[t] aside" whatever in the new methods *and* in the Bible they deem "not pertinent," "inessential," or " 'prehistoric' "[26] when writing on women's topics with Scripture—that is, irrelevant to the their faith perspectives and social agendas, or superceded by their modern desires and knowledge of women's subjection under ancient and modern patriarchy. But doing higher criticism *à la femme* was tricky and could end up legitimizing a project that cut women out; and whatever these women do with it serves the other projects they have on hand. Rather more than "heterogeneous" to the founding documents of biblical criticism, their efforts were also constitutive of a new feminist discursivity that extended in bold new directions the special language and common reading practices developed by many hands across the broader historical field of English women's *biblical*-social interpretation.

The conventional linking of men *and* higher criticism with "Negation" deleted from the record the even more shocking public embrace of "Agnosticism" or "Atheism" by women such as the post-Unitarian Harriet Martineau and Annie Besant, a deconverted Puseyite who preached an extempore sermon against the divinity of Christ to the empty pews of her husband's church, left him for the National Secular Society, and wrote a piece of Atheist propaganda in 1885 assailing the Bible in English history as women's scourge and "a curse to the human race."[27] Women's public endorsements of "ultra" creeds opened another contentious subfield of Victorian religion-and-gender discourse by giving the popular press new types of female scandal to expose—or a new "woman problem" for periodical writers to solve by managing women's vexed relationships with "skepticism," this is, with men in *their* new "condition." Such efforts by liberal-minded friends of the sex did not go unanswered either. In the 1880s, Mary Ward crafted her own version of how a pious wife might accommodate herself to an "honest" husband in *Robert Elsmere* (1888), even as conservative writers with an emboldened sense of Woman's Mission were stepping up to defend their sisters from the aggressive masculine hegemony of "doubt."

CASES: WOMEN'S "CRITICISM" OF/AND THE CRITICS

Female hostilities on these lines had broken out in *Woman's Mission* in 1839, where Sarah Lewis, dancing in high righteous ire on the pinnacle of her lofty cultural functions, assails the "men [who] have been scanning [the gospel] with the intellect, and not with the heart!"—and she adds, "what wonder is it, then, that a system addressed to the heart, and intended to operate upon the heart, has eluded their researches! How are they repaid for these researches? by unbelief. . . ."[28] While her climactic "Religion" chapter mentions no works of historical criticism, Lewis was broadly responding to the implications of a kind of biblical scholarship that set the authority of man's critical reason over God's Word, and set aside the critic's emotional allegiances, while vaunting its objectivity and freedom from the "bondage of dogma." In reaching for the word "intellect" to sum up the wrongs of biblical criticism, she raises the spectre of "rationalism," a highly useful adversary for Woman's Mission argument, and the subject of John Henry Newman's Tract LXXIII (*On the Introduction of Rationalistic Principles into Religion*, 1836). Following a durable standard, Lewis judges "rationalism" for its corrosive effects on faith, its insufficiency for reading God's Word, and its biblical sin of "pride of intellect," "that proud curiosity which evermore leads men on to seek to be as gods, knowing good and evil," traits she also ascribes to the "sceptic," who rejects Christian humility because it insults his pride.[29] Picking up on the conservatives' tendency to bundle the infidelities of Paine, Voltaire, Hume, English deism, and "the Germans" into the demonizing mega-terms "rationalism" and "scepticism,"[30] Lewis blurs distinctions to construct her code for faithless masculine reason and poises against it the "enlightened" "intellec[t]" of the woman who naturally grasps Christianity's teachings of the "heart," "love and self-renunciation" (*WM*, 151, 150).

Lewis's attack on men's "scanning" of the Bible is embedded in, and helps to justify, a more extensive denunciation of nominal Christianity that comes down hard on clergymen's weaponizing of prooftexts, their "petty differences, and paltry contentions" on "inferior matters of the law, the tithe of mint and cummin, [which] perplex, and, alas! shake the Christian world" (*WM*, 143, 138, 137). Lewis holds these lapses of Christian spirit responsible for the "errors" of skepticism and metaphorically connects with its surface-skimming literalism, while she finds Christian men's arrogant denunciations as guilty of "the selfish principle" as their opponents (*WM*, 143, 138). By manipulating a series of hierarchical binary oppositions through her "Religion" chapter—*human v. God, intellect v. heart*, and *letter v. spirit*—she collapses together literalistic skeptics, rationalistic interpreters, and legalistic preachers, in order to trump all these erroneous "interpretations of men" with the Missionary Woman's truth, which she folds into the "spirit, not the letter" of "Christianity" (*WM*, 136). Theologians who neglect the doctrine of "regeneration" for the "scheme of redemption" also nearly fall on the "letter" side of these binary oppositions. While this sharply antithetical rhetoric betrays the female combatant engaged in a struggle between the sexes for "Religion" power in England and the cultural power that came with it, Lewis's discourse displaces this struggle onto a higher plane where abstract antitheses do battle for her, distancing the merely personal. They also position the writer as a defender of religion and assure her Woman's Missionary triumph—rhetorically—by aligning her "spirit" and "heart" with "God."

But when Lewis holds up men's "errors" for reproof, anger leaps through her correct Christian discourse of forgiveness, bursting the constraints she has placed on female character to be "poor in spirit" (*WM*, 139). She heaps scorn on "men loudly and boldly declaiming concerning the hidden purposes of God, as though they had secret intimation of them, calling down on any, and on whom they will, his eternal wrath, and clothing the Deity with their own bad passions and selfish dispositions," until "we are ready to lift up our eyes and ask, where sleep thy thunderbolts?" (*WM*, 143). Even taken as a snide literalistic proof, her words pack the fury of a woman's plea that God strike down these arrogant rivals to His power, and hers. At "thunderbolts," Lewis's American editor, who provides the prooftexts she omits, inserted an unintentionally ironic footnote supplying the proper gospel words: " 'Father, forgive them, for they know not what they do.'—D" (*WM*, 143n.).

For all her absolute certainty about "Religion," Lewis's discourse betrays a less perfect orthodoxy than might at first appear. When she cries, "Why will we not go to the Bible, not only for our rule of faith, but for our rule of life, for the renewal of our hearts, that they may be filled with righteousness, peace, and joy in the Holy Ghost?" (*WM*, 150), she gives the Scripture question an anticlerical and antidogmatic edge and privileges *over* reading the Bible as a doctrinal textbook a hermeneutics of religious experience, of being regenerated, the work of the Holy Spirit and uniquely Woman's Mission. When she declares the Bible woman's "charter of manumission," giving her "light, freedom, privileges . . . as a right, by the unerring fiat of the Son of God!" she generalizes from several of Jesus's encounters with women (without quoting or retelling) and, lifting off from the letter before it is fully read, allegorizes the text to find in it her own ideology (*WM*, 146, 147–48). This is the procedure of a Victorian "spiritual reader" free of the old typological rules, and no Verbal Inspirationist, who would have quoted the *ipsissima verba* with chapter and verse. Lewis merely borrows the discourse of inerrancy and uses Jesus's respectful words to women (whatever they were) to second her own fiat, answering feminist cries of the hour, that Christianity "at once settled the condition of woman, by exalting her own peculiar qualities in the moral grade" (*WM*, 146).

In these arguments, by going to "the Bible" Lewis means "the gospel"— not all the diverse and uncertain writings of the evangelists and apostles either, but "the essence of Christianity," love and self-renunciation (*WM*, 136). Despite her "Methodistical" notes ("the renewal of our hearts" and "joy in the Holy Ghost"), this displacement of the whole of the Scriptures and Judaism by a core of "essentials" attributed to "Christianity" alone betrays the liberal influence of the French treatise Lewis had originally intended to translate, M. Aimé-Martin's *De l'Education des Mères de familles* (1834), which dealt philosophically with its subject and had acquainted her with continental thought. Like Aimé-Martin and other writers of Victorian essential Christianities, she downgrades "the letter," throws doctrines overboard (Original Sin and Hell), declines to "speak of forms . . . or dogmas," and condemns narrow dogmatism, the "letter" of theology that misses Christianity's "spirit" (*WM*, 136).[31] In reading "the gospel" primarily as a moral code mothers must inculcate in their children, she also follows Aimé-Martin in turning to the uses of Woman's Mission the ethicizing of Christianity that had begun with the *Lex evangelica* of Erasmus in the Humanist Reformation.[32] This ethical line, intersected by the work of the "German rationalists," then by Romantic hermeneutics, which emphasized the "heart" of the interpreter, had most recently produced Dr. Arnold's "ethical condensation of the Bible," a response to the loss of biblical narrative as divinely-inspired history.[33] In this phase of essentializing, "the Christian character," the focus of moral gospel reading, was evolving into "a form of religious proof" in Broad Church writing, "reflecting back a coherent set of principles on the Bible, the church, and the nation" that was no longer retrievable from the uncertain text. This "hermeneutics of character" led Arnold to exalt the worship of Christ and his followers to embrace Christian manliness.[34] Sarah Lewis, who seems to assume the gospels' historicity but flies free of the letter, makes her own remedy for many lacks by building up the efficacy of female Christian character as a "gospel" and substituting her narrative of Woman's Mission as salvific, not only for Christianity and the nation but for the whole human race. If her chapter on "Religion" engages wider Bible-and-gender wars via its hermeneutics of faithful female suspicion, in these other respects her discourse has a surprisingly modern provenance. But while demonstrating that the "enlightened" female mind to which she appeals could not be entirely sequestered from contemporary trends, Lewis enters the broad current of liberal discursivity only to channel it into Woman's Mission. Possibly one unacknowledged function of her sharp rejection of the "sceptics" is to resist these modern tendencies in her own discourse.

Near the beginning of Victoria's reign, *Woman's Mission* issued an opening volley in a long and not entirely predictable women's war in print on the academic "men's Bible." Whether assailing the critics is the focus of the writing or folded into other agendas, whether the challenger is evangelical, Broad Church, dissenting, heterodox, or a firm unbeliever, whether her objections are emotionally charged or rationally considered, whether hostilities take the form of sarcasms fired at the enemy or more extended sorties, this female battle zone can be generally identified by several rhetorical features we find in *Woman's Mission*. Writing in the mode of a sermon or prophetic diatribe, the author overrides the expected Christian rhetoric of humility and forgiveness to make a direct hit on a particular man or group of men—no sly "insinuating unpopular opinions" here (Pattison, *E&R*, 420). This is the binary opposition underlying many of these texts; but one antithesis tends to generate others in combative discourse, and a very common structure in Victorian women's "criticism" is to set the authority of their superior sense and religious sensibility against men's setting their "reason" over God's Word. Operating of necessity by indirection too, these skeptics cover their transgressive boldness by placing their arguments on the highest possible grounds—God's "kingdom come...on earth" (*WM*, 154), the "essence of Christianity," "the Christian spirit," God's "character," eternal salvation, the good of humankind or the nation. In shifting upward on such wings, they seem to transcend conventional notions of female subjectivism while aligning themselves with ultimate power and truth in an unequal struggle that cried out for divine aid.[35] Meanwhile, references and tonalities in the discourse betray the writer's subject position in the Victorian gender system and manifest its contradictions. In Lewis's sarcasms the note of the marginalized woman's revenge bespeaks frustration at men's ownership of biblical studies and public religious discourse, even as it betrays the exaggeration in Woman's Mission claims to decisive influence over men's thinking.

Critical commentary on men's "researches" and "Negation" issued from a wider band of female opinion in succeeding decades and took aggressive new forms as Scripture questioning became more widespread and women found or established power bases from which to speak. One such fortified site was the Salvation Army pulpit. Catherine Booth's responses in the 1880s, a late stage in the game when the cause of historical-critical method was well advanced, register high on the Richter scale of Victorian women's religious social anger, and the passive–aggressive voice of the sidelined woman's revenge has become a battlecry. In a lecture of 1887, in which she proclaimed "the Christ of the Salvation Army" against "the sceptics and the infidels," she ran down "The Christs of the Nineteenth Century," turning an established theme about the influence of the *Zeitgeist* on religious conceptions back on the historical criticism school. Booth's "False Christs" include a semi-Straussian "*religious myth or good angel*, a kind of religious Julius Caesar, who did wonderful things ages ago, and who is somehow or other going to benefit in the future those who intellectually believe in Him now" but is not a present help in trouble. Another "imaginary Christ," recalling Renan's feminized hero, is portrayed as a "*beautiful example*—the most beautiful the world has ever seen; not Divine, yet the nearest to our conception of the Divine which even [these skeptics] think possible"—but supplies "no power by which to conform ourselves to the model."[36] The discourse of the "*good angel*" and "*beautiful example*" exemplified to Booth the

"effeteness" of so much modern "Christianity" with "no Holy Ghost in it":
it was like "a dead body, or a galvanic battery without the power," whereas
Jesus, "the type for us" all, "combined all the tenderness, sublime devotion,
and self-sacrifice of the woman with the intellect and strength of the man."[37]

In this sally, Booth seems not to have noticed or minded that this androgy-
nous or dual-sexed conception of Jesus was another nineteenth-century
Christ, sponsored by women's rising expectations and often repeated. It
simply followed for her from experience that the female sex could powerfully
convey the real Jesus Christ: she once told a West End audience she "would
rather have a Hallelujah Lass, a little child, with the power of the Holy
Ghost, hardly able to put two sentences of the Queen's English together, to
come to help, bless, and benefit my soul, than ... the most learned divine in
the kingdom without it ...."[38] Walking in "*obedience to the light*" did "not
mean running around to see what this person says and the other person says
about such and such a text, in order that you may escape from the real, practical meaning of the text!"[39] Here was Bengough's female Bible believer on
the rampage and at large—a more influential figure in "the Making of Modern
England" to William Stead than Cardinal Manning or Dean Stanley.[40]
Catherine Booth's whole career in promoting "Aggressive Christianity" was
the ardent practice of the biblical proofs she marshaled to defend "Woman's
Right to Preach the Gospel" in *Female Ministry* (1870); but her best proof
against the critics was her conviction, born of experience, that "what
God has put in me [could not] contradic[t] what He has put into this
book."[41]

Operating in the 1860s from journalistic pulpits and her own books,
Frances Power Cobbe critiqued the Christs of the nineteenth century on
Theist grounds with feminist undertones, first in an appendix to *Broken
Lights: An Inquiry into the Present Condition and Future Prospects of
Religious Faith* (1864). In this systematic assessment of each major party's
position in the current Bible wars, Cobbe's relentless exposure of men's
lapses in reasoning, wishful thinking, and verbal equivocation seems covertly
driven by a rather complicated womanly animus, even as she is demonstrating logically why none can meet the challenges biblical criticism was posing
to Christian belief.[42] Formally she argues from the "Rational" perspective
(Theism) and distinguishes it not from "the heart"—for Theists held that "in
each man's heart and soul must lie the ultimate test of all religious truth"[43]—
but from the "Historical" standpoint of all the Christian parties. She predicts
that the historical-critical method of the "Second Broad Church" will undo
their attempts to reconcile their views to Christianity by undermining the
historicity of the Scriptures on which its faith was based—good news to
Cobbe if it cleared the way for Theism, a fully philosophical creed based on
"Religious Sentiment" in humankind.[44] But biblical criticism would do
incalculable mischief to belief in the One God if the churches, flying in the
face of accumulating uncertainties about the gospels, continued to insist that
faith depended absolutely on the Christ recorded in Scripture history
(*BL*, 119–20).

Undaunted, even stimulated to ambition by these gaps in biblical knowledge, men were launching fresh efforts in the "search for the historical Jesus" when Cobbe was writing *Broken Lights*. So to her volume she added an appendix on the sensational entry in this competition for 1864, Renan's *Vie de Jésus*. While she concedes the literary brilliance of his portrait, Cobbe announces (three times) that he had "failed" to convey "the essential characteristic of his great subject" by treating "a subject essentially *spiritual* from a merely moral and aesthetic point of view," thereby "betray[ing] a very slight sense of the sanctity of the ideas" he subjects to "aesthetic criticism," and exasperating Cobbe in styling "the repentant Magdalenes" as " 'ces belles creatures.' "[45] But she most wants to clear the Theistic understanding of Jesus from any taint of association with Renan's views, which she expects "Traditionalists" will take as typical of all who "reject a supernatural revelation" (*BL*, 116). The author of *Vie de Jésus* soon drops to the background, and Cobbe launches into her own provisional "theory" of who Jesus was (*BL*, 119). She swiftly dispenses with his divinity by rehearsing critics' findings of how the "exaggerating homage, of adoring disciples" had "magnif[ied] the Prophet" by degrees into "the incarnate Logos" (*BL*, 121). Who was Jesus, then? Surely more, she insists against a common "Rationalist" position, than the "supreme Moral Reformer of the world" (*BL*, 125). Reaching higher for a Theist hermeneutical tool, she proposes "the Life of Jesus" as "the great ALLEGORY OF HUMANITY" (*BL*, 123). But Cobbe the ex-Evangelical is drawn back to the "influence" of a radiant figure who has "dazzled [the] eyes of Christendom" (*BL*, 130, 119). The "work" of he who "changed the bondage of the alien for the liberty of the sons of God" had to do with "the heart," not the "intellect" nor even "conscience," and brought "a new spirit" of "Regeneration" into the world (*BL*, 133, 130). Although Cobbe rejects Jesus's divinity, she feels she can apply the adjective "divine" to him—and capitalize "Him"—because his spirituality of "transcendent excellence," the divine quality in every man or woman infinitely multiplied, made Christ "the great REGENERATOR of Humanity" (*BL*, 135, 132).

Cobbe's colleague in heterodoxy, Francis W. Newman, saw a crypto-Evangelical Jesus-worship in her extravagant biblical terms in the Renan appendix and preached a sermon against it, *Discourse on Hero-Making in Religion* (1864).[46] In a chapter on "Change in the Idea of Christ" in *Dawning Lights* (1867), Cobbe toned down the biblical rhetoric but exploited Newman's tip by turning it against *men's* "hero-making," especially the First Broad Churchmen, whose "perpetual *talk* about manliness" she had lampooned three years before (*BL*, 69). Overtly they are the exemplars in her Theistic argument that exalting "the Humanity of [a] Christ" still formally held divine could injure belief in the Deity as the gospels' historicity continues to evaporate "in the minds of thinking men" until *nothing but* the human Jesus is left (*DL*, 93). But the tendency of this chapter's discourse also reveals Cobbe the female skeptic of men's thinking by bringing out the narcissistic character of these men's "ardent homage" to the "Divine Man" (*DL*, 88, 90). The chapter begins with a telling figure: "the magic black mirrors of the old necromancers," wherein each "gazer" sees an image "connected with his own character and fortunes" and discovers ever "more wonderful . . . revelations" the "more intently" he looks (*DL*, 85). If each Christian age has "beheld . . . a Christ of its own,"

> the portraits of Renan and of the author of Ecce Homo belong of necessity to our era of sentiment and philanthropy, . . . in which Truth and Goodness can be treated as matters of Taste, and in which the Enthusiasm of Humanity has reached that sad stage when it becomes self-conscious, and hangs, Narcissus-like, admiring itself in the lake of human tears. (*DL*, 86)

Cobbe was evidently no more charmed by Renan's Jesus than were Booth and Nightingale, as though these women knew in their bones that "beauty" like "Taste" is not spiritual power. Cobbe also "passe[s] by" *Ecce Homo* "in the great gallery as a beautiful work of art, historically worthless [as a] . . . portrait," but recognizes how Seeley's masculinized Christ fed the current veneration for "Christ's *human* character" (*DL*, 93, 87, 88). As Revelation proves fallible and historical method becomes "notoriously feeble," she observes, men find it necessary to bring in "[character] witnesses" to affirm Christ "a true man" and attest "the superior value of the impressions of upright men" who so recognize him (*DL*, 90). Her motifs of mirror, portrait, and gaze, then, suggest that this convergence of male character with Christ's is more than an intellectual "fashion" for "Maurice, Kingsley, Davies, Haweis and Brooke," whose "hearts visibly turn" to Christ the man and "direc[t] our eyes" to him in their sermons, with a "genial, reverent, and fervent sympathy" that is "spontaneous, genuine, and original . . ." (*DL*, 87–88). As Cobbe goes on and on in this complimentary vein, it is tempting to see her mimicking the self-congratulatory style in which these men wrote about other Scripture heroes too, notably Moses.[47] Ultimately the buildup collapses: all this is "Christolatry," best abandoned for "pure Theism," her gender-transcending creed (*DL*, 94 n.).

Despite differences of standpoint, a recurring motif in Victorian women's dissent from biblical criticism is their sense of the ridiculous: the critics, blind to their own limitations, "elude[d]" by a Scripture they have *made* elusive, go "running around" to check what each other thinks, worship at the altar of their own reason, and bond with beautiful Saviors or manly Christs as themselves. Cobbe's sarcastic wit abounds, often turning on an ironic biblical allusion: the First Broad Churchmen "conduc[t] the student to the verge of . . . difficulty, and then suddenly proffe[r] him, instead of an explanation, some beautiful moral or spiritual truth," and the earnest "inquirer for bread receives, not an ordinary stone, but a diamond or ruby, and is generally so pleased thereat as to forget to press his demand for food any further" (*BL*, 70). But Cobbe knew such failures mattered. "Underneath [the] thin ice" of learned men's debates, "over which the controversialists perform their evolutions with more or less grace and vigour," she sighted "an abyss—the abyss cold, dark, and fathomless—of utter scepticism" (*BL*, 5). As a Theist she felt duty-bound to address the "Great Problem," where would "belief in God, in virtue, and immortality" be grounded in future once the faith of the Fathers had crumbled (*BL*, 4)? Other women too were not just conducting a rearguard action when they asked where the critics' "denying" without "constructing" was leading and questioned the leadership (*ST*, 114). Matthew Arnold might scorn Cobbe's "New Road religio[n] of the future,"[48] but the question of the "Future Prospects of Religious Faith" struck a resonant chord for her sex, who were thinking hard about their own prospects too in the 1860s. The allied term for this forward yearning that keeps coming up in these women's texts is "regeneration." Even for religiously orthodox minds it was not a stretch to apply the doctrine of new birth to a faithless society that cried out for deeper change than "reform."

Mrs. Booth, whose organization styled itself "the Church of the future,"[49] questioned what practical "help in trouble" new-style "Christs" could offer and headed an Army of help. Tuned to the reality of relationships and consequences, these skeptical women also assume it is no use for the interpreter to strive to "see or imagine things as they truly are" (Jowett, *E&R*, 482) if his project is defined so narrowly that its practical social implications are obscured or neglected. The social was ineluctably yoked to the spiritual and could not be bracketed, as irrelevant to exegesis or high matters of Church order, without cutting God out; and to cut out God, who made and cared for all, was to sideline women and their concerns. This gendered subtext often underlies the passionate defenses Victorian women make of "God" against the critics in which they resist marginalization by discursively reoccupying the Center men seem to have abandoned.[50]

When Nightingale defended the "character" of God and queried the welfare of religion after the critics had done their work, she pegged its prospects to reform of the whole social mechanism.[51] Her indictment of a "time of indifference and unbelief" weaves elements of the social crisis into the religious crisis, which was not only a matter of personal "doubt" of the Articles or the Book:

> We do not believe in a type of perfection into which each man is to be developed, we do not believe in social progress, we do not believe in religious progress, we do not believe in God. Our *political* progress is the only thing which we do believe in; but as to any development of our Church, any improvement in society which shall modify the two great extremes of luxury and poverty, we do not so much as imagine it. In the last 300 years . . . we have retrenched a good deal, but we have put nothing in the place of [religion]. It has been all denying and no constructing." (*ST*, 114)

Nightingale's own free interpretations of the Bible and doctrine embedded in the ironic and transformative allusions of *Suggestions for Thought* (privately printed, 1860) everywhere assume the devolution of biblical infallibility, an enabling condition for new readings that belong to, yet are other than, both the founding documents of the faith and modern biblical criticism. But she also explicitly indexes her social religious vision to the destructive implications and blind spots of critical methods she otherwise generally accepts and makes bold to leap into the chasm their interrogations opened: "*What then?*—what follows from all this?"[52] The recognition that "the astronomy, the geology of the Old Testament have been *generally* rejected as not true," and "*some* now see that the political economy, the moral philosophy of the new Testament, is not always true provides an opening, an opportunity to announce that" the time has come when "whether mankind have a religion or not" depends "on the exercise of man's nature . . . ." The keyword in this curious locution is "exercise"—and those who "speculate" or "go to a book for authority" rather than to "experience for facts," she insists, cannot recognize this truth (*ST*, 29). The Bible's loss as an authoritative guide had put belief in orthodoxy's God at a crux that could only be resolved in a reconstructed social order that enabled the fullest possible unfolding of each person's gifts, and so "reveal[ed]" God by experientially revealing the "will" of a "perfect being" for humanity's perfection (*ST*, 6, 30). If this formulation put the developed individual's "character" in place of a flawed written Revelation, Nightingale did not think it substituted humanity for God.[53] Rather, she posited *God's* "character" as the "type of perfection" for human beings and reconceived the process of their perfecting as learning "His laws" through experience (*ST*, 44–45). In other ways too, *Suggestions*, which often works off what "society," "the family," or "men" say, enters into the critics' discursive formation only to trump it with God's plan for "mankind."

Behind these arguments were Nightingale's labors in the early 1850s, after years of wrenching inward conflict and open battle with her family, to train a clarifying hermeneutics of suspicion on all that had prevented her for years from answering God's "call" to a vocation, especially the formidable convergence of societal demands on the daughter with the "bibliolatry" of her Evangelical mentors. To reconstruct after denying—and make theological sense of her rage—she set out in 1851–52 to recast her social and religious beliefs into a philosophy that would rationalize her vocational desires in a system of what God wanted for England and the whole human race. Serving deeply subjective needs, the rather tangled manuscripts that became *Suggestions for Thought* operate a highly abstract, transcendent discourse—about "mankind," the "character" and "laws of God," "the Perfect"—that simultaneously addresses the vastness of her subject, matches the size of her ambition, and resists feminine personalism. But into this masculine mode of theological disputation, the woman's anger and passionate desire repeatedly irrupt, at most sustained length in the essay "Cassandra" at the end of Volume 2. For these and other reasons, *Suggestions* is a thicket of gender-and-religion tensions, coming from within the writer herself and from without.

These conflicts inform Nightingale's wrestling by post with Benjamin Jowett, which began when she sent him a copy of *Suggestions* for comment in 1860 and continued to his death in 1893.[54] In these letters religion questions and gender questions collide, collude, covertly inform and displace each other, are discussed together and delinked, fueling their intellectual debates with background tensions. The dialogue partners, both with their own contradictions, projections, and blinders, share a certain liberal discourse (and love of Plato) yet write past each other, coming at the issues from different places defined significantly by gender as well as class. When he turns his mind to the woman question, the subtleties of the Essayist on the interpretation of Scripture founder on binaries.

Jowett, the more "feminine" partner, fights with velvet gloves, feints, and gentle thrusts that can hit and miss his target. Nightingale, who does not miss his delicately-veiled criticisms, minces no words in putting her complaints against his party:

> . . . In reading almost all Theological Essays of the present day, I feel constantly inclined to say: there is everything in this Theology, except God, there is everything except the belief that there *is* a Truth, and we have to find it out. As to a search after a *Perfect God*, there is nothing.

> (Your man, M. Pattison, actually defines Theology to be: 'a speculative habit'. . . . Really, my dear soul. . . . Mansel: his Bampton Lectures [*The Limits of Religious Thought Examined*, 1858] seemed to me to have nothing in them that they ought to have, and everything in them that they ought not to have. And the 'Times' calls him: 'One of the most successful leaders of original thought').[55]

Nightingale's argument is pitched to the highest level but her words resonate with the outsider's complaint in 1871, when she felt she had "gone out of office." Through friends in the government, now gone, who had taken up her reform agendas, she had striven to lead England back to want what God wants: but where, without "God," would men like Mansel "lead"? "[A]mid all this paper & print about religion" on the bookstalls, she writes Jowett again, "I expect to find something about God. Not at all." Germany had "volumes upon volumes of profound and admirable criticism . . . there are, all over Europe, but especially in England, enormous masses of superficial controversy between Roman Catholicism, Protestantism, and even the minor sects of Protestantism . . . "—and then "all the ecclesiastical controversy, the 'geography of Palestine' = the 'Fifth Gospel,' " a slighting reference to Dean Stanley's *Sinai and Palestine in Connection with Their History* (1856). Amid such folly, how could she be faulted for "speak[ing] of 'the character of God', without 'coming to the point,'" as Jowett complained? After reviewing her theological first principles for him once again, she demands, "Art thou a master in Israel and knowest not these things?"[56] But the key to her obsession with God's "character" lay in a complex woman's personality and experience, which the Master of Balliol could not divine from his own.

Nightingale complained of Jowett's exegesis that there was "nothing very inspiring in denying the Miracles, or denying a Moral governor, or in negation at all," and that to "good people, who are really trying to be Christians" he offered "nothing definite in the place of what he takes away."[57] Neither would he compose the "Theodike" she begged him to write.[58] (Instead he urged *her* to write it; but *Suggestions* had circled round and round the problem of evil without catching it.) These were no abstract demands: the "practical" was an urgent ground of Nightingale's dissent from his party's "researches" and "speculative" theology, and concrete evils were rampant. For an impassioned reformer of public health and Army administration, as for the Salvation Army preacher, it was a sign of godless times that the learned held aloof from the hands-on practice of what Mrs. Booth called the "UNIVERSAL BROTHERHOOD OF MAN"—no "mere humanitarianism" but the Christian's true work in the world, bringing to the streets the "real," "plain, practical, common-sense meaning of the [biblical] text."[59] It was from her outlook on the ground that Nightingale launched her tirade against Dean Stanley, whose Palestine book and recent introduction to Sir C. W. Wilson's *The Recovery of Jerusalem: A Narrative of Exploration and Discovery in the City and the Holy Land* (1871) perfectly exemplified historical criticism twiddling its scholarly thumbs while London burned. "Is it possible," she asks Jowett, lashing out at the Dean of St. Paul's with the righteous ire of a Catherine Booth,

> that a man, the ecclesiastical head of the greatest religious establishment in the most important Metropolis of the world, who has, within 1/4 hr of his establishment, a population to be numbered by hundreds of thousands, ground down by vice and sin and pauperism and misery and physical deterioration, so that, to use the words of one pauper, 'we have nothing but misery in this world, and those — clergy tell us we have nothing to look to but misery in the next.'
>
> Is it possible that this ecclesiastical head looks to the historical and geographical criticism of Palestine as being the 'Gospel' which is to bring 'good news' to this wretched mass, who . . . are seething in hell already . . . ?[60]

In this same letter Nightingale remarks on one of Stanley's speeches that she "like[s]" him "better on Walter Scott than on Jesus Christ." She was not defending Christ's divinity—or doting on his "humanity": she and Jowett held Christ "a great reformer," but it was Nightingale who intuited his "deep and ingrained sense, a continual gnawing feeling of the miseries and wrongs of the world," which "impelled [him] to devote life and death to redress them."[61] She also does not pause to quibble over "gospel facts" when she observes that Christ "raised women above the condition of mere slaves, mere ministers to the passions of man, raised them by this sympathy, to be ministers of God" (*C*, 50). *Cassandra* then becomes Nightingale's own "fifth gospel" when she envisions an even higher raising, a "female Christ," an ideal woman, "who will resume, in her own soul, all the sufferings of her race, and . . . be the Saviour of her race." While this biblical type had catches for Florence Nightingale, and her "Cassandra" doubts whether "we see one woman who looks like a female Christ," with her "passion of the Spirit," her world-redeeming potential, and the ironic social lessons of her suffering and nonexistence, this figure of desire necessarily challenges Jowett's "*latitudinarian*" Christ and implicitly rebukes his liberal discursivity with no words for "a true woman or queen, a female Christ, as you say, to show the way."[62]

In her projection of a "female Christ," Nightingale sailed over the lowlands where progressive women with ties to evangelical reading communities were engaged in a more common strategy in Victorian women's Bible wars, (re)reading the Good Book to defend their sex. Charlotte Brontë presents a mock-serious portrait of these labors in the eighteenth chapter of *Shirley* (1849), where the novel's two heroines answer Joe Scott, a biblical literalist fond of quoting the Apostle: "Let the woman learn in silence, with all subjection. I suffer not a woman to teach, nor usurp authority over the man; but to be in silence. For Adam was first formed, then Eve."[63] Both Shirley Keeldar's saucy anti-Adamite reading of the fall story and the Protestant argument for woman's "right of private judgment" Caroline Helstone puts to Joe were well-established moves in women's counter-patriarchal interpretation (*S*, 322, 323). It is with distinctly modern notes in 1849 that Caroline deploys critical method with "a little ingenuity" to give I Timothy "quite a contrary turn," revealing St. Paul as a defender of woman's right to "'speak out whenever she sees fit to make an objection . . . to teach and to exercise authority as much as may be,'" while "'Man . . . cannot do better than hold his peace.'" By having her historicize I Timothy as written "for a particular congregation of Christians, under peculiar circumstances," propose that "the original Greek" may "have been wrongly translated, perhaps misapprehended altogether," and interpolate her own variants, Brontë wickedly fashions the critic's tools into a woman's weapon, sent up in a comic scene to absorb the shock. Meanwhile her dialogue tracks the shifting dynamics of male–female relations when higher criticism becomes heterogeneous to women's transformations and Bible sex doctrine is reversed.

Some extraordinary "talk about womanliness" opening this chapter, when, choosing the beauty of a summer's eve over the prospect of boring sermons in the church, the heroines "are alone" and "may speak what [they] think," gives birth to their interpretive powers (*S*, 314). Shirley's fantastical retelling of *Paradise Lost* as a throbbing epic about woman as the life principle through history—from the "first" mother of Titan "daring" on through the "millenniums" to the "vast heart" that "could conceive and bring forth a Messiah"—builds up a rich lode of heroinisms that nurture the imagining of a goddess-savior (*S*, 315). When Caroline scoffs at this "hash of Scripture and mythology," Shirley dispels skepticism with a vision of "mother Eve, in these days called Nature," speaking "face to face . . . with God" at "her evening prayers," a palpable presence whose mystic arms embrace Stilbro' Moor, the men's battleground (*S*, 315, 316, 314). Invoking pagan and biblical figures of women's spirituality, and celebrating their heroic struggles but issuing in peaceful contemplation and sorority, the whole scene plays by contrast to the novel's dramatization of men's industrial conflict and the militarized clerical muscularism of Mr. Helstone, a type recently celebrated in Kingsley's *Yeast* (1848). More generally, although *Shirley* is set much earlier it represents the Church's tangled "men problems" and their relation to social problems in the later 1840s, when Anglicanism was struggling with its legacies from the Oxford Movement after Newman's defection to Rome in 1845, and Broad Churchmen had lost the leadership of Dr. Arnold, who had died in 1842, even as Chartism was exposing the class injustice on which the Establishment rested. In Brontë's "Whitsuntide" chapter, placed right before the "pentecostal" outbursts of women's interpreting in chapter 18, the narrator, after defending the clergy in general, calls on "God" to "reform [the Church]!" (*S*, 17.298). But even though Dean Stanley's *Life of Arnold* (1844) was one of Charlotte's best-loved books, in her post-Arnoldian novel both ecclesiastical and social reform are made practically unlikely by the faulty *characters* of the community's leading men.

These failures are the burden of a later scene of dizzying disputation in which male and female characters' charges and countercharges rebound from Brontë's angry pen. After the workers' armed attack on Moore's mill has been repelled, the chief "fighting parso[n]," Mr. Helstone, defends his part in Kingsleyan fashion "as a man and a Briton; which characters I deem quite compatible with those of the priest and Levite, in their highest sense" (*S*, 21.355, 354). His unfortunate echo of the Good Samaritan parable lingers, as the radical layman Hiram Yorke declares the Church "in a bonnie pickle ... when parsons took to swaggering among soldiers, blazing away w' bullet and gunpowder, taking the lives of far honester men than themselves" (*S*, 355; here the "honest men" are Luddites). Shirley then lobs back to Yorke an even more sweeping indictment, of

> "all that *cant* about soldiers and parsons.... All ridiculous, irrational crying up of one class, whether the same be aristocrat or democrat—all howling down of another ... all party hatreds, all tyrannies disguised as liberties, I reject and wash my hands of.... When I hear [the curates] chatter about the authority of the Church, the dignity and claims of the priesthood, the deference due to them as clergymen; ... their small spite against Disssenters ... silly narrow jealousies ... palaver about forms, and traditions, and superstitions....when I behold their insolent carriage to the poor, their often base servility to the rich, I think the Establishment is indeed in a poor way, and both she and her sons appear in the utmost need of reformation...." (*S*, 356–57)

Lest this speech merely echo Arnold, anti-Puseyite rant, *or* radicalism, Brontë's heroine turns on Yorke and declares that when she recalls his "sarcasms on the 'fat bishops,' the 'pampered parsons,' 'old mother church,' &c." and his "sweeping condemnations of classes and individuals, without the slightest allowance made for circumstances ... then ... doubt clutches my inmost heart as to whether men exist clement, reasonable, and just enough to be intrusted with the task of reform" (*S*, 358). At this pass, the female critic might well wash her hands of the whole spectacle—of Christian men whose behavior honors Mammon and fashion, wrangling in 1849 over a Church in which, they forgot, women too had a stake. Mother Church had carried their line of Apostolic Succession from Christ the Son born of Mary for millennia—and still allowed no Shirley Keeldars or Caroline Helstones in "Her" pulpits preaching reform from "His" Book. So Brontë's excluded woman must do it, with different readings and unorthodox texts, outside the church building—or write novels.

TROUBLESHOOTING IN THE DOMESTIC BRANCH
OF BIBLICAL CRITICISM

In *Robert Elsmere* (1888), a work usually regarded as symptomatic of "a certain phase of liberal religious thought in the later nineteenth century," Mary Ward offered more than "the gospel of Rugby and of *Literature and Dogma*" missionized.[64] A female "Arnold of the third generation" (and no suffragist), she used the novel form to dramatize biblical criticism's intimate practical effects on domestic life and character—dynamics not dreamed of in Uncle Matt's books—and thereby challenged readers to ponder the troubled religion system and the sex/gender system together while contending with the phenomenon of an "authoress" who grasped "the deeper thought of the period."[65]

While book sales soared in Britain and America, commentators tried to write Mrs. Ward out of theological debate and William Gladstone led the pack.[66] His vigorous rebuttal slurs her mastery of the "negative speculatists" as "ransack[ing]" and shames her for offering so little to justify "abolish[ing] . . . the whole authority of Scripture," the Church, priesthood, sacraments, "and the whole established machinery which trains the Christian as a member of a religious society." He proclaims Ward fatally naïve to imagine that disencumbering the faith of antiquated theology, miraculous elements, and "revealed religion" would best fit Christianity to modern minds and lives.[67] Indignant that "a great creed, with the testimony of eighteen centuries at its back" has no articulate defenders in the book, Gladstone undertakes to supply it by delivering the tradition's massive "evidence from consent" and reasoning for pages like a scholastic. After parsing the Apostles Creed as a series of "propositions," he adds the proof that its "third division . . . is bound down like the second to earth and fact by the article of the Church, a visible and palpable institution"[68]—an assertion that would surprise Mrs. Booth's "Holy Ghost."

Although Gladstone withholds his heavy artillery from the disabilities of Mrs. Ward's sex, his gender-coded discourse insinuates fatal doubt of the female mind's productions. The "sense of mission" he can praise in "every page and line" yields only a "propagandist romance," in which the authoress, instead of "reasoning patiently from step to step" through the hero's deconversion, "skips in thought, over undefined distances, from stage to stage, as a bee from flower to flower. A creed may (as here) be accepted in a sentence, and then abandoned in a page." Elsmere's deconversion is a limp affair, engaging in no real "Battle of Belief" with a clergyman's proper weapons (presumably the "topics of defense"). Gladstone charges "the Elsmere gospel" with effete characteristics—subjectivism, over-enthusiasm, shallow thinking, naïvete about "sin"—and ridicules Ward's overly "affection[ate]" portrait of the hero, a paragon to whom "every knee must be made to bow." The New Christian Brotherhood he founds without the Christ of the creeds is even "larcenous," for its ethicism seizes the moral "goods" of "the patrimony of Christendom," "the dominant power of the world," and so belonging to "the patrimony of the race." New Christian Brothers may sport the "peacock feathers" of a "Christian civilization" for a time but "cannot reproduce" them. Mrs. Ward's gospel, with its "dead man in Judea" for inspiration in place of "the gospel of God manifest in the flesh," may teach high moral lessons but cannot give birth to a living faith.[69]

Gladstone does find Ward "pure-minded" and avers that what her "brilliant and subtle understanding" takes away from Christianity still retains a "hold upon the inner sanctuary of her heart." But for this critic no woman's character can make up for the loss of God's Word, Christ the Son, or the apostolic Church. These losses are conveyed through Gladstone's motif of male "dismember[ment]," most striking for its violent irruptions into his resolutely logical prose.[70] If a part of the Christian scheme is "torn away" from the "organic" body of Christian dogma, he warns, "the residue will bleed to death." If the hero expresses but an "emasculated form of human hope," the gospels have been "t[orn] . . . to shreds": "the parts which remain, or which remain legible, are vital parts; but this is no more than to say that there may remain vital organs of a man, after the man himself has been cut in pieces." Other threats of social-sexual losses are coded into Gladstone's *two* reminders to Mrs. Ward that Christianity raised woman's position and his query about "how the New Brotherhood" "is to deal with the great mystery of marriage, perhaps the truest touchstone of religious revolution." Despite Catherine Elsmere's faithfulness even beyond death's parting, to Gladstone's mind, where gender ideals are locked in eternal embrace with Established Christianity, the hero's early death merely cuts off a train of consequences whose "relentless force of logic," he insinuates, will dissolve faith and domestic ideology together with "aveng[ing]" force.[71]

In this scenario, the home branch of conflict over Bible questions reaches its crux when the stable "differences" of the sex-gender system are intersected by modern disturbances in the Scripture-theology system. Gladstone's ideal resolution is to crush the latter with the massive weight of Church tradition and let the natural state of the former reassert its stabilizing influence. The attempt to anchor the floating religion to the supposed stabilities of gender had been a common discursive reflex for decades even among more liberal observers who worried that religion questions were opening a "gulf between the sexes." Nightingale complained in 1852 that the contemporary male "cannot impart to [woman] his religious beliefs, if he have any, because she would be 'shocked,'" since "religious men are and must be heretics now" to a Church that demands "we must not pray, except in a 'form' of words, made beforehand—or think of God but with a pre-arranged idea" (*C*, 45). At mid-century she saw that the "gulf" had already opened up—not so starkly between women's "faith" and men's "doubt" as between gendered conceptions of what faithful thinking is, since Nightingale's "heretics" *are* "religious men." Her solution entailed raising up her sex to her own advanced notions of "woman's estate and . . . the ideas of the nineteenth century" (*C*, 55).

An anonymous male commentator on "Women and Scepticism" in *Fraser's Magazine* for 1863 proposed a different solution, *sans* education, to the domestic religion problem differently conceived: to serve men's domestic needs, relieve female suffering from false religious notions and unnecessary anxieties, and raise them up to the standards of male intellect, women must be brought over to the moderately liberal side of the gulf—without embracing Negation or leaving home or Church.[72]

This writer's story is set in the domestic branch of what might be called husbands' and brothers' criticism. He dispenses rather shortly with females of the "superstitious or fanatical" sort, whose views no "honest" Englishman would credit, and darkly warns that if women "choose to buy peace of mind at the expense of truth and liberty"—the shining liberal credo—they will forfeit the precious respect of the men they love. But he is more anxious to avert a less talked-about threat to the peace of English homes: a new type of female who rushes into ultra-skepticism at the first sign that "good men" she looks to for guidance no longer believe the Bible "true"—"an often inexpressibly painful" discovery that "appears to take from her the very foundations on which all her schemes of life and principles of conduct were based."[73] To prevent such hasty conclusions, this 'friend of the sex' undertakes to estimate for the "reasonable" female reader how much there is in "the sceptical view" (a lot, but not as much as hasty people think) and through the rest of the essay strives to reason, flatter, shame, and threaten her into accepting the stripped-down creed of "honest m[e]n"—belief in God, duty, and immortality.[74] One shudders at what Gladstone would say of his "Christianity."

In the end the writer returns his rescued lady to the Anglican pew, where she is to hold private, generalized reservations about the truth of dogma and Scripture and add no "criticism" of her own, "conten[t]" to leave the business of "patient and free inquiry" up to professional theologians and scholars.[75] Urging that she "has as good reasons for believing in a God and a future life as she has for believing in any of the established moral or social doctrines of her time and country," such as the doctrine "that polygamy or personal slavery are evils," precisely because they *are* established beliefs "on which the whole framework of society is based," he simultaneously secures his lady in the gender system by attaching her newly scripted creed to the hegemonic social ideas and practices of English culture. Indeed, "the more the parallel between a woman's belief in a future life and her belief in monogamy is considered, the more the truth of this will appear."[76] Of course if this "truth" were true, if the parallels held, it would be just as logical for the perplexed female to throw over monogamy with her exploded faith. ("Cassandra" would also put in an exasperated word here about how "established moral or social doctrines," *especially* about matrimony, crush a lady's desire for higher things. Cobbe, who wrote antislavery tracts for the Victoria Press, would raise both eyebrows: Was slavery evil only because people said it was? And was there no "slavery" in English homes?) In the course of twenty pages, this *faux* friend has opened a crack between his reconstructed female and the outmoded pious type—a crevasse into which a woman's "love" for "her" Bible must fall—but by the end the interlocking regimes of gender ideology and Church order are still in place.

Deeper in the murky subtext of this essay, an even more urgent cultural rescue operation is covertly going forward. For if women become disillusioned when fundamentalist preachers prove to be peddling self-serving lies, as this writer charges, and then resent "honest men" for taking their beliefs away, the unspoken danger is that women will lose faith in men as a class. To restore that faith and diminish the social threat of these skeptical women, he labors to prove the indispensability of the sound male mind amid the unsettlements of "skepticism" by building up his *ethos* with redundantly masculine discourse, invoking the values of male professionals, chanting attractive liberal mantras, displaying his global knowledge, and flexing his prowess in deductive argument. In a mazy syllogistic stretch about the "grounds of religious assent," he writes as though belief is a matter of determining the truth of propositions, rather than grounded in religious experience, tradition, familial attachments, or personal need, and finally reduces it to an utilitarian affair in which deciding on the doctrines one believes is no different from the way questions are decided in medicine or law.[77] This discursive drift away from addressing "the more intelligent part of the sex" into a masculine comfort zone especially marks "Women and Scepticism" as a public site of the gender battle it describes incompletely and strives to resolve in unconscious bad faith. Nor does this writer's practice inspire confidence in men's superior reasoning powers: as he attempts to map the marshy ground between rigid orthodoxy and ultra-skepticism, he contradicts himself, makes faulty analogies, gets stuck in awkward logical corners, zig-zags around hard questions, and hedges everything, slipping into gulfs of his own making and generating even more questions for his readers. Among them was a female class he does not profess to know: women grown disillusioned with liberals who engaged in just his sort of temporizing to resolve religious doubt, and who then had the temerity to recommend their own dubious path out of the swamp—or into it—to the other sex.

Seventeen years further on, a female commentator on "Agnosticism and Women" would identify this liberal writer's type: "Men do not see willingly that which they dislike to see" and

> prefer to hope that women will be slow to drive logic to its ultimate end; that they will still cling with womanly inconsistency to all that is refining and soothing in the old creeds; and that the newer and colder lights of their husbands and brothers will only serve to eliminate from those creeds the elements of superstition and fear which are now considered so debasing.[78]

By 1880 the great threat to domestic tranquility is no longer religious fanaticism or good men's questioning but advancing Agnosticism, which Bertha Lansbury is certain will make women "discontented" with domestic duties and "increase tenfold" their cry for equitable work outside the home. This latest Negation looms even larger on her apocalyptic landscape than the women's movement, with its foolish "pride of their equality with men," for an obvious reason: men are behind Agnosticism and they rule the age.[79]

Lansbury exhibits an advanced grasp of how the masculine hegemonic operates, helping to create desires it purports to fulfill in its manipulated subjects:

> ... in a day when intellect in women is valued more highly than it has ever been, they will not long be willing to hold a belief that is not shared by men.... Progress allures and fascinates all, and the rational mind ... is the god at whose shrine all desire to worship. With this atmosphere around them it is not possible that women, highly emotional in temperament and essentially timid in intellect, should long remain proof against it.[80]

In her analysis of power relations, the discourses of reason and now Agnosticism feed women's new aspirations to be "in the tide of intellectual fashion; to rise above ... 'prejudices,'" a word with sharper connotations for women by 1880, and to exhibit a rational mind "in sympathy with the men they admire." To Lansbury these cultural persuasions, rather than the actual contents of skeptical thought, "are often the most potent influences that sway a woman's mind towards the atheism of the present day." This slippage from "reason" and "Agnosticism" to "atheism" signals the arrival of that much-feared "endless possibility of discourse" unleashed by the Seven against Christ two decades before. But Lansbury's prose also deepens conflict over religion questions for her sex by locating the war within, on the site of woman's strength, the "heart," where culture was writing its latest atheistical doctrines over God's laws. Given the enduring importance of women's domestic affections, what Agnosticism menaces most are the "Prayer and Hope" they need in caring for "the old and sick, teaching the ignorant," tending deathbeds, and "watching" cheerfully " over "the well-being of those they love." Bravely carrying on Woman's Mission in its dark days, but swamping the bright vista Sarah Lewis had opened in 1839, Lansbury sees the outlook for skeptical "women of the future" as even more desperate than the "prospects of religious faith," for their "suffering" will be greater "than that of the martyrs of old. They, at least, died for a belief," not for the lack of one. Reneging on her own compliment to new respect for woman's intellect, forgetting she has accused *men* of hoping "women will be slow to drive logic to its ultimate end," or perhaps falling in with this strategy, she pleads with her imperiled sisters to close down thought before it reaches agnostic conclusions—and cries out for men's "mercy" on feminine souls.[81]

In May 1880 *The Nineteenth Century* published a "Reply" to "Agnosticism and Women" by a manly advocate bearing good news for the other sex. "The negative position of *knowing nothing* but *phenomena*," J. H. Clapperton declares, "is the only logical one to ... masculine intellects," and when women adopt it they find what men find, and more: "truth for delusion," "a standpoint from which clearness of thought and stability of feeling increase," and greater "intellectual courage, which," he concedes, "is not at present a universal virtue of the sex."[82] He sees that "men and women are already too much divided"—the *Fraser's* bridge had failed—and in revisiting the domestic argument he rises above the Woman's Mission position: woman's "*highest, most sacred* human interests require of her to enter into the struggle, and acquaint herself with the reasons why so many men are no longer Christians at heart."[83] But although he rings a new variation on essential masculinity, he rejects the view that female nature is "unchangeable" and makes the novel argument that, "human nature" being "infinitely modifiable," while a woman may "suffer, in passing from old creeds to new, still adaptation goes on...."[84]

If the Development Hypothesis has been imported into this discourse in woman's favor, the Agnostic's mantras override the aggressive call for women's rights in the 1880s. Perhaps Clapperton felt the feminists did not serve his cause, although women's aspirations could be appealed to, because their ideas did not seem "logical" or suitable as a creed. Maybe their ideology was competition. Most late Victorian suffragists did not propose that Agnosticism would fix the gender system and their skeptical discourse had political point. But the practical independence of campaigns for women's rights from the main arenas of religious controversy did not prevent these debates from impinging on feminists' interests and goals. If "Tory" women had retarded public acceptance of biblical criticism in England, an atmosphere of anxiety about its deepening inroads on constituted authority could only have made the advancing Cause more alarming; and even though the critics hardly conducted the new exegesis on women's behalf, anti-suffragist discourse forged effective scare tactics by linking women's social questioning with men's religious doubting, as Lansbury does. In popular literature on these later woman questions, as in earlier writing about the crisis of belief that took up woman as a problem, Victorian conflicts about religion, over definitions of gender, and between the sexes rage on.

NOTES

1. See Donald E. Hall, ed., *Muscular Christianity: Embodying the Victorian Age* (New York: Cambridge University Press, 1994); Herbert Sussman, *Victorian Masculinities: Manhood and Masculine Poetics in Early Victorian Literature and Art* (Cambridge: Cambridge University Press, 1995); Andrew Bradstock, Sean Gill, Anne Hogan, and Sue Morgan, eds., *Masculinity and Spirituality in Victorian Culture* (New York: St. Martin's Press, 2000); and Jude V. Nixon's essay in this volume (chapter 2). An older study is Norman Vance, *The Sinews of the Spirit: The Ideal of Christian Manliness in Victorian Literature and Religious Thought* (Cambridge: Cambridge University Press, 1985).

2. Thomas Hughes, *The Manliness of Christ* (Philadelphia: Henry Altemus, n.d.), 10–12.

3. Frances Power Cobbe, *Broken Lights: An Inquiry into the Present Condition and Future Prospects of Religious Faith* (London: Trübner, 1864), 69; hereafter *BL*.

4. Benjamin Jowett, "On the Interpretation of Scripture," 504, and Mark Pattison, "Tendencies of Religious Thought in England, 1688–1750," 420, both in *Essays and Reviews: The 1860 Text and Its Reading*, ed. Victor Shea and William Whitla (Charlottesville: University Press of Virginia, 2000). Hereafter *E&R*.

5. Frederick Temple, "The Education of the World," in *E&R*, 138, 163, 139.

6. *Must We Burn Our Bibles? A Few Honest Words About the "Essays and Reviews"; Addressed to Honest People, by an Honest Man* (Bristol: J. Wright, 1861), 5.

7. Jude V. Nixon, "'Kill[ing] Our Souls with Literalism': Reading *Essays and Reviews*," *Religion and the Arts* 5 nos. 1–2 (2001): 34–64; quoting Michael Foucault, *The Archaeology of Knowledge* (New York: Pantheon, 1972), 145.

8. See Frederic W. Farrar, *History of Interpretation* (New York: E. P. Dutton, 1886); J. Estlin Carpenter, *The Bible in the Nineteenth Century* (London: Longmans, Green, 1903). Cf. Cobbe on John Colenso as a "later Luther," in "Bishop Colenso," *The Christian Examiner* 83 (July 1867): 1.

9. Hall, "Muscular Christianity, Reading and Writing the Male Social Body," in *Muscualr Christianity*, 10.

10. Waterland, *Eucharist*, 2nd edn (1737), 315; qtd. in *The Compact Edition of the Oxford English Dictionary*, vol. 1 (Oxford: Oxford University Press, 1971), 1295.

11. Qtd. in Pattison, *E&R*, 396, from John Locke, *Essay Concerning Human Understanding* (1690), iv. ch. 19, para. 4.

12. See, for example, Mary Astell, *A Serious Proposal To the Ladies, for the Advancement of Their True and Greatest Interest*, By a Lover of her Sex (London: R. Wilkin, 1694); *A Serious Proposal To The Ladies, Part II. Wherein a Method is offer'd for the Improvement of their Minds* (London: Richard Wilkin, 1697); and *Some Reflections Upon Marriage. With Additions*, 4th ed., 1730 (New York: Source Book Press, 1970). Astell supplements Gen. 1:26–27 with Cartesian reason. The *imago dei* is a "first principle" in Mary Wollstonecraft, *A Vindication of the Rights of Woman* (1792), ed. Carol H. Poston (New York: W. W. Norton, 1988), 11–19.

13. Pattison faults Warburton's construal of Gen. 1:26— "the image of God, in which man was at first created, lay in the faculty of reason only" (*Works*, 3.620, qtd. 396)—as intellectually and theologically reductive, not for its androcentrism. Pattison betrays his in automatically leaving Astell, a highly respected Tory apologist in early eighteenth-century religious debate, out of his history. See *The Christian Religion, as Profess'd by a Daughter of the Church of England* (London: R. Wilkin, 1705), a work of Anglican systematic theology that simultaneously teaches women to "Think" about their faith.

14. Gerald L. Bruns, *Hermeneutics Ancient and Modern* (New Haven: Yale University Press, 1992), 149, discussing Baruch Spinoza, *Tractatus Theologico-Philosophicus* (1670); Jowett, *E&R*, 504.

15. Elizabeth Strutt, *The Feminine Soul* (London, 1857), 96; qtd. in *The Woman Question*, ed. Elizabeth K. Helsinger, Robin Lauterbach Sheets, and William Veeder (Chicago: University of Chicago Press, 1983), 2:176.

16. Florence Nightingale, *Cassandra* (Old Westbury, New York: Feminist Press, 1979), 46; hereafter *C*. I am using this accessible edition for "Cassandra" quotations. See also Mary Poovey, ed., *Cassandra* and *Other Selections from Suggestions for Thought* (New York: New York University Press, 1992), 205–32; hereafter *ST*.

17. Title-page epigraph, *The Girl's Own Text Book. Containing a text from the Old and New Testaments for every morning and evening in the year*, Selected by a Lady (London: J. F. Shaw, 1858); hereafter Girls.

18. *The Boy's Own Text Book, containing a text from the Old and New Testaments for every morning and evening in the year*, Selected by a Lady (London: J. F. Shaw, 1857), xv, ix. The resonant sentence about running the race combines allusions to verses in Hebrews, I Corinthians, Luke, Galatians, and John as well as their embedded Old Testament echoes.

19. Josephine Butler, "Woman's Place in Church Work," *Magazine of Christian Literature* 6 (April 1892): 31.

20. "His Majesty's Declaration" (1562), preface to the Articles of Religion, *The Book of Common Prayer* (Oxford: Oxford University Press, 1899), 676.

21. Benjamin Jowett, letter to Florence Nightingale (May 11, 1861, and August 1866), in *Dear Miss Nightingale: A Selection of Benjamin Jowett's Letters to Florence Nightingale, 1860–1893*, ed. Vincent Quinn and John Prest (Oxford: Clarendon, 1987), 6, 94; Daniel L. Pals, *The Victorian "Lives" of Jesus* (San Antonio: Trinity University Press, 1982), 3.

22. Hall, *Muscular Christianity*, 9. Cf. Walter E. Houghton, *The Victorian Frame of Mind, 1830–1870* (New Haven: Yale University Press, 1957), 216–17.

23. J. W. Bengough, "The Higher Criticism," in *Motley: Verses Grave and Gay* (Toronto: William Briggs, 1895), ll. 45–47, 1. I am indebted for this source to Suzanne Bailey.

24. Michel Foucault, "What Is an Author?" in *Bulletin de la Société Française de Philosophie* (1969), rpt. in *The Critical Tradition: Classic Texts and Contemporary Trends*, ed. David H. Richter, 2nd ed. (Boston: Bedford/ St. Martin's, 1998), 897, 898.

25. Gary A. Phillips and Danna Nolan Fewell, "Ethics, Bible, Reading As If," *Semeia* 77 (1997): 2; Josephine E. Butler, "Introduction," in *Woman's Work and Woman's Culture*, ed. Josephine E. Butler (London: Macmillan, 1869), vii–lxiv. Feminist interpretation is a subject in my book in progress, "The Victorian Woman's Bible: Interpretation and Cultural Discourse in Anglo-American Women's Letters."

26. Foucault, "Author," 898.

27. Annie Besant, *A World Without God: A Reply to Miss Frances Power Cobbe* (London: Freethought Press, 1885), 12. On her transformations see Besant, *Autobiographical Sketches* (London: Freethought Press, 1885); *Annie Besant: An Autobiography* (London: T. Fisher Unwin, 1893); and Carol Hanbery MacKay, "The Multiple Deconversions of Annie Wood Besant," in *Creative Negativity: Four Victorian Exemplars of the Female Quest* (Stanford: Stanford University Press, 2001), 96–134.

28. Sarah Lewis, *Woman's Mission and Woman's Influence*, 10th American ed. from the London 17th ed. (New York: International Book Company, n.d.), 142–43; hereafter *WM*. Two contemporary points of reference were D. F. Strauss's *Leben Jesu* (1835) and Charles Hennell's *Inquiry Concerning the Origin of Christianity* (1838).

29. "The Oxford School. No. II," *Eclectic Review* 4 (August 1860): 126, qtd. in *E&R*, 29; Samuel Wilberforce, "Essays and Reviews," *Quarterly Review* 109 (January 1861): 305, qtd. in *E&R*, 36; *WM*, 139.

30. Wilberforce, 284, 293, 294, qtd. in *E&R*, 35.

31. Aimé-Martin had railed on against the Inquisition, witch-burning, the "stake and fagot," slavery, and the like to demonstrate "the great error of the ages," that "Holy Scripture, has passed through the hands of men": "They have copied, falsified, interpreted! everywhere leaving the impress of their passions, and of their miserable sophistry; substituting error for truth; theology for religion; and man for God...." (*The Education of the Mothers of Families; or, the Civilization of the Human Race by Women*, trans. Edwin Lee [London: Adams, 1860], 182–87). Rather than examining the notorious passages he cites—for example, "Every tree which bears not fruit shall be cut down and cast into the fire" (cf. Matt. 7:19)—he simply declares that these "infamous doctrines...harmonize with the letter of theology" and are "opposed to the spirit of the Scriptures" (184, 185). Lewis follows his substitution of the theological for the biblical letter, which enables them both to ignore the fact that these horrific practices were often based on *Scripture's* literal sense. She also feigns ladylike ignorance of the passages that gave snipers so much ammunition, and sounds defensive as though she or her ideal is being attacked, when she challenges "the sceptic to...find in that blessed book one maxim of selfishness, one trait of malevolence, one word which can authorize the bad and unholy passions which, clothed in the garb of religion, have desolated society," her veiled reference to the "bloody pages" in "the history of interpretation of holy books" (*WM*, 143; Aimé-Martin, *Education*, 182).

32. To Aimé-Martin Jesus did not come to institute "dogma" or "a special form of worship" (or, apparently, "the scheme of redemption") but to teach "the sincere love of God and man," the Golden Rule. Mothers must learn and impart the "science of the moral laws of nature" based on "the spirit of the Gospel," which has "civilize[d] the world"—his "missionary" theme. See the anonymous review of *De L'Education* des *Mères de Familles, ou de la civilization de genre humain par les Femmes*, in *Westminster Review* 22 (June–April 1835): 508–09.

33. Sue Zemka, *Victorian Testaments: The Bible, Christology, and Literary Authority in Early Nineteenth-Century British Culture* (Stanford: Stanford University Press, 1997), 70.

34. Ibid., 91–92.

35. Figuring these displacements of the personal and social onto a "higher" theological level, as an upward movement, is not meant to exclude dynamics at work on other planes, such as women's use of social experience and observation as hermeneutical tools for understanding men's criticism, seeing what they are 'doing' to texts or how they "think" as mirroring their social behavior.

36. Catherine Booth, "The Christs of the Nineteenth Century compared with the Christ of God," lecture at Princes Hall, Piccadilly, in Booth, *Popular Christianity* (London: Salvation Army Book Depot, 1887), 6, 7, 8, 9–10.

37. Catherine Booth, "Notes of Three Addresses on Household Gods," in *Popular Christianity*, 180.

38. Catherine Booth, "The Holy Ghost," in Booth, *Papers on Aggressive Christianity* (London: S. W. Partridge, 1881), 12, 7.

39. Catherine Booth, "Conditions of Effectual Prayer," in Booth, *Papers on Godliness* (1882; London: Salvation Army, 1890), 62.

40. W. T. Stead, *Life of Mrs. Booth: The Founder of the Salvation Army* (New York: Fleming H. Revell, 1900), 16–17, 8.

41. Catherine Booth, *Female Ministry: Woman's Right to Preach the Gospel* (London: Morgan & Chase, 1870); Stead, *Mrs. Booth*, 38.

42. In *Broken Lights*, Part I, Cobbe discusses the "Paleologians" (High and Low Church), the "Neologians" (the "First Broad Church" of Arnold, Kingsley, and Maurice, and the "Second Broad Church" of *Essays and Reviews*), and "Parties Outside the Church." In "Where Is the Woman in This Text? Frances Power Cobbe's Voices in *Broken Lights*," *Victorian Literature and Culture* 31 (2003): 99–129, I argue that although she deliberately bracketed her feminism when writing on such subjects, the razor-edge logic she applies to all parties, her mastery of the terminology of deductive reason (honed in writing a celebrated treatise on Kant), many scholarly references, and ample use of satire, parodic mimicry, and bathos all betray the Cobbe who was campaigning for women's right to higher education in the 1860s and rejected "the idea that [males] embody the highest human values" (Barbara Caine, *Victorian Feminists* [Oxford: Oxford University Press, 1992], 147). The Kant treatise was *Essay on Intuitive Morals, Being an Attempt to Popularise Ethical Science*, Part I: *Theory of Morals* (London: Longman, Brown, Green, and Longman, 1855).

43. Frances Power Cobbe, *Dawning Lights: An Inquiry Concerning the Secular Results of the New Reformation* (London: Williams and Norgate, 1882), 22; hereafter *DL*.

44. Cobbe saw this "Religious Sentiment" as an anthropological, rather than historical, fact recorded in world scriptures and experienced by the individual through the "Divine Light" of "Reason and Conscience." On these grounds of Theistic belief, see *BL*, 157–192; on the attractions of Theodore Parker's Theism, see the "Preface" to vol. 1 and the "Notice, by the Editor" for vol. 2 of *The Collected Works of Theodore Parker*, ed. Frances Power Cobbe (London: Trübner, 1863); on how she came to accept this creed, see *The Life of Frances Power Cobbe, by Herself*, 2 vols. (Boston: Houghton Mifflin, 1894), 70–88.

45. *BL*, 117 and note. In retaliation for Matthew Arnold's condescending attack on her (and his defense of Renan) in 1864, Cobbe later ridiculed men who "err by over-anxiety to lose nothing that may by possibility be preserved of the past, endeared by sacred associations or by aesthetic charm," and "visit each shrine more as artists and archaeologists than religionists, seeking for something beautiful or venerable in each object to justify its retention in the purified temple . . ." (*DL*, 39). For Arnold's remarks on Cobbe, see "The Function of Criticism at the Present Time," *Lectures and Essays in Criticism*, vol. 3 of *The Complete Works of Matthew Arnold*, ed. R. H. Super (Ann Arbor: University of Michigan Press, 1962), 276, 278–80. Cobbe also deplored Renan's finding " 'une delicieuse parabole' " in the Prodigal Son story, which she had rewritten as parody in her Low Church chapter to discredit her father's cherished doctrine of the Atonement, which Jesus's story of the "Father's free and unbought pardon" does not teach (*BL*, 49n., 48). See Larson, "Where Is the Woman in This Text?" 110–11. Nightingale thought Renan's *Vie* was "*all* fine writing" and his Christ "the hero of a novel"—and was "revolted by such expressions as *charmant, délicieux, religion du pur sentiment*, in such a subject . . ." (letter to W. E. Nightingale [September 26, 1863], qtd. in Sir Edward T. Cook, *The Life of Florence Nightingale* [London: Macmillan, 1913], 1.486).

46. Francis W. Newman, *Discourse Against Hero-Making in Religion*, delivered in South Place Chapel, Finsbury, April 24, 1864 (London: Trübner, 1864).

47. Toppling an absurdity with her own linguistic excess was one of Cobbe's rhetor-
ical techniques. See *BL*, 107, 112, for her choice quotations on Moses and the
Pentateuch from Frederick Denison Maurice's *Claims of the Bible and Science*
(London: Macmillan, 1863) and Charles Kingsley's *The Gospel of the
Pentateuch: A Set of Parish Sermons; and David, Five Sermons* (London:
Macmillan, 1881). She also compares this Broad Church duo to "Moses and
Aaron" (*BL*, 59). In *DL*, she may have been making amends for these earlier
sarcasms.

48. Arnold, "Function of Criticism," 290.

49. W. E. Gladstone, " 'Robert Elsmere' and the Battle of Belief," *Nineteenth
Century* 23 (May 1888): 771.

50. The metaphor of the interior center or intimate circle is resonant for Butler's
defense of her relationship with Christ (and solidarity with outcast women)
against the demolishers of the Gospel of John. She sees male bias in the fact that
the Churches have always "missed or denied" the significance of the story of the
woman taken in adultery (John 8:1–11), and now "the learned" were "tak[ing
it] from me and all women" by proving the inauthenticity of John. "No doubt,
it would be a great relief to some men if it could be proved that Christ never
pronounced such a word of emancipation for a woman, or so terrible a censure
of the sins of men," she says, but maintains that their judgment "does not much
matter" to one "who has come very near to Christ about this question, and has
heard Him speak" ("Woman's Place," 31). Jowett had offered qualified support
for her complaint in citing this story as a "neglected" passage whose moral contrasted with present-day severities toward "the errors of women" (*E&R*, 497).
But it was still missing in J. Estlin Carpenter's turn-of-the-century lecture on
"The Fourth Gospel," where his whole approach hermeneutically guarantees
the loss of Butler's adulteress story (*Bible in the Nineteenth Century*, 383–451).

51. Nightingale sums up her view of God's "character" in a letter to her father,
W. E. Nightingale (September 26, 1863), qtd. in Cook, *Florence Nightingale*,
1.486. See also *ST*, vol. 1, part 1, "Belief in God" (5–38).

52. In "The Bishop and the Philosopher," Matthew Arnold argued that unlike
Bishop Colenso, Spinoza, having found out the Bible's faults, had manfully
addressed the question "the higher culture of Europe" wanted answered:
"*What then?*—what follows from all this?" (*Macmillan's* [January 1863], in
Lectures and Essays, 49).

53. Nightingale tries rather unsuccessfully to distinguish her view of the relation
between character development and "God's revelation" from the views of
"the Arnold school," whose "names...we reverence beyond most" but
whose "principles...we are hardly able to understand)..." (*ST*, 82, 83).

54. Nightingale had sent copies of *Suggestions* to five men including John Stuart Mill
when she applied to Jowett. Vincent Quinn and John Prest, eds., *Dear Miss
Nightingale,* report that her side of the correspondence was largely destroyed and
reproduce only drafts and copies in their edition (xii, xxxvii).

55. Nightingale to Jowett, draft (August 7, 1871), *Dear Miss Nightingale*, 212;
cf. Pattison, *E&R*, 393. She approves Pattison's statement, "*evidences* do not
constitute theology," but disagrees "with him as to what *is* 'theology'"
(*ST*, 87n.).

56. Nightingale to Jowett, draft (August 17, 1871), *Dear Miss Nightingale*,
215–16.

57. Nightingale, British Library Add.MS 45785 fo. 247, and Nightingale to Jowett (November 10, 1894), both qtd. in *Dear Miss Nightingale*, xxxiv.

58. Nightingale, letter (February 8, 1895), qtd. in *Dear Miss Nightingale*, xxxiii.

59. Catherine Booth, *The Salvation Army in Relation to the Church and State* (London: S. W. Partridge, 1883), 11; "Effectual Prayer," in *Papers on Godliness*, 62, 63.

60. Nightingale, draft (August 7, 1871), *Dear Miss Nightingale*, 213.

61. Quinn and Prest, *Dear Miss Nightingale*, xvii; Nightingale, C, 53.

62. Nightingale, C, 53, 45; Jowett, British Library Add.MS 45785 fo. 268, qtd. in *Dear Miss Nightingale*, xvii; Jowett to Nightingale (May 11, 1861), ibid., 6.

63. *Shirley* (1849), ed. Andrew and Judith Hook (Harmondsworth: Penguin, 1979), 18.322–23; cf. I Tim. 2:9–15.

64. Basil Willey, "How 'Robert Elsmere' Struck Some Contemporaries," *Essays and Studies* 10 (1957): 54.

65. Gladstone, "Battle or Belief," 767.

66. Mark M. Freed, "The Moral Irrelevance of Dogma: Mary Ward and Critical Theology in England," in *Women's Theology in Nineteenth-Century Britain: Transfiguring the Faith of Their Fathers*, ed. Julie Melnyk (New York: Garland, 1998), 141.

67. Gladstone, "Battle of Belief," 778, 777. Ward showed she had studied the Christian apologists and possessed a brilliant grasp of the development of continental criticism in "The New Reformation: A Dialogue," *Nineteenth Century* (March 1889), 454–80; cf. Freed, "Dogma," 142–44. In *A Writer's Recollections* (New York: Harper Brothers, 1918), she revealed her artistic reasons for excising so much of the argument; see Willey, " 'Robert Elsmere,' " 66–67.

68. Gladstone, "Battle of Belief," 769, 781, 787, 779.

69. Ibid., 767, 766, 782, 787, 772, 777, 783, 786.

70. Ibid., 771, 788, 771, 784, 782, 779. Another of his organic figures is "limb," of tree, man, or creed.

71. Ibid., 788, 782, 774, 778, 786.

72. "Women and Scepticism," *Fraser's Magazine* 68 (December 1863): 679.

73. Ibid., 697–98, 680.

74. Ibid., 679, 697.

75. Ibid., 698.

76. Ibid., 682.

77. Ibid., 683–86.

78. Bertha Lansbury, "Agnosticism and Women," *Nineteenth Century* 7 (April 1880): 619.

79. Ibid.

80. Ibid.

81. Ibid., 626–27, 620.

82. J. H. Clapperton, "Agnosticism and Women: A Reply," *Nineteenth Century* 7 (May 1880): 842, 840.

83. Ibid., 842. Clapperton warns that this "wide intellectual breach" will injure the "moral nature" of the boy who grows up amid "conflicting influences" (since a "mother must expect her boys to be logical, even if her girls are not so"); ibid., 844, 842.

84. Ibid., 843.

CHAPTER 4

"DECOMPOSING" TEXTS:
BROWNING'S POETICS AND
HIGHER-CRITICAL PARODY

Suzanne Bailey

In *Browning's Beginnings: The Art of Disclosure*, Herbert Tucker makes the intriguing suggestion that the higher criticism was "the Continental deconstruction of its day."[1] Certainly, the reception of the higher criticism in the Victorian periodical press and other sources foreshadows the kind of protests against linguistic and hermeneutical indeterminacy familiar to critics in more recent times. In parodies of the higher criticism, which take the hermeneutical principles of the higher critics to their logical extreme, a kind of interpretive anarchy prevails. For instance, one humorist uses the higher criticism as a pretext for rewriting Shakespeare, and produces a textual monster, in which Ophelia marries Romeo and Juliet runs off with Hamlet.[2] The author of *The Abraham Lincoln Myth, an Essay in Higher Criticism*[3] attempts to prove that Lincoln was a historical fiction, the product of unreliable textual evidence and imperfect eyewitness testimony. In "The Higher Criticism," a satirical poem by nineteenth-century Canadian humorist J. W. Bengough, texts and subjects-in-texts shift and dissolve in a manner we are more accustomed to associating with postmodernist texts and deconstructive readings.[4]

If the higher criticism is a neglected field in Victorian studies, it may safely be assumed that parodies and other humorous treatments of this subject have received minimal, if any critical attention. Yet not only does this material serve as a useful marker of the reception of biblical criticism, but parody itself amplifies the critical positions presented in these works, clarifying for present-day readers just what was at stake in the higher critic's approach to textual analysis. It is clear in Bengough's work alone that the higher criticism confronted Victorians with the specter of unstable texts and inaccessible historical subjects, quite apart from the challenges to religious belief it posed. Parodies of the higher criticism map the contested terrain of a nineteenth-century battle over the nature of fact, evidence, and historical knowledge, pitting the advocates of literal readings of texts against a nineteenth-century version of postmodernist textuality. By examining works from Bengough's poem to texts that are "decomposed"[5] and recomposed, I want to recover the Victorians' sense of the higher criticism as a discourse about historical evidence and oral tradition. Moreover, I argue that the preoccupation with texts and testimony, that emerges so clearly in these little-known works, accounts for similar elements in the poetry of Robert Browning, together with aspects of his poetics which, as Mary Ellis Gibson notes, seem to anticipate "his postmodern successors,"[6] particularly in his sense of the limitations of textual evidence and the possibility of multiple points of view on factual events.

Bengough's poem captures particularly well the indignation with which many Victorians confronted with the higher criticism. As in Browning's "Christmas-Eve" (1850), the higher critic in this poem represents a kind of intellectual snobbery as he wields the "scalpel of the scholar" and condescends to the uninitiated.[7] Though the narrator claims he has "no quarrel with learning" (line 57), his suspicion of the intellectual may be traced in his portrait of the higher critic, who stands "scholarly and cool" at the "portals of the new Negation school" (lines 1–2). The speaker counters with his mother, pitting her simple faith against the sophistry of the higher critic:

> My dear old mother, dead and gone, was a Higher Critic, too;
> This Book was hers—she loved it, and she knew it through and through.
> She told me 'twas from God direct, and she'd no doubt at all,
> The Patriarchs had really lived, as well as John and Paul. (Lines 45–48)

Of particular interest here is the speaker's sense that the higher criticism undermines the evidence for the existence of historical subjects. In the words of Bengough's higher critic:

> The story of Creation, of the Flood, and of the Fall,
> Are obviously poems, as is also Abram's call.
> Indeed, as to the latter, *he's* not literally *real*—
> Abram's but a noun of multitude—a Hebrew race-ideal. (Lines 17–20, emphasis added)

In this stanza, the speaker humorously confronts the possibility that a historical figure may be reduced to a kind of linguistic anomaly or, at the very least, must be understood as the product of historical myth, a projection of cultural *Sehnsucht*, as D. F. Strauss argued in *Das Leben Jesu*. Indeed, the vanishing historical subject, as it might be termed, is one of the most interesting epistemological issues raised by the higher criticism in the process of reconfiguring the grounds for historical knowledge.[8] As George Steiner notes, "dismemberment was all the rage" in nineteenth-century biblical and Homeric scholarship.[9] Over several centuries, culminating in England in the controversies of the 1860s, figure after figure in the Bible was shown by the higher critics to be, in historical terms, an unreliable narrator or fallible eyewitness. In the wry words of A. H. Clough, "Matthew and Mark and Luke and holy John / Evanished all and gone" ("Epi-Straussium," 1869, lines 2–5).[10] Similarly, in Browning's "Christmas-Eve" the higher critic whom Browning mocks speculates,

> Whether 'twere best opine Christ was,
> Or never was at all, or whether
> He was and was not, both—together. (Lines 863–65)

Critics have generally accepted the fact that Browning is skeptical about the implications of the higher criticism for religious faith.[11] As he states in "Easter-Day" (1850), "How comforting a point it were / To find some mummy-scrap declare / There lived a Moses!" (7.176–79). Yet while concrete evidence of the historical reality of the Bible might reassure the higher critic, it is not the foundation for religious belief, which can accept truths obliquely told: "[s]o, I would rest content / With a mere probability" (lines 126–27).

While Browning's personal faith may not be challenged, the extent to which the higher criticism informs his understanding of historical evidence has not been adequately recognized. Browning's interest in the higher criticism of the Bible and of Homer is evident in poems in which he explicitly refers to Strauss, Renan, or other higher critics. Yet one can go far beyond such material in assessing the extent to which insights derived from the higher criticism underlie epistemological issues in Browning's work. For instance, poems written throughout his career demonstrate Browning's ongoing concern with oral testimony and with what might be termed the attenuation or fading of the human voice in time, an issue that comes to him directly from the higher criticism and reflects the epistemological problem of the vanishing historical subject.[12] If knowledge of the past resides in textual and archeological evidence or in the traces of folk-memory, what kind of historical knowledge is possible? "History depends on testimony," as Mrs. Ward puts it in *Robert Elsmere* (1888), eloquently summarizing the impact of the higher criticism not only in terms of religious belief but also for its bearing on the understanding and reception of historical evidence.[13] Through the higher criticism, Victorians discover yet another principle of indeterminacy in the field of knowledge, an area of epistemological grayness that can only be countered by a leap of faith. As G. R. Gleig observed in "The Great Problem: Can it Be Solved?": "the testimony of experience, though of unquestionable weight, is not absolutely conclusive on any disputed point in history."[14] In this essay, published in *Blackwood's* in 1875, Gleig argues that

> in truth, there is no such thing as universal experience. Each man's experience is his own exclusively; he cannot share it with another. The results of your experience, when offered to me, are testimony, and nothing more, and I accept them as such if I have confidence, not in your integrity only, but in your fitness to deal with the subject under consideration.[15]

Browning is keenly aware of the potential distortion of testimony through time, and this trope appears from "Christmas-Eve" and "Easter Day" to his very last poems. As Browning's speaker notes in "Parleyings With Christopher Smart" (1887), the "tellings and re-tellings" of events that comprise oral tradition may produce historical fables:

> Or show or hide, clear late, accretion-clogged
> Now, just as long ago, by tellings and
> Re-tellings to satiety, which strike
> Muffled upon the ear's drum. (7.165–71)

Browning approaches the problem of testimony in many moods in the poems. The nature of oral testimony is a source of humor, for example, in "The Heretic's Tragedy" (1855), a poem in which Browning reconstructs a historical event, then deconstructs or at least self-consciously qualifies his narrative by noting that it is based on a "glimpse" of an event, as "distorted by the refraction from Flemish brain to brain, during the course of a couple of centuries" (epigraph to "Heretic's Tragedy"). In *The Ring and the Book* (1868–69), similar observations are transformed into moving meditations on the nature of history and memory:

> The act, over and ended, falls and fades:
> What was once seen, grows what is now described,
> Then talked of, told about, a tinge the less
> In every fresh transmission; till it melts. . . .
> Across our memory, dies and leaves all dark. . . . (12.13–19)[16]

The fragility, the sheer tenuousness of the human voice in time haunts this poem, as it does "A Death in the Desert" (1864) and other works, in which speakers ponder once-living memories, the sole traces of which survive in texts. They "[d]windle into [something] no bigger than a book," as the poet-speaker writes in *The Ring and the Book*, or live in collective memory in the form of legend or myth, like the gold hair of the saint in "Gold Hair: A Story of Pornic" (1864), or the lost rituals of the Druids in "Fifine at the Fair" (1872).

Some of the clearest and most interesting nineteenth-century commentary on unstable texts and vanishing subjects exists in parodies of higher critical apologetics: that is, in a little-known corpus of historical material.[17] The importance given in these works to the reconstruction of the past through documents and testimony underlines the extent to which such patterns in Browning's work derive from or, indeed, represent popular perceptions of the higher criticism. For example, the retrospective stance of John and other speakers in Browning's "A Death in the Desert" is the central premise of *The Abraham Lincoln Myth*, a spoof on the higher criticism, set in Africa in the thirty-seventh century A.D. In this work, a historian looks back from the future at events in the nineteenth century and argues that facts such as the existence of Abraham Lincoln must be discounted as mere myth and superstition.

Bocard Bramantip, Huxleyan Professor of Dialectics, extrapolates from the position of the higher critics to argue that testimony about Lincoln must be viewed as "the concrete poetic or legendary expression of great abstract underlying ideas."[18] The case against the higher criticism is argued by the Principal of the Law School of the University of Uganda, who systematically outlines, then counters, the key tenets of the "Scientific Historical Criticism."[19] Citing conflicting biographical evidence, together with the "perishableness of original documents,"[20] Bramantip's fictional opponent presents the views of the "destructive" critics, who uphold what he calls "the constant struggle for conformity to theory."[21] The humor in the essay stems from the implicit assumption that facts such as the birth of historical figures or the dates of particular events do indeed have an objective validity independent of texts; moreover, that anomalies in textual evidence do not rule out the possibility of making judgments about the past. The Principal cites a recent court case in which witnesses to an accident all swear they have seen different things: "One of them said the boy was running from the north to the south side of the street. Another said he was running from the south to the north side. One saw only one boy running. Another saw two boys, one chasing the other."[22] What a pity, he writes, the higher critics of the nineteenth century were not familiar with the laws of evidence that allowed the judge to adjudicate conflicting claims,[23] a sentiment that reflects the confidence of Browning's judges (the pope and the poet-speaker) in *The Ring and the Book*, a poem based on contradictory testimony and the reading of source documents.

Parodists of the higher criticism resist the reduction of the real to the textual, and attempt to turn the higher criticism on its head by demonstrating that any text can be shown to be riddled with gaps, silences, absence, and contradiction. Even serious attempts to discount the "decomposition" of the Bible contain examples of textual hair-splitting. James Carmichael attacks the higher criticism in a paper entitled *How Two Documents May Be Found in One: A Monograph in Connection with the Higher Criticism* (1895).[24] In *The Documentary Theory of the Higher Criticism* (1904), a study reviewing nineteenth-century Biblical criticism, the Rev. T. McK. Stuart deconstructs a text written by a higher critic by drawing on the critical methods of the new criticism. Humorists seized on the satirical possibilities of this textual cut-and-paste. In *Homeric Games at an Ancient St Andrews* (1911), subtitled "an Epyllium edited from a comparatively modern papyrus and shattered by means of the higher criticism," the author collates completely unrelated sources, and claims to discover that the game of "goff" was practiced by the ancient Greeks.[25] William Hawley Smith's parody of *Hamlet* is based on a similar premise, as the title suggests. *The New Hamlet* is "[i]ntermixed and Interwoven with a Revised Version *of Romeo and Juliet*, the Combination being Modernized, Re-Written and Wrought Out on New-Discovered Lines, as Indicated under the Light of the Higher Criticism" (1902). From such parodies, in which objects or characters escape the control of the original author under new rules of textual criticism, it is not far to the textual anarchy of Pirandello's *Six Characters in Search of An Author*.

While the examples I cite date from the turn of the twentieth century, they reflect the kind of mock-confusion also rife in satiric treatments of the higher criticism in the Victorian periodical press. While the German higher criticism of the Bible evoked largely scathing commentary in the 1840s and 1850s,[26] the Homeric controversy likely provided safer ground to explore the implications of the new textual criticism, since issues of religious belief were not at stake. Thus, an anonymous reviewer in the *Quarterly Review* in 1850, while railing at "the Strauss poison" and "the Teuton doctors," lets his rhetorical fancy run wild in condemning the excesses of "Wolfomania" and the philological investigation of Shakespeare, with its apparent undermining of authorial intent.[27] Lamenting the excesses of such criticism, which would have audiences read not "from left to right" but "in the real authentic way—that is upside down," he contends:

> Such is the art of extracting sunbeams from cucumbers—exhibited with equal success in the Homeric and the Shakespearian departments, and which—for so divine a system can never die—will, two or three centuries hence, no question, whitewash the author of Childe Harold from the odious imputation of having written Don Juan...will also inquire and decide who wrote the Waverley novels [—] did Scott exist?—had he any share in them?[28]

A similar collective delusion grips the ancient Romans in the humorous periodical *The Man in the Moon* (1848): "In the forum of Rome, the spot is still shown where Curtius is said to have perished; but modem scepticism has thrown very great doubts upon the whole affair, and has not even scrupled to insinuate that the awful void existed only in the brains of Roman romancers."[29]

The skeptical turn of this criticism is the outcome of what De Quincey described eloquently as the enquiry into "the dark fountains of origination" (1841).[30] It is the subject of Browning's "Development" (1889), an autobiographical poem contrasting the poet's childhood knowledge of Homer to his adult understanding of the text after reading "Wolf, [and] a dozen of his like" (line 68). While commending the course of his initiation into the study of Homer (through performance, translation, and finally, critical analysis), Browning also comments that "[n]o dream's worth waking" (line 84); in other words, the child's initial imaginative response to the reading experience is the more important one. The poem concludes with an image of the aging poet as reader, bent over his Aristotle. The poet's earlier comments on the death of dreams resonate ironically here, in lines that implicitly ask the reader to consider which interpretive mode constitutes the greater "disfiguration":

> Now, growing double o'er the Stagirite,
> At least I soil no page with bread and milk,
> Nor crumple, dogsear and deface—boys' way. (Lines 113–15)

Both the subject of "Development" and its characteristic rhetoric of fancy and fact may be linked to popular representations of the higher criticism,

most strikingly through an earlier anonymous satire on the Homeric controversy which employs similar tropes. "The Delights of Fiction, by an Old
Boy," published in *Fun* in 1865, also turns on the issue of literal and figurative readings and questions the relative value of fact and fiction. *Fun*'s "Old
Boy" writes:

> FICTION may be a sort of food
> For young digestions far from good;
> So sweet but wrong, like ice!
> In childhood I ne'er found it fail,
> But monkey-like, devoured my tale,
> And thought it very nice.

The speaker's progressive disenchantment sounds very much like the process
Browning describes in "Development," as a dose of the higher criticism
shatters the speaker's illusions. As a child,

> I thought Jove thundered, then, on high:
> I know, now, he's a thundering—WHY,
> He never did exist!
> And as for Venus! She and Mars
> Are only planets, bless their stars!
> And never lived and kissed
>
> So now I've given Fables up,
> And turn to Truth's dry Bitter Cup,
> And envy boyhood's fate:
> Indeed, I'm in so sad a plight,
> I've turned to Fact from Fiction quite,
> And half believe Colenso's right
> That five and three are eight.[31]

The existence of this poem by no means detracts from Browning's achievement in "Development," but rather deepens our understanding of the
broader cultural resonances of "fancy" and "fact" in Browning's work.[32]

    As a satiric mirroring of Browning's plight as reader, "The Delights of
Fiction" also demonstrates that not all Victorians approached the advent of
the higher criticism with earnest consternation. This sentiment is reflected in
Brownlow Maitland's facetious proposal that there ought to be founded
"Society for the suppression of cruelty to Scripture."[33] A similar, quizzical
view of scholars' activities is represented in the pages of *Punch*, which are
filled from the first issue with parodies of scholars and antiquarians, and with
send-ups of the interpretive problems posed by the discovery of ancient
manuscripts or inscriptions on artifacts. For example, a stock item in *Punch*
in the 1840s and 1850s consists of reports on the activities of the
"Antiquarian Society," which is constantly digging up and misinterpreting
buried evidence. Thus, in one instance, the Society engages in debate over
whether the inscription LEG found on a buried fragment refers to Roman

legions or whether it might possibly stand for "LEG," in reference to "the fact that Gray's Inn Lane was the first place that Caesar put his foot or *leg* upon."[34] The unearthing of the "Sniveyson Marbles" elicits similar flights of interpretive fancy,[35] while the "Antiquarian Discovery" of a Mr. Jones's washing bills, complete with *marginalia* in ink, provides valuable information concerning his domestic economy.[36]

A case might be made for parody or humor in these works as a means of diffusing Victorian anxieties about the recovery of historical fact: in other words, a case for parody as a strategy of containment. The repeated suggestion that textual or archeological evidence is open to multiple interpretations reflects developments in philology traced by Linda Dowling, which summon for Victorians, in her words, "the spectre of autonomous language—language as a system . . . in isolation from any world of human values and experience."[37] New discoveries in the criticism of ancient texts, biblical or classical, posed similar concerns. Not only might oral traditions be unreliable or at least unverifiable, but on what grounds was the authority of the interpreter or the intent of the author to be understood? It is fears such as these that William Henry Smith (1861) acknowledges in a review of Renan's *Etudes d'Histoire Religieuse*, in which he notes:

> [w]hen, in the later years of the Roman empire, men who had some tincture of philosophy attempted to reconstruct religion out of the traditions of paganism, they gave to the popular fable their own philosophical interpretation. They could proceed no other way. Nevertheless, it was manifest that the fable, if it so pleased them, might be interpreted in twenty different ways, that it lay there, in fact, at the mercy of the philosopher, to be reanimated by whatever wisdom he could supply.[38]

He adds, "But what these [original] thoughts were, who can guess? Or who can know when he has guessed rightly?"[39] The problem of original commentary is exacerbated over time, culminating in the interventions of the modem critic. Thus, in an article entitled "False Coin in Sacred Hermeneutics" (1882), Brownlow Maitland argues:

> [p]erhaps the most prolific source of modern wrestlings of Scripture is the desire to discover in it what the expositor himself wants it to say, or thinks that it ought to say. . . . What expositors of this stamp draw out of the text is not so much what is really in it, *as what they themselves have brought to it.*[40]

Pushed to an extreme, this position ends in both hermeneutical and epistemological solipsism, as G. R. Gleig (1875) suggests in "The Great Problem: Can it Be Solved?"[41] Browning's response to the interpretive double-binds of the higher criticism suggests a more self-conscious synthesis, for while sharing the humorists' skepticism about reductive modes of understanding, he fully registers the higher critics' sense of the limitations of oral testimony and of the interpreter's activity.

Browning's recuperation of dangerously expansive textual contexts is at issue in many of his poems. A case in point is an obscure, later work that has received scant critical attention, and certainly not in the context of the higher criticism. "Jochanan Hakkadosh" (1883) is an example of Browning's Orientalism, reflecting an interest in Jewish culture that, not coincidentally, he shares with George Eliot, the translator of Strauss and Spinoza. The poem is notable for its foregrounding of the materiality of language through Browning's use of Hebrew script and supplementary notes, which both mimic the dialogism of Talmudic commentary yet bear an important relationship to the poem's concern with the nature of knowledge and the role of the scholar. As in "A Death in the Desert," "Jochanan Hakkadosh" centers on a disciple's effort both to minister to a dying holy man and to record his last words. The poem is marked by Tsaddik's determination to learn the truths of existence through the Rabbi's words and by his anxieties about achieving a correct or authentic understanding to which he will give permanent form in writing. Thus, Tsaddik begs Jochanan:

"... show by prompt analysis
Which is the metal, which the make-believe,
So that no longer brass shall find, gold miss
Coinage and currency?" (Lines 586–89)

Jochanan's response suggests in effect that the "false coin" in hermeneutics lies precisely in attempts to fix meaning in abstractions rather than through lived experience. The gift of extended life, which Tsaddik wins for the Rabbi so that he can record Jochanan's wisdom, fails to produce the maxims he desires, and it is only when Tsaddik and others abandon the Rabbi that Jochanan has his vision of "[t]ruths in their primal clarity" (line 736). The dying Rabbi cannot fully articulate what he sees when Tsaddik returns, and his insight that one must live in the present is not registered by his disciple, who speaks only of recorded precedents as explanation for the Rabbi's prolonged life (lines 765–93).

The ending of "Jochanan Hakkadosh" is itself not without an element of parody, despite Browning's fidelity to his Hebrew sources. Certainly, the rare Victorian reader who could understand Hebrew would appreciate the tongue-in-cheek manner in which Browning undermines the authority of the texts to which the poet-commentator appeals. Just as the life of Jochanan Hakkadosh is artificially prolonged through the gifts of his followers, the poem itself resists closure. In a manner that one of the few commentators on the poem describes as "increasingly wild,"[42] it ends with three sonnets about the bones of the giant Og, of which biblical legend, we are told, there are multiple versions. The commentator appeals to the authority of a text, but its title reads in Hebrew "a web of many lies," a reference to legendary elements in Browning's historical sources.[43] Appropriately, the final image in the textual glosses is the thigh bone of Og in free-fall: "seventy years ago: / It fell and fell and still without a stop / Keeps falling, nor has reached the bottom yet" (3.12–14).

The poem's rhetorically "endless," hermeneutically dubious textual coda repeats the lesson of Jochanan Hakkadosh, who dies with the insight that "*ignorance [is] confirmed / By knowledge*" (lines 683–84). His disciple Tsaddik throws away the blank parchment he had hoped to "glorify with... text and gloss" (line 635). Yet while these are stock themes in Browning's work, what has escaped critical notice in this poem is Browning's attention to the progressive thickening of oral tradition and commentary through the words of Tsaddik and the poet's own textual notes. From the moment of the holy man's death, his story is woven into a textual tradition through the perspective of an eyewitness, who tries to explain the apparent miracle by reference to textual precedents. Browning's indebtedness in this work to Talmudic tradition has been amply demonstrated,[44] yet there are obvious parallels here to the higher criticism as well, with its foregrounding of eyewitness reporting and the multiple, textual sources of the Bible itself.

In "Jochanan Hakkadosh," as in other works, Browning's approach to texts and testimony reflects his grasp of Schleiermacher's insight that when examining historical, textual sources, "we will never discover a uniform picture...but only different shapes side by side."[45] While acknowledging, even reveling in such interpretive double-binds, Browning transforms the dark discoveries of the higher critics into a complex hermeneutical project. Speakers in the poems frequently stand on the edge of an interpretive abyss in their contemplation of receding historical contexts, composed of "facts" that cannot be distinguished from "fancies" or the accretions of oral tradition. At the same time, what Browning perceives as the inability of the scholar or system-maker to disentangle fact from fiction allows him to justify in his work both the importance of inspired readings and the special status of poetry as discourse. If the conclusion of "Jochanan Hakkadosh" confirms the speciousness of commentary, this inadequacy supports and lends credence to the poet's activity as artist. After all, Browning's intent in this poem is to present by means of fiction or poetry both a philosophy of life and a response to "faith, ruined through and through / By doubt" (lines 722–23). From Browning's awareness of these issues comes his confident sense that poetry itself, as fiction, may tell a higher truth.

NOTES

I would like to thank my research assistant, Claire Senior, for her invaluable help with the periodicals research for this project. I also gratefully acknowledge the financial support of the Social Sciences and Humanities Research Council of Canada. A shorter version of this essay was presented at the MLA Convention in 1998.

1. Herbert Tucker, *Browning's Beginnings: The Art of Disclosure* (Minneapolis: University of Minnesota Press, 1980), 8.

2. William Hawley Smith's *The New* Hamlet is a farce in which Shakespeare's *Hamlet* and *Romeo and Juliet* are combined and rewritten to give both plays

a happy ending. Smith also alludes to the Baconian controversy regarding the authorship of Shakespeare's plays ("Foreword"). Smith, *The New* Hamlet: *Intermixed and Interwoven with A Revised Version of* Romeo and Juliet (Chicago: Rand, McNally and Co., 1902).

3. Oliver Prince Buel, *The Abraham Lincoln Myth, an Essay in Higher Criticism* (New York: Mascot Publishing, 1894). First published in *Catholic World*, November and December 1893.

4. J. W. Bengough, "The Higher Criticism," in *Motley: Verses Grave and Gay* (Toronto: William Briggs, 1895), 163–66.

5. Textual "decomposition" is a term used by nineteenth-century critics. See, for example, the Rev. T. McK. [*sic*] Stuart's discussion of the "decomposition" of the Bible by the higher critics, in *Divine Inspiration vs. the Documentary Theory of the Higher Criticism* (Cincinnati: Jennings and Graham, 1904), 78.

6. Mary Ellis Gibson, ed., *Critical Essays on Robert Browning* (New York: G. K. Hall), 2.

7. *The Poems of Robert Browning*, ed. John Pettigrew, 2 vols. (New Haven, Connecticut: Yale University Press, 1981), line 58.

8. I use the term epistemology rather than hermeneutics here, for I want to distinguish between the question of whether and to what extent the past can be known, rather than how evidence about the past is to be reconstructed.

9. George Steiner, "Homer and the Scholars," *Homer: A Collection of Critical Essays*, ed. George Steiner and Robert Fagles (Englewood Cliffs, New Jersey: Prentice Hall, 1962), 2.

10. *The Poems of Arthur Hugh Clough*, ed. F. L. Mulhauser (Oxford: Clarendon Press, 1974). Mulhauser notes that "[a] rough draft entitled 'Epi-Strauss-ion' occurs in the 1847 *Notebook*" (662).

11. See for example W. O. Raymond, "Browning and the Higher Criticism," in *The Infinite Moment and Other Essays in Browning* (Toronto: University of Toronto Press, 1965), 19–51. Elinor Shaffer points to this deficiency in Browning scholarship in *"Kubla Khan" and The Fall of Jerusalem: The Mythological School in Biblical Criticism and Secular Literature: 1770–1880* (London: Cambridge University Press, 1975), 192.

12. Dorothy Mermin has examined the notion of the survival of the primitive in Browning's work, noting the connection to the higher criticism. See Mermin, "Browning and the Primitive" (Gibson, 202–225). Donald Hair draws attention to Browning's interest in what he terms "[textual] transcriptions," found in chapter Seven of *Robert Browning's Language* (Toronto: University of Toronto Press, 1999).

13. Mary Augusta Ward, *Robert Elsmere*, 1888 (New York: Oxford University Press, 1987), 197.

14. G. R. Gleig, "The Great Problem: Can it be Solved?" *Blackwood's Edinburgh Magazine* 117 (January 1875), 135.

15. Ibid., 135.

16. Robert Browning, *The Ring and the Book*, ed. R. D. Altick (New Haven: Yale University Press, 1981).

17. Shea and Whitla include some parodies of the higher criticism in their edition of *Essays and Reviews*. See "Satires by Lewis Carroll and Others" in Victor Shea and William Whitla, ed., *Essays and Reviews: The 1860 Text and Its Reading* (Charlottesville: University Press of Virginia, 2000), 818–46.

18. Buel, Abraham Lincoln, 3.

19. Ibid., 15.

20. Ibid., 44.

21. Ibid., 69.

22. Ibid., 61.

23. "Now, in a mind property indoctrinated with the methods of agnostic dialectics, these discrepancies would raise a doubt as to whether there any boy running at all—or any accident.... It is fortunate for the 'higher historical criticism' that it knows nothing of legal rules of evidence" (Buel, Abraham Lincoln, 62).

24. James Carmichael, How Two Documents May Be Found in One: A Monograph in Connection with the Higher Criticism (Montreal: Gazette Print, 1895), 98 ff.

25. Alexander Shewan, Homeric Games at an Ancient St Andrews: An Epyllium Edited from a Comparatively Modern Papyrus and Shattered by Means of the Higher Criticism (Edinburgh: J. Thin, 1911).

26. The work of James Martineau in the Westminster Review is one exception.

27. Anon, review of William Mure, A Critical History of the Language and Literature of Ancient Greece (1850), Quarterly Review 87 (1850): 438, 439.

28. Ibid., 440, 441. The anonymous reviewer elaborates on the parallels between Homeric criticism and the higher criticism, or in his terms, "the determined warfare against the Bible": "Homer has been not unjustly called, by Wolf himself, the Bible of Greece; and it would be easy to show in how many ways the Antichristian conspiracy might have hoped to see its proper object forwarded by the collateral . . . co-operation of those who essayed to shake everything that had been for thousands of years accepted as to the construction, and authority of the literary monument which approached nearest in claim of antiquity to the Hebrew Scriptures" (436–37). Victorian controversies about authorship, including debates about Shakespeare, prompt such articles as "Who Wrote Dickens?" and a satire by Robert Scott entitled "The Jabbberwock, Traced to Its True Source, by Thomas Chatterton" (Macmillan's, February 1872). See Anon., "Who Wrote Dickens?" Macmillan's Magazine 54 (June 1886): 112–15; Scott, "The Jabbberwock, Traced to Its True Source, by Thomas Chatterton," Macmillan's Magazine 25 (February 1872): 337–38.

29. The Man in the Moon 2 (1848): 175.

30. Thomas De Quincey, "Homer and the Homeridae," Blackwood's Edinburgh Magazine 50 (October 1841): 411.

31. Anon., "The Delights of Fiction, by an Old Boy," Fun, September 2, 1865.

32. The rhetoric of fact and fiction is omnipresent in Victorian culture, as George Levine and others have observed. As Levine notes, "[f]act is the province of science: the geological, philological, archaeological fact demonstrates the falsity of religious doctrine" ("Matthew Arnold's Science of Religion: The Uses of Imprecision," Victorian Poetry 26 [1988]: 144). Linda Shires connects Victorian parody to the "epistemological uncertainty" that, she argues, "appears as a prominent feature in [nineteenth-century] literature" ("Fantasy, Nonsense, Parody, and the Status of the Real: The Example of Carroll," Victorian Poetry 26 [1988]: 267).

33. Brownlow Maitland, "False Coin in Sacred Hermeneutics," Blackwood's Edinburgh Magazine 132 (November 1882): 559. Maitland takes this suggestion from an unnamed American journal and proposes applying it in an

endeavour to "[protect] the sacred volume from maltreatment by its open foes" (559).

34. *Punch* 3 (1842): 62.

35. *Punch* 4 (1843): 214.

36. *Punch* 2 (1842): 35. Similarly, J. W Bengough runs a satirical series based on the discovery of a series of Assyrian manuscripts in *Grip* in the 1870s.

37. Linda Dowling, *Language and Decadence in the Victorian fin de siécle* (New Jersey: Princeton University Press, 1986), xii.

38. William Henry Smith, "M. Ernest Renan," *Blackwood's Edinburgh Magazine* 90 (November 1861): 633.

39. Ibid., 633.

40. Maitland, "False Coin," 563; my emphasis.

41. Gleig, Great Problem, 135.

42. William DeVane, *A Browning Handbook* (New York: Appleton-Century-Crofts, 1955), 471.

43. DeVane, 472. Pettigrew translates the title of the imaginary text Browning cites as his authority as "A Collection of Many Lies" (1093). The title of the collection, *Jocoseria*, also suggests parody.

44. See DeVane, Browning; Judith Berlin-Lieberman, *Robert Browning and Hebraism: A Study of the Poems of Browning which are Based on Rabbinical Writings* (Jerusalem: [s.n.], 1934); Arnold Cheskin, "Jochanan Hakkadosh: Rabbi Ben Browning," *Studies in Robert Browning and His Circle* 12 (1984): 134–47; "Robert Browning's Climacteric Hebraic Connections With Emma Lazarus and Emily Harris," *Studies in Robert Browning and His Circle* 10 (1982): 9–22; " 'Tis Only the Coat of a Page to Borrow': Robert Browning's Hebraic Borrowings and Concealments for 'Jochanan Hakkadosh," *Browning Society Notes* 20 (1990): 31–38.

45. Friedrich Schleiermacher, *Brief Outline of Theology as a Field of Study.* Cited in the "Editor's Introduction" to *Luke: A Critical Study* [1825], ed. Terrence N. Tice, trans. Connop Thirlwall (Lewiston, ME: Edwin Mellen Press, 1993), 9.

CHAPTER 5

"OUR KING BACK, OH, UPON ENGLISH SOULS!": SWINBURNE, HOPKINS, AND THE POLITICS OF RELIGION

Renée V. Overholser

Recent critics have emphasized the centrality of the discourse of religion and politics in the Victorian era and, following Linda Colley's *Britons*, the importance of the Protestant providential narrative—that God directs his nation, and protects it from its enemies—in forming England's national identity.[1] In linking theology with politics, nineteenth-century English Protestants saw evidence of God's continuing present-day support for the Protestant constitution, which earlier had been responsible for the historic defeats of Roman Catholicism—the rout of the Spanish Armada, the defusing of the Gunpowder Plot—and which now contributed to the period's well-documented anti-Catholic feelings. This essay focuses on the providential poetry of Algernon Swinburne and Gerard Manley Hopkins within the context of Victorian England's religious politics.

No voice was more prominent in the overheated discourse of mid-century religious politics than that of the masterfully vituperative, radically republican Swinburne; no poetic representative of the Roman Catholic point of view less prominent than Gerard Manley Hopkins. It can be seen, however, that each made his own attempt to "graft . . . the Christian story into the English story" through the construction of radically opposing alternatives to the Protestant narratives, one calling for England's conversion to the cause of international revolution against the Roman Catholic Church and its supporters, the other calling for England's reconversion to its Roman Catholic roots.[2] I argue that in framing his own call, Hopkins appropriated—converted—elements of Swinburne's texts to the uses of his religion in revelatory ways.

The anti-Catholic feeling allied for centuries with England's national self-definition had been stirred by the 1829 Catholic Emancipation Act and the reestablishment of England's Roman Catholic hierarchy in 1859 (the "Papal Aggression"). Its continued potency, reduced but still prominent in the public sector, was reflected at mid-century in the press and in popular fiction, with the long-running battle within the Anglican Church over ritualism helping to keep the dangers of Popery in the public eye.[3] At its most extreme, as in the case of William Murphy's anti-Catholic rabble-rousing, feeling spilled over into the streets in the form of riotous civic unrest.[4] The situation was further exacerbated by a series of actions by Pope Pius IX over a fifteen-year period, the most contentious the proclamation of the doctrine of the Immaculate Conception of the Virgin Mary in 1854, followed ten years later by the anti-modernist *Syllabus of Errors*. The pope's actions were reinforced by Vatican Council I's declaration of papal infallibility in 1870–71, the crowning triumph of the Ultramontane party led in Rome as well as in England by Archbishop Manning.[5] Like other Englishmen, Swinburne and Hopkins reacted to these religio-political actions—Swinburne publicly, through a series of strongly worded poems and letters to the editor on religious politics, Hopkins, privately, in letters and in unpublished poems.[6] Both priest and patriot—his "patriotic song for soldiers" reads "Call me England's fame's fond lover, / Her fame to keep, her fame to recover"—Hopkins was also vigorously opinionated on contemporary politics, perhaps to a fault in his own view.[7]

Both Swinburne and Hopkins had begun life as High Church Anglicans, both underwent conversion to their new affiliations at Oxford, where they were students at Balliol within a few years of each other, and both developed their opposing religious and political views in the Oxford essay societies. In 1856 Swinburne was one of the founding members of Old Mortality, the undergraduate center for radical philosophical and political thought, the latter centered on outspoken support for the anti-papist actions of Mazzini and other heroes of the Risorgimento. Eight years later Hopkins became a founder and active member of the Hexameron society, which was formed specifically to "preserve men…with good church feeling" from the "snare of such societies as the Old Mortality."[8] Its High Church members opposed strongly the Old Mortality's skeptical, relativist "Rationalism," which Hopkins is reported to have defined as "Neologian theories generally" and for which he "had a simple remedy—the authority of the Church."[9] Scattered and brief critical comments in his letters reveal Hopkins's lifelong awareness of Swinburne's poetry.[10] While Swinburne's poetic technique is often compelling, Hopkins is repelled by the political and moral attitudes expressed. One of the "plagues of mankind" along with Hugo, Swinburne is faulted for "crying always in a high head voice about flesh and flowers and democracy and damnation" (*Letters to Bridges*, 39, 72–73). An 1885 ode on Irish Home Rule is "a rigmarole," its politics reflecting the lack of principles that its author shares with Gladstone.[11] While only the "long waterlogged lines" of the *Armada*, "that pitfall of the patriotic muse," come in for censure (*Letters to Bridges*, 304), we can assume that the censure extends to the poem's gleeful jeers at the Roman Catholic beliefs of the defeated Spanish aggressors against England.

By the mid-1860s Swinburne was the famed author of *Atalanta in Calydon* (1865) and *Poems and Ballads*, first series (1866). Hopkins, however, had disavowed the practice of poetry as he entered into the Society of Jesus in 1868, and for seven years he was to write only "two or three little presentation pieces as the occasion called for" (*Correspondence*, 14). He explained to Canon Dixon, "Our Society values, as you say, and has contributed to literature, to culture; but only as a means to an end. Its history and its experience shew that literature proper, as poetry, has seldom been found to be to that end a very serviceable means" (*Correspondence*, 94). In the light of the Jesuit attitudes he acknowledged and accepted, it is significant that the presentation pieces with which Hopkins began to break his poetic silence became the means to gainsay the Victorian period's most powerfully defiant heretic, through the medium of Swinburne's own distinctive voice.[12]

Hopkins's first poetic conversion of Swinburne's texts occurred in two Marian poems, "Ad Mariam" and "Rosa Mystica," written in English in the early 1870s. Like the two Latin Marian poems written at about the same time, they bear a relation to the doctrine of the Immaculate Conception.[13] The Church in 1854 had pronounced on the vexed question of how Christ could have been born from a womb tainted by original sin, since of necessity his mother had been born before her Son's saving redemptive Incarnation. The doctrine extended asexual impregnation back a generation: the Holy Ghost, the male agency of Christ's birth, was pure spirit; now Mary was declared "immaculate," free of original sin from the moment of her own conception.[14] Demanding faith, not reason, for belief, the doctrine was a "gauntlet flung" in the face of rationalism by a Church that felt itself to be under siege by the secular ideas condemned in the 1864 *Syllabus of Errors*, and its promulgation "signaled defiance" of those modernist ideas, at the same time reinforcing the power of the pope to declare "truth."[15]

One result of the proclamation was the resurgence of Marianism. On the Continent, for example, the figure of the Virgin appeared on French soil through the agency of child visionaries, indicating for Roman Catholic believers her actual physical presence in the natural world.[16] The apparitions reinforced the recently proclaimed doctrine—"I am the Immaculate Conception," the vision of Mary told Bernadette Soubirous at Lourdes—and also verified the existence of a supernatural realm that could directly affect current events, in France giving support to the Church's conservative nationalism.[17] While there were no widely reported Marian appearances in Victorian Britain, the importation of the Marian cult from the Continent into the largely Protestant country made the figure of Mary an "explosive ingredient in [its] social and racial mythology."[18] In contrast to English Protestants of all denominations and, indeed, to many Roman Catholics, the Jesuit order supported the doctrine of the Immaculate Conception, as did Hopkins himself.[19] As well, Hopkins recognized the possibility of the Virgin's intercession in events in the natural world. In 1877 he noted in a letter to his mother that his grandfather had died on the day "signalised by our Lady's overruling aid asked for and given at the victory of Lepanto," which he in turn took as a "token from heaven" that the Virgin had saved his grandfather's soul (*Further Letters*, 147–48).

With the increased prominence of Marianism, Algernon Swinburne, who earlier had sung of "the supreme evil, God" at the remove of an ancient Greek setting, entered England's contemporary ideological battleground.[20] The poems that were later collected in *Songs Before Sunrise* (1871) and *Songs of Two Nations* (1875) first appeared in journals and newspapers, and included gleeful attacks on the Roman Catholic Church and its doctrines as well as celebrations of the Church's nationalist enemies around the world.[21] The Virgin Mary came in for particularly derisive commentary. In "The Saviour of Society" Jesus, the "son of man, but what man who knows?" becomes incarnate through a mother "Whose misconception was immaculate / And when her time was come she misconceived" (*Poems*, 2:308). In "Dolores" Swinburne employs what Margot Louis has termed "demonic parody," inverting Marian language to draw parallels between the Virgin and the archetypal whore Dolores, "Notre-Dame des Sept Douleurs," "mystical rose of the mire" (*Poems*, 1:154–55). Frequently, Swinburne represents the Virgin Mary as the antonym to the ebullient eroticism of the great pagan goddesses, Venus chief among them, in "Hymn to Proserpine," for example, contrasting meek Mary, "a sister to sorrow," with the beauty and fecundity of Venus, "Clothed round with the world's desire" (*Poems*, 1:71).[22]

About 1873 Gerard Manley Hopkins wrote his first Jesuit poem in English. "Ad Mariam" is a devout celebration of the Virgin written to be hung in Our Lady's Gallery at Stonyhurst as part of the college's May Marian activities. The belief it expresses is Hopkins's, but the text originated with Swinburne: Hopkins parodies the first Chorus from *Atalanta in Calydon*, transforming the paean to the pagan goddess Artemis into a paean to the by now much-maligned Virgin.[23] Swinburne had based his poem on the Greek myth of the virgin huntress Atalanta, who becomes the means for vengeance by Artemis on the people of Calydon. His kingdom of Calydon is an eroticized world overseen by cruel, distant gods. The famous first Chorus celebrates the moment "When the hounds of spring are on winter's traces," as the Chief Huntsman prays to Artemis as both virgin and fecund moon goddess (*Poems*, 4:249). In turn, Hopkins's poem praises Roman Catholicism's fecund Virgin who, as the Immaculate Conception, is also associated with the moon.[24] Imitating the Chorus's eight-line stanza form, anapestic and logaoedic rhythms, varied rhyme pattern, diction, and patterns of imagery, Hopkins uses Swinburne's technique of parodic inversion to elevate the Virgin mother at the expense of the goddess, and Christian values over pagan ones. Swinburne, for example, had turned the Christian emphasis on sexual sin upside down: in Calydon "sin" equates with winter's frigid, snowy chasteness, and it is the absence of sexuality, not its presence, that is sinful: "For winter's rains and ruins are over, / And all the season of snows and sins; / The days dividing lover and lover" (*Poems*, 4:250). In "Ad Mariam," the "maid-month" of which Mary is "Queen" (*Poetical*, no. 94, line 24) brings relief from winter's "storm-months" (line 29): "We have suffered the sons of Winter in sorrow / And been in their ruinous reigns oppressed" (lines 9–10). In its play on Swinburne's "rains and ruins" "Ad Mariam" removes Swinburne's phrase from the Greek world and brings it into Christian providential history, for the "ruinous reigns" of Winter ended when the pagan "line of kings did cease" (line 26): those kings "like the storm-months smote the earth / Till a maid in David's house had birth, / That was unto Judah as May, and brought her / A son for King, whose name was peace" (lines 29–32). With the saving arrival of Christianity, Christ the King has supplanted the pagan "Princes strong for the sword and slaughter" (line 27). Further, in a gesture that echoes the purifying strategy of the doctrine of the Immaculate Conception, sexual sin is removed from Mary's natural world, the Calydonian nymphs and fauns expelled from the erotic pagan landscape Swinburne had celebrated.

In the case of "Rosa Mystica," the second Marian poem in English, the "echoes of Swinburne in the poem were specific allusions to his latest sensation, 'Dolores.' "[25] Again, Hopkins has recourse to the techniques, images, and meter of Swinburne, and again, an image whose source is the pagan past, is made to take its place within providential history, and it is sexually purified in the process.[26] The whorish "mystical rose of the mire" (*Poems*, 1:155) of Swinburne's poem is removed from the mire by Hopkins to become again the Rose of Sharon, restored to its traditional Christian role as a symbol of Mary. It is removed as well from the pagan world for, as "Galilee's growth," Hopkins's mystic rose "broke into bloom upon Nazareth hill" (*Poetical*, no. 96, lines 9–10). And, again, the poem relates to the Immaculate Conception, for the rose is in a "mystery" (line 1)—a traditional reference to Mary as "devoid of original sin" (*Poetical*, 308–09).

Gerard Manley Hopkins's Swinburnian Marian poems are minor efforts, but with "The Wreck of the Deutschland" Hopkins began to secure his later place as a major nineteenth-century figure. Like the Marian poems, the great ode shows evidence of a relationship with the work of Swinburne, and like them it relates to current doctrinal politics, in particular to the actions of Vatican Council I.[27]

In the summer of 1870 the bishops of the Church met in Rome in an atmosphere of crisis, "since the gates of hell trying, if they can, to overthrow the church, make their assault with a hatred that increases day by day."[28] The Council adopted two constitutions, the first a Dogmatic Constitution of the "one true catholic faith, outside of which none can be saved." In it, the Council affirmed Christ's "redemptive providence," which had been manifested in the past by "a closer union of the members with the visible head, and an increased vigour in the whole mystical body of Christ," but which was now under attack. The heresy of "naturalism...which spares no effort to bring it about that Christ...is shut out from the minds of people and the moral life of nations," has "plunged the minds of many into the abyss of pantheism, materialism, and atheism." In the face of this threat the pope and the Council "declare from this chair of Peter before all eyes the saving teaching of Christ," that God "can be known with certainty from consideration of created things" as well as from "external indications of his revelation, that is to say divine acts, . . . first and foremost miracles and prophecies." The statements that "divine revelation cannot be made credible by external signs," or "that all miracles are impossible" are declared anathema. The second Dogmatic Constitution on the Church of Christ proclaimed the doctrine of papal infallibility: the pope's *ex cathedra* doctrinal statements concerning faith or morals to be held by the whole church are without error. Finally, the Council upheld papal primacy: popes are "perpetual successors" to Saint Peter, who was constituted by Christ as "visible head of the whole church militant," and have primacy of jurisdiction over the whole church (*Decrees*, 5–23).

Because the doctrinal pronouncements and the political reactions they prompted have bearing on the poems discussed in this essay, they require brief elaboration. Behind the proclamation of the pope as the "visible head" is the doctrine of the "visible church," which exists both as a "conspicuous and public" society and as a "Divine society," the latter an "aspect of the Church . . . described by the Apostles in figurative language. They represent it as the Body of Christ," among other images. Membership in the Church is described as "incorporation in the visible body of Christ."[29] The divine society was established by Christ "to be the means of salvation for all mankind. For this end it is essential that its claims should be authenticated in a manner evident to all; in other words, it must be visible, not merely as other public societies are visible, but as being the society of the Son of God," recognizable by those who do not suffer "spiritual blindness to the claims of the Church."[30] Tropes of vision and of the body predominate, then, in discussions of the nature of the Church.

The political repercussions of the Council's actions were focused particularly on the Church's claims in civil matters and the possible disloyalty they might inspire in Englishmen. As a basis for debate the Council had published a *schema* based on the extreme positions taken in the 1864 papal *Syllabus of Errors*. The earlier document, for example, had anathemized those who maintained that "the Church ought to be separated from the State, and the State from the Church" and that "it is no longer expedient that the Catholic religion be the only religion of the State, to the exclusion of all other forms of worship."[31] These points were dropped in the final Constitution in favor of less precise wording, binding the faithful to submit to the pope "not only in matters of faith and morals, but also in those which concern the discipline and government of the church dispersed throughout the world" (*Decrees*, 21). For decades, however, strong statements on all sides of the issue had promoted discord, and as recently as 1866 Archbishop Manning had drawn a parallel between the "Visible Church and its mission to the world" and the British Empire: "The Temporal Power of the Popes is as manifestly and as fully ordained of God as the power of Queen Victoria."[32]

While the immediate issue before the Council in 1870 was the governance of Papal States, it goes without saying that interpreting the pronouncements, particularly in defining the borders between temporal and spiritual power and the relationships governing these powers, provided further sites of vigorous controversy. There were fears of extensions of papal power, specifically, Prime Minister Gladstone's suspicions that a conspiracy of Roman Catholics would attempt to restore Pius IX's temporal power in the Papal States by war and, by extension, elsewhere.[33] There were further fears of continuing defections in England through conversions to a resurgent Catholicism obedient to the authority of an absolutist foreign ruler, which dated back to the widespread Roman Catholic public calls for the "conversion of England" in the heady days following Archbishop Manning's restoration of the hierarchy.[34] However, attention for the moment was directed away from the Council's actions by a compressed concatenation of events that had been building for decades. France declared war on Prussia in July 1870; in September the Council suspended sessions precipitously, under military threat; and one week later nationalist forces, latter-day representatives of the revolutionary republican Risorgimento, invaded the Papal States, entered Rome in triumph and set up a secular Italian national government. Although it was to continue in Germany, the centuries-long war between papal and national authority in Italy was at last settled. The doctrinal basis of papal power, so recently dogmatized, remained; the papacy's temporal sway was severely restricted. The Council had been justified in its sense of being under threat from its enemies.

Two of the long-standing bêtes noirs of the English public, revolutionary republicanism and the Roman Catholic Church, had met head-on across the channel. Algernon Swinburne and Gerard Manley Hopkins replicated that contention within England itself. Energized and focused by the threats to republicanism brought to a head by the Vatican Council, Swinburne continued to publish his *Songs* on religious politics. Fears of the disordering republicanism championed in Swinburne's verse, however, were largely overshadowed by the popularity of the cause of Italy—hymned by Byron, Hemans, Clough, the Brownings—as well as by the English public's continuing appetite for anti-Catholicism.[35] In contrast, Hopkins, English patriot, but now a Jesuit priest on the margins of English national life, would have remained suspect. William Gladstone, for example, made clear his own fears and suspicions of the Jesuits in his 1874 polemic, *The Vatican Decrees in their Bearing on Civil Liberty: A Political Expostulation*, which sold a remarkable 145,000 copies. "I am not now going to pretend that either foreign foe or domestic treason can, at the bidding of the Court of Rome, disturb these peaceful shores," he wrote, yet "[i]t must be for some political object, of a very tangible kind, that the risks of so daring a raid upon the civil sphere has been deliberately run."[36] The actions of the Council, Gladstone felt, put into question the civil loyalty of all Catholics, and particularly that of the powerful Jesuits, "the deadliest foes that mental and moral liberty have ever known."[37] In his attack on the Society of Jesus, Gladstone seems to have reflected widespread educated opinion. In any event, the entry on the order in the ninth edition of the *Encyclopaedia Brittanica* holds the Jesuits accountable "for precipitating the Franco-German war of 1870," and concludes its historical review of the order as follows: "How, with [Pope Pius IX]'s support throughout his long reign . . . they contrived to stamp out the last remains of independence everywhere, and to crown the Ultramontane triumph with the Vatican decrees, is matter of familiar knowledge."[38]

The political implications of the Council were important to English Jesuits, and in the 1870s Hopkins and his fellow Jesuits followed religious political events closely, including reactions to Gladstone's "*Expostulation* with Catholics upon the Vatican decrees and syllabus."[39] Hopkins's St. Beuno's debating club team argued successfully that "in the present contest between Gladstone and Rome," Roman Catholic beliefs were "liable to misrepresentation"; still, "the position of Catholics has been in no wise changed by the decrees of the Vatican Council."[40]

On October 25, 1870, Hopkins described in his Journal the "knot or crown . . . of dull blood-coloured horns" that he had seen in the sky: "A little before 7 in the evening a wonderful Aurora, the same that was seen at Rome (shortly after its seizure by the Italian government) and taken as a sign of God's anger" (*Journals*, 200–01). Like the appearances of the Virgin Mary, the aurora was a possible miraculous sign, that is, a perceptible, visible indication of Divine Providence's action in the natural realm. Indeed, this was an interpretation that would have been supported by Vatican Council I, for as we have seen the Council had just declared that miracles exist as external indications of God's revelation. Hopkins's connection of the appearance of northern lights to contemporary political events was characteristic of the pervasive apocalyptic mood of nineteenth-century England.[41] Indeed, for millennarians, political change was to "take place entirely through supernatural means," not through human agency.[42] Hopkins believed literally in the Second Coming, preaching of it through traditional imagery: life is dark night because "Christ the light of the world is gone"; "there is no dawn, no dayspring, to tell of the day coming, no morning twilight, the sunrise will be sudden, will be lightning. . . . There are indeed to be signs, but none but believers will heed them."[43] An aurora, lighting up the night sky, might well be one of these signs.[44]

An event related directly to the contemporary religious politics, which Hopkins could also interpret as a possible miraculous sign and apocalyptic foreshadowing, precipitated a poem "to the happy memory of five Franciscan nuns, exiles by the Falck Laws, drowned between midnight and morning of December 7 [1875]." The nuns were aboard the doomed ship as a result of Prince Otto von Bismarck's *Kulturkampf,* itself a Prussian reaction to the pronouncements of Vatican Council I. In a series of repressive decrees the Prussian government replaced ecclesiastical authority with civil authority, in part by declaring that all Roman Catholic religious orders were dissolved and, when the Roman Catholic clergy refused to comply with the new legislation, the priests, brothers, and nuns were expelled.[45] While many English Catholics considered the deaths of the Franciscan Sisters as martyrdoms, the English public generally supported Bismarck,[46] and again in this instance the Jesuits, who had been prominent in resisting the Prussian legislation, were viewed unsympathetically. The London *Times* declared: "Roman

Catholics will not find it easy to enlist...sympathies on behalf of the Jesuits. ...Bismarck wishes to abate a very great nuisance, the nuisance of an unscrupulous conspiracy bent on dissolving society in order to accomplish certain impossible ends of its own."[47]

In the Deutschland disaster, Hopkins the Jesuit found a way to serve as priest, poet, and patriot, and on a larger canvas than in the Marian poems. The event had profound significance for Catholics; the subject had been suggested by his rector (*Correspondence*, 14). Both the event and the poem accord with important issues that Vatican Council I had addressed: secular enemies had made "assaults with...hatred" against the Church, refusing to submit to, and indeed, destroying, the "discipline and government of the Church" in Prussia. The event could be interpreted as one of the "external indications of [God's] revelation, that is to say divine acts," evidence of the "redemptive providence" which the Vatican Council had affirmed. And it presented Hopkins with another chance to square off against Swinburne, the prominent atheist.

While the startling originality of "The Deutschland" has long been a critical given, I would nevertheless argue that it continues the conversion of Swinburnian forms, images, and language, begun in the Marian poems that immediately preceded it but now accomplished with greater complexity. The great ode that I shortly explore is in fact bracketed by works that bear distinctive signs of another voice; it was to be followed by three other works from 1876, the "exceedingly Swinburnian" "Moonrise" (*Poetical*, no. 103), "The Woodlark" (no. 104), and "Penmaen Pool" (no. 105), with its "pronounced mechanical Swinburnian movement."[48] And, while Hopkins aimed with some success at "a more Miltonic plainness and severity" (*Letters to Bridges*, 87) in the 1879 "Andromeda" (no. 138), he returned to themes involving both contemporary religious politics and Swinburne.[49]

Swinburne's reactions to the Vatican Council and its surrounding events were predictably strong, and indeed can be seen as prime examples of the assaults against the Church by atheistic supporters of naturalism condemned by the Vatican Council. The resulting poetry was published in *Songs Before Sunrise*, a volume focusing on the dawning of republican Freedom in the context of the contemporary struggles in Italy.[50] It includes direct attacks on the pope and the Society of Jesus, expressing the culture's doubts about Roman Catholic patriotism in breathtakingly vituperative language. For example, offering "A Choice" between "Faith false or true, born patriot or born priest" (*Poems*, 2:300), Swinburne excoriates the enemies of "Freedom," in particular the pope, sardonically called "high-priest," "Pius the Ninth, Judas the Second" (2:296), and consigns him, along with kings and priests, to damnation: "Go down to hell. This end is good to see; ...Now the last Jesuit found about thee is / The beast that made thy fouler flesh his cell" (2:293). In the "priestless Rome that shall be" (2:272) they will be replaced by the secular "priests" of the Risorgimento, Mazzini and Garibaldi.

Swinburne announced the new politico-religious order in "Hymn of Man (During the Session in Rome of the Ecumenical Council)," written both in opposition to the Council and in support of the competing Anti-Catholic Council of Naples.[51] Swinburne described the poem as a " 'Te Hominem Laudamus,' to sing the human triumph over 'things'—the opposing forces of life and nature—and over the God of his own creation. ... It might end somehow thus with a cry of triumph over the decadence of a receding Deity: ... 'Glory to Man in the highest! For man is the master of things.' "[52] In the parody of the Christian providential pattern, man brings about his own salvation through revolutionary political action, freeing himself from the ruinous reigns of his oppressors and thereby becoming master, dominant over now-destroyed priests and kings. In the new dispensation the Christian God has disappeared. As his followers call out to him in vain to make himself known, the poet taunts them: "Cry aloud ... / Is he drunk or asleep, that the rod of his wrath is unfelt and unseen?"; "Hath he gazed on himself unto blindness, who made men blind to behold?" and again: "O God, Lord God of thy priests, rise up now and show thyself God" (*Poems*, 2:103–04). But no savior appears or is heard, and it is in the answering void that the poet proclaims his new "religion of man."

Swinburne has proclaimed himself a "choral-souled boy-priest" (2:169) who trumpets international republican revolution in order to convert both individuals and nations. In the *Songs* his trumpet sounds nowhere more loudly, nor more insistently, than in the ear of still unconverted England, who fails to join the march of nations toward freedom (2:151), although she is equally beset by "thunder-forging priests" (2:153) and other "mindless" "masters" (2:155). In other poems England sleeps, failing to keep "A Watch in the Night" through "Storm and thunder and rain" (2:27), in contrast to the exiles and martyrs to the republican cause in Germany and Italy. In "The Eve of Revolution," "eyes blinded," England sits "shamed and self-contemplative" (2:19), unable to see the goddess of liberty who rises out of the stormy seas, "clothed round with raiment of white waves, / [Her] brave brows lightening through the grey wet air" as she lifts up her "head republican" (2:17–18). Tropes of vision and images of a storm at sea similarly abound in "The Litany of Nations," where England prays to mother Earth to show the way to "the beacon-bright Republic far-off sighted" (2:69).

Facing off against the calls for revolutionary disorder, "The Deutschland" directly opposes the political and religious ends of Swinburne's contemporaneous poetry, at the same time abounding in Swinburnean echoes. Elisabeth W. Schneider has argued convincingly that Swinburne's metrical experiments provide "one of the mainsprings" of its sprung rhythm.[53] The ode's distinctive irregular form, a version of which Milton had used in the Hymn of the "Nativity Ode," had been reintroduced into English poetry by Swinburne in three odes published between 1866 and 1871, each of which involves themes specific to "The Deutschland": exile, martyrdom, and a cosmic event in which all nature is implicated.[54] The text is marked by images that can also be found prominently in Swinburne, above all of the chaotic sea, as well as by individual words and phrases. For example, the two poets play in similar ways on the meanings of the same words, "make" and "unmake," "utter," "master," and "thing."[55] In "The Deutschland," however, Hopkins's verbal echoes, rather than being directly parodic as in the Marian poems, are fragmentary, compressed, scattered. Some of the material that undergoes transformation had become part of general Victorian discourse—very few among the educated public would have failed to recognize that as winter leaves it is pursued by the hounds of spring—and perhaps the clusters of images and words had come unbidden in some cases. Nevertheless, the sheer number of embedded verbal fragments argues for a degree of intentionality.[56]

That "The Deutschland" repeats the distinctive content of Swinburne's providential political plots is more easily apparent. Like Hopkins's ode, they link natural disaster, visionary experience, martyrdom, and call for national conversion. In his major 1870 political poems, *A Song of Italy* and *Ode on the Proclamation of the French Republic*, for example, Swinburne represents humanity as held in bondage by a repressive government allied to the Roman Catholic Church. People and poet call upon the controlling force of the universe to make itself known and to bring about a release from oppression. Through tropes of vision, Swinburne represents the call as answered by the appearance of a giant body, often seen rising out of a destructively stormy sea, which is identified through a series of epithets as "Freedom," "Love," "Justice," "Republic universal." It is this protean figure that England fails to perceive on "The Eve of Revolution," and it is this figure that is to replace the Christian god who fails to appear in the "Hymn of Man." A figure that relates specifically to current religious politics occurs in the "Epilogue" to *Songs Before Sunrise*, which republican visionaries like the "Master" Mazzini can perceive for it appears "[b]etween the wave-ridge and the strand" (*Poems*, 2:226). It is identified as the "many-sided soul of man," personified as a "naked God / That treads on burning hours unshod." As well, the visionary leaders can foresee the republican future: "From wreck to wreck as the world swings ... / Know but that men there are who see / And hear things other far than we," among them a Rome free from the cruelties of "miscrowned" kings and popes. The rest of humanity, however, cannot "hear or see / The sounds and lights of liberty," but can "trace only where he trod / By fire in heaven or storm at sea," that is, can recognize the presence of divine mankind only through signs of disastrous natural events (*Poems*, 2:232–33).

Readers of Hopkins's narrative might discern visible traces of Swinburne's texts in the plot, images, and language. Swinburne memorializes the redemptive deaths of revolutionaries whose martyrdom to the cause of Freedom may inspire entire nations to follow them. Hopkins memorializes martyred nuns exiled by a repressive government that is the enemy, rather than the agent, of Roman Catholicism. It is a Roman Catholic nun, not a revolutionary leader or republican poet, who perceives a godlike figure rising from the sea. And Hopkins reverses Swinburne's repeated calls for the conversion of England to the cause of anticlerical revolution into a prayer for the conversion of England to the Roman Catholic Church.

In the central narrative section of "The Deutschland" the ship's passengers undergo a literal "Watch in the Night" through an exceptionally heavy storm, during which the "tall nun" (*Poetical*, no. 101, line 151) cries out: "Sister, a sister calling / A master, her master and mine!" (lines 145–46); she "Was calling 'O Christ, Christ, come quickly'" (line 191). "[W]hat did she mean?" the poet asks (193).[57] The effort to determine the meaning of the nun's words is a central action in the poem. Like Swinburne's republican visionaries, she has seen something that the rest of humanity cannot discern, and it is in vain that the poet asks the reader's participation in her direct apprehension: "Strike you the sight of it? look at it loom there, / Thing that she . . ." [ellipsis in original] (lines 219–20). Further, the stuttering verbal crisis of stanza 28 signals the inability of the poet's language to fully "utter" the veiled epiphanic experience, that is, "to read the nun's reading."[58]

The call of the nun has been answered by "Christ," risen from the stormy sea, "the uttermost mark / Our passion-plungèd giant risen, / The Christ of the Father compassionate, fetched in the storm of his strides" (lines 262–64). The figure that has appeared out of the deadly night is not represented visually beyond the words "giant risen." In the background, however, it may be possible to perceive, albeit dimly, the protean personifications that have repeatedly risen from Swinburne's seas, and Hopkins's language may make it possible to glimpse, further back, an even dimmer figure. Swinburne's giant "Freedom" is a politicized version of the goddess Venus: Freedom "Rose, as from the sacred seas / Love," "A woman like to love in face, but not / A thing of transient lot" (*Poems*, 2:249, 253). Earlier, the goddess of love herself had risen in a famous passage in *Atalanta in Calydon* as the chorus cried out that, because of the human disruption she creates, Venus's birth should have been accompanied by tumultuous storm: "under thee newly arisen / Loud shoals and shipwrecking reefs"; "All these we know of; but thee / Who shall discern or declare? / In the uttermost ends of the sea / The light of thine eyelids and hair" (*Poems*, 4:276–77). In "The Deutschland" one person can in fact "discern and declare / In the uttermost ends of the sea" a figure rising from the sea, but it is not that of Venus, pagan goddess of love, as Swinburne had it. The nun, "at our door / Drowned, and among our shoals," (lines 273–74) discerns rather the Christian God of love, for in Hopkins's ode it is Christ Himself who is "the uttermost mark, / Our passion-plungèd giant risen" (lines 262–63).

The taunted Christian God of the "Hymn of Man," who was silent and unresponsive to the cries of suffering peoples, appears in answer to an anguished cry that evidences further traces of Swinburne's presence. Hopkins's nun "Was calling 'O Christ, Christ, come quickly': / The cross to her she calls Christ to her, christens her wild-worst Best" (lines 191–92). In *Ode on the Proclamation of the French Republic* (1871), Swinburne assures France that in her "wild-worst hour" the country still has the power to be "free" (*Poems*, 2:290). In Hopkins's ode, "wild-worst" is conjoined with a powerful image found in "Hesperia": "As the cross that a wild nun clasps till the edge of it bruises her bosom, / So love wounds as we grasp it" (*Poems*, 1:175). Swinburne's speaker suffers the cruelty of "Hesperia's" controlling deity, the goddess Venus, without hope of any easing of love's wounds: the poem "involves a denial, not an affirmation, of consolatory divinities, either transcendent or immanent."[59] Hopkins has not banished Swinburne's erotic imagery from "The Deutschland," as he had in the Marian poems. Rather, the object of passionate desire transforms from a human lover into a divine one; the emotion becomes caritas, not eros. In her own "wild-worst" hour the nun re- "christens" Swinburne's phrase and image to declare that she does discern the consolatory presence of the Christian God of love, the "uttermost mark" that supplants the love goddess at the "uttermost ends of the sea." Further, the nun affirms not the power of revolutionary freedom but the joyous freedom of a faithful Christian who acknowledges the presence of her "master." "Venus," "Freedom," the "soul of man," are replaced by "Christ," the God made man, God of Christian love and of Christian freedom.[60]

Absorbing Swinburne's naming sequences, Hopkins strives to further identify the figure through a series of epithets: "There then! the Master, / Ipse, the only one, Christ, King, Head" (lines 220–21); "Pride, rose, prince, hero of us, high-priest" (line 279). The technique of the naming sequence repeats only the method, not the substance, of the multitudinous aspects of the controlling forces in Swinburne's earthbound universe, where "Freedom," "Love," "Justice," "Republic universal" mutate each into the other in the world's ever-changing flux.[61] For in Hopkins's cosmos, Christ the Incarnate Word steadies and controls, and the names through which Hopkins declares Him reflect the eternally stable reality of the Logos. Here, man is not the "master of things" as he was in the "Hymn of Man," nor is Mazzini the "Master," as he was in the "Epilogue." It is Christ who is the controlling force of the universe, "mastering" (line 1) the speaker in "The Deutschland" and "Master" over "things." And in the complete identification of the divinity with the natural world, He Himself, Ipse, is the "Thing." The ode ends with a "cry of triumph," as had Swinburne's "Hymn of Man." In the final exultant lines language regains its power to praise that Incarnate presence, if not fully to discern and declare: He is "Our hearts' charity's hearth's fire, our thoughts' chivalry's throng's Lord" (line 280). And, again, Hopkins has recourse to Swinburnean usages, for the "mannered string of possessives" that concludes the ode "may have been suggested by" Swinburne's line in "Blessed Among Women" "The world's heart's thanksgivings."[62]

In Swinburne's political volumes, the imagery of natural disaster represents the disorder necessary to bring about redemptive, human-centered revolution. The godlike people of many nations, inspired by the heroic martyrs of revolutionary republicanism, march forward toward an international order united under the banner of the religion of humanity. It is the all-important duty of the visionary poet to work for the conversion of his nation, so that England can open her eyes to perceive the reality of Freedom and join the march to the future. Like Swinburne, Hopkins works for the conversion of the entire nation, praying at the end of "The Deutschland": "Our king back. Oh, upon English souls! / ...More brightening her, rare-dear Britain, as his reign rolls" (276–78).[63] In Hopkins's providential national narrative, the people of England will unite under the authority of the universal Roman Catholic Church, dedicated to the reality of Christ's redemptive sacrifice. Disasters such as the wreck of the Deutschland must be seen as evidence of God's redemptive grace. Notably, apocalyptic language and imagery pervade both "The Deutschland" and Swinburne's political poetry.[64] However, there is a fundamental difference in the poets' conceptions of the trajectory of human history. For Hopkins, time will end with the Second Coming of Christ, the light of the world, and after the Last Judgement the "political justice" of God's timeless kingdom will be established.[65] In contrast, for the Swinburne of *Poems and Ballads*, first series, history is continual flux, the world subject to meaningless change without an end. In *Songs Before Sunrise*, however, as the volume's title suggests, Swinburne has developed a degree of faith in the possibility of a new political daybreak for mankind within time, to be reached, not through divine intervention, but through the willing deaths of human heroes.[66]

"The Deutschland" carries considerable political significance. Like the Marian poems, it touches on the much-disputed doctrine of the Immaculate Conception: the disaster occurs the night before the "Feast of the one woman without stain" (line 237). "The Deutschland's" call for the country's conversion to Roman Catholicism returns to an issue that had long roiled religious politics in England. And in his representation of Christ's miraculous appearance within the natural world, whether as an apparition or in the flesh, Hopkins may be treading on politically sensitive ground by touching on the issue of the Church's temporal power. The visible church militant is traditionally represented figuratively as the body of Christ; as G. H. Joyce explained, the "claims" of that aspect of the church (of which the pope had just been affirmed "visible head") must "be authenticated in a manner evident to all; in other words [the Church] must be visible, not merely as other public societies are visible, but as being the society of the Son of God," recognizable by those who do not suffer "spiritual blindness." The "prophetess" (line 136) nun does not suffer spiritual blindness: although the "brine / Blinds her," she "sees one thing, one" (lines 148–49); "There was single eye! / Read the unshapeable shock night / And knew the who and the why" (lines 226–28). The nun discerns the body of Christ as he has miraculously risen from England's stormy waters. A "high-priest,"[67] a "prince," a "King," he comes "royally reclaiming his own" (line 271), with more than a hint that he claims a temporal domain as well as a spiritual one.

It is Hopkins's belief that the vision of the martyred nun may well open the eyes of the people of England and inspire them to return to the fold of the Roman Catholic Church: her death may "Startle the poor sheep back!" (line 248). Hopkins attempts to address spiritual blindness directly, as Swinburne had in his exhortations to England to open her eyes to Freedom, by inviting English readers of "The Deutschland" to share the nun's vision, to "see," to "read," as well: "strike you sight of it? ...look at it loom there." Christ's body is visible to the nun and, through his belief in the miraculous nature of the event, to the poet, and he seems to say that if the poem is read with the eyes of faith (as the snowflakes in stanza 21 are to be) the vision, in all its significance, will also be unveiled within the text. The visionary poet and the visionary nun, together, may effect English conversions.

"The Deutschland" can be read, then, as an effort to convert its readers so that they, too, can see the reality of the nun's vision. Further, the entreaty to God to bring "our King back, oh, upon English souls!" can be read as a reference to the restoration of both the spiritual and the temporal power of the Roman Catholic Church; that is, as a hint that the Church is once again to reign over both the "souls" and the soil of England in fulfillment of God's providential plan. "The Deutschland" rewrites both Swinburne and England's Protestant providential narrative.

"The Wreck of the Deutschland" was not published in its entirety for forty years. Writing to Robert Bridges, Hopkins conceded that the poem "needs study and is obscure, for indeed I was not over-desirous that the meaning of all should be quite clear, at least unmistakeable" (*Letters to Bridges*, 50). The fact that its language contains "a great many . . . oddnesses" is certainly one reason that the Jesuit periodical *The Month* rejected it for publication. But the language of Hopkins's further explanation to Canon Dixon—that "when I offered it to our magazine . . . though at first they accepted it, after a time they withdrew and dared not print it" (*Correspondence*, 15)—itself needs explanation. Another reason "they dared not print it" could be the uncomfortable argument concealed in the thickets of its language. As John Henry Newman had considered the Vatican's promulgation of papal infallibility as "inopportune," so, too, might the Jesuit editors of *The Month* in regard to Hopkins's ode. In Gladstone's words, Jesuits, "the deadliest foes that mental and moral liberty have ever known," are heavily implicated in the Church's "daring raid upon the civil sphere," which "must be for some political object, of a very tangible kind."[68] In any event, Hopkins did not try to find another publisher, and by the time Robert Bridges's first edition of the poems appeared in 1918 the original context had been lost, not that it would have been of much interest to the New Critics, for whom Hopkins became a proto-Modernist.

Hopkins constructed a "serviceable" poetic by transmuting Swinburne's texts to the uses of Roman Catholicism. Both poets attempted to affect the formation of English national identity by constructing alternative internationalist providential narratives, prompted by, and incorporating, issues of religious politics that roiled nineteenth-century Englishmen. That they failed—that, in fact, the political contexts of their poems have largely been lost—does not negate the recognition of their belief in the power of poetry to change the world.

NOTES

1. David Hempton, *Religion and Political Culture in Britain and Ireland: From the Glorious Revolution to the Decline of Empire* (Cambridge: Cambridge University Press, 1996); Peter Bingham Hinchcliff, *God and History: Aspects of*

   British Theology, 1875–1914 (Oxford: Clarendon Press, 1992); Linda Colley,
   Britons: Forging the Nation 1707–1837 (New Haven: Yale University Press,
   1992).

2. Hinchcliff, *God and History*, 18. Gauri Viswanathan argues that "conversion is
   arguably one of the most unsettling political events in the life of a society," its
   rejection of national definitions posing a "radical threat," as in the case of John
   Henry Newman, whose conversion to Catholicism she sees as "an expression
   of political resistance to English secular nationalism" (*Outside the Fold:
   Conversion, Modernity, and Belief* [New Jersey: Princeton University Press,
   1998], xi, 16, xvii). Newman brought Hopkins into the Church, and political
   resistance could have been a factor in Hopkins's conversion as well.

3. Josef L. Altholz, "The Vatican Decrees Controversy, 1874–1875," *Catholic
   Historical Review* 57 (1971–72): 596; D. G. Paz, *Popular Anti-Catholicism in
   Mid-Victorian England* (California: Stanford University Press, 1992), 49–70.
   Controversy over the "elaborate ritual and vestments adopted in some anglo
   catholic or high church parishes [which] were associated with Rome and
   regarded by some as an insult to the Protestantism of the nation" culminated
   in the 1874 Parliamentary debate between Gladstone and Disraeli and the
   passage of the Public Worship Regulation Bill, a defeat for the High Church
   party ("Ritualism: *Hansard's Parliamentary Debates*," *Religion in Victorian
   Britain*, ed. Gerald Parson, vol. 3. [Manchester: Manchester University Press,
   1988], 301).

4. See Walter L. Arnstein, "The Murphy Riots: A Victorian Dilemma," *Victorian
   Studies* 19 (1975): 51–71.

5. For the effects of Roman Catholic religious politics within the context of
   English anti-Catholicism, see Altholz, "Vatican"; Arnstein's "Murphy," and
   *Protestant versus Catholic in Mid-Victorian England: Mr. Newdegate and the
   Nuns* (Columbia: University of Missouri Press, 1982); G. F. A. Best, "Popular
   Protestantism in Victorian Britain," in *Ideas and Institutions of Victorian
   Britain: Essays in Honour of George Kitson Clark*, ed. Robert Robson (New
   York: Barnes, 1967), 115–42; Matthias Buschkühl, *Great Britain and the Holy
   See, 1746–1870* (Dublin: Irish Academic Press, 1982), 126–70; Eamon Duffy,
   Saints and Sinners: A History of the Popes (New Haven: Yale University Press,
   1997), 221–35; E. R. Norman, "Introduction," in *Anti-Catholicism in
   Victorian England* (New York: Barnes, 1968), 13–104; Paz, *Anti-Catholicism*;
   and Dermot Quinn, *Patronage and Piety: The Politics of English Roman
   Catholicism, 1850–1900* (California: Stanford University Press, 1993).

6. Politics were also frequently the subject of Swinburne's private letters to
   friends. He limited his political participation to the written word, declining a
   Reform League request in 1868 to stand for Parliament (Rikky Rooksby, *A. C.
   Swinburne: A Poet's Life* [Aldershot: Scolar Press, 1997], 165).

7. *The Poetical Works of Gerard Manley Hopkins*, ed. Norman H. MacKenzie
   (Oxford: Clarendon Press, 1990), no. 175, lines 11–12; *Further Letters of
   Gerard Manley Hopkins Including His Correspondence with Coventry Patmore*,
   ed. Claude Colleer Abbott, 2nd ed. (London: Oxford University Press, 1970),
   155–58; Gerald Roberts, " 'England's Fame's Fond Lover'—the Toryism of
   Gerard Manly [*sic*] Hopkins," *Studies: An Irish Quarterly Review* 69 (1980):
   129–36.

8. Qtd. in Gerald C. Monsman, "Pater, Hopkins, and Fichte's Ideal Student,"
   South Atlantic Quarterly 70 (1971): 368.

9. Martin E. Geldart [Nitram Tradleg], *A Son of Belial: Autobiographical Sketches*, 1882 (Ann Arbor: UMI, 1990), 167–68. For Hopkins's Oxford career, see Daniel Brown, *Hopkins' Idealism: Philosophy, Physics, Poetry* (Oxford: Clarendon Press, 1997); Geldart, *Son of Belial*; Robert Bernard Martin, *Gerard Manley Hopkins: A Very Private Life* (New York: Putnam's, 1991), 23–170; Gerald C. Monsman, "Old Mortality at Oxford," *Studies in Philology* 67 (1970): 359–89, and "Pater"; Renée Value Overholser, *Hopkins's Conversions: The Case of A. C. Swinburne* (Ann Arbor, Michigan: University Microfilms, 1996); Alison G. Sulloway, *Gerard Manley Hopkins and the Victorian Temper* (New York: Columbia University Press, 1972), 9–63; Norman White, *Hopkins: A Literary Biography* (Oxford: Clarendon, 1992), 3–161; Tom Zaniello, *Hopkins in the Age of Darwin* (Iowa City: University of Iowa Press, 1988), 11–59. For Swinburne, see Georges Lafourcade, *La Jeunesse de Swinburne*, 2 vols. (Paris, 1928); Rooksby, *Swinburne*, 45–63. Lafourcade, *reunesse* 2:218–20, reprints Swinburne's essay attacking Ultramontanism, "Church Imperialism," originally published in 1858 in the Old Mortality organ, *Undergraduate Papers*.

10. Hopkins's references to Swinburne are guarded, cast most often as discussions of style rather than substance. Perhaps disingenuously in the context of the present essay, Hopkins writes that Swinburne's poetry is "a perpetual functioning of genius without truth, feeling, or any adequate matter to be at function on" (*The Letters of Gerard Manley Hopkins to Robert Bridges*, ed. Claude Colleer Abbott, 2nd ed. (London: Oxford University Press, 1970), 304.

11. *The Correspondence of Gerard Manley Hopkins and Richard Watson Dixon*, ed. Claude Colleer Abbott, 2nd ed. (London: Oxford University Press, 1956), 135–36.

12. Hopkins made clear his belief in the efficacy of poetry in promoting political ends in a congratulatory letter to Coventry Patmore in 1886: Patmore's poems "are a good deed done for the Catholic Church and another for England, for the British Empire" (*Further Letters*, 366).

13. The two Latin Marian poems are "Ad Matrem Virginem" (*Poetical*, no. 91) and "O praedestinata bis" (no. 93). See *Poetical*, 301–04.

14. Marina Warner, *Alone of All Her Sex: The Myth and the Cult of the Virgin Mary* (New York: Knopf, 1976), 236–64; Jaroslav Pelikan, "The Woman Clothed with the Sun"; "The Great Exception, Immaculately Conceived," in *Mary Through the Centuries: Her Place in the History of Culture* (New Haven: Yale University Press, 1996), 177–200.

15. Barbara Corrado Pope, "Immaculate and Powerful: The Marian Revival in the Nineteenth Century," in *Immaculate and Powerful: The Female in Sacred Image and Social Reality*, ed. Clarissa W. Atkinson, Constance H. Buchanan, and Margaret R. Miles (Boston: Beacon Press, 1985), 181.

16. Pope, "Immaculate," 190. The Virgin's main nineteenth-century appearances in France occurred at La Salette (1846), Lourdes (1858), and Pontmain (1871). See Hilda C. Graef, *Mary: A History of Doctrine and Devotion*, vol. 2 (New York: Sheed and Ward, 1965), 83–118; Pelikan, "The Woman."

17. Graef, *Mary*, 97; John Kent, "A Renovation of Images: Nineteenth-Century Protestant 'Lives of Jesus' and Roman Catholic Alleged Appearances of the Blessed Virgin Mary," in *The Critical Spirit and the Will to Believe: Essays in Nineteenth-Century Literature and Religion*, ed. David Jasper and T. R. Wright (New York: St. Martin's Press, 1989), 38; Pope, "Immaculate," 188.

18. John Singleton, "The Virgin Mary and Religious Conflict in Victorian Britain," *JEH* 43 (1992), 34.

19. *The Sermons and Devotional Writings of Gerard Manley Hopkins* ed. Christopher Devlin (London: Oxford University Press, 1959), 43–46.

20. Algernon Charles Swinburne, *The Collected Poems of Algernon Charles Swinburne*, 6 vols. (London: Chatto and Windus, 1905), 4:287.

21. The majority of the poems were written in direct response to political events. Publication of *Songs Before Sunrise* was delayed by its publisher's nervous reaction to the more blasphemous examples, a delay that threatened to make the book irrelevant: William Rossetti commented in August 1870, "it is only last night that Gabriel [Rossetti] happened to say how disastrous it is that just now—when anything of an excited political tone from you on foreign politics would ring through England and Europe—the book would be shelved" (qtd. in Rooksby, *Swinburne*, 183). As Rooksby remarks, "events on the Continent were to overtake the poems."

22. Swinburne's polemic is close to the language of the Evangelical press a decade or two earlier. In 1850 the *Kentish Observer* warned of the dangers presented by the influx into England of Irish Catholics, whom "Mr. Mastai Ferretti [Pope Pius IX] is now marshalling for the subversion of our Protestant institutions . . . and substitution of the old Roman worship of that Venus Astarte, blasphemously designated as the Virgin Mother of our Lord, of whom he claims to be the High Priest and Supreme Pontiff, by grant of the last Emperors, for the pure and Christian worship of our Apostolic Church" (qtd. in Paz, *Anti-Catholicism*, 49). A poem, "The Misconception as to the Immaculate Conception of the Virgin Mary," was published in *The Bulwark* in 1854–55 (Singleton, "Virgin Mary," 26).

23. Some of Hopkins's early editors experienced considerable uneasiness with "Ad Mariam." It was not included in Robert Bridges's 1918 edition of the poems, and Claude Colleer Abbott termed the attribution "incredible" until convinced by the discovery of a manuscript copy (*Letters to Bridges*, xvii). See *Poetical*, 305.

24. Marina Warner, *Alone of All Her Sex: The Myth and the Cult of the Virgin Mary* (New York: Knopf, 1976), 266–68.

25. Jerome Bump, "Hopkins' Imagery and Medievalist Poetics," *Victorian Poetry* 15 (1977): 108–09.

26. In "Dolores" the rose is red. Bump comments that Swinburne "attempted to revive the original legend of the rose which was white until Venus, hastening to the relief of Adonis, pierced her foot on a thorn and bloodied the flower" ("Hopkins' Imagery," 114, n. 29). In Hopkins's "Rosa Mystica" the rose is "White to begin with, immaculate white" (line 32); the color changed with the Crucifixion, "when the rose ran in crimsonings down the cross-wood!" (line 34).

27. For accounts of the Council, see Buschkühl, *Great Britain*; Duffy, *Saints*; K. Kirch, "Vatican Council," *The Catholic Encyclopedia*, 1912, on-line edition, 1999, August 8, 1999, <http://www.newadvent.org/ cathen/15303 a.htm>.

28. *Decrees of the First Vatican Council*, ed. Norman Tanner, August 16, 1999, 17, <http://abbey.apana.org.au/councils/ ecum20.htm>.

29. G. H. Joyce, "The Church," *The Catholic Encyclopedia*, 1908, on-line edition, 1999, August 6, 1999, 18, 27, <http://www.newadvent.org/ cathen/03744a.htm>.

30. Ibid., 22–23.

31. *Syllabus of Pius IX*, 1862, August 15, 1999, 4, 6, <http://listserv.american.edu/catholic/church/papal/piusix/p9syll.html>.

32. Henry Edward Manning, "Archbishop Manning on the Temporal Power," *The Temporal Power of the Pope in Its Political Aspect. Anti-Catholicism in Victorian England*, ed. E. R. Norman, 1866 (New York: Barnes, 1968), 189.

33. Altholz, "Vatican," 598.

34. Quinn, *Patronage*, 5. The movement had begun earlier. In 1838, for example, a Crusade of Prayer was launched among both foreign and British Catholics for the conversion of England (Sheridan Gilley, "Roman Catholicism," *Nineteenth-Century English Religious Traditions: Retrospect and Prospect*, ed. D. G. Paz [Westport, Connecticut: Greenwood Press, 1995], 46–47). Beginning about 1845 individual conversions resulted in "a considerable influx of educated men and women into the Roman Catholic Church," among them "450 Anglican clergy" and "over seventy peers and peeresses" (Gilley, "Roman Catholicism," 45).

35. Harry W. Rudman, *Italian Nationalism and English Letters: Figures of the Risorgimento and Victorian Men of Letters* (New York: Columbia University Press, 1940), 414–32.

36. William Gladstone, "The Vatican Decrees in their Bearing on Civil Allegiance: A Political Expostulation," in *Newman and Gladstone: The Vatican Decrees*, ed. Alvan S. Ryan (Notre Dame, Indiana: University of Notre Dame Press, 1962), 46, 48.

37. Qtd. in Gerard Manley Hopkins, *The Journals and Papers of Gerard Manley Hopkins*, ed. Humphry House and Graham Storey (London: Oxford University Press, 1959), 442.

38. "Jesuits," *The Encyclopaedia Britannica*, 9th ed.

39. Zaniello, *Hopkins*, 86; *Journals*, 262. Hopkins remarks, "Many good answers appeared and were read in the refectory," including a "dignified" reply by Dr. Manning, which was however one of "the least interesting." Gladstone had attacked directly Manning's statements on Temporal Power. Dr. Newman's reply, *A Letter Addressed to His Grace the Duke of Norfolk on the Occasion of Mr. Gladstone's Recent Expostulation*, "we read in recreation." Newman argued that Gladstone had been "misled in his interpretation of the ecclesiastical acts of 1870 by judging the wording by the rules of ordinary language," which lacked the precision of theological language (qtd. in Norman, *Anti-Catholicism*, 101). Earlier, Hopkins had listed "some events from the end of '69," including the opening of the Vatican Council, "Definition of the Infallibility," and details of the capture of Rome, and quoted the Italian Minister of Foreign Affairs on "The obligation of not attacking the frontiers" of the Papal States (*Journals*, 202–03).

40. Qtd. in Zaniello, *Hopkins*, 86.

41. Evangelical Protestant millenarians of the dominant "continuous historical" school read the Apocalypse of St. John as parallel to and signifying Western history from the birth of Christ until the end of time (Mary Wilson Carpenter, "George Eliot and the School of the Prophets," *George Eliot and the Landscape of Time: Narrative Form and Protestant Apocalyptic History* [Chapel Hill: University of North Carolina Press, 1986], 3–4), and identified papal Rome with St. John's Antichrist, the "reign of the beast." In contrast, the "futurists " associated with Roman Catholicism and, specifically, with the

Jesuits, "interpreted Antichrist as a power to appear in the future rather than as the pope" (Carpenter, *George Eloit*, 8, 22). Sulloway comments, "As a young man at Oxford, Hopkins himself was almost deafened by the prophetic cacophony. . . . The nineteenth-century Jesuits' predictions of doom for heretical England were as vehement as the Tractarians' or the Fundamentalist Dissenters'" (*Gerard Manley Hopkins*, 169). All groups would have read the revolutions supported by Swinburne as engines of divine retribution and signals that the end-times were coming.

42. Carpenter, *George Eliot*, 14.

43. *Sermons*, 40. In 1881 Hopkins wrote Robert Bridges that he anticipated that a supernatural sign evidencing England's preparation for the Second Coming might occur on December 1. The date marked the three hundred and thirtieth anniversary of the martyrdom of the Jesuit Edmund Campion, "from which I expect of heaven, some I cannot guess what, great conversion or other blessing to the Church in England" (*Letters to Bridges*, 135–36).

44. The aurora could have held further meaning for Hopkins. As a knowledgeable observer of natural phenomena (see Zaniello, *Hopkins*), he would have known that the magnetic disturbances associated with northern lights indicated cosmic electrical activity, further possible proof of the divine presence in nature: as he would later write, "The world is charged with the grandeur of God" (*Poetical*, no. 111, line 1).

45. Sean Street, *The Wreck of the Deutschland* (London: Souvenir Press, 1992), 11–34.

46. Germany figured prominently in England's national narrative. The development of Anglo-Saxon concepts of freedom was traced back to the German primeval forests (Hinchcliff, *God and History*, 14), and Bismarck was seen "as the defender both of Protestantism and of national liberty against a subversive church seeking to establish political and spiritual despotism. The affinity between the England of 'civil and religious liberty,' the Italy of the *Risorgimento*, and the Germany of the *Kulturkampf* was fixed in the public mind" (*Altholz*, "Vatican," 595). Frequent parallels were drawn between Gladstone and Bismarck, with approval by much of the English Protestant press, with understandable disapproval by the pope (Norman, "Introduction," 97). Nixon suggests a British source for Bismarck's nation-building: "Carlyle's adulation of Prussia and inflation of its greatness in *Frederick the Great* (1858–65; and translated into German) must have inspired Bismarck's German unification wars (1860–62) to forge the new German Republic (1871), declaring himself its first Chancellor" (Jude V. Nixon, " 'Return Alphias': The Forster/Carlyle Unpublished Letters and Re-tailoring the Sage," *Carlyle Studies Annual* 18 [1998], 116). I am indebted to Jude V. Nixon for this and other insights.

47. Qtd. in Street, *Wreck*, 177.

48. Elisabeth W. Schneider, *The Dragon in the Gate: Studies in the Poetry of G. M. Hopkins* (Berkeley: University of California Press, 1968), 84.

49. "Time's Andromeda" is "normally identified with the church on earth," Perseus with Christ (*Poetical*, 414, n. 4). The Perseus figure "evokes also St. George protecting his distressed Britannia" (Paul Mariani, *A Commentary on the Complete Poems of Gerard Manley Hopkins* [Ithaca: Cornell University Press, 1970], 154) from the "wilder beast from the West" (line 7), which W. H. Gardner identifies as representing the forces of "rationalism, Darwinism,

[and] the new paganism of Swinburne and Whitman" (qtd. in Mariani, *Commentary*, 152). Mariani adds to the list of "wilder" forces "utilitarianism, liberalism, Irish nationalism, Gladstone, and the general weakening of moral fiber among his own countrymen, [which] were constant sources of worry in Hopkins' letters" (152–53). In a later article Mariani identifies the "lewd" beast with "the complex demon of sexual anarchy," specifically the homosexuality associated with Whitman and Swinburne ("The New Aestheticism: A Reading of 'Andromeda,'" *A Usable Past: Essays on Modern and Contemporary Poetry* [Amherst: University of Massachusetts Press, 1984], 121).

50. Jerome J. McGann, *Swinburne: An Experiment in Criticism* (Chicago: University of Chicago Press, 1972), 240–43. Margot K. Louis reads *Songs Before Sunrise* as Swinburne's earliest attempts to answer the questions, "What symbolic system can adequately present the People, their suffering and their self-regeneration" and "replace the Christian myth of sacrifice and redemption? Above all, what can replace that mode of religious parody which has hitherto been central to Swinburne's art?" (*Swinburne and His Gods: The Roots and Growth of an Agnostic Poetry* [Montreal: McGill-Queen's University Press, 1990], 98). Swinburne's new method involves, in part, the development of a secular political typology, which reinterprets the Christian model, making, for example, "England, Italy, Garibaldi, or the people take the place of Christ" (George P. Landow, *Victorian Types, Victorian Shadows: Biblical Typology in Victorian Literature, Art and Thought* [Boston: Routledge, 1980], 154). For Rooksby, the volume constitutes "Swinburne's republican book of common prayer" (*Swinburne*, 184).

51. Rooksby, *Swinburne*, 171–72. Just before starting the "Hymn of Man," Swinburne might have read a translation of the Canones de Ecclesia, based on the 1864 *Syllabus of Errors*, which was published in the *Times* on February 10, 1870 (Louis, *Swinburne and His Gods*, 100).

52. Algernon Charles Swinburne, *The Swinburne Letters*, ed. Cecil Y. Lang, 6 vols. (New Haven: Yale University Press, 1959), 2:37.

53. Schneider, *Dragon*, 51–57.

54. Raymond Dexter Havens, *The Influence of Milton on English Poetry*, 1922 (New York: Russell & Russell, 1961), 684; Schneider, *Dragon*, 80. "To Victor Hugo" (*Poems*, 1:144–50) celebrates the French poet's self-exile, contrasting his move toward freedom favorably with Christ's slave-like death. "Blessed Among Women: To the Signora Cairoli" (*Poems*, 2:56–63) memorializes two of the Cairoli sons who died fighting with Mazzini against papal forces at Rome in 1867 (Arrigo Solmi, *The Making of Modern Italy* [Port Washington, New York: Kennikat Press, 1970], 126); through Marian language their birth is equated with the birth of Christ, their mother with the Virgin. "Ode on the Insurrection in Candia" (200–08) mourns, through the figure of Freedom, the deaths of heroes who died for Greece during an uprising in 1867.

55. Hopkins is renowned for the use of etymological word play, but Swinburne "works" a word in much the same way, that is, by "manipulating its different meanings, teasing it for complex suggestions and nuances" (McGann, *Beauty*, 249). Other critics have found scattered verbal and stylistic reminiscences, as well as more fundamental similarities. For a range of critical opinion on similarities and differences between the poets, see Isobel Armstrong,

"Swinburne: Agonistic Republican"; "Hopkins: Agonistic Reactionary," in *Victorian Poetry: Poetry, Poetics and Politics*, ed. Isobel Armstrong (New York: Routledge, 1993), 402–39; William E. Buckler, "The Poetry of Swinburne: An Essay in Critical Reenforcement," in *The Victorian Imagination: Essays in Aesthetic Exploration*, ed. William E. Buckler (New York: New York University Press, 1980), 227–59; Bump, "Hopkins' Imagen,"; Mariani, "New Aestheticism"; Thaïs Morgan, "Violence, Creativity, and the Feminine: Poetics and Gender Politics in Swinburne and Hopkins," in *Gender and Discourse in Victorian Literature and Art*, ed. Antony H. Harrison and Beverly Taylor (DeKalb: Northern Illinois University Press, 1992), 84–107; Overholser, *Hopkins's Conversions*; John Rosenberg, ed. "Introduction," *Swinburne: Selected Poetry and Prose* (New York: Random, 1968), vi–ix; Schneider, *Dragon*, 48–62; Robert C. Schweik, "Swinburne, Hopkins, and the Roots of Modernism," *University of Hartford Studies in Literature* 11 (1979): 157–72.

56. Father O. R. Vassall-Phillips, who served with Hopkins as a priest at St. Aloysius, Oxford, wrote: "It used to be said of [Hopkins] that he expressed surprise at not being allowed to keep by him Swinburne's *Poems and Ballads* whilst he was in the novitiate at Manresa" (*After Fifty Years* [New York: Benziger Brothers, 1928], 81). The story suggests that Hopkins intended to reply to Swinburne's poetry from the outset of his religious career.

57. Armstrong stresses the complexity of the question: it "means not only what did she mean or intend, to what was she referring, but what is the meaning of the nun's cry, *how* does she mean?" ("Swinburne," 435). MacKenzie summarizes the widely divergent opinion on the nature and meaning of the nun's vision (*Poetical*, 343–44). See also Hilda Hollis, "Advice Not Taken: Attacking Hopkins' Dragon Through Stanza Sixteen," *Victorian Poetry* 36 (1998): 47–57. The nun's cry echoes Christ's announcement in Revelation 22.7, "Behold, I come quickly." Jacques Derrida uses Revelation's repetition of the word "come" as exemplary of the indeterminacy of apocalyptic language: " 'Come' . . . addresses without message, without destination, without sender or decidable addressee, without last judgment, without any other eschatology than the tone of the 'Come' " ("On a Newly Arisen Apocalyptic Tone in Philosophy," *Raising the Tone of Philosophy: Late Essays by Immanuel Kant, Transformative Critique by Jacques Derrida*, ed. Peter Fenves [Baltimore: Johns Hopkins University Press, 1993], 167).

58. Armstrong, "Swinburne," 435.

59. David G. Riede, *Swinburne: A Study of Romantic Mythmaking* (Charlottesville: University Press of Virginia, 1978), 68.

60. In an 1886 letter to Coventry Patmore, Hopkins writes, " 'Freedom': it is perfectly true that British freedom is the best, the only successful freedom, but that is because, with whatever drawbacks, those who have developed that freedom have done so with the aid of law and obedience to law. The cry then shd. be Law and Freedom, Freedom and Law. But that does not please: it must be Freedom only." He adds, "Then there is civilisation. It shd. have been Catholic truth. That is the great end of Empires before God, to be Catholic and draw nations into their Catholicism" (*Further Letters*, 367).

61. Armstrong writes perceptively that for Hopkins, Swinburne's "language of flux would be inseparable from a politics of flux," that is, a "drift towards democracy . . . obliterating the uniqueness of individuals" ("Swinburne," 421).

62. Schneider, *Dragon*, 205, n. 8. Compare also Swinburne's vision of the "city perfect," "The hearth of man, the human home, / The central flame that shall be Rome" (*Poems*, 2:225).

63. The possibility of a national conversion, in this case of Wales, had been in Hopkins's mind a year before the Deutschland disaster: "my desire seemed to be for the conversion of Wales and I had it in my mind to give up everything else for that; nevertheless weighing this by St. Ignatius' rules of election I decided not to do so" (*Journals*, 258).

64. Sulloway, *Gerard Manley Hopkins*, 158–95.

65. Three sermons in Liverpool in 1880, intended to be on the "political justice of belonging to the Catholic Church" (68), give some insight into Hopkins's political philosophy, which remains unclear since the series was cut short by his rector. Christopher Devlin comments: "It seems that GMH had originally meant his trilogy to end in a demonstration that the Catholic Church *as an organized society* [emphasis in original] is the only possible successor to the lost kingdom of Paradise" (*Sermons*, 280, 68, n. 2).

66. Riede, *Swinburne*, 108–10. Swinburne wrote of his first meeting with Mazzini, "I know, now that I have seen him, what I guessed before, why, whenever he has said to anyone, 'Go and be killed because I tell you,' they have gone and been killed because he told them. Who wouldn't, I should like to know?" (*Letters*, 1:237). For Swinburne, as Louis explains, meaning is given to the "flowing years" through "the republic of love, in spontaneous political harmony between man and man." This will require a "spiritual and intellectual reformation . . . since political revolution should follow as a matter of course" (*Swinburne*, 104).

67. Christ was prefigured as "high-priest" in the order of Melchisedech, with "twofold dignity as priest and king" (John J. Tierney, "Melchisedech," *The Catholic Encyclopedia*, 1911, on-line edition, 1999, August 6, 1999, <http://www.newadvent.org/cathen/10156b.htm>).

68. Gladstone, "The Vatican Decrees," 46, 48.

PART II

RELIGION AND THE AESTHETIC IMAGINATION

CHAPTER 6

HEARING ADVENTURE: GIUSEPPE
CAPONSACCHI, BROWNING'S
"HOLLOW ROCK"

Joseph A. Dupras

The deep country of hearing, described in terms of geology more than in those of any other natural science, not only by virtue of the cartilaginous cavern that constitutes its organ, but also by virtue of the relationship that unites it to grottoes, to chasms, to all the pockets hollowed out of the terrestrial crust whose emptiness makes them into resonating drums for the slightest sounds.

—*Jacques Derrida,* "Tympan"

In Robert Browning's *The Ring and the Book*, Giuseppe Caponsacchi wants to share with silent auditors his perception of Pompilia's moral goodness and his grief from her murder. An impeachable legal and religious system underestimated the seriousness of her troubles and left her vulnerable to Guido Franceschini's villainy. Although the judges have much to learn about duty and charity from Caponsacchi's brief, transforming association with "the sad strange wife,"[1] the canon nevertheless feels guilty for not preventing the crime, which has further impaired his self-confidence and thus ruptured his ambitions as a man and as a priest. He has to retell his story because criminal circumstances and an aching conscience demand that he "help the august law" (line 108) while admitting his dishonor.

The preceding remarks merely echo what many others have written about leitmotifs in Browning's monologues, including those in *The Ring and the Book*: spiritual agonizing within and between speakers and auditors whom this dramatic genre enlists to mark what Bishop Blougram calls "the dangerous edge of things" (line 395); and a barbarousness that disorients personae and imperils their intellectual and moral balance. A few scholars with good sense have begun to delve into Browning's poetry "Deeper than ever the Andante dived" (12.861) by plumbing the subject of "overhearing." Herbert Tucker, for example, recommends that readers not "turn back at the threshold of interpretation, stopping our ears to both lyric cries and historical imperatives, and from our studious cells overhearing nothing."[2] And John Maynard, though not spending enough time measuring the acuity of either Browning's listeners or readers-overhearers, is correct that in "[t]he form of dramatized poem...[b]ecause of his initial uncertain relation to the speaker, the reader is driven to create a position for himself as listener."[3] Whereas numerous excellent studies chart Browning's finer optics, interpretive adventures await readers who plot his canon in terms of listening and deaf spots. The way Caponsacchi valorizes, or re-peals, his life's most telling experiences can test whether readers are keen enough to learn from Browning's refinement of a psychological branch of otoscopy practiced in numerous poems throughout his career. We have to enter eerie textual gaps, meet obliqueness head-on, and reach otoliths on "the other side of language" without sealing them: "The ability to listen, which allows us to hold firm and remain vigilant at the borders of obscurity, might be the condition that makes it possible for us to remain open to further linguistic and theoretical fields of concern."[4] The resulting benediction from some grand yet still small voice (in our heads?) will always warn us—like Caponsacchi—that it takes more than meets the eye to tell anything about human motivation:

> Let this old woe step on the stage again!
> Act itself o'er anew for men to judge,
> Not by the very sense and sight indeed—
> (Which take at best imperfect cognizance,
> Since, how heart moves brain, and how both move hand,
> What mortal ever in entirety saw?)
> . . .
> To-wit, by voices we call evidence. . . . (1.824–29, 833)

Aurality is a featured motif in Caponsacchi's central monologue because of how he "turned Christian" (line 474), and how as an *amicus curiae* he wants his audience to reform their moral faculties by hearing him quote Pompilia and by listening to his "poor excuse / For what [he] left undone" (lines 1480–81). The way Caponsacchi defines himself as auriculate and tries to affect others acoustically brings us within earshot of Browning, who throughout his career aspired to be not only one of the "Makers-see" (*Sordello*, 3.928) but also a "Maker-hear." Just as Pompilia reacts to her friendly canon's features, so readers must try to hear Robert Browning in "The *broad brow* that reverberates the truth, / And flashed the word God gave him, back to man!" (7.1796–97; emphasis added). Both Caponsacchi and Browning suspect that their respective audiences will "mouth and mumble and misinterpret" (line 1868). Yet the canon's close listeners are bound to realize that his "great adventure" (line 1003) has excavated his spirit, leaving it disconsolate and haunted. Caponsacchi's redeemed "hearing ear"

(Prov. 20:12) should have strengthened his hold on "the comfort, Christ" (line 2096), hope, and altruism. Instead, a throbbing self-consciousness gives him more pain now than it ever did. Pompilia's words, still echoing in Caponsacchi's mind, remind him that she once lifted him spiritually, but the sordid world, his astonishment, and his self-abasement twist his integrity.

Aural dimensions of creativity and religion are prominent early in *The Ring and the Book*. Browning bought the Old Yellow Book for almost a song, relied on listeners' reactions to the story to demonstrate that the "book" and his "ear's auxiliar / —Fancy" ("Flute-Music, with an Accompaniment," lines 80–81) were complementary, and found a musical context for developing a poem in "praise of God" (1.486). Leading readers by the ear, he wants to sharpen their listening skills before he fashions the subsequent monologues. But he knows there is not yet much to hear: "Here are the voices presently shall sound / In due succession" (1.838–39). For the next 500 lines, he rehearses the poem's remaining 20,000 lines. Book I, like Caponsacchi's monologue, is designed to produce or register a spiritual tinnitus, the good sense attuned to what Pope Innocent XII in his monologue calls "truth reverberate, changed, made pass / A spectrum into mind, the narrow eye" (10.1390–91). The divine Logos as a light in sound, a sound-like power in light, produces in the mind a spectral language of finer tone.[5]

We are often encouraged to imagine how the principals in this story sounded while the poet lifts their voices from the pages of the Old Yellow Book, and we become his partners in recovering what was "Talked over, bruited abroad, whispered away, / Yet helping us to all we seem to hear" (1.835–36). We comprise "an imaginary audience" (1.1213) participating in Browning's epistemology and pragmatics: "[H]ow else know we save by worth of word?" (1.837). From evidential "voices" we will have to locate truth and action mediated in resonant discourse, the "Uproar in the echo" (1.834), and to apply our senses to something unnameable, which his literary and spiritual powers have made "mistily seen, murmuringly heard, / Mistakenly felt" (1.758–59). To go from merely hearing Browning's evocations of historical figures to actively listening to their moral timbre, we have to audition diverse "music for the mind" (1.1216). Some of it, like Caponsacchi's "dire need to reconstruct his identity," is dissonant, harsh, and elliptical.[6]

Effete Caponsacchi, formerly a defendant, but now an apologist, struggles vainly to fortify his faith and save himself. The judges only want to know why a common marital dispute has become so sensational, so tragic, so embarrassing. He repeats his story while convinced that they continue to misconstrue its significance, which further agitates him. Language is a liability in representing the help he received from Pompilia:

> But she—
> The glory of life, the beauty of the world,
> The splendour of heaven, ... well, Sirs, does no one move?
> Do I speak ambiguously? The glory, I say,

> And the beauty, I say, and splendour, still say I,
> Who, a priest, trained to live my whole life long
> On beauty and splendour, solely at their source,
> God. . . . (Lines 117–24)

Caponsacchi prods his audience to hear these sentiments as almost idola-
trous, rather than as more evidence of his lust. The deliberate rhetorical
tempo will dispel, perhaps, his judges' restricted impression of an uncompli-
cated "hot-headed youth / Who lets his soul show, through transparent
words" (lines 128–29). His repetitive language is defiant and self-asserting,
yet also as reverent as that of the narrator-poet who evokes "voices" from the
Old Yellow Book, "Deep calling unto deep" (1.521). Pompilia claims in her
monologue that when Caponsacchi first spoke to her, she heard the Word in
his dedication to save her from spiritual death:

> All himself in it,—an eternity
> Of speech, to match the immeasurable depths
> O' the soul that then broke silence—"I am yours." (7.1445–47)

Caponsacchi's credibility and effectiveness depend on his ability to sound
again those "immeasurable depths" where he was "All himself" yet closest
to divinity, yet where sounding truth(ful) is complex and precarious. To the
idealistic canon, who "portrays Pompilia as absolute good and Guido as
absolute evil,"[7] those "immeasurable depths" are also moral crevasses that
test whether an adventurer has the qualifications to find a way down *and* out.
    In a review of *The Ring and the Book*, Robert Buchanan astutely notes
Caponsacchi's "listening awe."[8] Book 6 reveals that an antiphony between
his priestly calling and Pompilia's "voice immortal" (line 1601) shapes the
canon's identity. Nearly ordained, with "Just a vow to read! / [He] stopped
short awe-struck" (lines 267–68), having scruples about his worthiness:
"I know myself too weak, / Unworthy! Choose a worthier stronger man!"
(lines 270–71). The bishop allays such genuine concerns by suggesting that
devotion to God is a kind of *trompe l'oreille*, like that used by Jews in the
tetragrammaton (lines 276–89), and finally by assigning Caponsacchi to prove
his value by continuing to practice his "superior gift . . . making madrigals"
(lines 331–32). Four years later, after his apprehension for eloping with
Pompilia, the religious tribunal apprises Caponsacchi that he may have been
remiss in the "prosecution of [his] calling" (line 394) by becoming involved
in a marital dispute instead of devoting himself to more serious work:

> I heard, last time I stood here to be judged,
> What is priest's-duty,—labour to pluck tares
> And weed the corn of Molinism. . . . (Lines 150–52)

Such equivocal signals about how best to serve the Church do not enhance
Caponsacchi's self-worth but rather confirm that as a priest he has become
even more detached from honorable action—passion, love, and duty—with

which he desires to fill his life. Ordination was nothing like a daring "leap / Over the ledge into the other life" (lines 264–65), but rather was a misstep or misunderstanding. Listening, "an essential function in the attempt to identify and monitor possible predatory aspects of our knowledge,"[9] both empowers and petrifies him. By misplacing his "listening awe" in the Church, Caponsacchi cannot reach his goal—adding to his family's illustrious civic and spiritual service.[10]

Caponsacchi's first sight of the woman who will change his life carries not only pictorial significance but also acoustic markers. Pompilia's appearance at a theater is like a Raphael painting displayed in his Pieve cathedral that shatters his indifference to "matin-song" (line 401). His associate, Canon Conti, immediately begins to whisper about Pompilia's dire situation, and a day later mixes vespers with whispers. Conti's olla-podrida of Latin and gossip has comical elements, recalling the polyglot monk in "Soliloquy of the Spanish Cloister" and exemplifying the Lacanian principle that language keeps us in stitches. Furthermore, Caponsacchi is beginning to stew ethically because neither his conscience nor ears have heard enough about an "other life" beyond the clergy, which would be less vexatious than the current one. Although Caponsacchi is "Mindful of Christ," he also owes allegiance to social respectability, "the other potentate / Who bids have courage and keep honour safe" (lines 155–57). Thus he initiates his desperate plan to leave for Rome where introspection, he hopes, will settle his life's mission—or at least keep him from further debasement as a coxcomb. This acoustical juxtaposition of worship with worry sets the tone for much of what follows, as Caponsacchi struggles to rearrange his life affected by Pompilia's call and scored by clerical procedures. Her voice, even before he first hears it, seems to be a happier alternative to the theology he reads but cannot enact:

> [W]hen the page o' the Summa preached its best,
> Her smile kept glowing out of it, as to mock
> The silence we could break by no one word,—
> There came a tap without the chamber-door,
> And a whisper. ... (Lines 500–04)

Pompilia is not visiting the priest, although given his need and anticipation, readers as well as he desire her appearance. Margherita, Guido's maid, is delivering a letter supposedly from Pompilia, but in this and subsequent correspondence Caponsacchi does not detect her true voice. A spiritual faculty, superseding the sensual ear, is Caponsacchi's credential to rebuke his judges, who infer that Pompilia wrote the letters. Resorting to his image of Raphael's Madonna, he claims that what they think they have heard is not "venom issued from Madonna's mouth" (line 673) but their own physical and moral waste.

Even after first meeting with Pompilia ("While [he] stood still as stone, all eye, all ear," line 724), Caponsacchi struggles to keep her spiritual summons foremost in his moral consciousness because he now has his "own fact, [his] miracle / Self-authorised and self-explained" (lines 919–20). Someone's believing in him makes all the difference between his feeling weak or strong. Listening to Pompilia positions Caponsacchi where he can follow a desired path beyond gallantry to social awareness, and inwardly beyond egoism to willpower. His aurally induced "fact" is moral focus on himself that provides a place for him to act, confirming that "[w]hat I hear, unlike what I see or touch, is not set over against me; it is set *into* my consciousness, mixed into my reflexive awareness of my own presence."[11] However, as if Pieve's stones had immediately cried out in response to Caponsacchi's religious infidelity, he detects "the church changed tone" (line 995), recalling him to dispassion rather than a due occasion of earnestness that Pompilia proffers: "Now, from the stone lungs sighed the scrannel voice / 'Leave that live passion, come be dead with me!'" (lines 1000–01). There is irony in Caponsacchi's wavering, tremulous dedication, which even he perceives: Pompilia has unwittingly cooperated with the Church to help create a sound barrier between herself and an impressionable rescuer. Moreover, the Miltonic allusion in "scrannel" ("Lycidas," line 124) offers Browning's readers a way to hear beyond Caponsacchi's spiritual and psychological range. Ideally, in advance of the priest's recounting this ethical and ecclesiastical pressure, alert readers are already prepared to distinguish acoustical signs of a corrupt Church mimicking Christian values. Our sensation of genuine Christianity's reverberating, tonic uproar becomes a salutary burden, which sometimes we might play ourselves (albeit awkwardly), if we know our own stops.

Caponsacchi stresses that his divided allegiances came mainly from an ear-splitting "conch-ience," which deranges his sense of obedience. He struggles to deny that he was afraid, which would have compromised his honor as well as prevented self-sacrifice, the keystone of his moral wisdom. In the middle of this dramatic monologue Browning has his character rereading Aquinas, hearing vespers, and reading the office to stiffen his professional backbone. Caponsacchi hears his conscience predominantly through interior monologues, which were impossible before Pompilia spoke to him:

> Sirs, I obeyed. Obedience was too strange,—
> This new thing that had been struck into me
> By the look o' the lady,—to dare disobey
> The first authoritative word. 'T was God's.
> I had been lifted to the level of her,
> Could take such sounds into my sense. (Lines 1010–15)

Pompilia enables "Obedience," literally a *hearing* that causes Caponsacchi's rededication to the Church. Nevertheless, his procrastination and rationalizing about ministerial courage, duty, and solace are signs that he cannot stay at her "level." Caponsacchi expects to weasel out of obeying Pompilia's summons, but her voice again turns him from a distracted misreader ("Aquinas blazed / With one black name only on the white page," lines 1025–26) into a reformed activist. He climactically shuts Aquinas's *Summa* to find a moral alliance with St. Thomas, the disciple who "bade all doubt adieu" (line 1104) at the Assumption of the Virgin Mary. In a quest for "immolation" (line 953), Caponsacchi, armed with "a sword in case of accident" (line 1122), seems ready to die fighting his demons, as well as Guido. Yet Browning allows us to overhear the thoughts of a monologist who was cracking under the pressure to sustain the moral stamina to believe in himself, as well as to save Pompilia.

Caponsacchi's "miracle" of faith is aurally reinforced as he and Pompilia flee Arezzo for Rome, but his exalted role as "the excepted man" (line 1129)— expected, like Christ, to foot trod moral enemies (1 Cor. 15:25–27)— is nonetheless severely challenged despite its auspicious start.[12] This journey shows Caponsacchi at his best and worst, determined to prove himself saved and a savior, yet defensive about his initiative. He waited for Pompilia

> With a tune in the ears, low leading up to loud,
> A light in the eyes, faint that would soon be flare,
> Ever some spiritual witness new and new
> In faster frequence, crowding solitude
> To watch the way o' the warfare. ... (Lines 1133–37)

The counterpoint, elision/pseudo-hypercatalexis, alliteration, and rhyme reveal Caponsacchi at a mystical pitch, prepared to battle evil and dutifully displaying his skills before a worthy spiritual audience.[13] But Caponsacchi's self-confidence receives several jolts as he travels with Pompilia, whose words haunt and sometimes embarrass him. He does not like to be reminded that she "called" him ("I did not like that word," lines 1233–34), but he especially dislikes her recalling him to his clerical duties:

> At eve we heard the *angelus*: she turned—
> "I told you I can neither read nor write.
> ...
>   ...but you—
> Who are a priest—wherefore do you not read
> The service at this hour? Read Gabriel's song,
> The lesson, and then read the little prayer
> To Raphael, proper for us travellers!"
> I did not like that, neither, but I read. (Lines 1266–74)

If Pompilia is really illiterate, she knows more than we think she should about the significance of the Annunciation and Raphael's role in helping Tobit, Tobias, and Sarah. Readers, like Caponsacchi's audience, are having their own faith in miracles and truthful discourse tested. Yet Browning has good reasons to draw attention to biblical contexts for these travelers as they make the most of each other. When Pompilia reminds Caponsacchi of his office, she empowers him to suppress her demons, but only temporarily. Caponsacchi takes his cue from Pompilia's strength to be her guardian angel on this "way o' the warfare," which eventually will prove his downfall.

The effect of promptly responding to Pompilia is like a benediction for Caponsacchi, who is quite vain about his developing relationship with her, especially when she begins to call him friend and wants their journey to be "life-long" (line 1312) because it transcends sensuousness:

> "Yours is no voice; you speak when you are dumb;
> Nor face, I see it in the dark. I want
> No face nor voice that change and grow unkind."
> That I liked, that was the best thing she said. (Lines 1316–19)

Caponsacchi's actions speak louder than words, but his inaction haunts him almost as powerfully as Pompilia's speech and silence: "[I]n his retrospective reflection there is a consistent interplay between pride in his efforts to save Pompilia and a terrible frustration at having to acknowledge his weakness."[14] Without using his priesthood as an excuse, he tries to extenuate his faint-heartedness at Castelnuovo when he could not brave Guido. The villain's words immobilize Caponsacchi who, were he not a priest, ideally would have killed Guido on the spot. When the poet-priest should have used his own sword, he loses himself—and his heroic chance—in thoughts of language and literature: "And while I mused, / The minute, oh the misery, was gone!" (lines 1498–99). This muffled misery—oath misery—is being caught with his guard, not his pants, down. "Listening awe" incapacitates him, and he feels uncomfortably akin to swifter Guido, who was stunned more by Pompilia's verbal attack than by her swordcraft: "No matter for the sword, her word sufficed / To spike the coward through and through" (lines 1550–51).

As Caponsacchi concludes his account of traveling with Pompilia, he tries again to impress the judges with his own moral authority, which he doubts he possesses. Besides counting himself an imposter, ironically he is soul-sick from recuperating his (in)famous surname:

> Though he has learned a great lesson, he has also suffered a ghastly disap-
> pointment for which he cannot wholly blame external forces—Guido, for
> example, or the judges or the system. So, as we gradually learn, he is not nearly
> so sure as he seems to assert and is compensating for fear with a measure of
> bravado.[15]

Caponsacchi talks as if he were in custody and as if the news of Pompilia's fate were a way to torture some secret out of him that he had not disclosed months earlier. What he knows cuts two ways: "The priest who needs must carry sword on thigh / May find imperative use for it" (lines 1774–75). Yet he was also not manly enough to use it. The shattering of his callow knightly pretensions and self-assurance torments the priest who wanted to be a savior, besides the man who expected to be fearless. With the announcement of Pompilia's end, he has to believe his own ears, which reverberate the fact that he too was a "coward through and through."

In Caponsacchi's adventure, his "ears" are not only on his head but also in his psyche, as portals of imagination and conscience. Though earmarked to enhance a family reputation for bravery, he is merely scarred when his leadership potential lapses. Pope Innocent values the priest's hearing compared with men who should have helped Pompilia in an authentic moral conflict. Because Caponsacchi was not

> too obtuse
> Of ear, through iteration of command,
> For catching quick the sense of the real cry,— (10.1197–99)

he acted like a true wayfaring Christian. Hearing this papal testimonial, we must not forget, however, that the priest was no Giovanni on the spot and that his hesitation endangered Pompilia. The pope innocently prefers to think that Caponsacchi, "whose sword-hand was used to strike the lute" (10.1200), actually used his terrible swift sword; the priest himself knows that as a swordsman, a "warrior-priest," he did not "show mettle" enough to prevent a sordid murder (10.1095, 1202). Furthermore, Innocent attributes to him more acuity than is warranted: everyone should "see this priest, this Caponsacchi, stung / At the first summons" (10.1555–56). Indeed, the priest was better than an unstung hero, but his immediate audience and wary readers hear someone whose sense of personal disgrace disconnects him from life. Pope Innocent, if he heard Caponsacchi's bleeding heart and self-conviction, would be disappointed but, perhaps, not surprised: "Deserve the initiatory spasm,—once more / Work, be unhappy but bear life, my son!" (10.1210–11). The pope later reevaluates Caponsacchi: "his own mere impulse guides the man— / Happily sometimes" (10.1913–14)—unhappily hereafter because passion, his "formula for living,"[16] is ethically unreliable. On the brink of post-Christian moral relativism, Innocent worries that such a man, "the first experimentalist / In the new order of things,—he plays a priest" (10.1909–10)—is a poor replacement for St. Augustine. Caponsacchi, "a frustrated aspirant to an unattainable heroism,"[17] misplays the role of St. George, and he is not much of a priest either. He is, instead, as Browning suggests, a quitter who, before leaving the stage, sounds off.

Caponsacchi's listeners represent the corrupt world that failed to shield Pompilia. He aims to put them in their place, yet while he is in despair about his own station, there is a chafing propinquity that turns a hearing into everyone's trial. The aftermath is an affirmative answer to one of Jacques Derrida's penetrating questions about o(n)tological distress: "In order effectively, practically to transform what one decries (tympanizes), must one still be heard and understood within it, henceforth subjecting oneself to the law of the inner hammer?"[18] The authorities will probably misunderstand Caponsacchi again: "the first telling somehow missed effect" (1.1044), and now "the same result of smiling disbelief" (line 1709) may recur. If so, he will have repeated himself—without lessening the burden of "aspiration here, achievement there, / Lacking omnipotence to connect extremes" (lines 489–90). Even if he could put "A word in [their] ear" (line 57), he is not omnipotent, and cannot even convey the power of a spiritual plea from

Pompilia "recalled inside [his] head, way past the ear; a tenuous yet monumental voice."[19] He now and forever relives what he recognizes as his des-
tiny: not like Christ or some cavalier who goes "trippingly...up to the
height / O'er the wan water" (lines 266–67), but someone unsound who
cannot justify his own ways. Like the poet-narrator of Book I, Caponsacchi
feels that Pompilia was "Saved for a splendid minute and no more" (1.588),
and that his Roman listeners discredit his spiritual credentials. Having failed
to save Pompilia's body, he fears he is losing his soul again because of
miscommunication equivalent to inaction:

> I fear
> You do her wit injustice,—all through me!
> Like my fate all through,—ineffective help!
> A poor rash advocate I prove myself. (Lines 1960–63)

This is not false modesty to embarrass his listeners, but rather a confession
that his current ineptitude virtually reprises his former status as Pompilia's
impeached savior manqué.[20] After his first view of her, he knows instinctively
that her debased condition offers him a life-saving/surrendering opportunity, a way to escape his soul's abysm, which has widened and deepened since
his forced dissociation from her. Now Caponsacchi has only mortifying
voices and ears that, instead of closing "the gap 'twixt what is, what should
be" (line 487), measure it with the smallness of an almost tragic man.

   The poet-narrator of Book I informs us how to hear Caponsacchi ("he
speaks rapidly, angrily," 1.1070) and, underrating the monologist's remaining insecurities, claims that the "perplexed puppet" (1.1021) put his past
behind him. Apparently a joint obedience between the Church and the
world no longer affects "the seeming solitary man, / Speaking for God"
(1.1072–73). Like Lacan, Browning is manipulating readers' "multifarious
wires" (1.1019), like his persona's, to demonstrate not only that being
God's deputy is formidable, but also that the proper study of mankind is
man's whorled, linguistic being, a sentiment the pope echoes:

> Therefore *this* filthy rags of speech, this coil
> Of statement, comment, query and response,
> Tatters all too contaminate for use,
> Have no renewing: He, the Truth, is, too,
> The Word. (10.372–76; emphasis added)

The most formidable challenge for readers as well as Caponsacchi is always
to be renewing their credentials as a poet's or God's deputies: "Man and
priest—could you comprehend the coil!" (1.1017); and "his strange course /
I' the matter, was it right or wrong or both?" (1.387–88).[21] Caponsacchi, an
"ambiguous creature" (10.1226), cannot unwrap himself from this tighten-
ing coil in order to eliminate the cochlear pressure caused by a spiritual ear-
piercing. He pulls rank (rather than a sword) and plans to continue his
priestly duties, but imagines being "unfettered by a vow, unblessed / By the

higher call" (lines 2082–83). What the poet-narrator says about Guido's second monologue—"the true words come last" (1.1281)—also applies to Caponsacchi's collapse from his own defects and perplexities into an ellipsis, which marks his variance from a perfect spiritual circle: "So I, from such communion, pass content . . . / O great, just, good God! Miserable me!" (lines 2104–05). Pompilia's voice fills this ellipsis and the textual space following it; the typography of *The Ring and the Book* measures what the auditors cannot. And the appeal ("O") to God cannot compensate for Caponsacchi's existential woes as he "awakes / To the old solitary nothingness" (lines 2102–03), the same "absolute nothingness" (line 1931) he imagines a living Guido would face. Caponsacchi does not "grow healthy" (line 753), as Pompilia expects of him, because although he can "comprehend the coil," it nevertheless threatens his "symmetric soul" (10.1134). Pope Innocent doubts Caponsacchi can "teach others how to quit themselves, / Prove why this step was right, while that were wrong" (10.1921–22). Although Caponsacchi tries to be more poised than when he first testified before these same authorities, who intimidated someone they considered immoral, he is too wounded, vulnerable, and tightly wound to analyze (that is, unloosen) what it takes "to quit," or acquit, oneself.

A despised audience's vulgar minds cannot clear his conscience, and he has convinced himself that such attention to "mundane love that's sin and scandal too" (line 130) prevents the judges from hearing his message about a greater Love, "the comfort, Christ" (line 2096). What they need to learn approximates what Caponsacchi needs, another chance for acquittal, undoing his fatal "fate all through,—ineffective help!" with Pompilia:

> To live, and see her learn, and learn by her,
> Out of the low obscure and petty world—
> Or only see one purpose and one will
> Evolve themselves i' the world, change wrong to right:
> To have to do with nothing but the true,
> The good, the eternal . . .
> . . .
> Just as a drudging student trims his lamp,
> Opens his Plutarch, puts him in the place
> Of Roman, Grecian; draws the patched gown close,
> Dreams, "Thus should I fight, save or rule the world!" (Lines 2085–90, 2098–101)

The young, dashing, idealistic canon wants control he never has had—and never will have. His "imagined life" is either above an inferior world, or in an ideal world still needing him as a savior or ruler. If Caponsacchi's religious elders can learn anything from him, it may be the disadvantages of being a self-conscious, yet impulsive, instinctual man, who has to live in disgrace, who is "So very pitiable, . . . / Who had conceivably been otherwise" (lines 2070–71), and who desperately resorts to "speech that smites" (1.1070) because it is a handy, though unreliable, device. Caponsacchi's tongue is now a sharp sword with which he wounds auditors but also disadvantages himself: "In other words, can one puncture the tympanum of a philosopher and still be heard and understood by him?"[22] One judge weeps (line 1884), but the lack of verbal interplay in a dramatic monologue helps Browning shape the self-destructive fearful symmetry within Caponsacchi between dignity ("I stand here guiltless in thought, word and deed," line 1861) and degradation ("shame of faultiness," line 1889).

Whereas Caponsacchi initially heard "priest's-duty" as a vow to uphold religious doctrine, his own priest-study confirms his attitude that passion and action must be complementary. He now wants his auditors to understand that "priests / Should study passion; how else cure mankind, / Who come for help in passionate extremes?" (2078–80). Ironically, study rather than action has prevented Caponsacchi from meeting Pompilia's expectations: "You would die for me" (line 861). As the priest reviews his life, climaxing in failure to protect an abused wife, he recognizes he is neither the man nor the priest he wanted to be. And the monologue itself—still more talk than exploit—takes him no closer to his goal:

> [L]et me
> Make you hear, this time, how, in such a case,
> Man, be he in the priesthood or at plough,
> . . .
> How he is bound, better or worse, to act. (Lines 152–54, 159)

The man-priest originally intended to prove his masculinity in the "new bait of adventure" (line 685) with Guido. When Caponsacchi was his own audience, expecting Guido's trickery instead of Pompilia's appearance, he vaunts:

> I began to laugh already—"he will have
> 'Out of the hole you hide in, on to the front,
> Count Guido Franceschini, show yourself!
> Hear what a man thinks of a thing like you,
> And after, take this foulness in your face!'"
> The words lay living on my lip. . . . (Lines 696–701)

This remembered soliloquy, with its inlaid daring, proves Caponsacchi could talk the talk. Now, he and his derelict auditors know performance is more difficult. Guido was merely "a thing" to Caponsacchi before their encounter at Castelnuovo. The latter, more emotionally than physically restrained from fully defending Pompilia and thereby making himself a Christian soldier, is humiliated. Having failed the passion/action test that he thought he was man-priest enough to pass, Caponsacchi is near(ly) nothing, almost "a nonentity, / For what is an idea unrealized?" (10.1501–02).

Caponsacchi can neither recall what was undone nor recriminate without regretting his contretemps and demerit. Burdensome talk counteracts the benefit of Pompilia's former spiritual tonic:

> Alike abolished—the imprisonment
> Of the outside air, the inside weight o' the world
> That pulled me down. Death meant, to spurn the ground,
> Soar to the sky,—die well and you do that. (949–52)

Browning stretches these monosyllabic lines to rate what the priest reckons he lost by not laying down his life for his friend. Caponsacchi has lapsed from a blessed mood into the uproarious, too intelligible world which he now wants to abandon. From "the first Spring" (line 946) he shared with Pompilia in April and in spirit, Caponsacchi by the following January has passed into a long winter of discontent. He has to live defeated by Guido, whom he considers a coward (line 2001), and whose death at the hands of a priest would have meant "man redeemed" (line 1478). Although Caponsacchi wanted to "die well" as a martyr, he conversely feels he should have killed his enemy. A survivor, unable to die or live the way that would make his "great adventure" successful, Caponsacchi exists in the ruin of his "miracle." Being auriculate, he has gotten an earful of logocentrism, which not only has morally reconstructed him but also has broken his spirit because he has no hope of acquitting himself in the hollow, tympanic, and coiled space where words strike.

Caponsacchi owns his testimony only faintly redoubles Pompilia's accent on his auricular character. Her words filled him with the potential to align his soul's "symmetry" with "God and man, and what duty [he] owe[s] both" (line 942). This potential is wasted, he thinks. He neither died heroically nor lives wholesomely now with such basic disappointment in himself and the Church. Yet, to help his listeners fathom the crises, as well as lifelong urgency, of desire and deed, he must try to resound the spiritual uproar permeating his consciousness and signaling a compression of time between Christ's Crucifixion and Last Judgment:

> [W]hat is it you ask
> By way of explanation? There's the fact!
> It seems to fill the universe with sight
> And sound,—from the four corners of this earth
> Tells itself over, to my sense at least.
> But you may want it lower set i' the scale,—
> Too vast, too close it clangs in the ear, perhaps;
> You 'd stand back just to comprehend it more:
> Well then, let me, the hollow rock, condense
> The voice o' the sea and wind, interpret you
> The mystery of this murder. God above!
> It is too paltry, such a transference
> O' the storm's roar to the cranny of the stone! (Lines 64–76)[23]

Caponsacchi's obdurate listeners have been so full of themselves that they cannot perceive what is so obvious to him: Pompilia's life and death have a logocentric design. His acoustical, mediating role, learned from obedience and demanded by tragic circumstances, may not earmark them because they want to "stand back just to comprehend" (mis)deeds, instead of changing their spiritual sensorium so they can interpret (for) themselves. Only if they live closer to the moral uproar—where "hearing . . . is already within the sphere of hurt"[24]—will they feel what makes such a man happy or miserable, as well as what difference this "mystery" makes to their ethos, their ties with "God above" and the mundane.

Caponsacchi wants his audience to recognize their defects and potential by having them imagine they were along for the ride to hear what moral goals they ought to set for themselves as men and priests. Pompilia's voice strikes Caponsacchi on the fault line in his character between who he is and the nobleman he wants to become. At one point on the way to Castelnuovo, Pompilia touches upon the character of manhood, a subject that has troubled Caponsacchi since he first saw her. She asks him:

> Tell me, are men unhappy, in some kind
> Of mere unhappiness at being men,
> As women suffer, being womanish?
> Have you, now, some unhappiness, I mean,
> Born of what may be man's strength overmuch,
> To match the undue susceptibility,
> The sense at every pore when hate is close?
> . . .
> Yet rocks split,—and the blow-ball does no more,
> Quivers to feathery nothing at a touch;
> And strength may have its drawback, weakness scapes. (Lines 1235–41, 1246–48)

Giuseppe Maria Caponsacchi, perhaps trying to avoid being perceived as epicene, does not record his answer to these questions of gender identity. Anyway, he has already remarked that his first perception of Pompilia's difficulties made him feel that he "had a whole store of strengths / Eating into [his] heart, which craved employ" (lines 495–96). The judges have to find the same answer in their hearts by learning how the combination of power and weakness is not unbecoming Christlike men who make the "abysm [into which] the soul may slip" (line 488) an inspiring rather than frightening hollowness.

Caponsacchi, being "the hollow rock," remains earthbound and enervated, not the soaring, dynamic person he wanted to become especially after Pompilia's summons. It is paltry to be Caponsacchi, a hollow man whose message about the redemptive power of love, passion, duty, and sacrifice may be incommunicable in sepulchral language, "this filthy rags of speech" (10.372), just as he has lost himself in "the mystery of this murder," which deafens and defines him. A world transformed by Pompilia's Christlike knowledge and innocence is a world another decibel closer to the apocalypse. Although Caponsacchi "turn[s] Christian" under Pompilia's influence, his failing to "quit himself" turns him from a would-be "excepted man" (line 1129) into an unaccepted, unbecoming Everyman, "an unclean thing, and all [his] righteousnesses are as filthy rags" (Isa. 64:6). His change not only humbles and humanizes him but also further bruises his sense of masculinity, ethical as well as sexual, which has afflicted him throughout the adventure—wanting to prove his manhood to Pompilia and his muscular Christianity to a hypocritical Church. He has to believe ruefully that "his good is—knowing he is bad" (line 144). His emptiness resembles kenosis; yet as a broken man, he is no rock on which to (re)build the Church. Caponsacchi detects in the way Christianity is sometimes practiced "a crack somewhere, something that's unsound / I' the rattle!" (lines 1879–80). Moreover, what he hears is partly his own fault. His life and monologue demonstrate a spiritual acoustics depending on ethical space and psychological boundaries. He lacks Pompilia's "fine ear," "experienced ear," for God's decree to cherish life (10.1065, 1090). To Browning and his personae who are our *aides-d'oreille*, such a difference between the ears is profound, labyrinthine, and giddy. *Différance* spans the uproarious far cry and its lasting echo of humanity exercising itself with passion and intellect, "when hearts beat hard, / And brains, high-blooded, tick…" (1.36–37). Readers with grit are never too late or preposterous—that is, too ear-ly—to be turning around their sense of Browning's playfully earnest canon.

NOTES

1. Robert Browning, *The Ring and the Book*, ed. Richard D. Altick (New Haven: Yale University Press, 1981), 6.493. Subsequent citations to Caponsacchi's monologue, Book 6 of *The Ring and the Book*, will provide only line references. Parenthetical citations to Robert Browning's poetry are from *Robert Browning: The Poems*, eds. John Pettigrew and Thomas J. Collins, 2 vols. (New Haven: Yale University Press, 1981).
2. "Dramatic Monologue and the Overhearing of Lyric," in *Lyric Poetry: Beyond New Criticism*, eds. Chaviva Hošek and Patricia Parker (Ithaca: Cornell University Press, 1985), 243.
3. "Speaker, Listener, and Overhearer: The Reader in the Dramatic Poem," *Browning Institute Studies* 15 (1987): 107–08.
4. Gemma Corradi Fiumara, *The Other Side of Language: A Philosophy of Listening*, trans. Charles Lambert (London: Routledge, 1990), 91.
5. In the same vein Fiumara says: "A philosophy of listening can be envisaged as an attempt to recover the neglected and perhaps deeper roots of what we call thinking, an activity which in some way gathers and synthesizes human endeavours" (*Other Side*, 13).
6. Constance W. Hassett, *The Elusive Self in the Poetry of Robert Browning* (Athens: Ohio University Press, 1982), 67. As my essay witnesses, Roman Jakobson's following remarks about Hölderlin also pertain to Caponsacchi's monologue:

> The basic fact underlying the schizophrenic poet's verbal art and creative power is their dichotomic character—the stark contrast between the

immense loss of his ability to take part in conversations with people around him and his strangely unimpaired eagerness and talent for effort-less, spontaneous and purposeful improvisations. Anything connected with dialogue—the mutual address, the exchanges with questions and answers, the speaker's achievement, and the hearer's attention, the endowment of meaning to one's own utterances and the ability to grasp those of one's partners—the whole technique of conversation—could only be imitated with great effort and even then, not completely; it was confused and had mainly been lost. ("The Language of Schizophrenia: Hölderlin's Speech and Poetry," trans. Susan Kitron, in *Verbal Art, Verbal Sign, Verbal Time*, eds. Krystyna Pomorska and Stephen Rudy [Minneapolis: University of Minnesota Press, 1985], 137.)

7. Clyde de L. Ryals, *The Life of Robert Browning: A Critical Biography* (Oxford: Blackwell, 1993), 164.
8. Qtd. in Boyd Litzinger and Donald Smalley, eds., *Browning: The Critical Heritage* (New York: Barnes & Noble, 1970), 319.
9. Fiumara, *Other Side*, 21.
10. Donald Hair superbly validates his claim that "[c]onversion . . . is the govern-ing pattern of Caponsacchi's experience, and it takes the form of discovering that words are . . . living powers" (*Robert Browning's Language* [Toronto: University of Toronto Press, 1999], 193). However, Hair misestimates that Browning "is not much interested in . . . the echo which is the aural equivalent of the [mental] mirror" (300).
11. Lawrence Kramer, *Music and Poetry: The Nineteenth Century and After* (Berkeley: University of California Press, 1984), 98.
12. Perhaps using the word "excepted" as a pun on "expected," Browning would thereby parody Caponsacchi's hubristic sense of himself as savior—likely to be St. George in the poet's canon—to foreshadow Pompilia's moral envoy and guardian not quite meeting her (much less his own) expectations of alacrity and deliverance.
13. Deborah Vlock-Keyes says that "in Browning personality is generated through syncopation—a subversion, in poetry, of metrical order" ("Music and Dramatic Voice in Robert Browning and Robert Schumann," *Victorian Poetry* 29 [1991]: 232).
14. E. Warwick Slinn, *Browning and the Fictions of Identity* (Totowa: Barnes & Noble, 1982), 119.
15. William E. Buckler, *Poetry and Truth in Robert Browning*'s The Ring and the Book (New York: New York University Press, 1985), 135.
16. Michael G. Yetman, "Giuseppe Caponsacchi: 'A Very Reputable Priest'?" *Baylor Browning Interests* 21 (May 1970): 23.
17. Alexander Pettit, "Place, Time, and Parody in *The Ring and the Book*," *Victorian Poetry* 31 (1993): 102.
18. Jacques Derrida, "Tympan," in *Margins of Philosophy*, trans. Alan Bass (Chicago: University of Chicago Press, 1982), xiii.
19. Roland Barthes, *A Lover's Discourse*, trans. Richard Howard (New York: Hill and Wang, 1978), 114.
20. "Speech, in the poem [*The Ring and the Book*], indicates that one has not yet connected. . . . Speaking, then, provides only a lesser knowledge, a fragmen-tary understanding. That Caponsacchi is unable to do more than tell his story

(and he will probably tell it again and again and again) implies that his vision has been shattered. When he loses Pompilia, he loses his intuited understanding of the whole" (Kris Davis, "Browning's Caponsacchi: Stuck in the Gap," *Victorian Poetry* 25 [1987]: 66).

21. In *Sordello*, Browning suggests more convolutedly—however familiarly—that our willingness to listen patiently must fit any ethical and interpretive curiosity or passion if we are to venture inside the poet's luxuriant head(ing) for history. Vis-à-vis Browning's canon and our listening to it/him, the following quotation is a paronomastic uproar that requires more amplification and modulation than I can give here. Nevertheless, readers who are denizens of noisy scholia are being taught how to hear the poet's craft and position (i.e., *wave script dash, hortatory's plash, margins I lent out*, and *demon-sent long stresses*):

> Noontide above; except the wave's crisp dash,
> Or buzz of colibri, or tortoise' splash,
> The margin's silent: out with every spoil
> Made in our tracking, coil by mighty coil,
> This serpent of a river to his head
> I' the midst! Admire each treasure, as we spread
> The bank, to help us tell our history
> Aright: give ear, endeavour to descry
> The groves of giant rushes, how they grew
> Like demons' endlong tresses we sailed through,
> What mountains yawned, forests to give us vent
> Opened, each doleful side, yet on we went
> Till. . . . (3.655–67)

22. Derrida, "Tympan," xii.

23. Cf. Wallace Stevens's "The Rock":

> In this plenty, the poem makes meanings of the rock,
> Of such mixed motion and such imagery
> That its barrenness becomes a thousand things
>
> And so exists no more. This is the cure
> Of leaves and of the ground and of ourselves.
> His words are both the icon and the man.
>
> The rock is the gray particular of man's life,
> The stone from which he rises, up—and—ho,
> The step to the bleaker depths of his descents. . . . (Lines 55–63)

24. Geoffrey H. Hartman, *Saving the Text: Literature/Derrida/Philosophy* (Baltimore: Johns Hopkins University Press, 1981), 128.

CHAPTER 7

FAITH, ROMANCE, AND IMAGINATION: NEWMAN THE STORYTELLER

Bernadette Waterman Ward

John Henry Newman found in stories instruments of such power that they turn even a "black day" of mayhem, theft and death into a thing "blessed." Stories exercise the imagination; and thus they differ from mere illustration, or instruction, which seek to banish rather than reveal mystery. Newman's understanding of the place of story in the spiritual life—"real" life— challenges us to confront the narrow, blunting, scorched-earth lovelessness that has until even this day passed for the work of the imagination in our culture. As we consider "black days" of violence, it is worth considering that even the September 11 terrorists have been discussed in print as men whose imaginations were marinated in gory American disaster movies.[1]

Newman indeed warned of the dangers of exposing one's imagination to corrupting images: "Oh, thoughtless, and worse, how cruel to yourselves, all ye who read what ye should not read, and hear what ye should not hear! . . . Oh, how you will despise yourselves, oh how weep at what you have brought on you!"[2] Nevertheless, Newman was willing to imagine something corresponding to what the terrorists imagined—the difference being that he imagined it from the perspective of the victims of the violence—and it was not exclusively with pity that he considered the fate of such victims. In his *Apologia pro vita sua* Newman pointed out that he had long ago "said of the Bishops, that, 'black event though it would be for the country, yet we could not wish them a more blessed termination of their course, than the spoiling of their goods and martyrdom.'"[3]

The black events shadowing us were perpetrated by jihadists, who certainly wished to kill and spoil their "infidel" victims (no doubt including any available Christian bishops in that category). But the motives that fueled the imaginations of jihadists are not necessarily religious. Only two years before, two suburban Colorado boys with no discernible religion worked to bomb and terrorize their whole school. Eyewitnesses claimed that they singled out enthusiastic Christians for particular mockery, intimidation and murder, especially if other Christians were looking on. Some of their victims aroused popular veneration as martyrs in the ancient sense for their refusal to deny Christianity. At the time, the editorial page of the *New York Times* was full of musings about the overactive imaginations of the killer teens.

Like the Gestapo in Anthony Hecht's famous poem "More Light," the young murderers in Colorado sought to provoke their victims to a type of moral collapse that confirms the killer's absolute power to overwhelm and limit the imagination of the victim.[4] Though legend has it that Ernest Hemingway defined courage as the total lack of imagination, in fact a trammeled imagination works against courage. Terrorists are all alike in seeking to limit the ideas of their victims to just two: submission or unrelieved suffering. Those who resisted through faith in other possibilities gained courage and, through courage, liberty. Such faith was a supreme act of imagination, in the context of Newman's thought; the failure of imagination was all from the side of the murderers. For in Newman's understanding, the imagination has an infinite reach. It is essential to the ability to love, to human dignity; imagination is the key ingredient in free will. Newman seizes upon imagination as the very fount of what he calls the "real"—that which can call the heart to action, as opposed to the "notional," a mere abstraction which cannot move a human will, however well constructed the concept. Only through imagination can the infinite—the good, the true, Love Itself—rise to the level of reality in our lives.

There is much evidence showing that Newman found imagination a delicate and dangerous power; his *Oxford University Sermons* often warn young men about the kinds of stories they allow themselves to be told. Jaime Ferreira has pointed out that Newman preached seriously about the "danger of wish-fulfillment, illusion, fantasy—the illegitimate overextension of imagination. But what is more unexpected is that he also warns of the danger of using imagination as the limiting standard for determining what is possible." Ferriera emphasizes Newman's warning that a stunted imagination "tethers us in our search for truth."[5] In his understanding of what storytelling does for a human being's moral capacities, Newman tries to make his hearers aware that there is a kind of failure of imagination that is a disaster far greater than the spoiling of one's property and even the taking of one's life. In the final analysis, Newman, with his roots in Romanticism, sees imagination not as a thing to be repressed, but, despite all dangers, to be set free.

Newman prized the way imagination offers liberation from constraint, even from fear, and for the sake of that liberation he promoted traditional Christian tales. The great story that Newman told himself was the story of the Church: of the slow revelation of doctrines and creeds; of its saints under persecution; of its heroes who heard the voice of the Holy Spirit, princes of the church or the common crowd of the faithful, rising above the confusion of the world and the devil to triumph in orthodoxy. Newman was fascinated by antiquity, and wanted to learn the story, detail by detail, from the beginning;

and as he did, he found that the story changed him: "here, in the middle of the fifth century, I found, as it seemed to me, Christendom of the sixteenth and the nineteenth centuries reflected. I saw my face in that mirror, and I was a Monophysite" (*Apologia*, 217). In this moment we can see the great strength and the great weakness of Newman as a storyteller. It is a gripping moment; but how many of his readers have ever looked in any sort of mirror and seen a Monophysite staring back? How many would know one if they saw one? The Monophysite controversy is not much of a live issue in America in the twenty-first century; and it wasn't in Newman's England either. A friend at Oxford advised him that there was no more boring subject in all the history of the Church than the early Councils. Indeed, the ante-Nicene fathers are not popular reading today. Yet, despite Newman's rather esoteric interests, and the alien vocabulary, that seminal moment of revelation is moving. This seems odd in the absence of any particularity of detail and circumstance in which the readers—in the nineteenth century as well as ours—could recognize some similarity to their own lives.

The rich sense of the interaction between one's times, one's surroundings, and one's spirit, in all the concrete detail of daily life, was the province of the great novelists of Newman's day. The realist tradition was triumphant in Hardy and Dickens, Trollope, and George Eliot. Victorian masters of fiction made their readers feel as if they found a whole world inside the novels, one that, like our own, the reader could only partly know; literary critics can still debate endlessly about the secret feelings of the fictional people in these tiny worlds. Key moments are constructed like a grand edifice, of thousands of little bits of concrete everyday experience from which readers must infer and imagine the inner lives of characters, as if building up data for a sociological study. As we contemplate the mystery of how the innumerable circumstances contribute to characters' feelings and actions, we enrich our understanding of the mystery of the people we meet in the many dramas of our larger world. But although he is an emblematically eminent Victorian, Newman's novels and other narratives do not rise to that characteristic Victorian excellence: the connection of closely observed detail to the moral drama of human life.

Newman's handling of setting and plot hardly seem Victorian at all. Even in *Callista*, the painstakingly researched "novelistic" slices of local color—the locusts, the witchcraft, the intervention of a Greek philosopher, the mob rising into persecution and itself being attacked by the authorities, the three types of Roman marriage[6]—fascinating as they are, all seem a mere distraction from the passionate loneliness of the main characters, satisfied finally only in God. Perhaps finding Newman's novels wanting in characteristically novelistic roundedness of detail, some criticism decries Newman's novel plots as predictable.[7] But certainly no one can accuse him of adhering to Victorian plot conventions. In Newman's *Callista*, the hero runs off to a refuge from deadly peril, without a trace of shame—and without the virtuous girl he loves, whom he leaves behind to die. And after Newman puts the lovers through familial misunderstanding, prison, and deadly threats to bring them into a lovely spiritual harmony with one another, he never even lets them see each other alive again, much less get married. No ordinary template for Victorian novels could have predicted a tenth of the events of *Callista*. Trollope, Thackeray, and Dickens can never resist at least one tidy marriage, and even graver novelists like Eliot, Gaskell, and Hardy at least include marriage, however grimly, among the chief events of their heroes' lives. All of them carefully craft circumstances to justify their characters' decisions and settle their plots without divine intervention.[8]

His enormous popularity as a preacher in his day, and the continuing weight of Newman as a moral authority in his church, attest that Newman indeed understands the drama and mystery of human character in decision as few others have; but circumstances fall away under his pen. Crucial incidents in *Callista*, like Agellius's illness and the demonic possession of Juba, arrive by Divine fiat, without anything like the thousand little hints and preparations one might expect from a Victorian steeped in the scientific and sociological preoccupations of Newman's time. The interaction of circumstance with character is evidently unimportant to him.

Loss and Gain is similarly eccentric for a Victorian novel. For one thing, nobody important gets married. For another, almost nobody does anything externally more startling than getting on a train or going to church. The drama is all internal, and the novel's pacing seems almost calculated to undercut any understanding of the working of circumstances upon the mind. Wild, luminous moments in Charles Reding's tenderly unfolding yearning for God—the chat in the garden with his sister; the session of prayer at the roadside cross, near the mysterious penitent; the kiss of the man who will later become a Passionist priest; the marvelous adoration of the Blessed Sacrament in the end—jostle against a rowdy crowd of charming but acidly satiric setpieces that are so much at odds with the hero's emotional development that they seem to have crashed the party from some other novel. Distracted by the fun of the innumerable conversations that Newman sprinkles with barbs against private judgment or the Anglican follies of his day, we lose sight of Charles for two momentous years while he develops toward Catholicism in the house of a sketchily drawn Anglican clergyman. And when Charles makes up his mind to become a Roman Catholic, Newman grants him only a brief, harrowing interview with his mother. Newman wrote the novel soon after his own conversion; no doubt Newman's own wounds were still stinging from his sister Harriet's "terrible letters." But, to use an example from another style of storytelling, imagine the way George Eliot would have steeped the mother's language, for such a scene, in the rich colors of family history and complex feelings about her son and dead husband.[9]

As Charles travels by train to be received into the Catholic Church, a novelist like Eliot might have played the tones of the English countryside, punctuated with country steeples and colored with memory and longing, into a crescendo of poignant desire and fear and loss. Newman instead gives Charles one philosophically weighty railroad conversation with a Catholic priest traveling incognito, and then sends in a vaudeville show of religious cranks: John the kitchen-boy Irvingite, whose sect proposes to create new

Apostles; a lady with a twirling parasol who wishes Charles to nominate his favorite doctrines for her new religious body; Zerubbabel, who wants bloody sacrifices renewed on the Temple Mount; Mr. Batts of the Truth Society, whose doctrine is that truth must be sought but cannot be found; the author of Kitchens' surefire "Spiritual Elixir," who is afraid of crosses; a wildcat Swedenborgian; and a crusty old Anglican who deplores Charles's social disgrace but is grateful that he hasn't made worse mistakes, like losing the family money. No doubt these zanies reflect the actual hounding of converts by unsavory religious zealots, for converts' names were published in the newspapers to facilitate such persecution. The scenes are funny; they're philosophically very keen at times; but they seem to be intruders from a comic rather than a passionate courtship dance between a man and his God. Such stories there are; C. S. Lewis's *Surprised by Joy* is merciless to his fatuous early self. But the character of Charles Reding is ardent and humble, not combative and self-satisfied, and the parade of absurdities develops neither his character nor the structure of the plot. Newman takes on the role of a controversialist, combating the isolation and persecution of Catholic converts and mocking the instability of private judgment in Protestantism. He is not seeking a unified emotional effect for his readers, or balancing character and incident to serve the grand architectural sweep we identify as the shape of the great Victorian novel.

Technical tools of plotting and pacing, of tone and choice of detail, are not Newman's primary interests when he's telling a story. His central preoccupation sheds some light on why he could look at himself, a fellow of Victorian Oxford—and see a fifth-century Greek-speaking heretic from Asia Minor. What Newman cares about is what he called "romance"—though it is not much like what is ordinarily called "romance" in novels. Newman admired, for instance, the cleverness of Jane Austen's tightly plotted, beautifully paced art. In Austen, as in any consummate English novelist, circumstance is chosen carefully and narrated minutely so as to blossom forth to the revelation of character, which in its turn is revealed to be deeply shaped by circumstance. Austen's heroine always falls in love and finally marries the right person. That rightness is precisely calibrated in terms of social and moral worth, and the couple is guaranteed lifelong prosperity. Nevertheless, as her characters go off two by two into matrimony, Newman laments, "Miss Austen has no romance—none at all!"[10]

Romance for Newman is not sexual love, nor the favorable settling of the hero's fortune and marriage prospects, nor even dramatic events. Rather, romance is the passionate commitment of one's self to another—he considered his ordination "espousals" of this sort. For Newman—who thought that the world might be a dream and was certainly a symbol, and to whom only two beings had any sure existence, himself and his luminous God—there was only one story, really, and it did not matter where in the shadowy physical world it happened, or when it happened, or how it happened. The central event of romance is that assent of the whole self to a relationship. The "unromantic" Austen always approaches love as mediated and properly held in check by class and finances and the acceptance of social convention; but Newman can see a monophysite in Victorian England because race, class, gender, and historical position do not matter: the one thing that matters is the decision to trust or not to trust the Holy Spirit at work in the people of God. In that commitment is romance; and the commitment is a free decision above all circumstance.

That is why it is not in dramatic structure but in the vignette, which enshrines the defining moment, that Newman's stories have power; and there they have power indeed. Certainly Newman honed his skills for the pulpit, where the apposite vignette cannot well expand itself to a novel. But even in his longer, scholarly writings, as Newman tells the stories of the saints—Chrysostom, Athanasius, Basil—his narrative meanders dully through mere lists of events until suddenly a personality leaps forth, forever defined in some glowing act or utterance. Newman prefers, when he learns of a saint, "to have any one action or event of his life drawn out minutely." Thus "we have a view of his character, his tastes, his natural infirmities, his struggles and victories over them, which in no other way can be attained." Newman prefers to give excerpts from saints' letters, or their reported words, because the passionate self there flashes forth most truly; thus we hear of St. Basil confronting the imperial vicar, who was trying to force him out of his episcopal authority. The vicar had the saint stripped to a single garment, revealing a body ravaged by jaundice; then the persecutor, executioners at hand, threatened to tear out Basil's liver. Then we hear Basil's own voice, combining the martyr's insouciance with the invalid's peevishness: "Thanks for your intention; where it is at present, it has been no slight annoyance." Learning of Basil's danger, Newman records, "the city rose...as bees smoked out of their home. The armourers, for whom the place was famous, the weavers, nay the women, with any weapon which came to hand, with clubs, stones, firebrands, spindles, besieged the vicar, who was only saved from immediate death by the interposition of his prisoner."[11] Here is not only a moment of triumph for the Church but a slice of the wry character of a man nevertheless courageous through the Holy Spirit. Yet when such full history of a saint is lost to knowledge, Newman does not despise the collective act of Christian imagination that has rushed in to supply the defect:

> The Christian lives in the past and in the future, and in the unseen; in a word, he lives in no small measure in the unknown. And it is one of his duties, and a part of his work, to make the unknown known; to create an image within him of what is absent, and to realise by faith what he does not see. For this purpose he is granted certain outlines and rudiments of the truth, and from thence he learns to draw out into its full proportions and its substantial form,—to expand and complete it; whether it be the absolute and perfect truth, or truth under a human dress, or truth in such a shape as is most profitable for him.[12]

The creation of a saint's legend is only one case of the understanding Newman had of all human perception—that we know the world through acts of faith and will, rather than as mere recorders. In the *Grammar of Assent*, the mere incursion of facts into the intellect is insufficient to make an idea "real"; reality emerges through memory and experience—even if it is only the experience of trusting the person who delivers the information. In the development of his epistemology, Newman freely acknowledged the influence of the Romantic poet, Samuel Taylor Coleridge, whose work "instilled a higher philosophy into inquiring minds, than they had hitherto been accustomed to accept" (*Apologia*, 202). Coleridge speaks of our world as unable to come to life, to come into full reality, without being interpreted.[13] Uniting poet and philosopher, Coleridge says: "Imagination ... I hold to be the living power and prime agent of all human perception, and as a repetition in the finite mind of the eternal act of creation in the infinite I AM." Without this act of will—for human imagination is the will acting upon the memory, to choose what to recognize—he says, "all objects (as objects) are essentially fixed and dead."[14] In his use of the Divine Name from the Book of Exodus, Coleridge implies that human perception and affirmation participate in God's creative work, and grant a new reality to the "dead" world. Newman builds on this sense of participation in perception in the *Grammar of Assent*, where humans can only assent to what is "real"—what is able to move the will. "Reality," in Newman's sense, can only enter the mind through the exercise of the imagination.

Reality is a personal and historical thing. Newman says that we recall and select realities among the particular sensations in memory. It is not an abstract idea of Peach but some single peach, remembered, that takes on for Newman the reality of all peaches in the world.[15] Moreover, within each human being, each peach, each story, realities exist in potency, unrealized by anyone's particular experience of that person, that tale, even that orb of fragrant fruit. Others—someone color-blind, or someone with different cultural training—may have some entirely different experience of a thing, and yet know truth about it, perhaps a truth invisible to others. To encounter reality is to encounter something that could reveal some other aspect of itself to another person; it is an encounter with mystery. Every reality opens this mysterious possibility, and every commitment we make to a belief in some reality is at its best a passionate commitment—an act of romance, founded upon an act of imagination.

In the *Apologia pro vita sua*, Newman says he turned to Coleridge from "the need which was felt both by the hearts and intellects of the nation for a deeper philosophy." He speaks of the "dry and superficial character of the religion of the last generation, or century"—a demand for impersonal, compelling evidence of the worth of religion because faith in the Christian community as the transmitter of doctrine had withered (*Apologia*, 202). German scholars had begun to mistrust the ancient Roman historians, making plausible arguments that they served as mere organs of political parties, slaves to either cultural delusions or the lust for power. Nothing they said could be trusted without corroborating archaeological artifacts.[16] However, a clever scholar could use such artifacts and draw judiciously upon these flawed texts to "scientifically" reconstruct the past by "inference" made necessary by the "absence of original records," which was the natural result of discrediting the historians.[17]

Suspicion about the reliability of texts spread to the Bible as well, fueled by French scholarship, which had in the preceding century made the story of Genesis a redaction of differing "source documents" that could be "recovered" on the basis of the words used for God in each pericope.[18] The "science" that caused the crisis of belief in the nineteenth-century crisis was historical text criticism, not biology. Newman put it plainly:

> Protestants, appeal to Scripture, when a religious question arises, as their ultimate informant and decisive authority in all such matters; but who is to decide for them the previous question, that Scripture really is such an authority? . . . Religious Protestants, when they think calmly on the subject, can hardly conceal from themselves that they have a house without logical foundations, which contrives indeed for the present to stand, but which may go any day—and where are they then? Of course Catholics will bid them receive the canon of Scripture on the authority of the Church, in the spirit of St. Augustine's well-known words, "I should not believe in the Gospel, were I not moved by the authority of the Catholic Church." But who, they ask, is to be voucher for the Church, and for St. Augustine?[19]

To treat the Bible as a completely objective artifact, untouched by human influence, rather than a story told by a community, is to make it into a dusty document for historians to dispute. The dead letter is open to the types of inference that had corroded history into an exercise in "disdain for antiquity" (*Apologia*, 135).[20] Bishop James Ussher had created a timetable based on a strictly literal reading of the Old Testament; geology and biology cast his chronology into doubt. Those who trusted the words of the Bible more than the community that had preserved it were thrown off balance, and many felt that they had to reject either God or science. Some religious people retreated from making any definite intellectual claims for religion, and located all faith in feelings.

Newman spurned as nonsensical an anti-intellectual approach to Christianity. One could demand neither from the Bible nor from "scientific" history a truth that could bring absolute certainty, and preclude any need for the act of will that makes a dead letter emerge into reality. In other words, even the "scientific" is founded upon some sort of need for faith. Nothing "objective" is sufficiently within our experience to move the will, for knowledge requires a knower. A knower's personal assent is required even for direct divine vision, like Peter's encounter with an angel who freed him from prison, which he could not be sure was reality.[21] It is hopeless, even morally wrong, to seek to purge knowledge of the taint of human witness. Newman's faith rested in "an argument from Personality, which in fact is one form of the argument from Authority" (*Apologia*, 135). Instead of trusting in his private conclusions about the written artifact of a Bible, Newman trusted in the community that had taught him what the Bible meant in its life. Newman preserves a reverence for even the historically thinnest legends of saints' lives because he is not ashamed to trust in the Christian community as it tells its stories.

Trust requires commitment; commitment requires real apprehension; and real apprehension, in its turn, requires imagination. What Christians are to really apprehend in trusting the word of the Christian community is the virtue of their predecessors. The German scholars had rifled Roman and then Biblical history for the most narrowly partisan and personal motivations for the writing of each text. They had recognized not human freedom but the overwhelming narrowing of the field of human action when controlled by the strongest desires—those oriented, as the Scholastics say, to self.

The desires centered on the self certainly lead to much duplicity, but not inevitably; they are not to be despised. Newman argues that we as humans are to seek our true happiness in God. To desire God is the virtue of Hope, and in Newman's *Discussions and Arguments on Various Subjects* he mocks the pride that despises the hope of reward from God as unworthy. Yet rightly do we pity or despise those whose lives are oriented only toward self—addicts and obsessives who cannot liberate themselves from need, cupidity, or fear in order to be able to do what they should rightfully do. We do not honor the enslaved will; we respect freedom, which has imagination for its root.

By imagination human minds can recognize and sympathize with other selves, even with animals or plants or ecosystems; we can know what's good for them, because we can imagine them as in some way like ourselves. Having a real apprehension of the good of the other is what enables people to be attracted to those goods as well as to the good oriented to self. Any good thing attracts a person who can really apprehend it. Freedom is being able to choose which good to regard in a given moment, our own or other goods. Like God, a free being can choose among good things, without choice necessarily involving evil. Newman finds that human beings are not bound by necessity to choose only the good for the self; humans are free, as God is, because they have imagination. In fact, one can choose poverty, chastity, silence—one can even freely choose obedience.[22] Those who most achieve this freedom, which wills the good of all beings as much as the good of the self, are those who have the mind of Christ. They are most free and therefore most loving, for there is an infinite scope to the love of one who is not bound to self.

A free imagination is therefore not compelled by desire for food, sex, entertainment, power, money, or any of the million other obsessions; to be overcome by such desires is to become like an abandoned hulk on the ocean: helpless, undirected, the wreck of an image of God. If all one's choices are already made, contracted to the next fix, the next drink, the next scheme for filling some aching, craving pit of ambition—then one's human personhood itself is twisted and cramped. Because desire is infinite, it is an eternal frustration to limit it to some finite space—self, tribe, country. It is a truth common to the point of banality that sensual attempts to satisfy infinite desire simply become more and more desperate; people even find themselves exploiting fear to stimulate enough adrenaline to distract the desperate soul from the howling emptiness within. Newman knew this too, and said, as he advised the young to limit the garbage to which their imaginations are exposed, "At this day surely there is a special need of this warning; for this is a day when nothing is not pried into, nothing is not published, nothing is not laid before all men" ("Ignorance," 260). And in that sermon Newman was not even envisioning an age when a mere click of the mouse or flick of a dial could bring us habitual acceptance toward, mental practice of, and even interactive participation in meaningless sexual couplings, aggressive physical revenge, or cynical humor, cramping the imagination with less effort than ever before.

Yet every functioning human being has, however damaged, some ability to imagine the desires or benefits of other beings, and act upon those perceived realities. We see that someone is tired or hungry; we understand what this is. We also understand when someone wants attention, money, or power at our expense. But such understanding has a different tenor in the great saints, according to Newman:

> They are versed in human knowledge; they are busy in human society; they understand the human heart; they can throw themselves into the minds of other men; and all this in consequence of their natural gifts and education. While they themselves stand secure in the blessedness of purity and peace, they can follow in their imagination the ten thousand aberrations of pride, passion and remorse. The world is to them a book, to which they are drawn for its own sake.[23]

"For its own sake"—that is the great freedom in Newman's view of the imagination: to be liberated from the need to love the world merely for the sake of oneself. That book which is the world is closed to terrorists, whose failure to love things for their own sakes is the deep failure of their lives. Their corrosive ambition, their war against all humanity outside their own cause, is like the hell envisioned by Newman's Callista—an ultimately lonely feeding off of self, trammeled and self-devouring, focusing on all things only as they enhance the killers' sense of power.

Newman says that St. Paul's "vivid imagination enabled him to throw himself into the state of heathenism, with all those tendencies which lay dormant in his nature carried out, and its infirmities developed into sin." Therefore, "he is tender towards (*sic*) the weak from a sense of his own weakness" (*Sermons*, 117, 125). The real use of the imagination is the use Christ made of it: to pour oneself out for the good of others, in the virtue of charity. And then, as Newman says of St. Paul,

> A man who thus divests himself of his own greatness, and puts himself on a level with his brethren, and throws himself upon the sympathies of human nature, and speaks with such simplicity and such spontaneous outpouring of heart, is forthwith in a condition both to conceive great love of them, and to inspire great love towards himself. (*Sermons*, 125)

Moreover, the very fact that we can recognize these desires and act on them implies a much larger freedom; we can recognize good in things that are simply good in themselves—happy children, peaceful nations—without needing to secure our own profit. We can see this good as something worthy of being pursued; we can be heroes, we can seek the truth, we can be saints. In charity, we seek to lead others to the good they truly desire because we understand its likeness to the good we truly desire.

The great step needed for faith, the indispensable step, is to recognize that others too have this desire for the good, the true, and the beautiful, and that they can act upon it. But if we refuse to believe in the infinite yearnings of the human heart, we can recognize only the most narrow and crabbed of motives in the works of others—like the suspicious German historians who dared not allow that the historians of Rome might have a simple desire to speak the truth. The refusal to believe in the disinterested love of another person for what is good makes it impossible to have religious faith. Faith springs from accepting the idea that those who tell us about God are motivated not by baseness and greed but by a desire to speak the truth and do good. Newman sees as sin the refusal to accept that they love not merely the good of themselves but our good, and that they approach us with charity. People can choose to believe or refuse to attend to that reality of the desire for good in another person's soul. The virtue of faith is an act of free will because it requires a constant affirmation of this attention to the goodness of fellow creatures. If we choose the right stories, they train the imagination to understand such virtue in others; to attend to stories can be a discipline of faith.

Therefore Newman encouraged the writing of English saints' lives, just as his hero St. Philip Neri "substituted, for the chivalry or the hurtful novels of the day, the true romances and the celestial poetry of the lives of the saints" (*Sermons*, 281). Convinced that "Revealed Religion should be especially poetical,"[24] Newman advanced poetry as a vehicle for bringing the Oxford Movement into far more homes than ever had contact with his little cadre of ritualistic Anglican priests; "The Dream of Gerontius" made it possible for his readers to imagine the concerns of the Last Things and the state of Purgatory. Imagination fulfills the need to keep the good before one's eyes and in the reality of one's experience, to see in memory the noble and the good. Newman emphasized the need to keep nobility of heart before the eyes of our imaginations, to renew one's apprehension of the ability of others to seek truth, and the love engendered by good. It was because he was able to attribute good desires to others that Newman could accept the Fathers' flexible approaches to the Bible. He trusted the good faith of the community more than the sort of judgment that expects only evil and suspects that the people of ancient times were more corrupt morally than the manuscripts they had preserved for their posterity were corrupt textually. Thus Newman developed, as he said, "freer views on the subject of inspiration than were usual in the Church of England at the time" (*Apologia*, 131) and escaped with both his equanimity and his keen intellect intact during the hurricane

of doubt that devastated so much of English Christianity. Newman notes
that it is often a consequence of habituation to sin, one's own or that of others, that one's heart hardens so that it refuses to recognize virtuous impulses
in others'. Such people, lost to faith, he says,

> are very sceptical about the existence of principle and virtue; they think all men
> are equally swayed by worldly, selfish or sensual motives, though some hide
> their motives better than others, or have feelings and likings of a more refined
> character. And having given in to sin themselves, they have no higher principle
> within them to counteract the effect of what they see without . . . and they use
> their knowledge to overreach, deceive, seduce, corrupt, or sway those with
> whom they have to do. ("Ignorance," 1717–18)

Well before our time Newman could foresee the deadening effect of an
intensely cynical and snide popular culture that attacks every permanent commitment among human beings, so that the imagination has nothing to feed
on but its own darkest fears. Newman had much to say about how private
judgment becomes at length the justification for the most desperate states of
decay in the human spirit. Even within our own society, in a desperate effort
to feel that something matters, people look to more and more exercise of
their own power, to even violence. Only the destruction of the self is accomplished by such delusive assertions of the self's power of commitment. The
terrorist, self-absorbed and suicidal, is the emblematic case of this desperation.

Newman urged his parishioners to commit themselves instead to the way
of the saints, who know by imagination the sin that surrounds them and, "by
reason of the grace which dwells within them, they study it and hold con-
verse with it for the glory of God and the salvation of souls" (*Sermons*,
117–18). A saint can pity the disappointment of the infinite yearning of the
souls whose imaginations are desperately stunted. The stories of saints must
be told to keep alive the very capacity for understanding virtue: single-
hearted chastity, noble humility, firm resolve, joyous endurance, gentle gift,
heroic charity. A story, rather than a plan, a diagram, or an example, hints at
this infinity of the unknown in any person, in any culture or situation.
Newman is a storyteller because he cares about that capacity for infinite
yearning, the soil from which faith and charity spring.

NOTES

1. Neal Gabler offers this theory not only for the attackers but for their victims in
   the *New York Times*, September 16, 2001, sec. 4.2; cf. Martha Bayles, "Closing
   the Curtain on 'Perverse Modernism,'" *The Chronicle of Higher Education*,
   October 16, 2001, B14.
2. "Ignorance of Evil," in *Parochial and Plain Sermons* (London: Longman,
   Green, 1891; reprint, San Francisco: Ignatius Press, 1997), 1716.
3. John Henry Newman, *Apologia pro Vita Sua*, ed. Philip Hughes (Garden City,
   New York: Doubleday Image Books, 1956), 162.
4. Nancy Gibbs, "In Sorrow and Disbelief," *Time Magazine, Online*, May 2,
   1999, http://www.time.com/time/archive/preview/from_newsfile/0,10987,

1101990503-23541,00.html; Peter Jennings, interview with Mrs. Schnerr, mother of surviving Columbine massacre-victim Val Schnerr, ABC Evening News, April 28, 1999; James Dobson, radio interviews with Columbine murder witnesses, *Focus on the Family*, May 5 and May 15, 1999.

5. M. Jamie Ferriera, "The Grammar of the Heart," in *Discourse and Context: An Interdisciplinary Study of John Henry Newman*, ed. Gerard McGill (Carbondale, Southern Illinois University Press, 1993), 131.

6. The three levels of Roman marriage correspond, by the way, with startling modernity to what in America can be recognized as our own legal categories: domestic partnerships, marriage with no-fault divorce, and covenant marriage.

7. Ann Carson Daly, "Ever Old, Ever New: The Novelistic Heart of Newman," at http://www. ewtn.com/library/HUMANITY/FR89406.TXT, 10.

8. John Henry Newman, *Callista, A Tale of the Third Century*, ed. Alan G. Hill (Notre Dame: University of Notre Dame Press, 2000).

9. John Henry Newman, *Loss and Gain*, ed. Alan G. Hill, The World's Classics (Oxford: Oxford University Press, 1986).

10. Qtd. in Ian Ker, *John Henry Newman, A Biography* (Oxford: Oxford University Press, 1988), 138.

11. John Henry Newman, *Historical Sketches*, vol. II (Westminster, Maryland: Christian Classics, 1970), 13.

12. John Henry Newman, "A Legend of St. Gundleus," in *The Lives of the English Saints, Written by Various Hands at the Suggestion of John Henry Newman*, ed. Arthur Wollaston Hutton, vol. 3 (London: Ballantyne, Hanson & Co., 1901), 5.

13. Patricia Ball, *The Science of Aspects: The Changing Role of Fact in the Work of Coleridge, Ruskin and Hopkins* (London: Athlone Press, 1971), 5.

14. Samuel Taylor Coleridge, *Biographia Literaria*, ed. James Engell and Walter Jackson Bate, vol. 1 (New Jersey: Princeton University Press, 1983), 304.

15. John Henry Newman, *Essay in Aid of a Grammar of Assent* (Notre Dame: University of Notre Dame Press, 1979), 40.

16. Herbert Butterfield, *The Origins of History* (New York: Basic Books, Inc., 1981), 195–97.

17. This process is described with complacent approval in the next generation by the *Encyclopaedia Britannica*, 11th ed. [1910–11], s.v. Barthold Georg Niebuhr.

18. Butterfield, *Origins*, 194–95.

19. John Henry Newman, *Discussions and Arguments on Various Subjects*, new ed. (London: Longmans Green & Co., 1891), 367.

20. Newman seems to have been theologically unruffled by evolutionary theory; cf. Newman, *Grammar of Assent*, 206–07.

21. Newman's *Philosophical Notebooks* (ed. Edward Sillem, vol. 2 [New York: Humanities Press], 1970) cites this example from Acts 12: 8–11.

22. See Annie Dillard's witty account of this liberty in her essay "Living Like Weasels," in *Teaching a Stone to Talk* (New York: Harpercollins, 1982).

23. John Henry Newman, *Sermons Preached on Various Occasions* (London: Burns & Lambert, 1862), 106; cf. discussion by John C. McCloskey, "The Apostolate of Personal Influence in the Work of Cardinal Newman," at http://www.catholicity.com/cathedral/mccloskey/newman.html.

24. John Henry Newman, "Poetry, with Reference to Aristotle's *Poetics*," in *Essays and Sketches*, vol. I (New York: Longmans Green & Co, 1948), 76.

CHAPTER 8

A "THOUSAND SOLACES" FOR THE MODERN SPIRIT: WALTER PATER'S RELIGIOUS DISCOURSE

Lesley Higgins

> *Fundamental belief gone, in almost all of us, at least some relics of it remain—queries, echoes, reactions, after-thoughts; and they help to make an atmosphere, a mental atmosphere, hazy perhaps, yet with many secrets of soothing light and shade, associating more definite objects to each other by a perspective pleasant to the inward eye against a hopefully receding background of remoter and ever remoter possibilities.*

—*Pater*, Miscellaneous Studies

Friends and colleagues of Walter Pater who tried to revise public opinion after his death in July 1894 attempted to "restore" the once-notorious don's reputation by insisting that, in his later years, he had returned to the Church of England's pious embrace. A renewal of religious orthodoxy was invoked to sanitize a life—and a literary canon—and to rescue all from any taint of "decadence." Subsequently, some Pater critics have obeyed similar impulses, insisting that the near-conversion that Marius undergoes, in *Marius the Epicurean*, is autobiographical signal and fictive fact. Marius's experiences, they contend, constitute indirect proof that the author himself eventually re-endorsed Christian piety, and thereby either repudiated or mitigated the relativism and anti-Christianity expressed in his earliest writings.[1] Other critics have vehemently insisted just the opposite: that to speak about religious suppositions in Pater's writings is to destabilize his importance as a seminal figure in radical *fin de siècle* culture. Some would have it both ways: Pater attempted to "reconstruct" and "reclaim" a vague Anglo-Catholicism that enfolded aestheticism, decadence, and homoeroticism.[2]

Dispensing with any interest in Pater's own devotional needs or activities,[3] this essay suggests that critical nervousness about the possible role of religious *dogma* in Pater's life and texts has occluded the pivotal place of religious *discourse* throughout his writings, both published and unpublished. Most importantly, such an oversight has obscured the extent to which these discursive practices provided an important response to "the conditions of modern life" as Pater encountered them in the late nineteenth century.[4] Rather than rehearse my argument in terms of the most familiar Pater texts, however, this essay concentrates on several unpublished works-in-progress in which the full breadth and resourcefulness of these discursive enterprises are revealed.[5] These hitherto unexamined manuscripts include "Art and Religion," "The Aesthetic Life," "The History of Philosophy," "Thistle," and "Moral Philosophy." Taken as a whole, the unfinished fragments and essays are both summary and symbol of the always-incomplete answers Pater constructed.

Speculations on the proper relationship between cultural productions and the burden of modern existence culminate, in the "Winckelmann" essay, in the following passage: "What modern art has to do in the service of culture is so to rearrange the details of modern life, so to reflect it, that it may satisfy the spirit. And what does the spirit need in the face of modern life?"[6] Variously enunciated, the latter question energizes the Pater canon from aesthetic criticism and travel essays to fiction and philosophical speculations. For it is the *spirit* that remains fundamental in Pater's writings: it is anterior to morality, myth, and religion. Hence his initial disagreement with "Coleridge's Writings": "Coleridge thinks that if we reject the supernatural, the spiritual element in life will evaporate also, that we shall have to accept a life with narrow horizons, without disinterestedness, harshly cut off from the spirits of life in the past. But what is this spiritual element? It is the passion for inward perfection with its sorrows, its aspirations, its joy" (*CW*, 57). This "modern" spiritual condition, of "a soul permanently ill at ease" (*MS*, 82), can generally be defined as post-Kantian existence intensified by Darwinian scientific discourse. To quote the "Prosper Mérimée" essay, "After Kant's criticism of the mind, its pretensions to pass beyond the limits of individual experience seemed as dead as those of old French royalty" (*MS*, 11).[7] The unfinished "Art and Religion," on the other hand, identifies religious discourse as an important site of resistance to the encroaching and often "sterile" (*AR*, 58) scientism of the age. The "levelling down of man to the merely physical world," as "natural organism" only, Pater contends, loses sight of "minimum distinctions within the region of mind itself" (*AR*, 16r). Consequently, one forgets that human beings are "allied to a wonderful world of intellectual culture of man in history, of man in possession of {a} sagacious political life, of ^a thousand solaces^ for his spirit in music and the like, in the wonderful story of his religious history" (*AR*, 17r, 18r).

"The Aesthetic Life," one of the more complete and polished manuscripts, begins by considering then-contemporary convictions that religion is *passé*:

> We live (it is said daily) amid the wreck of religious theories of the unseen; while philosophy itself, turned suicidal, proclaims that all theories which propose to carry us beyond our own fleeting experience are not merely obsolete, but essentially vicious in aim.... The true history, the progress, of the human mind might seem to be that of its disillusion. And if metaphysical philosophy has thus renounced all pretension to carry us beyond time and space, on the other hand, its surviving antagonist, the empirical philosophy ... has, in inverse proportion, narrowed the ... spiritual, the imaginative, horizon. The magnificent forethought of creation, the creative energy itself, are replaced by slow worms' work. (*AL*, 1r, 2r)

"[R]eligious faith," the text contends, remains one of the more successful means to "under-arch the void with an ideal which is also a great possibility" (*AL*, 4r). At the very least, the "modern mind" has "come to a <delicacy> {<fineness>} refinement, . . . ^a versatility,^ a spiritual cunning" (*AL*, 29r).

Prompted, then, by such "spiritual" queries, Pater's texts have a double motive: first, to dismantle the absolute truth claims of Christianity, interrogating its doctrinal paradigms and especially its somatic regime; and second, to reaffirm, as an alternative, the imaginative and idealistic potential of historically specific religious discourses. Having refused or refuted the main ontological and eschatological props of the Christian system, the texts endorse instead the benefits of religious intuition, creativity, communality, and consolation. (This is very different from suggesting that Pater is another Victorian "reconciler," who, like Benjamin Jowett or Matthew Arnold, tried to reconcile the seemingly competing discourses of religion and science.[8]) Fundamentally, Pater's writings stress the importance of religion as cultural practice: useful and vital for the production of values and art, but not, historically speaking, indispensable. Put another way, Pater eschews the truth claims of any one *religion*—an established church's system of worship—and promotes instead the social, spiritual, and aesthetic possibilities of *religiousness*.

Pater's texts, I would argue, repeatedly disavow the transcendent or apocalyptic promises of organized religions, yet never doubt the rudimentary human significance of religious discourse. The essay "Art and Religion," for example, denies "the old arg[umen]t of an universal rel[igious] sense or intuitive innate sense of the divine, a rel[igious] faculty, as they say," yet insists that there is an "intuitional function" that can be "organised in the Xn ch[urch]" (*AR*, 34r) or expressed through art. The "Art and Religion" manuscript includes notes for three linked essays: Essay 1 would "show[] the reasonableness, the fitness to the artist, of the precept—Be as rel[igious] as possible." Essay 2 would "show[] that Amiel won't do—is a loss of ideal." And Essay 3 would "limit[], yet assert[], the claim of cath[olicis]m" (*AR*, 1r). All would be animated by the following observation:

> Rel[igion]—what a cheerfulness it gives to work—symp[athy] with others is an ideal—... endless hope—what a dignity & int[erest] it gives to life—more than

that disparate view—what a sense of security, of largeness, in work—More, the artist acquires happiness—rel[igion] releases from unhappiness—a gr[eat] burden of unhappiness wh[ich] retards w[or]k. (*AR*, 2r)

It is not the purpose of this essay to impose a Foucauldian analysis on Pater's writings.[9] Instead, and more significantly, the discussion proposes several ways in which Pater's analyses anticipate Foucault: through the consistent theorization of the formation and function of knowledge/power relations in religious systems; an insistence on the historicity of religious discourse; the analysis of the way in which the ultimate object of devotion and impenetrable knowledge—the deity—is constructed by a society (thus fulfilling an imaginative as much as a spiritual need); the argument that each cultural epoch "produces" (Pater's term) its own dreams and ideals (*HP*, 1r); and the attention paid to issues of subjectivity and "the aesthetics of existence."[10] Crucial to the writings of each man is an anti-metaphysical hypothesis, and genealogical rather than teleological or originary intentions.[11] In "Nietzsche, Genealogy, History," Foucault argues that, "A genealogy of values, morality, asceticism, and knowledge will never confuse itself with a quest for their 'origins,' will never neglect as inaccessible the vicissitudes of history."[12] Pater had expressed a similar argument in *Plato and Platonism*: "Fix where he may the origin of this or that doctrine or idea . . . , the specialist will still be able to find us some earlier anticipation of that doctrine, that mental tendency" (*PP*, 31). In Pater's essays, as in Foucault's, not the *Ursprung* or origins of religions but the historical operations and consequences of religious systems, sentiments, and practices are stressed. Pater rethinks and reimagines religious discourse, I would argue, similar to the way Foucault, meditating on Nietzsche's writings, rethinks history. "It is not the unavoidable conclusion of a long preparation," to quote "Nietzsche, Genealogy, History," but "a scene where forces are risked in the chance of confrontations, where they emerge triumphant, where they can also be confiscated."[13]

As a cultural historian, therefore, Pater stresses the assimilative and nonexclusive developmental flux of Western religions, pausing to consider the social or personal impact of religious sentiments rather than explicate specific beliefs. "Who would forego," the "Pascal" essay demands, "in the spectacle of the religious history of the human soul, the aspects, the details which the doctrines of . . . grace . . . embody?" (*MS*, 71). Inscribing in his works an acute "temporal perspectivism,"[14] Pater reassesses, microcosmically, the way in which many religions—particularly Christianity—organize the individual within time, and focuses, macrocosmically, on historical "periods of anachronism, survival, or transition"[15] in which religious discourses compete with one another. Although readily identified with or by specific individuals— the condemned Socrates's desire for an afterlife, Marcus Aurelius's inadequate Stoicism, or the dilemmas of a late nineteenth-century English agnostic— each "locus of emergence," to borrow Foucault's phrase, reminds us of the extent to which the "time-spirit" or "the genius of the age more or less insensibly control[s]" the enunciating subjects (*EL*, 3r).

To pursue the argument further, I would like to outline several crucial facets of Pater's engagement with religious discourse. Specifically, the discussion addresses the ways in which Pater's writings stage a contest between religious "authority" and a relativistic theory of knowledge; the social benefits of polyphonous discourses; and religion and subjectivity. Mention is also made of the function of "religious yearning" as defined in Pater's essay "Moral Philosophy"; and the construction of a "religious personality" sketched in several manuscripts (extensions of a project first attempted in "Diaphaneitè").

RADICAL RELATIVITY

From his first, privately circulated essay to his last, partially completed manuscript, Pater's texts grapple with the consequences of denying "any form of absolute or wholly objective knowledge."[16] As "Coleridge's Writings" announced in 1866, "To the modern spirit nothing is or can be rightly known except relatively under conditions" (*CW*, 49). In "Moral Philosophy," drafted and revised while Pater was working on *Marius the Epicurean* in the early 1880s, he returns to the premise

> I have been dwelling on at ^^so much^^ length—that all ^human knowledge^ is but relative; that is to say, that, all man's ideas, and views, the forms in which he mirrors his experience as a whole, or any part of it, are consequences of his position at a particular time and place, each true indeed from its own point of view but false ^or inadequate^ at the next point, and all alike mere phases in the mental career of one ^the very essence of^ whose <very> life physical and spiritual is mutation ^itself^. (*MP*, 4r)

Such a refusal of what Foucault terms a fundamental "will to knowledge" could be, Pater admits, intellectually and morally paralyzing. Pater, however, is challenged by the way in which "the relative spirit, by dwelling on the more fugitive conditions or circumstances of things,... giv[es] elasticity to inflexible principles" (*CW*, 60). What can be known *about* and *through* religious discourse is radically reduced, but the latter can nonetheless prevent the individual from "abandon[ing] oneself" (*CW*, 48), or capitulating hopelessly, to "a certain *nihilism*" (*MP*, 4r), an "abyss" of unmeaning. This thorny issue preoccupies "Moral Philosophy." "At the present day," the essay observes,

> there are two circumstances which powerfully affect the {condition} [or] state of general philosophy: first the weakened hold of religious authority on the modern intellect and secondly the doctrine of the relativity of human knowledge[.] Perhaps the authority of religion over the human intellect can at no period be said to have been really unquestioned—at no period of the old pagan religions[,] at no period again in the Christian world[,] as for instance in the age represented by Saint Bernard—the great epoch of its culmination according to some writers—in which however it is directly... ^confronted^ by the

innovating ideas of Abelard. But the question is one of degree and the authority of a system of religious ideas to ^direct or^ limit...men's speculations has certainly been most readily questioned during the last three centuries. (*MP*, 2r, 2v, 3r)

"Dogmatic faith" and the features of an "assured system" are quietly repudiated in this text—and yet, the essay suggests, "And yet it is the religious authority which has ever been at bottom the most effective sanction of morals[,] the...clearest explanation of *duty* being that it is something owed to a persona whose claims on one include those of one's neighbour and...^one's self^ " (*MP*, 3v). Religion, the essay concludes, must be bracketed, positively, with *custom* rather than absolute truths—"religious yearning" can produce stability and cultural coherence without taking refuge in false assurances of transcendence.

> To do or abstain from doing a thing in deference to custom might seem the leading treat of a weak character. Yet customariness!—how we prize it! Order,... {KOSMOS} how many of the best associations the words awake in us! How much {really consists[,] depends on the religious}....For the essence[,] the principle of such deference to custom if you really look hard at it and raise its... {relations by} but one degree is sympathy[,] sympathy with a body of persons outlined perhaps but vaguely in our minds[.] (*MP*, 10v)

An anti-systematic position is always maintained in Pater's texts; they never waiver from their critique of the potential destructiveness of institutionalized discourses. (Otherwise, one suffers as did Emerald Uthwart: "He found himself in a system of fixed rules, amid which, it might be said, some of his own tendencies and inclinations would die out of him through disuse" [*MS*, 211].) Hence the number of priestly figures in Pater's canon (including an unfinished "portrait" of a "saintly" yet "different" French priest) who are tested and consequently fail in their proscribed roles. As Wolfgang Iser remarks, "It is the polemics against closed systems which throw the liberating impulse of the relative spirit into proper relief. Pater's scepticism is negative (rejecting the norms of the absolute spirit) and positive (bringing to light the undefined and undefinable)."[17]

SOCIAL INSTINCTS, RELIGIOUS ACTS

Paterian interest in the social dimensions of religious practices should not be underemphasized. As *Marius the Epicurean* and *Gaston de Latour* vividly enact, the beneficial public "dispersion" of religious ideals and rituals extends to the creation of nurturing communities. Cathedrals such as Notre-Dame d'Amiens and Notre-Dame de Troyes (the subject of another fragment) are similarly valued for the "popular" experiences of construction and utilization (*MS*, 119) that they represent. Medieval monasticism, on the other hand, is frequently censured in Pater's writings because of its "very exclusive" nature that "has verily turned its back upon common life, jealously closed inward upon itself" (*MS*, 141).

Literally and metaphorically, public religious activities offer "a pict[ure] of worship" that, according to "Art and Religion," "sceptical young men are to be sent back to—w[oul]d you like to have no share in this greatest of all societies?" (*AR*, 53r). Knoepflmacher, for one, has always criticized such "sentiments" because they "reduce religion to the ritualistic sensations of sympathy and joy"; Marius, he complains, is "left with only . . . ritual, the visible form of faith, . . . depicted as the only principle capable of self-renovation."[18] I would counterargue that Pater has identified the way in which religious rituals—the most visible and concrete discursive practices, embodied spectacles both public and communicative—provide a time and space and a "mental atmosphere" (*MS*, 15) for the development of moral "impressions." Importantly, they help to promulgate personal and collective "sanity." As Marius learns, "Ritual, in fact, like all other elements of literature, must grow and cannot be made—grow by the same law of development which prevails everywhere else, in the moral as in the physical world" (*ME*, 2:126). (Pater's religious discourse is indelibly marked by a development plot constructed from the writings of Heraclitus and Darwin.)

According to the "Art and Religion" manuscript, religious discourse articulates "a certain social instinct," a "cons[cious]ness of the . . . community in a general way" (*AR*, 35r). Furthermore, the lived communal reality of religious practices animates moral teachings, rendering them "as concrete as possible" (*AR*, 52r). "On a larger scale," one learns in "Moral Philosophy," "that concession to [religious] custom becomes . . . *assent* and that vague body to which we in thought defer becomes incorporate as *humanity*" (*MP*, 11r).

MODELS OF SCEPTICISM AND ASSENT

At the same time that the community provides, in a "general way," a "company" of " 'enthusiastic' souls" (*AR*, 22r), religion exercises a more specific agency through the notion of a hieratic *doppelgänger*. Florian Deleal is but one of several figures in Pater's fiction who discover a special "companionship" and come to depend upon a "sacred double of their life, beside them" (*MS*, 193–94). In *Marius the Epicurean*, several characters rehearse for the role before Marius meets the worthy Cornelius. In terms of Pater's own writings, two figures repeatedly function as intellectual and spiritual "doubles"—Michel de Montaigne and John Henry Newman.[19] The textual presence of just one of these men would obviously provide decidedly "skeptical" or "assenting" "under-currents"; the presence of both ensures "delicate balances" (*GDL*, 104).

The function of skepticism in religious and philosophical discourses is essayed in "The History of Philosphy." The latter is almost Miltonic in its evocation of a prelapsarian or "unconscious" Greek age, "harmonious with itself," which was supplanted by "conscious speculation" (*HP*, 2v). "For philosophy begins," the composition insists,

> only when, under one of many possible guides—Heraclitus in the old world, and Berkeley or Fichte in the new—we enter into a sort of secondary consciousness,

in which the common sense of every-day becomes the subject of dispassionate criticism. . . . And it is a step which can never be retraced. The mind which has once broken the smooth surface of what seemed its self-evident principles can never again be as natural as a child's, nor perhaps will it ever find an equivalent for its earlier untouched healthfulness in that rationalised conception of experience, and man's relation to it[.] (*HP*, 3r, 3v)

The essay goes on to compare "ancient" and "modern" philosophical skepticism, preferring the latter's interest in "reason" to the former's "over-sophisticated" (*HP*, 5r) dedication to "a somewhat narrow metaphysical speculation" (*HP*, 5v).

The skepticism of Montaigne is therefore exceptional for its positive resourcefulness. A featured presence in *Gaston de Latour*,[20] Montaigne is also repeatedly invoked in the manuscript essays for his efforts to achieve a balance between belief and disbelief. (Pascal's indebtedness to Montaigne is also stressed as Pater explores the portentous role of doubt and denial in the circulation and dissemination of religious discourse.) Because of his crucial role in a tradition of "reaction," Montaigne occupies a cardinal place in the discussion of "Art and Religion":

> And in this aspect, phase of his [Montaigne's] curious individuality, he seems char[acteris]tic of a class; of a class of sceptics who have reserves, of various colours & degrees, on a certain matter based on their own special char[acteris]tic {—after a survey of the controversy.} of int[uitiona]l sincerity; {he} Mont. represents a general {in some instances very surprising} concession on the part of humanism {after all} to at least the questionableness of the rel[igious] view & explanation of things. He is one factor in a trad[itio]n of reaction wh[ich] upsets a certain generalisation [space for a word] as if rel[igio]n had only {thus questionably} been [truth?] at a particular time. . . . Augustine, Rousseau are others—a trad[itio]n of reaction of wh[ich] a hist[ory] might be written . . . a trad[itio]n of inability, actually to accept what might seem to be the {proper} real {moral from the premises} conc[er]n of a negative <ph[ilosophi]c> culture, of a ph[ilosoph]y of denial. (*AR*, 8r)

"Art and Religion" is only one of several manuscripts that is overwhelmed by its own efforts at contextualization. In this particular case, questions of "art" and even "art and religion" are delayed for more than fifty pages as the essay attempts to come to terms with "religion." In the process, Montaigne's "reactions" are counterbalanced by a consideration of John Henry Newman's special and difficult intuitional belief. "When we speak of int[utiona]l believers," Pater observes,

> perhaps the im[ag]e occurs of one of those mystic souls, like STC [Samuel Taylor Coleridge] or F.D.M. [F.D. Maurice] The uses & charm of this type of rel[igious] mind.
>
> But after all such [space for a word] as these, have no real difficulties; minds evasive; or they misrepresent, or their assent not real; they are no sceptics; at least, their scepticism is apart from, or independent of evid[ence].

> But there has been a trad[ition]n of int[uitiona]l belief very diff[erent]t from this—men who have immense difficulty, who yet receive entirely—& this on evid[ence]. Their position defined by scepticism [with] belief. . . .
>
> Instances—such were; {—} such in our own day, time, is Card. N. (*AR*, 57r)

The textual significance of Cardinal Newman's writings in the development of Pater's own "grammar of assent" and dissent deserves a separate essay. For the purposes of this discussion, I would simply remind the reader that Newman's discursive and personal presence is felt throughout Pater's canon. "Coleridge's Writings" finds little to praise in "STC's" own texts, but pauses to commend "writings which really spring from an original religious genius, such as those of Dr. Newman" (*CW*, 57). The production of "The Writings of Cardinal Newman" was extended yet incomplete—the manuscript, which occupies thirty-six sheets, is in various stages of preparedness; changes in script and writing implement indicate that portions of the essays were written and edited at different times. Central to this fascinating text is Pater's conviction that "Two <great> leading theological ideas especially" Newman has "thus made his own . . . the ideas of *Assent* and *Development*" (*WCN*, 7r):

> The "Theory of Dev/t"—the theory, like the bk.—{belongs} corresponds to a later phase in N's life, as also in the natural order of ideas; it is his justification of, or apology for the ch[urch] of R[ome]. But the greater & more permanent influence of N. at least for those who look at his work from without {is} lies not so much in his application of the idea of Dev/t in apology for the ch[urch] of R[ome] as in his theory of Assent his apology for rel[igio]n generally; though the fact that this remarkable effort in Xtn, in rel[igious] apology, sh[oul]d be the work of one who deserted the ref[ormatio]n ch[urch] may well seem a matter of serious consideration. The theory of Assent, if we may the use the term fixed by a vol[ume] of his later life a line of thought traceable in some of his earliest writings, is worked out specially, in his vols of [University Sermons] . . . and finally in that later vol[ume] pub[lishe]d in [space for date], The Grammar of Assent. (*WCN*, 8r)

In this and other essays, Pater positions himself as one of "those who look at" Christianity "from without"; it is a subject position that makes possible informed and engaged, yet distanced, enunciations. Like the multifaceted Cardinal he admired so profoundly,[21] Pater interrogates the "whole conjoint effects of the claims of religion" (*WCN*, 12r). Unlike Newman, however, Pater insists that "I want to look at it, from a p[oint] of view, certainly diff[eren]t from N's—humanly speaking, as they say—i.e. as an outsider <might> must look at it, noting what he sees, as <a> phen[omen]a of human mind, not of divine {gifts} grace" (*WCN*, 20r). A Montaignesque imperative or impetus always emerges in Pater's texts.

MULTIPLE VOICES, MANIFOLD RELIGIONS

J. Hillis Miller has evocatively described Pater's writings as "a palimpsest of discordant voices impossible to reduce to a single monologic meaning."[22]

The metaphor is borrowed from *Plato and Platonism*, which examines how, in the history of ideas and sensations, the "seemingly new is old also, a palimpsest, a tapestry in which the actual threads have served before" (*PP*, 38). Religious discourse, according to Pater's canon, is similarly polyvalent—not the revelation of a single truth but a web of truths featuring often antithetical warps and woofs. This rejection of doctrinal and sectarian exclusivity has drawn the criticism of many, including Knoepflmacher,[23] who would like Pater (and his fictional characters) to follow only one path—preferably straight, medium to narrow in width—toward Christian absolutism. But time and again a Paterian text demonstrates that the beliefs of one religious sect are not only insufficient, but temporally unstable. We shall always be able to discern what the "Pascal" essay terms "two opposed, two counter trains of phenomena . . . too large and complex a matter, as it is, to be embodied or summed up in any one single proposition or idea" (*MS*, 70). Analogously, an incomplete study of "Plato's Ethics" declares at the outset that any notion that "certain inward dispositions of the soul" should "be capable of reduction to one or another single exclusive formula . . . is more than could be expected" (*PE*, 1r).

One reason why so many of these manuscript projects remained unfinished might be that Pater realized his iconoclastic, historically informed ecumenicity would be ill-received. "Theology is a great house," the controversial "Coleridge's Writings" first announced, "scored all over with hieroglyphics by perished hands" (*CW*, 58). Within the house, as subsequent texts reaffirm, "there are a thousand intermediate shades of opinion, a thousand resting-places for the religious spirit" (*CW*, 52). Consequently, Pater's revisionist writings refuse to distinguish between the authenticity of ancient Greek and Roman religions and Christianity. Furthermore, they do not relegate pre-Christian religious discourses to the categories of "heathen beliefs" or, even more pejoratively, "myths." (In this Pater reaffirms the opinion expressed in Max Müller's *Introduction to the Science of Religion*.[24]) Hence Pater's insistence on the "religion of sanity" observed by the Lacedaemonians (*PP*, 226–27), and Marius's realization that the religion of his youth is "but one voice, in a world where there are many voices it would be a moral weakness not to listen to" (*ME*, 1:44).[25] As I have argued elsewhere, Pater repeatedly insists that Demeter and Persephone are chthonic *religious* figures, and should be respected and feared as such.[26] "Demeter and Persephone" is designed to restore "the mysticism" associated with these divinities from an "*earlier*, matriarchal culture" (*GS*, 79); to reestablish the "religious elements" of the "Eleusinian ritual"; and to reassert that "there were religious usages before there were distinct religious conceptions, and these antecedent religious usages shape and determine, at many points, the ultimate religious conception, as the details of the myth interpret or explain the religious custom." The emphasis on "usage" and "impressive religious rites" reminds one that Pater is always interested in the efficacy of worship, the personal and cultural benefits of "transforming daily life, and the processes of life, into a religious solemnity" (*GS*, 121–22).

TECHNOLOGIES OF THE SELF

Pater's fictional "portraits" dramatize—and carefully locate in specific historical and cultural "moments"—the production and instrumentality of "techniques of the self."[27] Not only would I suggest that Pater's notion of "self-culture" (*TR*, 229) anticipates and affirms Foucault's theory of the " 'cultivation of the self,' "[28] I would argue that both are highly critical of Christianity's potentially tyrannizing and deformative role in "subjectification."[29] The common ground of their critique is an appreciation of the ancient Greek emphasis on "the *techne* of life," an ethical code of conduct (and control) that did not punish individuals for acknowledging themselves as "subjects of desire" and polymorphous sexual practices.[30] Within Christianity, on the other hand, "self-formation" had to be

> constantly examined because in this self were lodged concupiscence and desires of the flesh. From that moment on, the self was no longer something to be made but something to be renounced and deciphered. Consequently, between paganism and Christianity, the opposition is not between tolerance and austerity, but between a form of austerity which is linked to an aesthetics of existence and other forms of austerity which are linked to the necessity of renouncing the self and deciphering its truth.[31]

The compulsory morality, and compulsory heterosexuality, of Christianity "was imposed on everyone in the same manner," thus organizing people within "a unified, coherent, authoritarian moral system."[32] Pater's interrogation of these repressive "practices of the self" is most apparent in arguments made against Christianity's somatic regime.[33] The latter transformed the human *body* and its pleasures into the *flesh*, a demonized and demonizing realm of sin, secrecy, and temptation.[34] Pater counters this disciplinary discourse, with its rigorously policed boundaries between the "licit and illicit,"[35] by insisting upon the primacy of the body in "self-culture," ancient or modern. In essays and fiction alike, writing the body is a recurrent "under-thought" and textual practice. As importantly, Pater refuses to dichotomize body and soul. (In this, too, he concurred with Max Müller, who championed philosophy's attempts to reconcile the "living body" and the "living soul.") Any "religion of sanity" praised by Pater emphatically includes, and endorses, "bodily sanity" as well (*ME*, 1:41).

"The Child in the House" is an exemplary study in the diverse "practices of the self" Pater sanctioned.[36] At a crucial phase in Florian Deleal's emotional and "mental growth"—after he has cultivated a "desire of physical beauty"—"religious sentiment" is introduced as an affirmative, resourceful *techne* that "presented itself to him as a thing that might soften and dignify, and light up as with a 'lively hope,' a melancholy already deeply settled in him. So he yielded himself easily to religious impressions, and with a kind of mystical appetite for sacred things" (*MS*, 192–93).

The Paterian ideal of a "diaphanous" character or "temperament"—an argument pursued in the essays "Moral Philosophy" and "The Aesthetic

Life"—is the quintessential product of affirmative "techniques of the self."
"Might such a temper," he inquires in "The Aesthetic Life," "extend itself
further still & modify{ing} practice generally, present itself...{as a
ph[ilosoph]y}? Briefly, {modify the interests of other lives} {as a theory or
prin. of service to other men's lives...}...it w[oul]d not be difficult to intimate its tendencies...its sympathies,...in politics, in morals, in rel[igio]n"
(*AL*, 37r). Such intimations undoubtedly inform Pater's tentative outline for
Thistle, the novel that would have constituted a trilogy with *Marius the
Epicurean* and *Gaston de Latour*. According to one sketchy note for the project, Thistle discovers "something different from all those forces" in circulation at the beginning of the nineteenth century—"a something represented
best by Newman":

> The beginning of this cent[ury] in Eng[lan]d.
> Rousseau & Voltaire, have been.
> Kant, has been—opening a double way.
> The Fr[ench] rev[olutio]n has been.
> STC, Keats, Shelley, Wordsworth, Byron, are around.
> He finds, defines, realises, something diff[eren]t from all those forces—a some-
> thing rep[resente]d best by Newman—of whom in a way, & amid quite other
> cond[ition]s, outward & inward, he is an anticipation. (*Th*, 3r)

"What he needs," the text would have demonstrated, "is a larger-soul[']d life
than his own—the working-out of the spiritualities of what then, *is*. In this
way, might be indicated, the *permanent* tendency, strength, truth of the
19th c[entury]" (*Th*, 7r).

RECONCILING "RELIGION AND CULTURE, HOLINESS AND BEAUTY"

Finally, I would like to consider Pater's assertion that religion, broadly
defined, is indispensable "if life is to be kept from being a mere grasping,
undirected random grasping"—"some provisional expl[anatio]n, wh[ich]
true or no, & certainly not wholly verifiable, may at least throw over" (*AR*,
28v) the materialism and *ennui* of the age. Religion *and* art, he insists,
should be considered as alternative sites for the production of values; they
are complementary, not competitive, and never mutually exclusive. Pater is
echoing, in part, the opinion of Lessing, who observed that, "Only a misunderstood religion can distance us from the beautiful, and it is a proof of
true religion, properly understood, that it should bring us everywhere back
to the beautiful."[37]

A new, inclusive definition of spiritualized "culture" is the goal of "The
Aesthetic Life," a manuscript which declares that, although art "might seem
the rival or the makeshift of [Christianity], must needs confess after all intimate contact with a [religion]...the greatest correction for the materialism
there is[.] It is the business of culture (or morals, of [religion] surely) to
pluck gratefully the flowers that blossom year by year" (*AL*, 38r, 39r). Not

surprisingly, the essay entitled "Art and Religion" insists upon the conjunction and interdiscursive vitality of aesthetics and religiousness, suggesting in fact that a Christian church "weighty with associations, deeply rooted in hist[ory]—complex" is one in which "even a life of high artistic egotism, like Goethe's, really finds its place" (*AR*, 6r). Fundamentally, Pater's concern is practical as much as it is spiritual. "What shall we do with" religion, the outline for "Art and Religion" begins—"How can we have profit of it—this system, so complex, that has come down to us, & *will* confront us?" (*AR*, 1r). Pragmatically and imaginatively, Pater suggests that religiousness provides an emotional "release" that makes possible artistic production. Hence his abiding appreciation of any and all artists who are "inspired above all else by the majesty, the majestic beauty, of religion—its persons, its events, every circumstance that belongs to it" (*MS*, 68).

In his "Pascal" essay, Pater revisits the physical "inspiration" of Isaiah, whose lips were touched with hot coals when God commissioned him (6:6–7). The burden of such a gift is considered for the "impassioned servant of religion whose lips have been touched with altar-fire, whose seriousness came to be like some incurable malady, a visitation of God" (*MS*, 68). Seriousness, however, is deemed preferable to the absence of any such informing passion, or commitment to do what is most difficult yet most illuminating. Clearly, Pater's texts neither serve an established religion nor show disservice to the personal and cultural efficacy of religious ideals and practices. Instead, the writings negotiate a relationship with institutionalized religions that is always *para*-doxical. Although great pains are taken to demonstrate that religious discourse produces both its subjects and its objects, Pater's texts nevertheless educate would-be readers to the possibilities of what he terms "the whole range of things spiritual" (*AL*, 29r). Within the context of the published canon only, the "religious" passages and inquiries—as in the "Raphael" essay, for example—seem like unexpected, even unwarranted irruptions or digressions. But when unpublished manuscripts are read in conjunction with the published works, new patterns of concern and intellectual investigation become apparent. An engagement with religious discourse was, one discovers, continual throughout Pater's career; "what does the spirit need" echoes throughout polished essay and unfinished fragment alike.

Citing the essays on Michelangelo and Luca Della Robbia, Ian Small has reminded us of the importance of "incompleteness" in Pater's aesthetic. Rather than suggesting that a "work is unfinished" or otherwise defective, the "quality of incompleteness . . . [is] a constituent feature of it in the sense that it allows the individual spectator partly to construct his own experience of that art-object."[38] Similarly, Pater's religious discourse must be "completed" by the individual reader, who thereby constructs his or her own informed spiritual experience. It may be unsettling to some to realize that the energy or purposefulness of religious discourse, as envisioned and enunciated by Pater, is fundamentally *centrifugal* rather than *centripetal*, but this should certainly come as no surprise. The truth claims of systematic faiths are repeatedly

refused in Pater's texts, but the multifaceted benefits of "religious aspiration"—
including the creation of a community, the religiousness of assent, spiritual
consolation, and the "release" that makes possible artistic production—are
stressed with surprising regularity and engagement.

NOTES

1. The antithesis of this argument is the "Decline-of-Walter" critical narrative,
   which laments that "the rebellious aesthete who had written *The Renaissance*...
   turned into a prophet of conservatism" (Robert and Janice Keefe, *Walter Pater
   and the Gods of Disorder* [Athens: Ohio University Press, 1990], 123). Keefes's
   book is but the most recent example of this thesis; even U. C. Knoepflmacher
   refers to the way in which Pater eventually "revoked" the Hellenism of
   The Renaissance (*Religious Humanism and the Victorian Novel: George
   Eliot, Walter Pater, and Samuel Butler* [New Jersey: Princeton University
   Press, 1965]).
2. Ellis Hanson, *Decadence and Catholicism* (Cambridge, Massachusetts: Harvard
   University Press, 1997), 177. Hanson's book insists that the erotic and the
   spiritual are linked in Pater's writings; his discussion of "maternity, male com-
   radeship, and aesthetics" is informative. Yet, as James Najarian states, Hanson's
   definitions of Catholicism and decadence are "circular: Catholics are decadent,
   decadents are Catholic.... Hanson needs to define what Catholicism is for his
   purposes—is it a set of private beliefs, an institution, a denominational affiliation, or merely an aesthetic stance? The context of critical views one expects
   from a work of scholarship is often thin, so that the exercises in hunting down
   Catholicism seem oddly uninformed and impressionistic. There is little historical, doctrinal, or liturgical specificity.... Hanson avoids defining Catholicism
   in order to find more of it" (James Najarian, review of *Decadence and
   Catholicism*, by Ellis Hanson, *Journal of Pre-Raphaelite Studies* 8 [1999]: 170).
3. Although I would acknowledge that "all [Pater's] work in varying ways is
   obscurely autobiographical.... No writer could be more reticent and evasive than
   Pater, less likely to speak directly about himself. Nevertheless, everything Pater
   wrote is an indirect form of self-exploration" (J. Hillis Miller, "Foreword," in Jay
   Fellows, *Tombs, Despoiled and Haunted: "Under-Textures" and "After-Thoughts"
   in Walter Pater* [Stanford: Stanford University Press, 1991], xviii), I am not
   interested, as Hanson is, in "defining Pater" (70).
4. Pater's exploratory enunciations were neither part of "the rash of reactionary
   cultural formations" in the 1880s and 1890s nor an attempt to "reinvent" a
   "transcendental metaphysic which can promise if not deliver a guarantee on
   truth against the existential uncertainties and social ambivalence of modernity"
   (Griselda Pollock, *Avant-Garde Gambits 1888–1893: Gender and the Colour of
   Art History* [London: Thames and Hudson, 1992], 53). It is useful to compare Pater's approach to "art as consolation" with that of Vincent van Gogh
   and Paul Gauguin; see Pollock for a discussion of religious painting in the
   1880s as an "avant-garde gambit" (52–59).
5. The manuscripts, which are housed in the Houghton Library, are quoted with
   permission. Great thanks are due to the staff of the Houghton Library, Harvard,
   and to Dr. Sharon Bassett, who is editing the manuscripts. Due to the unfinished
   state of most manuscripts, the following editorial symbols have been

used: < > WHP's cancellations; { } interlinear text (WHP had not decided whether to make the addition/correction); —indicates WHP's dash; &.c., WHP's mark; [ ] my editorial additions.

6. Walter Pater, *The Renaissance: Studies in Art and Poetry*, ed. Donald Hill (Berkeley: University of California Press, 1980), 184. The following Pater texts and abbreviations are used in this essay: "Aesthetic Life," *AL; Appreciations, with an Essay on "Style"* (London: Macmillan, 1910), *AP*; "Art and Religion," *AR*; "Coleridge's Writings" (*Westminster Review* 85 [January 1866]), *CW*, "English Literature," *EL; Greek Studies* (London: Macmillan, 1910), *GS*; "The History of Philosophy," *HP; Marius the Epicurean*, 2 vols. (London: Macmillan, 1910), *ME; Miscellaneous Studies* (London: Macmillan, 1910), *MS*; "Moral Philosophy," *MP; The Renaissance, TR*; "Plato's Ethics," *PE; Plato and Platonism* (London: Macmillan, 1910), *PP*; "The Writings of Cardinal Newman," *WRN*.

7. In his review of "Coleridge's Writings," WHP first surveys the possibilities of religiousness in a post-Kantian world: "Repressing his artistic interest and voluntarily discolouring his own work, [Coleridge] turned to console and strengthen the human mind, vulgarized or dejected, as he believed, by the acquisition of new knowledge about itself in the 'éclaircissement' of the eighteenth century" (*CW*, 50).

8. Knoepflmacher, *Religious Humanism*, 6.

9. Jay Fellows provocatively argues that "Gracq and Foucault . . . are *this* text's prior authors, themselves Paterian 'afterthoughts' (the Foucault of extended sequences of *Madness and Civilization* might well, after all, have claimed for his own, with uncanny justice, the discarded or erased 'Aesthetic Poetry' of Pater, as well as 'Apollo in Picardy.') . . . It is not so much that Pater may have influenced them, Gracq and Foucault, as it is *as if* they, after the fact . . . had influenced him—*as if*, further, the idiosyncratic dynamics of Paterian belatedness might be efficacious at the point where logical absurdity meets the justice of poetic license" (*Tombs*, 5–6).

10. *The Foucault Reader*, ed. Paul Rabinow (New York: Pantheon Books, 1984), 343.

11. As Foucault observes, "A genealogy of values, morality, asceticism, and knowledge will never confuse itself with a quest for their 'origins,' will never neglect as inaccessible the vicissitudes of history" (*Foucault Reader*, 80).

12. Ibid., 80.

13. Ibid., 92–93.

14. Fellows, *Tombs*, 117.

15. Steven Connor, "Conclusion: Myth and Meta-Myth in Max Müller and Walter Pater," in J. B. Bullen, ed., *The Sun Is God: Painting, Literature, and Mythology in the Nineteenth Century* (Oxford: Clarendon Press, 1989), 213. Connor is echoing the argument of U. C. Knoepflmacher, who addressed the historical specificity of Pater's fictional plots more than thirty years ago. "All of Pater's protagonists," he remarks, "belong to transitional periods of history. They move in a Roman Empire yielding to a new faith; in a sixteenth-century France purging its medievalism through bloody religious wars; in a semifeudal Germany yearning at once for foreign enlightenment and for a native culture" (162).

16. Gerald Monsman, "Introduction: On Reading Pater," *Walter Pater: An Imaginative Sense of Fact*, ed. Philip Dodd (London: Frank Cass, 1981), 1.

17. Wolfgang Iser, *Walter Pater: The Aesthetic Moment*, trans. David Henry Wilson (1960; Cambridge: Cambridge University Press, 1987), 17.

18. Knoepflmacher, *Religious Humanism*, 21, 215.

19. This "doubling" or counter-pointing strategy is evident throughout Pater's canon, a means of enriching the discussion or analysis through apposite comparisons. In *Plato and Platonism*, for example, Plato is juxtaposed with Heraclitus, Athens with Sparta; in the unfinished "Dante" manuscript, the correlation of Dante and Giotto makes possible an interdisciplinary, cultural critique.

20. Gaston finds himself poised between two opposed systems of thought: "two worlds, two antagonistic ideals, were in evidence before him. Could a third condition supervene, to mend their discord?" (*GDL*, 38). Montaigne functions as the "two-sided" thinker who is capable of achieving "delicate balances" (*GDL*, 104). Similarly, the "young man" invoked in *Plato and Platonism* must utilize his doubt to generate a personal creed for "an age which thirsts for intellectual security, but cannot make up its mind. *Que scais-je?* it cries, in the words of Montaigne; but in the spirit also of the Platonic Socrates, with whom such dubitation had been nothing less than a religious duty or service" (*PP*, 195).

21. "The Writings of Cardinal Newman" was designed to address Newman's poetry, literary criticism, published sermons, theological texts, and the *Apologia*.

22. Miller, "Foreword," xv.

23. Knoepflmacher, *Religious Humanism*, 217–19.

24. Max Müller, *Introduction to the Science of Religion: Four Lectures Delivered at the Royal Institution in February and March 1870* (Varanasi: Bharata Manisha, 1972).

25. I would therefore disagree with Knoepflmacher's assertion that "next to *Plato and Platonism*," *Marius the Epicurean* is "the most ambitious formulation of Pater's lifelong search for a religious creed" (*Religious Humanism*, 190).

26. See Lesley Higgins, "But who is 'she'?: Female subjectivity in Pater's Writings," *Nineteenth-Century Prose* 24, no. 2 (1997): 37–65.

27. *Foucault Reader*, 342.

28. Michel Foucault, *The History of Sexuality, Volume 3: The Care of the Self*, trans. Robert Hurley (New York: Vintage Books, 1988), 43.

29. Saul Rabinow, "Introduction," *Foucault Reader*, 11.

30. Michel Foucault, *The History of Sexuality, Volume 2: The Use of Pleasure*, trans. Robert Hurley (New York: Vintage Books, 1985), 5; *Care of the Self*, 65.

31. *Foucault Reader*, 366.

32. Foucault, *Use of Pleasure*, 21.

33. Ibid., 32.

34. Foucault identifies "a Christian tradition that consigned pleasure to the realm of death and evil" (*Use of Pleasure*, 16); Pater dramatizes the tradition in texts such as "Denys L'Auxerrois" and "Apollo in Picardy."

35. Michel Foucault, *The History of Sexuality, Volume 1: An Introduction*, trans. Robert Hurley (New York: Vintage Books, 1990), 37.

36. Foucault, *Care of the Self*, 65.

37. Gotthold Lessing, *Gesammelte Werke*, 2 vols. (Munich: Carl Hanser, 1959), 2:1014–15.

38. Ian Small, "Pater's Criticism: Some Distinctions," *Walter Pater: An Imaginative Sense of Fact*, ed. Philip Dodd (London: Frank Cass, 1981), 32–33.

CHAPTER 9

"AMEN IN A WRONG PLACE": CHARLES DICKENS IMAGINES THE VICTORIAN CHURCH

Natalie Bell Cole

THE RIGHT REVERENT AMEN

When Dickens visits churches, either as the narrator of a novel or as a travel writer and tour guide, he depicts these buildings as signs of a dilemma that is both personal and cultural.[1] How, Dickens asks, can we apply Christian ethics to social practices within and beyond the material church, even as most churches cease to be vital locations for practices of faith and worship? Moreover, since churches are ubiquitous in urban and rural Victorian England and function as emblems of cultural flux, the observant Dickens cannot help but encounter and represent them. Dickens's work anticipates Philip Larkin's "Church Going," which articulates the compulsion to visit the church site coupled with a confusion about what is sought there:

> Yet stop I did: in fact I often do
> And always end much at a loss like this,
> Wondering what to look for; wondering, too,
> When churches fall completely out of use
> What we shall turn them into....[2]

Like Larkin, Charles Dickens bears witness to church sites/sights and how their meanings are being transformed in his lifetime. In the process, he discovers in the nineteenth-century English church a rich trope for the paradoxes of Victorian life: vitality persisting in the face of decay, permanence altered by change, theatricality contesting with earnestness, the wonder and threat of urban spaces that dislocate tradition, yet yearn for the transcendent. Murray Baumgarten poses part of the problem when he calls London's new train stations "the cathedrals of the new technological order."[3] In a London, as Joss Marsh writes, "always building, building, building," Dickens's varied representations of the material church demonstrate the tension he felt between what Peter Eisenman sees as "a nostalgia for the security of knowing" and Dickens's own conviction that nineteenth-century landscapes had no indelible record except in memory.[4] Consequently, a Dickensian discourse of faith can be located in church settings as diverse as the entropic city church palpably resolving into a dust tasted by every parishioner; the failing monumentality of St. Paul's Cathedral; and uncanny and unexpected church settings that help stage renewals of vitality and faith. This essay seeks to initiate an examination of the diverse ways religion, and especially the material church, can be interpreted in Dickens's canon, with particular attention to his some of his late essays from *The Uncommercial Traveller*, published between January 1860 and October 1863. While Michael Cotsell and John Drew have insightfully examined this collection, neither has focused on the church as a trope illuminating Dickens's understanding of Victorian faith.[5]

Dennis Walder (1981) and Janet Larson (1985) provide the most comprehensive discussions of Dickens's religious beliefs and representations of religion in his characters, plots, and use of language.[6] Walder describes Dickens's view of Christianity as "[participation] in a popular Romantic tradition of non-dogmatic Christianity through his...reiterated conviction of the irrelevance of religious 'forms,'" and "a religion based on deep feelings about man, nature, and God," underscoring Dickens's dislike of anything sectarian, dogmatic, intolerant, or exclusive.[7] Thus, in *David Copperfield*, for example, it is not David's Anglican faith but the natural and human sanctuaries of the Swiss Alps and Agnes Wickfield that combine to rehabilitate David back into work, love, and spiritual renewal. Zemka, following Larson, summarizes and emphasizes Dickens's adherence to a self-sufficient *New Testament* ethos.[8] Both Walder and Larson locate Dickens in relation to Victorian currents and cross-currents of faith, Larson explaining that Dickens "deplored the acrimonious religious debates of his day," but was well aware of them, and Walder emphasizing Dickens's Unitarian-inflected, liberal Christianity: "[Dickens] strongly supports the basic intention of the liberal Christian manifesto, *Essays and Reviews* (1860), to reconcile Christianity with the intellectual tendencies of the age and so save religion and the Church." Humphry House voices it even more succinctly: "The Established Church is firmly built into the Dickens landscape."[9] While these are important compasses in analyzing Dickens's thinking about faith, they only *begin* to orient the Dickens reader. One has only to reconsider the unsolvable clues to Dickens's noted "reticence" about expressions of religious faith in his work: his *Life of Our Lord*, seminal to his children's religious education but suppressed from wider circulation until 1934; his rigid, and to some, rabid and inexplicable, response to Millais's *Christ in the House of His Parents* (1850); and the tumbling-down church buildings and hard to be endured church services in much of his canon that are the particular focus of this essay.[10] Articulations of a Dickensian faith by J. Hillis Miller and Robert Polhemus point to the quagmire critics must enter when they seek to explore a subject like religious faith. Polhemus sees the Victorian novel as "a means for imagining forms of faith that would augment, or play off orthodox religious visions," and Miller finds Dickens's novels, while "they do not express orthodox religious doctrine…are religious in that they demand the regeneration of man and society through contact with something transcending the merely human."[11] It is my contention that examining representations of the church and faith in the novels in conjunction with related representations in his familiar essays further elucidates Dickens's struggle to identify and reformulate his own, and the Victorian cultural need, for the transcendent.

Dickens's contemporaries assessed his representations of religion in various, and at times, contradictory ways. Reviewing *Martin Chuzzlewit* in the mid-1840s, one reviewer reassures readers that "No man has dreamed of Mr. Dickens's politics, or cared to inquire after his religion; he has stood among us, belonging to us all"; only a decade later a reviewer of *Bleak House* chastises Dickens: "He is at once the creation and the prophet of an age which loves benevolence without religion."[12] Philip Collins notes that "journals of a denominational allegiance were apt to criticize [Dickens] on doctrinal grounds," especially Catholic periodicals such as *The Dublin Review* and *The Rambler*, and High Church organs such as *The Christian Remembrancer*.[13] House notes that the evangelical press "attacked Dickens not only for his satire but also for the absence in his work of any doctrinal language and the almost total absence of church-going of a proper public-kind."[14] But it is precisely Dickens's representations of the church-going that is both public and private, church-places, and his ability to reimagine and recreate the church as sanctuaries of various kinds that demand further exploration.

In "City of London Churches" (1860) Dickens gives us a parabolic reading of the interplay of decaying churches, vitiated faith, and persistent human vitality. A modest-sized, underpopulated city church and its congregation are found "in a very advanced stage of exhaustion."[15] However, the unruly play of some boys irreverently revitalizes the moribund service, as one holds his breath to frighten his aunt, while the other boys' suppressed laughter goes off "like crackers." The inebriated clergyman misinterprets the disruption, supposing only that somebody has said "Amen in a wrong place" ("Churches," 111–12). Dickens vividly communicates his sense of losing his place as practitioner of Anglican faith, as a city dweller, and as a nineteenth-century citizen. A church oblivious to play and human energy must indeed be endangered. Thus a metaphoric "amen in a wrong place" pervades Dickens's canon, as he reiterates a fatigued practice of faith and laments the scarcity of "true, practical Christianity" within the institutional church ("Shipwreck," 32).[16] Additionally, Dickens continues throughout his work to represent a material church whose inextricable linkage to the nineteenth-century city both troubles and fascinates him.

Dickens's canon, starting with sketches, essays, and novels in the 1830s, began to grapple with what "amen in the right place" might be, whether inside or outside of the church. Dickens remains interested in the attendant rituals and forms of worship. Dickens's convictions about Sabbatarianism and his linking of church-going to middle-class respectability appear most notably in this decade in an essay and novel, *Sunday Under Three Heads* (1836) and *Oliver Twist* (1838).

In his passionate plea for the clergy and institutional church to be instruments of social justice rather than oppressors of the poor, his essay *Sunday Under Three Heads* names the strict new rules proposed for the Sabbath's "saintly venom," particularly poisonous to the poor. "The propriety of opening the British Museum to respectable people on Sunday, has lately been the subject of much discussion," writes Dickens, arguing for intellectual stimulation, physical exercise, and "wholesome" amusement for working-class folk on Sundays.[17] Dickens points to the disappearance of the faithful in houses of worship:

> Look into your churches—diminished congregations, and scanty attendance. People have grown sullen and obstinate, and are becoming disgusted with the faith which condemns them to such a day as this, once in every seven. And as you cannot make people religious by Act of Parliament, or force them to church by constables, they display their feeling by staying away. (*Sunday*, 653)

Thus Dickens associates Sabbatarianism with a loss of freedom and a coercive authority, and suggests, instead, an ideal church led by a country clergyman whose discourse is "plain, unpretending, and well adapted to the comprehension of the hearers" (*Sunday*, 659), and who had successfully established "a very animated game of cricket" in a meadow just beyond the churchyard. This balance of worship in church and active pleasure in leisure on the Sabbath epitomizes Dickens's Romantic faith linked with nature, and his holistic understanding of an interconnected bodily and spiritual health.[18] Additionally, Dickens imagines here a church leadership that does not exclude the pleasure of sport from the Christian life, but rather provides the materials and space for such a game, a perspective later articulated by Thomas Hughes in *Tom Brown's Schooldays* (1857).

Dickens, however, feels more bound by religious convention in *Oliver Twist*. As noted by Leonore Davidoff and Catherine Hall, "Respectability was coming to include church-going, family worship, the observance of the Sabbath, an interest in religious literature."[19] Nine-year-old Oliver Twist had never been to church or had any formal religious instruction, yet he is exhorted by a member of the workhouse board to "pray for the people who feed you and take care of you," an occasion satirically commented on by the narrator: "It would have been *very* like a Christian, and a marvelously good Christian, too, if Oliver had prayed for the people who fed and took care of *him*."[20] Oliver's rescue into middle-class prosperity and family brings with it an idealized encounter with the Maylies's country church:

> There was the little church, in the morning, with the green leaves fluttering at the windows; the birds singing without: and the sweet-smelling air stealing in

at the low porch, and filling the homely building with its fragrance. The poor people were so neat and clean, and knelt so reverently in prayer, that it seemed a pleasure, not a tedious duty, their assembling there together. (*OT*, 32:239)

This passage appears to be Oliver's point-of-view, offered in free indirect discourse as Dickens's third-person narrator drifts into Oliver's consciousness. Dickens seems unaware of any irony of association between the regimented piety of the workhouse and the insistence on the orderliness of the "lower orders" in the country church. Two significant aspects of Victorian religious services are implied here: a dread of church attendance as a "tedious duty," and an illustration of how social hierarchies are maintained even within a church service. Also important here is Dickens's tendency to valorize country churches in contrast to his frequent portrayal of decaying, dusty, urban churches, and his romantic impulse that associates the church service with the natural world outside. Oliver's religious instruction continues at home, as each week he studies "a chapter or two from the Bible," and reads aloud from it to his new friends, feeling "more proud and pleased, than if he had been the clergyman himself" (*OT*, 32:239). No mention is made of liturgy or preaching, or of an actual clergyman officiating at the service. The idea that the Maylies are characters who practice charity as "Christian by nature rather than by formal adherence" gets to the heart of the matter:[21] Oliver has had Christian behavior modeled for him in their taking him into their home and family after the house-breaking—the church-going simply completes his rehabilitation into a happier (and more respectable) life. In essence, Oliver undergoes less of a spiritual conversion than the reader, who is exhorted to follow the Maylies's example and care for the poor.[22] Still, the fact that regular church-going, presented as natural and reverent, becomes routine in Oliver's life must not be overlooked. Dickens, desiring to "[touch] the religious consciousness of a vast reading public" in the 1830s, still believes churches can teach habits of reverence.[23]

The 1840s marked an important decade in Dickens's life and his representations of the church. Dickens traveled to America, was attracted by Unitarianism, published four novels and four Christmas books, and wrote his *Life of Our Lord* for his own children.[24] Most important for this study are Dickens's depictions of city and country churches; of church sacraments such as baptism and marriage; and his most explicit articulation of a Christology that appears throughout his canon, although not unambiguously.

The village church as Little Nell's refuge and death site in *The Old Curiosity Shop* has drawn much critical attention. Humphrey House emphasizes its thanatognomonic function as "a monstrous curio rather than a great relic of civilization," and "more a mausoleum than a sanctuary."[25] In contrast, Robert Polhemus reads this church through what he calls Dickens's "erotic faith," expressed by how the child "Nell actually haunts and usurps the church, allegorically taking it over. Dickens has her being and memory literally merged into the physical site of faith, the religious structure." As Polhemus explains, Nell becomes a site for sublimated desire that protects children and affirms the value of virginity and female spirituality, while the novel itself is "a secular, popular, literary cathedral, an accretive Gothic textual structure with chapels that emphasize different kinds of faith and include all kinds of beliefs in the crazy architecture of its fiction."[26] Larson might question Polhemus's broad definition of faith, but she too sees Little Nell as one of "Dickens' favorite fictions"—"the intercessory female in Victorian fiction."[27] Certainly the child-woman-angel Nell cannot be associated with the city church. Dickens opposes urban churches to English country churches by contrasting their respective confusion and noise, peace and silence.[28] As Nell and her grandfather hurry out of London to the suburbs, they pass

> mounds of dockweed, nettles, coarse grass and oyster shells, heaped in rank confusion—small dissenting chapels to teach, with no lack of illustration, the miseries of Earth, and plenty of new churches, erected with a little superfluous wealth, to show the way to Heaven.[29]

The "mounds" (foreshadowing the dust mounds of *Our Mutual Friend*) of wilderness and waste are juxtaposed to the implicitly superfluous places of worship—chapels and new churches—that constitute the urban wasteland from which Nell and her grandfather flee. Metropolitan chapels and churches, often caught up in contentious debates over doctrinal differences, are well placed, the narrator says, to teach the "miseries" of a secular life, and new churches (usually Anglican) are signs of that Church's vanity and wealth, too far removed from the lives of working-class congregations. Exiting London, one could

> [look] back at old Saint Paul's looming through the smoke, its cross peeping above the cloud (if the day were clear), and glittering in the sun; and casting his eyes upon the Babel out of which it grew until he traced it down to the further outposts in the invading army of bricks and mortar whose station lay for the present nearly at his feet—might feel at last that he was clear of London. (*OCS*, 116)

The Cathedral emerges from the "Babel" of the city, and becomes to the city escapee a visual sign not of salvation, but of chaos. The cross "peeps" and "glitters" but cannot console, aid, or sustain Nell's life. When Nell reaches the village church, its "sweet reality" exceeds even her visions of it (*OCS*, 46:347). Her attention is "exclusively riveted" by this church:

> It was a very aged, ghostly place; the church had been built many hundreds of years ago, and had once had a convent or monastery attached; for arches in ruins, remains of oriel windows, and fragments of blackened walls, were yet standing; while other portions of the old building, which had crumbled away and fallen down, were mingled with the churchyard earth and overgrown with grass, as if they too claimed a burying place and sought to mix their ashes with the dust of men. (*OCS*, 46:348)

The village church features mounds and overgrown grass similar to the sub-urban wasteland on London's outskirts, but the dominant tone is elegiac. While the churches of the city may appear ill-suited to their task, the village church is actually falling apart, returning to the soil, an even less hopeful position for this emblem of institutional faith. If the church bells here commune with the dead (*OCS*, 52:388), so do Nell and the narrator. Still, Dickens gestures to themes of Christian resurrection and Nature's regeneration. First, Nell gardens among the churchyard graves (an image Dickens returns to in "City of the Absent" [1863]) and second, this rural community of believers who worship Nell's goodness adorn her bride-like corpse with winter leaves and berries gathered from the natural world encroaching on the ruined church. Nell's death follows the Victorian Christological tradition of patient suffering unto death, but this tradition is problematized by her grandfather's madness in the face of loss (possibly underscoring for the reader the correct way to "read" Nell's death, as a celebration of innocent Christian suffering). The presence of the physical church is both irrelevant and intrinsic to Dickens's meaning—irrelevant as a source of solace or theology, intrinsic as a ruin emptied of meaning, displaced by the sanctity of Nell herself. Nell's death, so long a dividing line between Victorian readers and readers today, casts a shadow forward to *The Uncommercial Traveller* essays of the 1860s, marked as they are by their refusal to soften the suffering the narrator witnesses or to model what Michael Cotsell calls "the grace, finally, of unprotestingly, religiously, dying."[30]

THE LIFE OF OUR LORD AND THE UNLIKELY DISCIPLE

Dickens returns to the city church in *Dombey and Son*, a novel composed at the same time Dickens wrote *The Life of Our Lord* for his children's religious instruction. Sue Zemka, examining Victorian Christology, has discussed the concurrence of the Christmas books, *Dombey and Son*, *The Life of Our Lord*, and Dickens's correspondence about fallen women with Angela Burdett-Coutts. She argues that "of all Victorian novelists [Dickens] was the most inclined to use images of childhood and femininity as vehicles of a secular gospel of feeling," and this is certainly borne out in Florence and young Paul Dombey.[31] But other important conjunctions between these two texts exist as well. Dickens's reluctance to preach his religious beliefs in his fiction, his "discretion" in pronouncing upon religion subjects,[32] appears in a letter written only a few days before Dickens's death. This letter, written in connection with his composition of *The Life of Our Lord*, finds its counterpart in characters reluctant to profess but compelled to moral action, such as Captain Cuttle. Dickens wrote to John Makeham:

> I have always striven in my writings to express veneration for the life and lessons of our Saviour; because I feel it; and because I rewrote that history for my children—every one of whom knew it from having it repeated to them, long

before they could read, and almost as soon as they could speak. But I have never made proclamation of this from the house tops.[33]

Dickens's awareness of religious controversy, what he called "unseemly squabbles about 'the letter' which drive 'the Spirit' out of hundreds of thousands,"[34] achieves expression in *Dombey and Son* through its criticism of the Established Church's empty forms and the secularized and egotistical appropriation of the sacraments. Christ's humility, his need to serve and compassionate, and his solidarity with his apostles appear throughout *Dombey and Son*.

In regard to church rituals and ceremonies, Dickens's understanding of the intrinsic theatricality of Victorian experience celebrates the human propensity for dramatization. However, he is also suspicious about how such theatricality may diminish or obscure the sincerely religious purpose of such rituals as baptism and marriage.[35] Religious forms risk losing their spiritual significance to become merely staged events, a risk dramatized in *Dombey and Son*'s icy baptism and in the contrasted weddings of Mrs. Edith Granger to Paul Dombey and Florence Dombey to Walter Gay.[36] At infant Paul's baptism, the "chill and earthy" church becomes associated with the icily prideful father, who serves wine at the christening breakfast so cold that it forces a scream from one of the guests. The "strange, unusual, uncomfortable smell and the cadaverous light" inside the church suggest physical burial rather than baptismal rebirth (*DS*, 5, 55). The narrator chastises Mr. Dombey for not attending to the religious significance of the ritual:

> It might have been well for Mr. Dombey, if he had thought of his own dignity a little less; and had thought of the great origin and purpose of the ceremony in which he took so formal and so stiff a part, a little more. His arrogance contrasted strangely with its history. (*DS*, 5:57)

Mr. Dombey refuses to acknowledge Paul's divine Creator and to share Paul with his Heavenly Father (Dickens introduces this blasphemous rivalry early on, with the phrase "*anno Dombei*" [1:2]). In *The Life of Our Lord*, Dickens tells the story of John's baptism of Jesus, and John's humble posture: "Why should I baptize you, who are so much better than I!" (*LOL*, 22). Dickens writes this role reversal into Paul and Dombey's relationship, with Dombey unaware of Paul's innocence, of his innate generosity, and of what a parent can learn as a child's disciple. John Carey has claimed that Dickens "did not seriously accept" that "the ceremonies of Christianity had a vital spiritual meaning," and notes Dickens's inconsistent treatment of the sacraments in *Pickwick Papers* compared to those in *Dombey and Son*.[37] But significantly, *Dombey and Son*'s chronological proximity to *The Life of Our Lord* opens up another possibility. Dickens may purposely write *this* scene of baptism into *Dombey and Son* in order to underscore Mr. Dombey's lack of humility: "His arrogance contrasted strangely with its history" (*DS*, 57), thereby thematically linking it with the emphasis on humility as a cornerstone of Christian conduct in *The Life of Our Lord*. Dickens reiterates this central tenet of his faith in a letter to the Reverend David Macrae in 1861: "All my strongest illustrations are derived from the New Testament . . . all my good people are humble, charitable, faithful, and forgiving" (*Letters of Dickens*, 9:556–57).

Dombey is not alone in using the church to stage his own importance, in complete disregard of the spiritual roots of church ritual. As Dombey's second marriage looms imminent, the narrator describes both the interior of the church and the neglected Church of England liturgy: "And now, the mice, who have been busier with the prayer-books than their proper owners, and with the hassocks, more worn by their little teeth than by human knees, hide their bright eyes in their holes" (*DS*, 31:436). The wedding scene itself has the quality of a combined performance and business transaction for bride and groom; ironically, more emotionally involved are the onlookers in the gallery, the uninvited guests who choose to witness the wedding for reasons of their own—Miss Tox, Mr. Toots, and Captain Cuttle. Their presence in the balcony suggests the inherently theatrical nature of the ceremony, as well as their desire to experience, albeit vicariously, some sacrament that would transcend their accustomed loneliness.

In contrast to her father's wedding, Florence Dombey's marriage to Walter Gay serves as the necessary corrective to the previous wedding of commodity-driven exchange. Although the modest church in which they marry exhibits almost as much dust as a churchyard, the ceremony is redeemed by the authentic love of the participants. The Dickens narrator, still aware of the ceremony's aspect of performance, describes it thus:

> The amens of the dusty clerk appear, like Macbeth's to stick in his throat a little; but Captain Cuttle helps him out, and does it with so much goodwill that he interpolates three entirely new responses of that word, never introduced into the service before. (*DS*, 57: 807)

Amens in the right place, Dickens suggests, will come from human goodwill and genuine practices of faith that make up in strong feeling what they lack in shallow form. Captain Cuttle's responses show that there can be no superfluity in expressions of genuine feeling. His lusty *amens* usher this loving union into the larger community, a union rescued from the dust and grave of marriages made through commerce.

Larson, however, reads Cuttle differently, finding his religion "sentimental" and unable to articulate "what principles should guide the novel's more complex world."[38] The character of the Captain can also be read through *The Life of Our Lord*'s emphasis on treating others with generosity, healing pain and illness, and celebrating redemption. One of the miracles of Christ Dickens relates to his children is that of "a poor man who had his hand all withered and wasted away," and whom the Pharisees forbade Christ to heal on a Sunday (*LOL*, 38). It is on a Sunday when Walter Gay, seconded by Captain Cuttle, applies to Mr. Dombey for help to repay his uncle's debt, incurred, significantly, in assisting a friend. The loan is a gift of love from Paul to Florence, and "the phenomenon" of Cuttle waving his hook politely at Miss Tox and Mr. Dombey is no match for the phenomenon of Dombey loaning money to a subordinate. Dickens invokes the Christology of *The Life of Our Lord* both in Cuttle's steadfast friendship and pursuit to help Walter, as well as in Paul's redirection of his father's wealth.

Furthermore, Cuttle, ridiculous though he may be, combing his hair with his hook, brandishing his sugar tongs about, fracturing scripture right and left, acts with serious religious purpose on crucial occasions. Indeed, there is no contradiction here between Cuttle's comic absurdity and his faith, if we accept Polhemus's idea that "Dickens's comic vision is based on seeing the world as both funny and potentially good . . . and on the drive for liberty of mind, exuberance of spirit, pleasure, and imaginative regeneration." A comic disciple, or as McKnight might call him, a "holy fool," Cuttle keeps the faith in the Little Midshipman, an oasis of fidelity in the commodity-driven city, sitting down alone to read from the burial service in the Book of Common Prayer in remembrance of Walter, thought to be dead at sea.[39] His solemn private acknowledgment of Walter's death contrasts Mr. Dombey's denial of the deaths of his wife and son, losses that exacerbate his denial of Florence's love for him. Dickens links the inability to grieve with the inability to love. Walter, an orphan, has no earthly father, and his uncle Soloman Gills has disappeared. Natalie McKnight, examining fathering in Dickens's work, explains, "The ultimate father in Dickens's world would, of course, be God. . . . In *The Life of Our Lord*, Dickens stresses aspects of Jesus and God that most match his fictional depictions of good fathers."[40]

Cuttle, an excellent surrogate parent, makes a home for the runaway Florence, complete with food, fire, and affection, becoming an earthly father to emulate a spiritual Father. *The Life of Our Lord* mentions the importance of "kind friends and good homes" (*LOL*, 28); "Jesus, always, full of compassion" (*LOL*, 30); the restoration to life of a daughter and brother (*LOL*, 32, 82–83); and the lack felt by the "poor" and "bad" from "not having parents and friends to take care of them when young" (*LOL*, 62). Cuttle tries to sustain Florence in body and spirit; he strives to create a homelike, domestic atmosphere for her despite his modest means, arranging items on her dressing table and carefully preparing a hearty meal that her sorrow prevents her from eating. Florence experiences the Midshipman as a sanctuary remote from the selfish mercantilism epitomized by Dombey, her failed father, when the Captain tells her that she is as safe in the loft of the shop as "at the top of St. Paul's Cathedral, with the ladder cast off." In this image, Dickens transforms the precarious isolation of a ladderless dome into a golden, protective womb from which Florence can emerge at will. It is a rebirth into domestic security, the first step toward the reformation of family. Gaston Bachelard, examining the metaphoric space of the nest as an image of "rest and quiet," quotes the poet Adolphe Shedrow: "I dreamed of a nest in which the trees repulsed death."[41] Dickens imaginatively transforms the monumental majesty of Saint Paul's into a nurturing and death-defying "nest" for Florence, a place where her bruised self can heal. The Wooden Midshipman, the small unsuccessful shop down on London's streets, is transformed not only by Dickens's analogy between it and St. Paul's, but through its proximity to three sites of British commercial power: the Royal Exchange, the Bank of England, and the East India shipping company (*DS*, 4:32). Thus the home fires Cuttle tends have associations of sanctuary, sacred space, nationhood, and cultural permanence. This is a different Saint Paul's than the symbol of chaos in *The Old Curiosity Shop*.

Cuttle's wedding gift to Florence, a wooden chest engraved with the name *Florence Gay*, symbolizes an ark that has kept them all afloat—that their shared human suffering would be redeemed by a future reunion. Thus, Cuttle's *amens* do not stand alone, but are part of his belief in powers greater than the self. Cuttle's sincere amens affirm Walter's and Florence's union by locating it in a loving human family whose members reverence marriage. Cuttle does not need to be aware of his discipleship; it is enough that Dickens had it in mind as he worked out the story of *Dombey and Son* and explained Jesus's love for orphans and other outcasts:

> Whosoever shall receive one such little child in my name receiveth me [and], He chose them [the disciples] from among poor men, in order that the poor might know...that Heaven was made for them as well as for the rich, and that God makes no difference between those who wear good clothes and those who go barefoot and in rags. The most miserable, the most ugly, deformed, wretched creatures that live, will be bright Angels in Heaven if they are good here on earth. (*LOL*, 59, 27–28)

Dickens's "Romantic" religion of a liberal, inclusive, tolerant faith in *Dombey and Son* is reconstituted within the walls of the Little Midshipman, with benedictions pronounced by Captain Cuttle.

THE CHURCH "ALWAYS ON THE WAY TO BECOMING"

Julian Wolfreys describes the act of "writing London" and of representing the event of the city itself as "always on the way to becoming," a constant flux, motion, and denial of stability or stasis.[42] Similarly, the Victorian church in Dickens's lifetime is "always on the way to becoming," as it loses authority and seeks to revitalize itself in the midst of a London depopulating at its urban core.

If Dickens was inclined in his fiction during the decade of the 1850s to turn away from church services toward human beings unselfishly serving others outside church walls, he was in good company. In 1851, Horace Mann's census of public worship showed that "five and a quarter million people had chosen to stay away from public worship on census Sunday," with attendance "lowest of all in London."[43] House noted that "the evangelical press attacked Dickens not only for his satire but also for the...almost total absence of church-going of a proper public kind."[44] Critics accused Dickens of substituting humanitarianism for religion, and fellowship for worship. Margaret Oliphant asked, "Are a 'pipe and a pint of beer' so much better than even the miseries of church going?"[45] Dickens answers this resoundingly in the affirmative in *David Copperfield, Bleak House*, and *Little Dorrit*, especially when church-going involved evangelicals of the Anglican or Dissenting sects. An unsigned reviewer of *Little Dorrit* writes in 1857 that Dickens "soars above all considerations of sect, above all narrow isolations of creed; and, though a more deeply religious writer is not to be found . . . he is never disputatiously theological or academic."[46] Dickens articulates his impatience with the esoteric "ologies" of sectarianism the decade before, but these feelings guide him in the 1850s:

> Disgusted with our Established Church and its Puseyisms, and daily outrages on common sense and humanity, I have carried into effect an old idea of mine, and joined the Unitarians, who *would* do something for human improvement, if they could; and who practice charity and toleration. (*Letters of Dickens*, 3:455–56; Dickens's emphasis)

Dickens's concern about religious intolerance led to his repeated satirizing of the hypocritical evangelical preacher (Reverend Chadband in *Bleak House*) and the Puritan Anglican believer too intently focused on damnation rather than redemption (the Murdstones in *David Copperfield*, Miss Barbary in *Bleak House*, Mrs. Clennam in *Little Dorrit*). Yet beyond this specific target, Dickens continues to suggest what the church is ceasing to be and what it may become through imaginative transformation.

In *David Copperfield*, the church is not only the scene of David's childhood oppression by the "austere and wrathful" Murdstones, but more significantly, the place where David's ability to rescue himself through storytelling begins. David Parker argues that the adult narrator and storyteller David Copperfield may be seen in Phiz's illustration, "Our Pew At Church," a male figure leaning against a pew in the right foreground, scanning the church service and congregation with "tense alertness."[47] Parker's positioning of Dickens's character and narrator within David's own church scene nicely suggests the internal/external possibilities offered by church-going, making the church both a private refuge and public stage. One could people-watch or mentally construct scenes of one's own, and Dickens describes instances of both. The child David, watching Miss Murdstone's "dark eyes roll around the church when she says 'miserable sinners,' as if she were calling all the congregation names," quite naturally links a wrathful Old Testament with the Murdstone domestic tyranny of hate and punishment; but the rolling eyes are also the stage gesture of a histrionically "religious" woman.[48] In David's earliest childhood, his imagination had transformed the church and its pulpit into a stage for playing at military daring: "what a good place it would be to play in, and what a castle it would make, with another boy coming up the stairs to attack it" (*DC*, 1:15).[49] Near the end of the novel, after his three years abroad, the adult David, now a successful writer, comes home to a London greatly altered. David's newly disciplined heart accepts the loss but nostalgically hopes for something immutable:

> [I] observed that an old house on Fish-street Hill, which had stood untouched
> by painter, carpenter, or brick-layer, for a century, had been pulled down in my
> absence; and that a neighboring street . . . was being drained and widened; I half
> expected to find St. Paul's Cathedral looking older. (*DC*, 59:820)

David's temporary disorientation prepares for his new awareness of Agnes as
an erotic and marital partner.[50] St. Paul's appears again as a unique feature
of the city, a constant in a constantly changing city. This only works for
Londoners, however, since his former nursemaid, Peggotty, visiting London
while David proves her husband's will, rejects the real St. Paul's in favor of
the replica Cathedral painted on her sewing workbox (*DC*, 33:475–76).
David may be amused by Peggotty's tenacious hold on her previous vision
of St. Paul's, but Dickens once again demonstrates the comforting power of
imagination in the face of disparate, and often disconcerting, urban chaos.
Arlene Jackson has interpreted Peggotty's preference for the crude replica as
"an opting for the past and the domestic as opposed to the imposing, public
reality of the actual St. Paul's."[51] The complexity of these juxtaposed images
invites further discussion in another place.

Dickens, described by Steven Marcus as the "poet-novelist of the modern
city,"[52] presented his readers with a sensory overload that resisted order.
Walter Bagehot puts it this way: "Everything is there, and everything is dis-
connected. . . . His memory is full of instances of old buildings and curious
people, and he does not care to piece them together."[53] "The old buildings and
curious people" that crowd Dickens's pages invite and challenge readers to
discover and decode them. Following Michel Foucault, Julian Wolfreys talks
about a Dickensian "architexture," that is, representations of the city that
"privilege the narrative over the monumental, movement over the static"
and represent London as the "city-as-the-event, a city always on the way to
becoming, . . . always readable as antithetically positioned to the closure of
narrative."[54] Further, "the event of the city, or the buildings composing that
city, are frequently opposed, or used to subvert, forms of oppressive, monumental structure, in the forms of institutions, authorities, practices, discourses."[55] Such representation denies to churches the fixed meaning that
would make them symbols of moral and social stability for some Victorian readers. One cannot read Dickens's work without becoming aware of St. Paul's
Cathedral as the most frequently mentioned church in Dickens's London
landscape, a visual "event" and destination for the Victorian tourist, as
Pegotty has already demonstrated.[56]

In *Old Curiosity Shop*, the Cathedral is inextricably linked with urban
chaos; in *Dombey and Son*, it transmutes danger into safety, with associations
of the stability of nationhood; in *David Copperfield*, it can mean defiance of
the real (Peggotty), as well as mutability and permanence (David). But this
London monolith, towering over the city, is much more than a sign for the

Church of England and the British nation-state, for over and over again Dickens reinscribes it with other possible meanings. It has an almost organic centrality, reminiscent of the medieval church described by Lewis Mumford: "the great church is central to the town, in every sense but a geometric one."[57] It is, as Dickens's aged Master Humphrey says, the heart of the metropolis that "when it should cease to beat, the City would be no more."[58]

In *Bleak House*, Dickens invokes the Cathedral's religious and geographical prominence in the city, making it the perfect ironic counterpoint to the "nothinkness" of the crossing-sweep Jo, homeless, illiterate, and seen as a "lower animal" by his "betters." At first the physical and moral authority of the monumental Cathedral seems evident, but gives way as the narrator pans across the larger scene that includes Jo down near Blackfriar's Bridge, "munching and gnawing," looking up at the cathedral.[59] The reader watches Jo as he views

> the great Cross on the summit of St. Paul's Cathedral, glittering above a red and violet-tinted cloud of smoke. From the boy's face one might suppose that sacred emblem to be, in his eyes, the crowning confusion of the great, confused city; so golden, so high up, so far out of his reach. There he sits, the sun going down, the river running fast, the crowd flowing by him in two streams—everything moving on to some purpose and to one end—until he is stirred up, and told to "move on" too. (*BH*, 19:271)

The Cathedral's magnitude, architecture, and vertical position over the polluted city may indeed for some readers symbolize orderliness, cultural centrality, and transcendence of the city's material dirt and spiritual malaise. However, Dickens positions the Cathedral as the "crowning confusion" of a contradictory culture that misdirects its wealth and energies, reiterating and further elaborating the image of the Cathedral used in *The Old Curiosity Shop*. The "two streams" further emphasize the temporal urgency (the setting sun and racing river) and human exigency (the child whose essential humanity is denied as he is "moved on" from place to place). The reader views "the city-as-event" and becomes aware of the spatial and moral distance between the religious institution of the church and the lives of the poor, a traverse that Dickens dynamically tracks in this passage. Jo's cultural and spiritual illiteracy is not so much the point as Dickens's recasting of St. Paul's Cathedral, a "sacred emblem," as a narrative "city-event" that gains significance precisely through its proximity to Jo. Its enormity at first threatens to erase Jo and human need from the reader's moral line of vision. This "city-event" shifts to include Jo's perspective of the chaos at ground level, as told from the narrator's perspective as he visually shifts from street to sky and across bridge and river. Radically, Dickens reorders the scene so that this vagrant boy transcends at street level the remote, lofty, golden dome of the Cathedral.

Dickens echoes this perspective, albeit more tentatively, in "On an Amateur Beat," when the Uncommercial Traveller, while noting the "beautiful" proportions of St. Paul's, describes it as remote from the people below it: "it had an air of being somewhat out of drawing, in my eyes. I felt as though the cross were too high up, and perched upon the intervening golden ball too far away" ("Amateur," 382). St. Paul's was a personal favorite destination of Dickens's, along with the Monument (built to commemorate the Great Fire of 1666); scaling these structures with his feet and revisiting them in his head and writing made Dickens not only the poet-novelist of the city but its ardent social critic.[60]

Clearly, then, the presumed order and authority of London governmental and church landmarks can be ironically undercut by their physical proximity to the inhabitants of "the open streets":

> Within so many yards of this Covent-garden lodging of mine, as within so many yards of Westminster Abbey, St. Paul's Cathedral, the Houses of Parliament, the Prisons, the Courts of Justice, all the Institutions that govern the land, I can find—*must* find, whether I will or no—in the open streets, shameful instances of the neglect of children.... ("Short-Timers," 239)

Here the modest yet authoritative personal viewpoint (from the narrator's own lodging) is placed alongside the monolithic and quintessentially British structures, creating the visual effect of these towering monoliths being "pulled down" to the level of the street to witness the distress of the poor. In this essay, as in *Bleak House*, Dickens places churches on a level with governmental institutions that fail to enact social justice or to provide moral inspiration. Church architecture, unlike *David Copperfield*'s angelic human lamb, points upward only to underscore, ironically, religion's diminished role in Victorian society. If, as Richard Stein argues, "city-seeing" challenges the individual to establish identity in relation to urban surroundings, to "position oneself" within the city,[61] then Dickens's prominent inclusion of churches in his city-seeing challenges readers to realign their vision to see the disjunction between revered yet static monuments and always reviled and unstable social "Others."

Dickens's symbolic animation of St. Paul's as London's "heart"—as the circulatory, emotional, and spiritual center of London's "body"—shows a conflicted desire for fixed meaning despite that heart's vulnerability, mutability, and inevitable death. Dickens imagines both the vitality (continuity) and mortality (discontinuity, transformation) inherent in urban scenes and ways of seeing.

With a cinematic eye that pulls back for an overhead shot, Dickens considers the idea of the church as a centering force, a means to ordering the disordered city, when he invites the reader to draw an imaginary circle around the Cathedral, that "Heart of London":

> Wealth and beggary, vice and virtue, guilt and innocence, repletion and the direst hunger, all treading on each other and crowding together, are gathered round it. Draw but a little circle above the clustering housetops, and you shall have within its space everything, with its opposite extreme and contradiction,

close beside. . . . Does not this Heart of London, that nothing moves, nor stops,
nor quickens,—that goes on the same let what will be done,—does not it
express the City's character well? (*MHC*, 107–08)

Yet, St. Paul's imperviousness to the lives around it undercuts whatever moral
centrality it may be presumed to have; its height fails to provide the transcendent moral force symbolized architecturally in its verticality. Tu Yi Fu
Tuan explains the vertical/horizontal tension between churches and cities as
"[symbolizing] the antithesis between transcendence and immanence,
between the ideal of disembodied consciousness (a skyward spirituality) and
the idea of earthbound identification."[62] In Dickens's imaginary circle,
St. Paul's is metaphorically scaled down to the surrounding housetops, just
one more dividing and obstructing wall in a city filled with paradoxical
human experiences. Similarly, in *Little Dorrit* Dickens shows the church
functioning only as an accidental shelter, when Little Dorrit and the mentally
disabled Maggy, locked out of the Marshalsea, spend the night in a church
vestry, their heads pillowed by the church's burial register. The practical help
of shelter for the homeless is not seen by many Victorians as the church's
responsibility; Little Dorrit is suffered to be there only because her birth
record is housed in that church, and she has the notoriety of being one of
the church's "curiosities," having been born in the Marshalsea and never left.
The verger or sexton's practical kindness comes about randomly, since the
vestry is being painted. This is a church barely adequate as shelter, and offers
no ascertainable spiritual inspiration. Dickens does give one note of hope,
however, in the verger's remark about the mystery of whose births and
deaths will be written in future registries. Even the mundane verger wonders
about the unknowable, that evidence of human vitality so dear to Dickens.[63]

Finally, then, while Anglican clergyman of Dickens's era could proclaim the
power of church architecture to "arouse feelings of awe and reverence in its sug-
gestiveness of the supernatural and the Unseen,"[64] Dickens remains more interested in the individual human lives carried on concentrically in the church's
vicinity, finding them untouched by the church's spiritual presence. Such contrast foreshadows the good clergymen created in the fiction of Dickens's
last decade, the Anglican clergymen Frank Milvey (*Our Mutual Friend*) and
Septimus Crisparkle (*The Mystery of Edwin Drood*), whose good works and
goodwill transcend the boundaries of church buildings, however imposing,
as well as the narrowness of church forms and prejudices. Milvey and Crisparkle
care for the poor, the orphan, the Jew, and the foreigner, again underscoring
Dickens's New Testament emphasis on tolerance and kindness, even in the face
of opposition from wives (Milvey's) and mothers (Crisparkle's).[65]

"AS GOOD AS A PLAY": THE
HISTRIONIC CHURCH

The inability of most clergy to put church doctrine into practical action, the
disconnection between church form and function in the public mind, the

disaffection of the public for church-going, and the increasingly difficult relationship between church and city all find voice in Dickens's fiction and essays. David Hempton's study of Victorian religion and popular culture finds that "buildings alone did not create religious cultures, they merely serviced them," and that "religious identities were not foreclosed by the growth of cities in the nineteenth century, they simply became more eclectic and more intricate."[66]

Those who do attend church services do so with mixed motives, as Dickens makes clear in several *Uncommercial Traveller* essays, particularly in "City of London Churches," an essay written and published early in the *Uncommercial Traveller* series (seventh of the thirty-six essays). Dickens's own narratorial stance is complicated by mixed motives, described by John Drew as a combination of a compulsion to "read" the city and interpret it to other Londoners; a sense of "the marketability of the process"; and a missionary zeal that blends "aggression" and "evangelicalism."[67] Harking back to his *Sunday Under Three Heads* argument concerning sabbatarianism, Dickens, in "City of London Churches," offers a tongue-in-cheek apology for Sunday travel, excusing it because his destination was city churches. He relieves the reader with the promise not to offer scholarly classifications of churches: "no answer to any antiquarian question . . . shall harass the reader's soul"; rather, his motivation is "pleasure" concerning "their mystery" ("Churches," 108–09). But this makes matters worse rather than better, if Dickens is truly mindful of a Victorian reverence for Sundays, since curiosity about urban "mysteries" also characterizes the sensation novel and increasingly yellow Victorian journalism.[68] The Uncommercial Traveller's persona survives the "burial alive"[69] in deserted city churches, threatened by the depopulation at the urban core, only by seeing the Victorian church as a part of the theater of the London scene.[70]

Dickens's theatrical treatment of urban scenes is well known due to J. Hillis Miller's seminal essay on Dickensian realism. Dickens not only stages street scenes, but invites readers to consider similarities between the theater and the church. For example, in *Great Expectations* Mr. Wopsle, famous for how he "punished the amens," leaves the theater of the church where he is parish clerk to act Shakespeare on a makeshift London stage, underscoring the performance opportunity inherent in church services, a point also made by John Jasper's singing in the Cloisterham Cathedral in *The Mystery of Edwin Drood*. A further significant example of Dickens's linking of church and theater comes in *Two Views of A Cheap Theatre* (1860), which compares a Saturday night at the Britannia Theater, Hoxton, to a Sunday evening in the same building.

On the first night the theater hosts a Pantomime and a Melodrama, while the second is devoted to a religious service; Dickens attends both. He first joins the working-class audience on Saturday night and describes it as a "we" experience: "as a community we had a character to lose"; "we could never weep so comfortably as when our tears fell on our sandwich" (*Cheap Theatre*, 56, 58). But when he writes about the church service, he laments the clergyman's addressing the audience as "fellow-sinners," suggesting, instead, the more inclusive "fellow-creatures," an echo of Joe Gargery's inclusive sympathy to the convict when he calls Magwitch a "poor miserable fellow-creatur" (*GE*, 5.36). The clergyman's inability to touch "one pulse" of the congregation declares the church service a less unifying and perhaps less morally uplifting use of the theater than the spectacular performance of the previous evening. Here Dickens inverts the cultural fear of "catching something in a theatre" to express the desirability of congregations "catching faith" in church. Deborah Vlock comments: "That theatre audiences could themselves be infected, and enter into acts of performance, had interesting implications for novel readers as well, certainly for readers of Dickens."[71] Comparing church services and congregations with play-acting and perform-ance in "City of London Churches," Dickens parodically emphasizes the fever of the Victorian theater that characterized some High Church services:

> I came upon one obscure church which had broken out in the melodramatic style, and was got up with various tawdry decorations, much after the manner of the extinct London may-poles. These attractions had induced several young priests or deacons in black bibs for waistcoats, and several young ladies inter-ested in that holy order (the proportion being, as I estimated, seventeen young ladies to a deacon), to come into the City as a new and odd excitement. It was wonderful to see how these young people played out their little play in the heart of the City, all among themselves, without the deserted City's knowing anything about it. ("Churches," 115)

The theatricality of *Sketches by Boz* applies equally to *The Uncommercial Traveller* essay just quoted: "London…comes to seem a place where every-one is in one way or another engaged not in productive work but in perform-ing or witnessing scenic representations."[72] The church infected ("broken out") with melodrama abounds in theatrical motifs such as stage sets, cos-tumes, the sensational nature of Victorian theater ("a new and odd excite-ment"), and play-acting.

The church can also be a place for "acting-out," as Dickens's "Wapping Workhouse" (1860) illustrates. The narrator, ostensibly touring the women's wards in order to investigate "the many shameful sick wards for paupers" and to draw the public's "merciful attention"[73] to these substandard conditions, encounters a professedly pious inmate who begs to be allowed to go to wor-ship services. She is denied permission, however, because "[O]n the last occasion of her attending chapel…[she] had secreted a small stick, and had caused some confusion in the responses by suddenly producing it and belabouring the congregation" ("Wapping," 46). Humorously told, this anecdote links church worship with overt acts of violence, madness, and an acting-out of frustration by an inmate of one kind of prison (the workhouse) whose deliverance into a house of worship (yet another prison?) is no deliverance at all.

Dickens also depicts the inherent "showmanship of the church" through its visual spectacle and role as a touristic destination for his characters.

Peggotty's sightseeing with David has already been mentioned, but there is also *Nicholas Nickleby's* John Brodie, "wrapt in admiring wonder" at the gargantuan sight of St. Paul, exclaiming, "a soizable 'un, he be" (*NN*, 39:501). Westminster Abbey also attracts the eyes and visits of those who try to gain knowledge of and pleasure in the city. As Peter Mandler notes, "historical tourism—and English historical consciousness in general—was a particularly populist form of respectability."[74] When Pip and Herbert begin their friendship in *Great Expectations*, Pip asks him to lend a hand in his less formal education as a gentleman, such as helping him with etiquette at table. Herbert also introduces Pip to favorite leisure activities of Londoners: "In the evening we went out for a walk in the streets, and went half-price to the Theatre; and the next day we went to church at Westminster Abbey, and in the afternoon we walked in the Parks" (*GE*, 22:174). Here attending a church service is on a par with theatre-going and *flaneurie*, a leisure pursuit that involves the experiential consumption of the London sights.[75]

"A HUNGER IN HIMSELF TO BE MORE SERIOUS": UNCOMMERCIAL DEATH AND REDEMPTION

Philip Larkin's church-goer discovers "a hunger in himself to be more serious" as he visits old churches.[76] Dickens also feels this hunger, as the novels and essays of the 1860s attest. The cacophony of bells from four churches "clamouring for people" to attend services in "City of London Churches" sounds the waning influence of religion in the nineteenth century even while relentlessly declaring the physical presence of the church. The eighteen "pious warehouse[s] of red brick" in *Hard Times* (1854) also feature a "barbarous jangling of bells," appropriately discordant amidst Coketown's architectural identity crisis in which hospitals, prisons, and churches appear interchangeable (*HT*, 5.23). With their "metallic throats," urban churches offer more grim reminders of mortality, "[leaving] a resonance in the air, as if the winged father who devours his children, had made a sounding sweep with his gigantic scythe in flying over the city" ("No Thoroughfare," in *Christmas Stories*, 539).

In *Our Mutual Friend*, urban darkness and chaos infect city churches, underscoring the oft-reiterated link in Dickens's work between time, death, and the city:

> The towers and steeples of the many house-encompassed churches, dark and dingy as the sky that seems descending on them, are no relief to the general gloom; a sundial on a church-wall has the look, in its useless black shade, of having failed in its business enterprise and stopped payment forever. (*OMF*, 2.15, 393)

These churches near Leadenhall Street and its market, although literally encircled by homes, fail to act as a unifying agent or antidote to the city's prevailing signs of death, imaged by "dark," "gloom," and "black shade." Furthermore, the metaphor of bankruptcy permeates even the churchyard, connecting it to the urban commodity culture that surrounds it. Alexander Welsh describes it: "the hurry and activity, the commerce, even the emotional ties of the city of destruction are so many signs of death, which will soon bring all to a stop."[77] More "signs of death" appear in Bradley Headstone's doomed proposal to Lizzie Hexam in a nearby churchyard. His menacing offer of marriage occurs next to a nightmarish dirt plot in need of Victorian sanitary reform:

> [A] paved square court, with a raised bank of earth about breast high, in the middle, enclosed by iron rails. Here, conveniently and healthfully elevated above the level of the living, were the dead, and the tombstones; some of the latter droopingly inclined from the perpendicular, as if they were ashamed of the lies they told. (*OMF*, 2.15, 394)

The literally unhealthy elevation of "the dead" emphasizes the tombstones' loss of perpendicularity, a visible falling-away from spiritual transcendence. These headstones "lie" about the lives of the departed, and comment ironically on Headstone's infatuation with Lizzie. This space, contiguous with the traditional sanctuary of the church, ironically becomes a prison where Lizzie hears Headstone's proposal against her will, and a court where her brother indites her for disloyalty and for declaring herself an enemy to his version of "respectability."

The dust heaps, recycled waste, and bodies in *Our Mutual Friend* (1865) are repeated in *The Mystery of Edwin Drood* (1870), and are also a dominant trope of "City of London Churches," where congregations "wink, sneeze, and cough" on the "snuff" made by "dead citizens in the vault below" ("Churches," 110). Living and dead mingle:

> We cough and sneeze dead citizens through the service. . . . We stamp our feet to warm them and dead citizens arise in heavy clouds. Dead citizen stick upon the walls, and lie pulverized on the sounding-board over the clergyman's head, and, when a gust of air comes, tumble down upon him. ("Churches," 110)

Dickens, the master re-animator, creates a contested church arena where the living and dead vie for air and space. With Dante's *Inferno* in mind, Alexander Welsh comments on the omnipresence of the dead, which "gives Dickens's London something like an image of classical hell."[78] Yet the palpable presence of the dead does more than this. For who is more marginalized finally, who more risks being obliterated by the changing times and changing England, than the multitudinous, anonymous dead? Every time Dickens evokes the dead he allies himself with them as a chronicler of the city, including the story of its churches and the people inside them, and implies a hope that his stories likewise will persist. The image in *The Mystery of Edwin Drood* of children growing "small salad out of the dust of abbots and abbesses" and making "dirt pies of nuns and friars" recuperates the dead past into a living present through the imaginative force of creativity and play.[79] While hope exists in Cloisterham's dust and dirt, its presumed "holy" space, the Cathedral, is a space of death, inextricably linked with mortality and inexorable time:

> Old Time heaved a mouldy sigh from tomb and arch and vault; and gloomy shadows began to deepen in corners; and damps began to rise from green patches of stone; and jewels, cast upon the pavement of the nave from stained glass by the declining sun, began to perish. . . . In the free outer air, the river, the green pastures, and the brown arable lands, the teeming hills and dales, were reddened by the sunset. . . . In the Cathedral, all became grey, murky and sepulchral. . . . (*ED*, 93)

The color found in nature is extinguished in the Cathedral, whose physical darkness suggests a moral darkness epitomized by the corrupt John Jasper and prejudiced Dean. The Dean, disengaged from the real lives of his congregation asserts: "We clergy need do nothing emphatically" (*ED*, 188). In addition to the image of the Cathedral as a giant, darkened sepulcher, it houses "a sea of music," which "beat its life out," having "lashed," "surged," and "pierced" the surrounding building (*ED*, 93). This deadly music, described as an assault rather than an inspiration, indicates how great a distance High Church worship services are from teaching the New Testament message Dickens holds dear. In this final novel, not even the muscular Christian Reverend Crisparkle can counter the deadly dominance of the Cathedral over the town and its inhabitants. Instead, Dickens must shift the scene to London, to recuperate the losses of Cloisterham.

Shifting away from death to evidence of London's vitality, Dickens concludes his "City of London Churches" with churches whose riverside placement links them with the city as a world marketplace. These churches give olfactory hints of the secular adventures that lie beyond them:

> From Rood-lane to Tower-street, and thereabouts, there was often a subtle flavour of wine: sometimes, of tea. One church near Mincing-lane smelt like a druggist's drawer. Behind the Monument, the service had a flavour of damaged oranges, which, a little further down towards the river, tempered into herrings, and gradually toned into a cosmopolitan blast of fish. ("Churches," 115)

The potpourri of the marketplace reminds readers of the omnipresence of commercial London, and humorously counters the tangible odor of "dead citizens" with evidence of the human appetite for life. Significantly, the vitality of the city penetrates the church and reawakens its attendees to city life outside the church's walls.

As Dickens concludes this self-styled "pilgrimage" of London churches, his ambivalence becomes stronger about how to read what he has witnessed. His narrator evaluates and puzzles over the English church's place in London, Micawber's "modern Babylon." Some churches bear inextricable connection to the movement and contemporaneity of the nineteenth century, an intimate association between a practice of faith and an industrial power, such as "the church where the sails of the oyster-boats . . . almost flapped against the windows,

and "the church where the railroad made the bells hum as the train rushed by
above the roof." But many churches have become instead, "Monuments of
another age," spaces of "singular silence…unknown to far greater numbers of
people speaking the English tongue, than the ancient edifices of the Eternal City,
or the Pyramids of Egypt" ("Churches," 116). Instead, they should be what
Michel Butor calls "the places which speak, which tell us of our history and ourselves."[80] Prominent in Dickens, as in Carlyle and Victorian inheritors such as
Freud, is the fascination with metaphors of excavation, with unearthing buried
remains.[81] Like St. Peter's in Rome or the Pyramids, these nearly abandoned
churches may retain some spiritual power at their core, even if most living
citizens do not seek it out in church spaces. The comparison above of the
"secret" location of city churches to great buildings in Rome or the Pyramids
is itself an act of excavation, in which Dickens "digs out" the hidden city church
for the reader's rediscovery. He thereby acknowledges that they are buried, but
retrievable. Although resilient in ages past to fires and plagues, churches in
Victorian England have become "tombs" and "Monuments of another age,"
chiefly valuable as artifacts of "the time when the City of London was really
London" ("Churches," 116). Yet, throughout the Traveller's "uncommercial"
wanderings through city churches, the "real" London, Dickens argues, is the
London of a twilight faith that the Traveller, even while resisting, is compelled
to witness.

Dickens's criticism of "amen in the wrong place" is equally a striving to
locate amen in the right place, to find a reverence for God combined with a
reverence for humankind; to do so, he must find a church that has been literally, not only imaginatively, transformed. He does so far from London, in
a Welsh village near Anglesey. There he finds clergyman, church community,
and a material church that enact his ideal of "true, practical Christianity"
in their rescue efforts following the wreck of the Royal Charter and loss of
500 lives. This is the subject of "The Shipwreck," from *The Uncommercial
Traveller* (January 28, 1860).

The Anglican clergyman, Stephen Roose Hughes, has turned his church
into a mortuary, and given his time over to the "agonised friends" of the
dead and to the dead themselves, identifying them whenever possible, and
giving them Christian burials in his church's cemetery. Inside the church,
practical Christianity has displaced doctrinal Christianity, symbolized in the
removal of the pulpit to make room for the drowned. The church bears signs
everywhere of its transformation into a mortuary:

> the very Commandments had been shouldered out of their places, in the bring-
> ing in of the dead; the black wooden tables on which they were painted, were
> askew, and on the stone pavement below them, and on the stone pavement all
> over the church, were the marks and stains where the drowned had been laid
> down. ("Shipwreck," 32)

In addition, pitch has been burnt to disinfect and purify the air, and the
Communion Table has next to it boots belonging to some of the drowned.
The rearrangement of this place of worship into a mortuary continues to

reflect the narrator's awareness of the competing claims of physical death and spiritual redemption, and of documentary reporting and inspirational story-telling. The displacement of traditional worship services by the need to shelter and identify the dead allows for a fuller practice of Christianity than the worn rituals depicted in churches elsewhere in Dickens's canon. The reader, along with the narrator, is invited to see and reconstruct:

> The eye, with little or no aid from the imagination, could yet see how the bodies had been turned, and where the head had been and where the feet.... Here, with weeping and wailing in every room of his house, my companion [Reverend S. Hughes] worked alone for hours, solemnly surrounded by eyes that could not see him, and by lips that could not speak to him, patiently examining the tattered clothing, cutting off buttons, hair, marks from linen, anything that might lead to subsequent identification, studying faces, looking for a scar, a bent finger, a crooked toe, comparing letters sent to him with the ruin about him. ("Shipwreck," 32–33)

More striking even than the selfless energy of the clergyman are the metonymic eyes and lips that "stand in" for the deceased, forming an eerie church congregation. The entire essay fictively reconstructs events at the safe distance of two months after the wreck of October 25, 1859, in the "Christmas season of the year" ("Shipwreck," 31). Dickens implies in his reconstruction a writerly kinship with the reconstructive work of the disaster community that labored to protect the sanctity of the dead and thereby redeem the enormous waste of the wreck. This figurative kinship is needed to modify the threatened exploitation of the tragedy by the writer "marketing" the wreck to readers snugly ensconced in front of their hearths, an ironic distance Dickens makes use of early in the essay: "O reader, haply turning this page by the fireside of Home, and hearing the night wind rumble in the chimney, that slight obstruction was the uppermost fragment of the Wreck of the Royal Charter..." ("Shipwreck," 29).

If indeed "[t]here were distinctive patterns of men's spiritual experience" in Victorian England, as the editors of *Masculinity and Spirituality in Victorian Culture* posit, then Dickens's interest in reporting the Christian heroism of this clergyman figures importantly in our understanding of Dickens's religious beliefs.[82] While John Drew has attributed "Dickens's almost morbid interest in the burial process" to the fact that four of Dickens's relatives by marriage had drowned in this shipwreck, and we need also to consider Dickens's abiding fascination with what John Carey calls "stilled life," corpses that "border the country between people and things,"[83] it can also be argued that Dickens has found in Hughes's example a way to celebrate the Christian man as worker, detective, survivor, and consoler, with no concomitant feminization. Sue Zemka, in looking at *The Life of Our Lord* and *Dombey and Son*, notes Dickens's anxiety in representing characters or situations that seem driven "by a prurient curiosity," finding in "the Dickensian Christ a nodal point of tension in the organization and authority of sentimental narratives."[84] The genre of the familiar essay, though, releases Dickens from some of this tension, by allowing him to eschew the mediating female found so often in the fiction, and to locate saving grace in an adult male. Also writing about representations of Christ and Victorian masculinity, Sean Gill claims that "what was often at stake in such endeavors was the author's sense of self as a man."[85] Thus Dickens's reconstruction of the shipwreck's aftermath and valorization of Hughes's Christianity speaks directly to Dickens's own redemptive drive as a man and an author, including his attempts to imagine and depict practices of faith.

At the essay's spiritual climax, the Traveller moves from the church as mortuary to the churchyard as the scene of Christian burial. According to the Traveller's account, the Reverend Stephen Hughes helped to identify and/or bury 145 bodies that washed ashore after the wreck, often acting as a mediator between grieving relatives and the body they sought; he and his family shielded the relatives as much as possible from the horror of so many corpses. Reverend Hughes, Dickens's exemplum of "true practical Christianity," is also credited with writing 1,075 letters to the grieving survivors of those lost in the wreck. When the Traveller repeatedly noticed "the awful scene of death he had been required so closely to familiarize himself with for the soothing of the living," Reverend Hughes admitted that the experience left him able to eat and drink little but coffee and bread. Through these details, Dickens unambiguously establishes the Reverend's heroic fortitude and compassion, thus allowing the Traveller to make in this essay a strong statement of where the most vital faith is found:

> I seemed to have happily come, in a few steps, from the churchyard with its open grave, which was a type of Death, to the Christian dwelling side by side with it, which was the type of Resurrection. I shall never think of the former without the latter. ("Shipwreck," 35)

It is not in the church building, nor in the churchyard, but in the home of the Christian hero Reverend Hughes that Dickens asserts the strength of religious belief, always united with good works. In Wales, "where so many were so strangely brought together," the Traveller's tourism takes a serious turn, and Dickens manages to write more reassuringly about the redemptive opportunities of faith and death than he ever managed to again.

In other *Uncommercial Traveller* essays, churches have yet to be galvanized into practices of faith like those in the "Shipwreck," because city churches and city writing lack the stability and cohesiveness of this idealized Welsh community,[86] and because Dickens unflinchingly sees the church where genuine faith is practiced as an anomaly. Finally, Dickens's longing for a church congruent with New Testament good works and his impulse to relocate *amens* to other human spaces have a transcendence all their own.

NOTES

I would like to thank my colleagues Jude Nixon at Oakland University, Rob Garnett at Gettysburg College, and Monika Brown at Pembroke State University, for their helpful comments and suggestions.

1. John Drew and Joss Lutz Marsh (1993) both describe Dickens as a tour and travel guide. See Drew, "*Voyages Extraordinaires:* Dickens's 'Travelling Essays' and *The Uncommercial Traveller*," Parts 1, 2, *Dickens Quarterly* 13, nos. 2, 3 (June–September 1996): 76–96, 127–50; Marsh, "Imagining Victorian London: An Entertainment and Itinerary (Chas. Dickens, Guide)," *Stanford Humanities Review* 3, no. 1 (1993): 67–97.

2. Philip Larkin, "Church Going," in *Collected Poems* (London: Marvell and Faber and Faber, 1988), 97. Thanks to my colleague Rob Anderson at Oakland University for drawing my attention to the Larkin poem.

3. Murray Baumgarten, "Fictions of the City," in *The Cambridge Companion to Charles Dickens*, ed. John O. Jordan (Cambridge: Cambridge University Press, 2001), 111.

4. Marsh, "Victorian London," 81; Eisenman, qtd. in Julian Wolfreys, *Writing London: The Trace of the Urban Text from Blake to Dickens* (London: Macmillan, 1998), 176.

5. See Michael Cotsell, "*The Uncommercial Traveller* on the Commercial Road: Dickens's East End, Part Two," *Dickens Quarterly* 3, no. 3 (1986): 115–22, who calls the East End essays "great because they articulate discomfort" (116), and Drew, "*Voyages Extraordinaires*." Drew uses work by Michel Butor and Walter Benjamin, and notes that "the travel motif becomes a vehicle for social and cultural criticism, a medium for assessing that most Victorian of pre-occupations, change" (Part 1: 87).

6. Important discussions can also be found in Humphry House, *The Dickens World*, 2nd ed. (London: Oxford University Press, 1965); Norris Pope, *Dickens and Charity* (New York: Columbia University Press, 1978); Barry Qualls, *Secular Pilgrims of Victorian Fiction* (London: Cambridge University Press, 1982); and Sue Zemka, *Victorian Testaments: The Bible, Christology, and Literary Authority in Early Nineteenth-Century British Culture* (Stanford: Stanford University Press, 1997).

7. Dennis Walder, *Dickens and Religion* (London: George Allen and Unwin, 1981), 91.

8. See Zemka, *Victorian Testaments*, 129.

9. Walder, *Dickens*, 175; Janet Larson, *Dickens and the Broken Scripture* (Athens, Georgia: The University of Georgia Press, 1985), 9; House, *Dickens World*, 110.

10. I call these various moments in Dickens's life and work "clues" because they gesture toward the mystery of Dickens's faith; but I don't mean to imply that a single "solution" is possible or even desirable. Rather, I want to draw attention to the difficulty and complexity of making any kind of absolute pronouncement on Dickens's religious beliefs. Walder describes the difficulty of defining Dickens's representation of religious beliefs in his fiction as "complicated by his independence of easily identifiable systems of worship, by his intuitive and shifting point-of-view, and, it should be added, his discretion" (171). Zemka, on the other hand, suggestively discusses the conflicts at play in Dickens's correspondence about Urania Cottage, scenes of Christian enlightenment in *Dombey and Son*, and the version of Christ's life in *The Life of Our Lord*. Dickens attacked Millais's first major religious painting in "Old Lamps for New Ones," *Household Words*, June 15, 1850 (leading article), reprinted in *The Amusements of the People and Other Papers: Reports, Essays and Reviews, 1834–51*, ed. Michael Slater (Columbus: Ohio State University Press, 1996), 242–48. Dickens was particularly repulsed by "Two almost

naked carpenters." Leonee Ormond discusses Dickens's reaction to the Millais painting in the context of Dickens's responses to other contemporary artists' work in "Dickens and Painting: Contemporary Art," *Dickensian* 80, no. 1 (1984): 2–25.

11. Robert Polhemus, "Comic and Erotic Faith Meet Faith in the Child: Charles Dickens's *The Old Curiosity Shop ("the Old Cupiosity Shape")*," in *Critical Reconstructions: The Relationship of Fiction and Life* (Stanford: Stanford University Press, 1994), 71, and J. Hillis Miller, *Charles Dickens: The World of His Novels* (Bloomington: Indiana University Press, 1958), 315.

12. William Howitt, "Charles Dickens," *The People's Journal*, June 3, 1846, 8–12; qtd. in *Dickens: The Critical Heritage*, ed. Philip Collins (New York: Barnes and Noble, 1971), 205, and [James Augustine Stothert], "Living Novelists," *The Rambler*, January 1854, n.s. 1, 41–51; qtd. in *Dickens: The Critical Heritage*, 294.

13. Philip Collins, "Introduction," *Dickens: The Critical Heritage*, 12.

14. House, *Dickens World*, 119.

15. Charles Dickens, "City of London Churches," in *All the Year Round*, May 1860, reprinted in *The Uncommercial Traveller and Other Papers 1859–1870*, eds. Michael Slater and John Drew (Columbus: Ohio State University Press, 2000), 111. All references to essays originally appearing in *The Uncommercial Traveller* are from this edition: "The Shipwreck" (26–40); "Wapping Workhouse" (41–51); "Two Views of a Cheap Theatre" (52–62); "City of London Churches" (105–16); "The Short-Timers" (237–47); "On an Amateur Beat" (377–85).

16. Excellent introductory material is provided at the beginning of each essay in this Dent Edition of *The Uncommercial Traveller*.

17. Charles Dickens, *Sunday Under Three Heads*, in *The Uncommercial Traveller and Reprinted Pieces Etc.*, *Oxford Illustrated Dickens* (Oxford: Oxford University Press, 1989), 650; hereafter *Sunday*. Unless otherwise noted, all references to Dickens's works are from the *Oxford Illustrated Dickens*.

18. Bruce Haley, *The Healthy Body and Victorian Culture* (Cambridge, Massachusetts: Harvard University Press, 1978), writes, "...there was a general tendency [by Victorians] to broaden the concept of health metaphysically to suggest an integration with external, spiritual laws" (19).

19. Leonore Davidoff and Catherine Hall, *Family Fortunes: Men and Women of the English Middle Class, 1780–1850* (Chicago: University of Chicago Press, 1987), 76.

20. Charles Dickens, *Oliver Twist*, 32.239; hereafter *OT*.

21. Walder, *Dickens*, 4.

22. Qualls elucidates how Dickens is influenced by Thomas Carlyle's conversion pattern, and explains: "The pilgrim's questions *Who am I?* and *What shall I do to be saved?* have amazing potency in his novels" (85, 87).

23. Walder, *Dickens*, 4.

24. Charles Dickens, *Life of Our Lord* (New York: Simon and Schuster, 1934); hereafter *LOL*. Walder gives this history: "Perhaps the most significant act from the religious point of view taken by Dickens was when he decided to attend the Little Portland Street chapel of Edward Taggart (1804–58). He had begun to attend Thomas Madge's Essex Street Unitarian chapel on his return from America, but it was Taggart's funeral sermon on W. E. Channing, whom Dickens had met in Boston, which attracted him to Little Portland

Street on 20 November 1842. There he found that he and Taggart shared 'that religion which has sympathy for men of every creed and ventures to pass judgement on none'" (*Dickens*, 12).

25. House, *Dickens World*, 34–35.

26. Polhemus, *The Old Curiosity Shop*, 76, 74.

27. Larson, *Broken Scripture*, 271–72.

28. Walder notes, "Dickens's lack of confidence in urban religion" in *OCS* (69). Andrew Sanders links *The Old Curiosity Shop*'s romantically rural church with Wordsworth's "Essay on Epitaphs," appended to *The Exursion* in 1814 (*Charles Dickens: Resurrectionist* [NewYork: St. Martin's Press, 1982], 14–17).

29. Charles Dickens, *The Old Curiosity Shop*, 15:115; hereafter *OCS*. David Hempton has commented on the challenge facing the institutional church in Victorian times: "The real test for churches and voluntary religious organisations in the first half of the nineteenth century, therefore, was how well they could adapt to the realities of urban living, and more particularly, how much support they could attract from a predominantly youthful and mobile working class" (*Religion and Political Culture in Britain and Ireland* [Cambridge: Cambridge University Press, 1996], 120).

30. Cotsell finds the essays and their failure to console the reader "out of key with [Dickens's] fiction" ("*The Uncommercial Traveller*," 121). Like Cotsell, I find this honesty makes the essays particularly valuable in the study of Dickens's work.

31. Zemka, *Victorian Testaments*, 120.

32. Walder, *Dickens*, 171.

33. To John Makeham, June 8, 1870, *The Letters of Charles Dickens*, ed. Madeline House, Graham Storey, and Kathleen Tillotson, 12 vols. (New York: Oxford University Press, 1965–2001), 12:547–48.

34. To Rev. R. H. Davies, December 24, 1856, in *The Letters of Dickens*, 8:244–45; qtd. in Larson, *Broken Scripture*, 9.

35. Deborah Vlock comments: "Often, attacks on the theatre were themselves acts of "theatrical" display, which suggests that the institutions, implicitly or explicitly pitted against performance, like family, church, and government, depended on a healthy industry to provide them with voices and to secure their own identities" (*Dickens, Novel Reading, and the Victorian Popular Theatre* [Cambridge: Cambridge University Press, 1998], 56–57).

36. In "The Bloomsbury Christening," from Dickens's *Sketches by Boz*, the christening service itself is perfunctorily performed. The officiating clergyman has six more church rites to administer, the theological import of the christening is reduced by the child's father to the vague phrase, "all that sort of thing," and godfather Dumps, miserable to find himself partaking in this ritual, almost drops the infant into the baptismal font. Altogether, the baptism "went off in the usual business-like and matter-of-course manner" (*Sketches* 476), and proves to be merely a delay in getting to the real festivities, an evening party given by the parents. While amusingly rendering the cranky Dumps' reluctant god-parenting and the parents' worship of their new offspring, Dickens also portrays the loss of meaning in this religious form.

37. John Carey, *The Violent Effigy: A Study of Dickens' Imagination* (London: Faber and Faber, 1973), 56–57. I thank Professor Rob Garnett, Gettysburg College, for drawing my attention to Carey's argument.

38. Larson, *Broken Scripture*, 101.

39. Polhemus, *The Old Curiosity Shop*, 72; Natalie McKnight, *Idiots, Madmen, and Other Prisoners in Dickens* (New York: St. Martin's Press, 1993), 35–38.

40. Natalie McKnight sees Dickens connecting himself as an author to Christ the story teller, who "guides his flock through creative language" ("Dickens's Philosophy of Fathering," *Dickens Quarterly* 18, no. 3 [2001]: 136).

41. Gaston Bachelard, *The Poetics of Space*, trans. Maria Jolas (Boston: Beacon Press, 1969), 98, 103.

42. Wolfreys, *Writing London*, 5, 18, 171, passim.

43. Hempton, *Religion*, 118–19.

44. House, *Dickens World*, 119.

45. Pope, *Dickens and Charity*, 20.

46. Unsigned review of *Little Dorrit*, 1857, qtd. in *Charles Dickens: The Critical Heritage*, 363.

47. David Parker, "Our Pew at Church," *The Dickensian* 88, no. 1 (1992): 40–42.

48. Charles Dickens, *David Copperfield*, 4:52; hereafter *DC*.

49. In *The Mystery of Edwin Drood*, philanthropy becomes the "castle" under attack, and Mr. Honeythunder the childish, bullying man who misguidedly defends his own brand of coercive do-gooding. Playing in church could also be ascribed to Wopsle in *Great Expectations*, and John Jasper in *Drood*.

50. Arlene Jackson discusses images of the church in the text and illustrations of *David Copperfield*, including the important associations Agnes Wickfield has with memory and sanctuary ("Agnes Wickfield and Church Leitmotif in *David Copperfield*," *Dickens Studies Annual* 9 [1981]: 53–65).

51. Jackson, "Agnes Wickfield," 57.

52. Steven Marcus, *Dickens: From Pickwick to Dombey* (New York: Basic Books, 1965), 278.

53. Walter Bagehot, "Charles Dickens," *National Review*, October 1958, vii, 458–86, reprinted in *Charles Dickens: The Critical Heritage*, 390.

54. Wolfreys, *Writing London*, 18; Wolfreys's work is indebted to Michel Foucault, *The Archaeology of Knowledge*, trans. A. M. Sheridan Smith (New York: Pantheon, 1971), in which Foucault sees history as archaeology, having an "interest not in continuity but in discontinuity (threshold, rupture, break, mutilation, transformation)" (5).

55. Ibid., 145.

56. Walder calls the cross of St. Paul's "a familiar, almost obsessive image for the novelist" (*Dickens*, 165).

57. Lewis Mumford, *The City in History: Its Origins, Its Transformations, Its Prospects* (New York: Harcourt, 1961), 306.

58. Charles Dickens, *Master Humphrey's Clock and A Child's History of England*, 6.107; hereafter *MHC*.

59. Charles Dickens, *Bleak House*, chapter 19; hereafter *BH*.

60. Letter to Thomas Beard, January 28, 1837: "I want a walk;—we can have a stroll on Monday, if you are not engaged. The top of the Monument is one of my longings; the ditto of St. Paul's, another" (*Letters of Dickens*, 1:238).

61. Richard Stein, "Street Figures: Victorian Urban Iconography," in *Victorian Literature and the Victorian Visual Imagination*, ed. Carol T. Christ and John O. Jordan (Berkeley: University of California Press, 1995), 238.

62. Qtd. in Marilyn Faulkenberg, *Church, City and Labyrinth in Bronte, Dickens, Hardy and Butor* (New York: Peter Lang, 1993), 18.

63. *Little Dorrit*, 14:177.

64. Michael Hall, "What Do Victorian Churches Mean? Symbolism and Sacramentalism in Anglican Church Architecture 1850–1870," *Journal of the Society of Architectural Historians* 59, no. 1 (2000): 89.

65. In *The Mystery of Edwin Drood*, John Jasper's apparent hypocrisy as choir-master at Cloisterham Cathedral is worth noting: he is never in better voice, performing the hymns and sung responses of the Anglican Church, than on the day during which he is (presumably) plotting his nephew's murder.

66. Hempton, *Religion*, 122, 142.

67. Drew, *Voyages*, 133, 140.

68. Judith Walkowitz notes "a streak of voyeurism" in the work of journalists such as Henry Mayhew, and the preoccupation with prostitutes shared by Gladstone and Dickens, among others, which characterized mid- and late-century Victorian England (*City of Dreadful Delight: Narratives of Sexual Danger in Late-Victorian London* [Chicago: University of Chicago Press, 1992], 21). Zemka also notices the tension in Dickens's attitude to the fallen women for whom Urania Cottage was designed, between a Christological motive of spiritual reclamation and a prurient interest in female sexuality (*Victorian Testaments*, 141–45).

69. A suggestive phrase, used by Dickens in "City of London Churches" to describe two churchgoers, an old man and a female child, descending into a cellar after church. This idea of live burial appears elsewhere in Dickens's canon and in the work of his contemporaries. See Book I, chapter 6, "The Shoemaker," in *Tale of Two Cities*, describing Dr. Manette, "the buried man who had been dug out," and Mary Elizabeth Braddon's *Lady Audley's Secret*, "Buried Alive" (Oxford: Oxford University Press, 1987), referring to the incarceration of Helen Talboys/Lucy Graham/ Lady Audley in a Belgium mental asylum (3.6). Matthew Arnold's poem "The Buried Life" (1852) locates the desire to unearth the individual's repressed desires, that "buried life," "in the world's most crowded streets" (*The Poems of Matthew Arnold*, ed. Kenneth Allott and Miriam Allott, 2nd ed. [London: Longman, 1965], lines 45–48).

70. "The problem of City churches first raised its head over a century ago, in the 1850s, when the City's population began to fall dramatically in proportion to that of Greater London" (Hermione Hobhouse, *Lost London: A Century of Demolition and Decay* [London: Macmillan, 1971], 58).

71. Vlock, *Dickens*, 36.

72. J. Hillis Miller, "The Fiction of Realism: *Sketches by Boz, Oliver Twist*, and Cruikshank's Illustrations," in *Dickens Centennial Essays*, ed. Ada Nisbet and Blake Nevius (Berkeley: University of California Press, 1971), 105.

73. John Drew cites this 1866 letter written by Dickens six years after writing "Wapping Workhouse" to the secretary of the newly formed Association for the Improvement of the Infirmaries of London Workshouses" ("Wapping," 41). "Wapping Workhouse" appeared originally on February 18, 1860 in *All Year the Round*.

74. Peter Mandler, " 'Wands of Fancy': The Historical Imagination of the Victorian Tourist," in *Material Memories*, ed. Marius Kwint, Christopher Breward, and Jeremy Asynsley (Oxford: Berg, 1999), 129.

75. See Drew, "*Voyages Extraordinaires.*" Drawing from Walter Benjamin's often-cited work, Drew comments on the "notion of flaneurie . . . [and] the ambivalent response of the artist to the experience of traversing the modern city" in relation to Dickens's persona in *Uncommercial Traveller* (Part 2: 134).

76. Larkin, "Church Going," 98.

77. Alexander Welsh, *The City of Dickens* (Cambridge, Massachusetts: Harvard University Press, 1986), 59.

78. Ibid., 65.

79. Charles Dickens, *The Mystery of Edwin Drood* (Oxford: Oxford University Press, 1989), 3.18; hereafter *ED*. Faulkenburg discusses Dickens's church in *Drood*, concluding that "For Dickens the true church is a spirit residing within the person so that Tartar's private rooftop garden metaphorically issues a call to moral transcendence more effective than that of the institutional Cathedral tower" (27).

80. Qtd. in Drew, *Voyages Extraordinaires* (Part 1: 129).

81. Lawrence Frank, "*Pictures from Italy:* Dickens, Rome, and the Eternal City of the Mind," *Il Confronto Letterario* (Padua, Italy) 14, no. 2 (1997): 239–43 passim, claims that Dickens, like Freud, found in archaeology a metaphor for the processes of the human mind.

82. Andrew Bradstock, Sean Gill, Anne Hogan, and Sue Morgan, eds., "Introduction," in *Masculinity and Spirituality in Victorian Culture* (Houndmills: Macmillan, 2000), 2.

83. See Drew's headnote to "The Shipwreck," 27. Drew also provides the historical context for Dickens's composition of this essay and Carey, *The Violent Effigy*, 101–02.

84. Zemka, *Victorian Testaments*, 142, 137–38.

85. Sean Gill, "Ecce Homo: Representations of Christ as the Model of Masculinity in Victorian Art and Lives of Jesus," in *Masculinity and Spirituality in Victorian Culture*, ed. Andrew Bradstock, Sean Gill, Anne Hogan, and Sue Morgan (Houndmills: Macmillan, 2000), 165–67.

86. Alexander McKee gives an account of the community's response at variance with Dickens's account of the community's disinterestedness (*The Golden Wreck: The True Story of a Great Maritime Disaster* [London: Souvenir Press, 1961], 146).

CHAPTER 10

"POETRY IS WHERE GOD IS": THE IMPORTANCE OF CHRISTIAN FAITH AND THEOLOGY IN ELIZABETH BARRETT BROWNING'S LIFE AND WORK

Alexandra M. B. Wörn

What could a stronger awareness of the presence of Scripture and theological reflection in Elizabeth Barrett Browning's life and work contribute to our understanding of her poetic achievement? In this essay I suggest that knowledge of her engagement with biblical and theological texts can help to enrich our understanding of Barrett Browning's poetry. Most scholars have tended to approach her verse with an interest in its feminist, aesthetic, and political aspects,[1] but its religious and theological aspect has not received an equal amount of attention. Work on her biography and her poetry often appears to underplay the influence of Christian spirituality as well as intellectual engagement with the Bible and theological literature on her thought.[2] However, in Barrett Browning's writings and in her life, spirituality and theological reflection held a central place; in her essay on English poetry we read that "[n]ature is where God is. Poetry is where God is."[3] In what follows I explore the importance of Scripture and theological thought in Barrett Browning's life and work implicit in these lines, and furthermore show her "creative and original engagements with religious texts and theology."[4]

I intend, in particular, to do justice to the relationship between Barrett Browning's poetry, theory of poetry, and Christian faith, and to show how each has influenced the other. I demonstrate that for Barrett Browning poetry, nature, and God were interlinked. She understood poetry to be a response to nature, which was created by God. Barrett Browning's religious family background is necessary for a proper understanding of the development of her religious thinking. Her poetry reflects the tension between the religious ideas she inherited, particularly from her father, and those she would later hold in more or less conscious opposition to what she had been instructed.[5]

Elizabeth Barrett Browning was raised in a religious family of freethinking Congregationalist Christians.[6] The Congregationalist emphasis on the free movement of the Spirit and distrust of giving binding authority to creedal statements resulted in a freedom of religious thought in Barrett Browning's father, in turn inherited by his daughter, and would prepare the ground for much of her later creativity.[7] Since Mr. Barrett had an immense influence over his daughter, it was only natural that the religious life of the Barrett family was formative on her.[8] "As a child ... [Barrett Browning] went occasionally with her father to the nearest Congregationalist chapel, ... [however] the Barrett household was pious in feeling rather than strict in observance."[9] The danger of excess in this religious freedom experienced by the young Elizabeth can be seen in her own recognition that she was "in great danger of becoming the founder of a religion of [her] own" where Christianity was merged with Greek pantheism (*BC*, 1:351). Different but equally individual spiritual convictions took form in Mr. Barrett's heart and mind, a deep and intense religiosity independent from canons of orthodoxy accepted in traditional theological circles of his time, yet having a strictly Calvinistic emphasis.

The early death of Mrs. Barrett in 1828 had an immense impact on the family. Mr. Barrett's strong faith increased in piety, but he was "beginning to interpret God's word in his own strange way,"[10] and the whims of Mr. Barrett's religious thought were increasingly attributed by him to the will of God.[11] Mary Barrett's death was understood by her husband as a sign of God's mercy, that God had released her from disease and weakness.[12] The independence of his religious thinking after his wife's death led him more and more in this "strange" direction, moving gradually further away from an understanding of God as gracious toward a doctrine sketched in Pelagian colors where salvation also requires works of a good and holy life. Barrett Browning's father became obsessed by the idea of an utterly corrupt world; he was preoccupied with the evil he saw around him. This knowledge induced him to cultivate a negative understanding of humanity placed in opposition to the perfections of the divine. Mr. Barrett subscribed to a neat, more or less black-and-white dualism: the evil of the earth on the one hand, and the purity of heaven on the other.[13]

This polarized understanding is evident in some of Barrett Browning's earlier works, in ballads such as *Isobel's Child* and *The Romaunt of Margret*, both published in her 1838 volume *The Seraphim, and Other Poems* (*CW*, 2:1–29). The reader can witness the poet's struggle: she was torn between her unhappiness with the apparent imperfections of the earth together with her longing to escape from its sorrows, and her recognition that this black-and-white view of good and evil was undermined by evidence of selflessness and perfection in the human being.[14]

From the late 1830s onward, Barrett Browning began to emancipate herself gradually from her father's Pelagian thinking. She explored and developed a doctrine that, in contrast to her father's, located divine glory in the imperfections of the world. This was to begin hesitantly with *A Drama of Exile* (1844), continuing with her love verse as well as her political poetry, and was fully realized in *Aurora Leigh* (1856).[15] Through these works we can trace Barrett Browning's self-emancipation from Mr. Barrett's bleaker vision of the world toward a more Romantic-Platonic idea of the world as participating profoundly in the glory of the divine.

Elizabeth Barrett Browning, "by her own testimony, at the age of twelve, ... was declaring her religious independence."[16] However, it is interesting to ask from what she was actually distancing herself: she was not only distancing herself from Mr. Barrett but also from established religious forms in general, since she felt her faith should be determined and shaped by her personal life experience:

> I revolted at the idea of an established religion—my faith was sincere but my *religion was founded solely on the imagination*. It was not the deep persuasion of the mild Christian but the wild visions of an enthusiast. I worshipped God heart and soul but I forgot that *prayers should be pure & simple as the Father I* adored[.] ... I trusted with enthusiastic faith to His mercy "who only chasteneth whom he loveth." (*BC*, 1:351, emphasis mine)

Barrett Browning followed in the footsteps of her family in that she did not wish to associate herself with anything established: she detested classification. It was not astonishing, therefore, that she had been called "orthodox by infidels, and heterodox by churchpeople ..." (*LEBB*, 2:420).[17] "Arminians in general w^d. call [her] a Calvinist,—while Calvinists w^d. call [her] an Arminian" (*BC*, 8:22). This showed that Barrett Browning was struggling from the very beginning with the established churches and any priesthood other than Christ's. Her faith was in keeping with the fundamental teachings of all churches, for she believed "in the Divinity of Christ, in Atonement and Grace, Judgement and Life Everlasting," yet remained faithful to her Congregationalist upbringing "in the practice of [her] faith by direct relation of ... [her] soul to God, without intermediary of hierarchies or rites, by reliance on the Bible, and with toleration of other sects."[18]

Barrett Browning was also unhappy with the theology as practiced in the universities: she intended her thought to break free from the neat concepts and categories of the philosopher-theologians. In a letter to Robert Browning dated March 20, 1845, she confessed that all is well "as long as I keep out of the shadow of the dictionaries & of theological controversies, & the like ..." (*BC*, 10:134). True to the spirit of Congregationalism, Barrett Browning was trying to create her own theology in her poetry where the highest authorities were Scripture and experience gained from life; theologians and the established churches were granted second place. The diary she kept between 1831 and 1832 tells us that she read seven chapters of the Bible daily and "in as simple a spirit as [she could] ...."[19] We also know from a letter to a friend that "[f]rom motives of a desire of theological instruction ... [she] very seldom read any book except God's own ... [she was] apt to receive less of what is called edification from human discourse on divine subjects, than disturbance & hindrance" (*BC*, 8:107).[20]

Nevertheless, Barrett Browning had all the competences of a serious biblical scholar. She had a firm grasp of Ancient Hebrew and Greek.[21] Her reading and translating of the Old Testament most probably influenced and deepened her thinking about the relationship of the Divinity and humanity of God. The lack of dualism in Hebraic thought must certainly have been one of the influences on her desire for experiencing the God incarnate in this world, rather than a longing for transcendence. Glennis Stephenson writes:

> [i]n the early religious poems, to withdraw from the world, to embrace God..., may seem an attractive proposition, but the romantic ballads soon challenge the idea that God's love alone can provide happiness....Earthly life and earthly love are shown to be the source of sorrow as well as joy, but they still appear preferable to the perfect placidity of heaven and divine love.[22]

Barrett Browning's interests were not only scriptural; she was also well read both in the Greek Fathers, the English divines, and the general theological literature of her age. She had

> read rather widely the divinity of the Greek Fathers, Gregory, Chrysostom, & so forth, & [had] of course informed [herself] in the works generally of [the] old English divines, Hooker's, Jeremy Taylor's, & so forth. (*BC*, 8:107)

Moreover, her essay on *The Greek Christian Poets* (1842; *CW*, 6:168–239), resulting from four papers she had written for the *Athenaeum* in 1842, was an analysis and a translation of twenty-one Theologian-Poets ranging from the fourth to the fourteenth century. Her treatment of the selected poems of the Greek Church Fathers and their successors showed a deep knowledge, competence, and confidence in her material.[23] Barrett Browning's reverence and high estimation for Gregory of Nazianzus deserves mentioning, for he seems to have been a major influence on her thought especially in the 1830s and early 1840s.[24] In her eyes, Nazianzus was an unjustly "neglected" fourth-century Church Father: "I have read with admiration and delight various parts of his poetry and his prose. His devotion is fervent and sublime, as all his thoughts and his feelings."[25] In the introduction to her translations of three of Gregory Nazianzus's hymns, Barrett Browning refers to the influence that Gregory specifically, and the Greek Fathers more generally, had on her poetry:

> for whenever through the cloud of this folio of them [meaning the Greek Christian poets] we catch a glimpse of the luminous soul, we fall back upon ourselves for an increase of praise. (*CW*, 6:348)

Hence, Barrett Browning had a very broad theological knowledge. This, along with her Congregationalist faith and the religious understanding of Mr. Barrett, was one of the main influences on her poetry.

A third, and perhaps the most important influence was simply Barrett Browning's love for the stories and poems of the Bible, which in their richness in content and freedom of form, and their way of engaging the religious-poetical imagination, was in stark contrast to the aridity of the scholars. She was not enamored with the distinctions and categories of many a standard theological textbook. Her intention was to stay close to the narrative and verse forms she admired so much in Scripture. For Barrett Browning, the best way to convey truth is that way for which the Bible itself provided the model. She felt her religious convictions were best expressed through poetry just as truth was best expressed through verse, allegory, and story in Scripture. Through poetry, Barrett Browning also felt that the evil and sorrow in this world was preserved and not argued away, just as the stories and verses of both Testaments are not free of contradictions and ambiguities. In her poetry Barrett Browning articulated her religious struggles as well as those that tend to receive more attention by scholars. Thus, Barrett Browning stands as a poet sensitive to and fully aware of theology without ever wanting to become a theologian herself. Despite her familiarity with this discipline, she held her distance from it as she did with the established churches themselves, favoring the freedom of verse inspired by Scripture rather than the dryness of theological prose.

As a poet, then, Barrett Browning was searching for new poetic forms of expression and new ways to express how God related to his created order. In doing so she was liberating herself from the religious pessimism of her father and his clinging to the dead. "[N]ew *forms*...as well as thoughts" was what she sought. To her "[t]he old gods [were] dethroned. Why should [she] go back to the antique moulds...classical moulds, as they are so improperly called"? One should "aspire rather to *Life*—& let the dead bury their dead" (*BC*, 10:135). This allusion to Matthew 8:21 and following, where Christ exhorts the true disciple to leave burying his own father and follow him, illustrates how Barrett Browning, unlike Mr. Barrett, finds glimpses of God and his goodness in human life and vitality.

The struggle to affirm life as she felt Christ had done is exemplified in Barrett Browning's work in the gradual but drastic shift in her depiction of God. Her understanding of God moved from divine remoteness to the closest intimacy with his creation.[26] This is borne witness to in several of her more mature poems, such as *A Drama of Exile* (1844) and the *Sonnets from the Portuguese* (1850), where the lyric female subject—Eve and the subject of the *Sonnets*—is infused with selfless, perfect love, imaging the attributes of the divine in his created order. From the publication of *The Seraphim, and Other Poems* (1838) onward, the characters in Barrett Browning's poems seem to be allowed to be both more intimate in relationship with God and to be more godlike. The perfect union of Adam and Eve in love for one another evident at the end of *A Drama of Exile* is made the sign of God's tender presence in the world, since here Christ is portrayed as a mediating figure "rejoic[ing] in the physical and sensuous world, in the joining of the lovers and the intimacy of union."[27] The perfect love between two human beings participates in the eternal love between the three persons of the Trinity; human love is not, as Mr. Barrett would have thought, totally other than divine love. Later and more radically in *Aurora Leigh* (1856) Aurora herself is elevated to the title of Christ.[28] Like Christ, Aurora is called the morning star, the dawn, the new morning; she, like Christ, but as a woman, serves humanity in proclaiming the truth "in love and in life"[29] through her poetry. Romney, Aurora's addressee, says "[y]ou have shown me truths, / ... truths not yours, indeed, / [b]ut set within my reach by means of you ... " (*'Aurora Leigh': Aurora Leigh, CW*, 5, book 8, lines 608, 610–611). Here Barrett Browning is re-envisaging the traditional male role of the poet as priest, indeed, of the male Christ himself as Logos-bearer, in the new form of a female; thus, she is expressing old religious truths while making them her own.

Returning to the initial quotation, "[n]ature is where God is. Poetry is where God is" (*CW*, 6:294), I now look at nature in its theological meaning for Barrett Browning. An obvious place to begin is her treatment of the Paradise narrative in Genesis 1–3. Barrett Browning refers to it in three of her literary essays, *A Thought on Thoughts* (1836), *The Book of the Poets* (1842), and the already mentioned *The Greek Christian Poets* (1842), as well as in *A Drama of Exile* (1844). Through the essays and *Drama*, Barrett Browning's own interpretation of Paradise unfolds. Seen together, they offer quite a comprehensive insight into her reading of the Creation and the Fall.

A Drama of Exile, compared to *Aurora Leigh*, is arguably Elizabeth Barrett Browning's more neglected work. Cynthia Scheinberg shows that here the poet clearly displays her competence in Hebrew and Greek, "while also invoking the Hebraic through a complex use of the figure of 'exile.'" Barrett Browning was wrestling here with two important issues: first, the notion of exile "and her claim to authoritative scriptural interpretation," and second, feminism "and her position as a woman writer." Thus, Scheinberg rightly concludes that in the *Drama* Barrett Browning "not only invokes her 'experience as a woman,' but also her experience as a scholar" and refuses to remain "'an exile' herself from the worlds of both Biblical exegesis and literary ambition."[30]

As has been stated, in the *Drama* Barrett Browning's first motif was exile from Paradise—the "new and strange experience of the fallen humanity, as it went forth from Paradise into the wilderness" (*CW*, 2:143).[31] Adam and Eve had left all behind: perfect truth, beauty, and goodness. Alison Milbank, in her monograph *Dante and the Victorians*, shows how exile, metaphysical or geographical, is the "Victorians' dilemma."[32] This dilemma was the quest for a spiritual and transcendental home, something that the figure of Dante and his treatment of the Paradise narrative seems to offer. Barrett Browning confirms Milbank's observation when she writes in her preface to the *Drama* regarding Adam and Eve's banishment: "[I should be] with my EXILES,— I also an exile!" (*CW*, 2:144). Thus, the poet herself declares her solidarity with society's problems—a few years later, she even exchanged the metaphysical exile for geographical exile in Florence, Italy. Not only the poet herself felt exiled; in the drama there was not a single character who was not in exile: angels, humanity, animals and the earth, Christ, Lucifer, Adam and Eve, organic and inorganic nature.

The second motif is Eve's grief. Eve's expression of her deep sorrow is her "consciousness of originating the Fall to her offence . . . [and] considering that self-*sacrifice* [henceforth] belonged to her womanhood" (*CW*, 2:143–44). In a letter dated 1843, Barrett Browning wrote to her friend Richard Hengist Horne that her primary design in composing *A Drama of Exile* was

> the development of the peculiar anguish of Eve—the fate of woman at its root. . . . The principal interest is set on Eve—"the first in the transgression." *The first in the transgression* has been said over & over again, because of the tradition,—*but first & deepest in sorrow*, nobody seems to have said, or, at least written of as conceiving. (*BC*, 8:117)

In her emphasis on Eve's contrition rather than her sinfulness, Barrett Browning was concerned about reestablishing Eve to her basically good nature against the traditional interpretation of her as temptress. Simultaneously, Barrett Browning was rehabilitating nature to reflect God's goodness and woman as fully participating in it.

Exile from Paradise and the desire to return to our true nature, which the Paradise image symbolizes, was a metaphor for what Barrett Browning saw religious poetry doing: restoring us from our lifeless, exiled condition of ignorance to what God intended us to be. According to Barrett Browning, poetry was inspired by the remembrance and anticipation of Paradise, and in turn brings both, its remembrance and its anticipation, into the minds of her readers. Thus, Barrett Browning's verse can and could effect a conversion back to God for its reader. This was also evident in her prose reflections on the nature of poetry, for example in *A Thought on Thoughts*:

> Poetical Thought!—. . . [t]he glory of the earth, more than its glory, is burning in her eyes with a deep, mystical, unquenchable fire—with a fire which no weeping will quench. The lashes are wet, but the eyes burn still. Burning, wandering, melancholy eyes! *The sword of the cherubim, which drove from the world its vision of beauty, left one in her soul*, and from the depths of that soul she gathers it, and spreads it over the withering land, and wailing sea, and darkening sky; and tries to call them as God *called* them ere the ruins came, "*very good.* . . ." (*CW*, 6:355–56, emphasis mine)

In this essay Barrett Browning claims that the cherub had left a mark of the immaculate on the poet's soul. In *The Greek Christian Poets* she explains further what this meant, suggesting that the understanding a poet has regarding creation and Fall is significant: it distinguishes a good from a bad poet. The "vision of beauty" the cherub left on the poet's soul is the right understanding of Paradise, the Paradise that is lost: "there have been poets, not a few, singing as if earth were still Eden; and poets, *many singing*, as if in the first hour of exile..." (*CW*, 6:176). Barrett Browning, following her Christian Platonic instincts, sees the poet as one who reminds human beings that the sparks of the divine are still in them in spite of their fallenness. She writes to her friend Mary Russell Mitford:

> the uses & object & essentiality of poetry...[are] a depicturing of our fallen corrupted humanities...without their noble self-abjurations and their yearning after what is not self. (*BC*, 3:179)

Consequently, the poet's task is to return to her spiritual home—except it is a home lost and left behind. This loss has to be acknowledged and articulated poetically. The "very good" has to be seen through the lens of fallenness: this ability is the mark of purity on the poet's soul, which is the sign of her calling.[33]

Barrett Browning claims that all true poetry has to attempt to return to Eden and be a reminder to us that the imperfect world we know was originally created in perfection, for nature is God's art. Poetic art is humanity's response to God's perfect and primal art, that is nature, but it is no mere imitation of it. In nature, God has "hidden" a "spiritual significance" in "sensible symbol[s]" (*CW*, 6:272). But poetic art

> looks past the symbol with a divine guess and reach of soul into the mystery of significance....Art lives by nature, and not the bare mimetic life generally attributed to Art: she does not imitate, she expounds. (*CW*, 6:272)

In these very Neo-Platonic lines, Barrett Browning brings together art and nature as two "accomplishment[s]" of God (*CW*, 6:272). The link between these three primal categories in Barrett Browning's concept of religious art—nature, God, and poetry—cannot be reasoned apart into independent principles. The "right use of the right poetry of Art" (*CW*, 6:294) means appreciating how it is intertwined with nature and with God. Any poet who wanders over hills, past trees and rivers, and exclaims, "here only is nature," misunderstands the character of the "poetical" since "[n]ature is where God is. Poetry is where God is" (*CW*, 6:294). Barrett Browning expands her definition of nature to make it include human creation without falling into an irreligious naturalism:

> let us make room for it in the comprehension of our love!—for the coral rock built up by the insect and the marble column erected by the man. (*CW*, 6:294)

Like the sculptor in marble the poet in words by writing does not act antagonistically to nature but fulfills it. The task of a true poet like that of nature is to be a creator of symbols to remind human beings of God (*CW*, 6:310).

I now return to Barrett Browning's understanding of Paradise as the origin of true poetry. The "vision of beauty," the goodness undefiled, is to be spread into the world.[34] The poet's mission is, thus, to transport the memory of the undistorted good into the fallen world:[35] the poet is the one who is remembering ultimate Nature.[36] Barrett Browning sees poetry as a bridge between Paradise—the perfect state and perfect union with God—and the fallen world, bringing the reader back to a mindfulness of God. This "vision of beauty" is the clear poetic mind that is able to reflect, though only in a limited manner, God's ultimate good. Thus, the poet, Janus-faced, can be described as someone who is standing outside the gates of Paradise, looking both ways: she gazes back to the ultimate good, and looks at the unregenerated world. The poet works with fallen nature yet possesses an inward vision, a reflection of Paradise, which is the image of God.

The poet's ability to possess such a "vision of beauty" is understood by Barrett Browning as the result of God's original intention to create nature and human beings as good, and Christ's incarnation and death as the means by which God's original intention could be fulfilled. The incarnation is the occurrence of divine grace where the cherub has returned to leave another "vision of beauty" in the poetic heart. Christ's death and resurrection provides Barrett Browning with a model for understanding the activity of the poet as one who can transform fallenness into goodness and by whom the whole of creation is as it were renewed. She writes:

[w]e want the touch of Christ's hand upon our literature, as it touched other dead things—we want the sense of the saturation of Christ's blood upon the souls of our poets, that it might cry *through* them in answer to the ceaseless wail of the Sphinx of our humanity, expounding agony into renovation. (*CW*, 6:176)

This yearning was articulated by *The Greek Christian Poets:* it is "perceived in art when its glory [...] [is] at the fullest" (*CW*, 6:176). Barrett Browning sees poets, like Christ, as called by "the saturation of Christ's blood" upon their souls to renovate humanity. She believed that they have a special status in unfolding the beauty of God's creation hidden from the ordinary view. The true poet has a special calling to interpret the biblical message in terms of real beauty and truth and goodness:

[o]h what an unspeakable poetry there is in Christ's religion!...[M]en look on it coldly because without understanding, & do not even cry aloud for an interpreter. (*BC*, 3:179)

A Drama of Exile offers examples of Elizabeth Barrett Browning, as a true poet, reading scriptural material to show "what an unspeakable poetry there is in Christ's religion" (*BC*, 3:179). Through the poet's presentation of her own interpretation of the biblical narrative the reader is introduced to her poetic vision of intact, fallen, and redeemed creation. In the *Drama* (*DE, CW*, 2:142–228) we get an insight into the way in which Barrett Browning was preserving yet transforming the strong Christian beliefs inherited from her family. Based on Genesis 3:24, *A Drama of Exile* begins with "the first step of Humanity into the world-wilderness, driven by the Curse ... [and] flying along the great Sword-glare" (*BC*, 8:117). Adam and Eve "are seen in the distance" fleeing Paradise (*DE*, line 149). God had driven "out the man; and at the east of the garden of Eden [had] placed the cherubim, and a sword flaming and turning to guard the way to the tree of life" (Genesis 3:24). In the opening scene the fallen archangel Lucifer, the archetype of exile, appears on stage to recite the introductory monologue. He greets the reader with great elation: "[r]ejoice . . . /[m]y exiled, my host! / Earth has exiles as hopeless as when a / Heaven's empire was lost" (*DE*, lines 1–4). Lucifer speaks elatedly on the condition of fallen creation where beauty, goodness, and truth are perverted. The keeper of Eden's gate, the archangel Gabriel descends to shed a different light on the matter. The dialogue that follows is a battle over the dominion of the earth, where both good and evil are laying claim to the throne.

Lucifer announces that all creatures henceforth will fall and be exiled, since God "saves not" (line 17). But Gabriel challenges Lucifer on his understanding of God's nature. He retorts that through "heaven and earth" God "moves freely" and "overflows/ [t]he firmamental walls with . . . / . . . love" (lines 113–17) and compassion. "If thou, [Lucifer], hadst gazed upon the face of God / [t]his morning for a moment, thou hadst known / [t]hat only pity fitly can chastise. . . . " (lines 125–27). Lucifer is unmoved by Gabriel. He continues to envision a future where "evil will increase and multiply / [w]ithout a benediction" (lines 195–97). Gabriel responds: "Nothing more?" (line 197). Lucifer in his blindness, has, like Barrett Browning's own father, forgotten the goodness of God, for Gabriel answers, "God is more" (line 199). "[L]eave the earth to God!" (line 202), Gabriel entreats the fallen angel. Lucifer, however, does not grant Gabriel's plea.

While Gabriel and Lucifer disagree, Adam and Eve take their fearful flight from Eden. The former undefiled beauty of Paradise represented by a chorus of various Eden spirits—the spirits of rivers, trees, birds, and flowers—accompanies their journey. The requiem these "orphaned spirits" (line 235) sing recalls the good order that once was. The spirits lament:

> God gave [the Eden spirits] golden cups, and [they] were bidden
>   To feed [humanity] so.
> But now [their] right hand hath no cup remaining,
>   No work to do,
> The mystic hydromel is spilt, and staining
>   The whole earth through. . . . (Lines 237–42)

Nature, once perfect in Paradise, is now tainted through the Fall. In the silence following the Eden spirits' song, Adam and Eve "[pause] a moment on this outer edge / [w]here the supernal sword-glare cuts in light / [t]he dark exterior desert" (lines 390–92). They look back and see a "spectacle of cloud / [w]hich seals the gate" of Paradise "up to the final doom" (lines 395–96). They reflect on how they once had lived and how "they have [now dropped] heavily / [i]n a heap earthward" (lines 417–18).

At this point in the *Drama*, Eve sinks to the ground bidding Adam: "[b]ruise my head with thy foot,—as the curse said" (line 429). Here Eve wrongly takes on herself the curse God put on the snake in Genesis 3:14–15: "cursed are you among all animals. I will put enmity between you and the woman, [she] will strike your head." She identifies with the snake, who is the true tempter, and believes she should be punished. She implores Adam:

> O Adam, Adam! by that name of Eve—
> Thine Eve, thy life—which suits me little now,
> Seeing that I now confess myself thy death
> And thy undoer, as the snake was mine,—
> I do abjure thee, put me straight away,
> Together with my name! Sweet, punish me!
> Oh Love, be just! . . . (Lines 420–26)

But Adam does not leave Eve to equate herself with the snake's depravity and "writhe on the ground feed[ing] on ashes" (line 436); instead, he calls her his "beloved," his "Eve," his "utter life and light" (lines 438–39, 441), and confesses his own sinfulness:

> . . . [i]f we have fallen,
> It is that we have sinned,—we: God is just;
> And, since his curse doth comprehend us both,
> It must be that his balance holds the weights
> Of first and last sin on a level. What!
> Shall I who had no virtue to stand straight
> Among the hills of Eden, here assume
> To mend the justice of the perfect God,
> By piling up a curse upon his curse,
> Against thee—thee? (Lines 441–49)

Here Barrett Browning introduces a noteworthy twist into her interpretation of the Genesis narrative: whilst remaining deeply attached to the message of Scripture, she raises Eve's status in relation to Adam's, contrary to more traditional accounts. The poet wants to portray an Adam who allows Eve to be an equal to him. Barrett Browning's Adam is a man who emphasizes time and again: "I am deepest in the guilt, / [i]f last in the transgression" (lines 458–59), and acknowledges that he only "stand[s] / [u]pright, as far as can be in this fall" (lines 489–90) because of Eve. Adam knows her love gives him back his human dignity; the "discrowned brow" (line 493) will receive the crown lost through sin.

The only good left in exile is love. Through Eve's love, Adam can stand upright despite his sinful disposition: he is, as Martin Luther would say, *incurvatus in se ipsum*, that is, he is curved in upon himself. Eve's love is the antidote to Adam's sinfulness, and, reciprocally, through Adam's love she can live in this fallen condition. "Because I comprehend / [t]his human love, I shall not be afraid / [o]f any human death" (lines 503–5), she says. The love revealed here is the one that "makes . . . [the heart] strong" (line 546).

In *A Drama of Exile*, Barrett Browning shifts away from traditional, more misogynistic interpretations of the Paradise narrative to a fairer depiction of

Eve. The love of Eve as everlasting and all enduring embodies a standard notion of female love; however, although this love was generally seen as weak and passive in the literary traditions she has inherited, Barrett Browning presents a richer vision of Eve as a loving, caring and doubting woman. In a further interesting departure from traditional Christian readings of Genesis and the Fall, she makes Adam unveil and proclaim Eve's strength by acknowledging that he cannot live, that is, he cannot stand upright, without her. He follows Eve into exile from Eden and from the "sword-glare / [i]nto the outer darkness of the waste" (lines 548–49). Eve is the strong one: she leads Adam, and he follows her accompanied "[f]aint[ly] and tender[ly]" (line 561) by a chorus of invisible angels who are a sign that humanity is not left alone and that heaven is on Adam and Eve's side.

The "waste" (line 549) into which Adam and Eve are exiled is interpreted by Barrett Browning as lovelessness, the consequence of listening to Lucifer. The encounter they have with the fallen archangel is an ominous anticipation of the turmoil in which they would henceforth have to lead their existence. Lucifer plants doubts in their minds about love and faith, friendship, beauty and truth, suggesting that these things have no real existence. When Eve meets Lucifer, she immediately asks Adam to hold her hand. She knows that "[i]t is Lucifer— / [a]nd we have love to lose" (lines 646–47). Here we encounter Barrett Browning's own interpretation of fallen human nature. For her, to live in exile means to live in a "desert" (line 649) where the ability to love and be loved is easily lost. The fallen archangel endeavors to lure Adam and Eve into his own hopeless state by making them doubt love and the good. Lucifer's plan is to flatter them and make them believe that they themselves are "new gods" (line 672) who can pardon all sin: he tries to awaken their pride, and, thus, have them sin against God's grace. Instead, however, the two human beings preserve the right humility in remembering their love for one another: "Adam loved Eve. Jehovah pardoned both! / Adam forgave Eve—because loving Eve" (lines 680–81).

Eve entreats Adam to leave the discussion with Lucifer, because "it is not good to speak with him" (line 739). Yet Lucifer does not allow them to depart, asking coquettishly, "[a]m I beautiful?" (line 751). Lucifer then gives a glimpse, albeit a perverted one, of undefiled, original beauty. He says: "as I praise God, / [u]nwillingly but fully,... I stand / [m]ost absolute in beauty" (lines 754–56). This beauty, like the higher beauties of just and righteous lives, rather than the lower beauties of comely physical forms, is the quality a godly person has, and shows her participation in genuinely divine worship. It is the opposite of the person *incurvatus in se ipsum*. But this dwelling in beauty is beyond Lucifer on account of his fallenness.

The vision of beauty offered by Adam can still be achieved, at least in part, in exile, but it requires love:

> The essence of all beauty, I call love.
> The attribute, the evidence, and end,
> The consummation to the inward sense,

Of beauty apprehended from without,
I still call love....
...
So, without love, is beauty undiscerned
In man or angel. Angel! Rather ask
What love is in thee, what love moves to thee,
And what collateral love moves on with thee;
Then shalt thou know if thou art beautiful. (Lines 777–81, 784–88)

Through this understanding of beauty as enabled by love, original beauty becomes visible through divine worship. Lucifer, however, does not comprehend the vision of beauty offered by Adam, for he says: "Love! what is love? I lose it. Beauty and love / I darken to the image. Beauty—love!" (lines 789–90). Here Adam and Eve realize that the archangel's fall has been so deep that he has lost his ability to love. Adam remarks to Eve: "Think that we have not fallen so! By the hope / [a]nd aspiration, by the love and faith, / [w]e do exceed the stature of this angel" (lines 795–97).

As the first night dawns on exiled earth, Adam and Eve become aware of their future condition. "[T]he wide melancholy earth / [g]ather her hills around...[them], grey and ghast, / [a]nd stares with blank significance of loss / [r]ight into...[their] faces!" (lines 896–99). Adam and Eve experience fear, for they are uncertain of their new, fallen life and the fallen nature of the world. "O life / ...what is this?" (lines 907–08), Eve cries. Adam comforts Eve, reassuring her and himself that there is no "cause for fear," for "[t]he circle of God's life / [c]ontains all life beside" (lines 909–10). Yet fear still persists, for they remember how they fell and "spoilt...[life's] sweetness with...[their] sin" (line 927). This fear is also sensed by the spirits of organic and inorganic nature, who were forced to flee from Eden in spite of their innocence. They arise and chant a tune that offers no consolation to the distressed. They curse humanity for having "drag[ged]...[the world] downward / unto...[their] ruin" (lines 1123–24). "[They] fasten / ...[their] sorrow's fang upon...[the human] souls dishonoured" (lines 1120–21). Nature's spirits wailing and crying signify the pain innocent creation henceforth has to suffer. "I wail, I wail!" they shout. "Do you hear that I wail? / I had no part in your transgression—*none*. / ... *I* was obedient" (lines 1127–28, 1131). Adam and Eve are tortured by their rebukes. Eve entreats Adam: "I choose God's thunder and His angels' swords / [t]o die by, Adam, rather than such words. / Let us pass out and flee" (lines 1141–43). "We cannot flee. / ...the creatures' cruelty / [c]urls round us" (lines 1143–45), Adam replies.

But when the first "vision of Beauty" had been lost in the Fall, the "agony is beyond what...[Adam and Eve] can bear" (line 1750), and they are "taunted and perplext / [b]y all these creatures...[they had] ruled yesterday" (lines 1752–53). The second "vision of Beauty" appears in the figure of Jesus Christ himself. God does not thunder, but comforts with his presence: "I AM HERE!" (line 1758). Christ has come to grant Adam and Eve "[p]erfect redemption" (line 1818) from their affliction "through the hope and through the peace / [w]hich are ... [his]" (lines 1819–20). Here Adam and Eve witness amidst the fallenness the first signs of the goodness that is to come. Christ takes Adam and Eve with him on his earthly ministry. Blessing them and instructing them in the ways of a righteous life as he did with his disciples, Christ emancipates both Adam and Eve from their "childhood" in Paradise to their "exiled adulthood."[37] Christ reveals himself as love, and strengthens Adam and Eve in their love for God and for one another. His love teaches them to be compassionate to one another and work for the kingdom of God here on this earth (lines 1842–97).[38] Barrett Browning's understanding of the incarnation, however, heavily accents the importance of the feminine role: Eve, as the representatives of all mothers, will bear children. "God ... [in turn] *shalt* be seed" (line 1909), he will be implanted in and born of a woman. Thus, sin will be redeemed through God as man but born of a woman.

To confirm the reality of his promise, Christ is transfigured in front of their eyes into his humanity and suffering. He shares with them the knowledge and hope of "the new worlds' genesis / ... the gradual humming growth / [o]f the ancient atoms and first forms of earth" (lines 1939–41), which will be borne out of his death on the cross of Calvary: "[h]owbeit in the noon of time/ [e]ternity shall wax as dumb as Death" (line 1951).

> [A] new Eden-gate
> Shall open on a hinge of harmony
> And let you through to mercy. Ye shall fall
> No more, within that Eden, nor pass out
> Any more from it. (Lines 1990–94).

Christ's promise to Adam and Eve, the "first sinners and first mourners" (line 1995) is that his death will save them from their sinfulness and bring them back into relationship with God. He encourages them to "[l]ive and love,— / [d]oing both nobly because lowlily! / Live and work, strongly because patiently!" "with constant prayers" (lines 1995–97, 2000). For Christ tells Adam and Eve that he

> ... [will] wrap round [him] [their] humanity,
> Which, being sustained, shall neither break nor burn
> Beneath the fire of Godhead, will tread earth
> And ransom you and it, and set strong peace
> Betwixt you and its creatures. (Lines 1969–73)

Here Barrett Browning follows once more her beloved Greek Fathers in choosing this image of Christ "wrapping his human nature around his divine" and taking it with him into heaven; thus he redeems Adam and Eve's fallenness in God's purity. Christ opens humankind's way to the new Eden wherein they "shall fall / [n]o more ... nor pass out / [a]ny more from it" (lines 1992–94). His resurrection lifts them up out of the darkness and death of exile into the light and life of the redeemed world. It is love divine incarnated in Christ that has the capacity to save human beings from sin and evil. Through Christ love is seen as stronger than death since he is the first to rise out of his grave into new life. At the end of the *Drama*, Christ finally vanishes leaving Adam and Eve standing in ecstasy as they perceive the transformation of the earth around them and know that being exiled does not mean being abandoned by God.[39]

I hope to have illustrated that Elizabeth Barrett Browning's poetry and theory of poetry is suffused by religious considerations. She was steeped in biblical and theological knowledge, with a special preference for Scripture and the writings of the Greek Fathers. Barrett Browning read Scripture as a devotional exercise for the most part of her life. She was additionally indebted to philosophy, Platonism in particular, which her juvenilia, early poetry, and essays, as well as her conception of God, nature, and art, illustrate.[40] For Barrett Browning, God permeated every fiber of life, and was present throughout nature. A comparison of the earlier with the later poems show that this was a hard won religious vision, in strong contrast to and in tension with her father's faith. Thus, the religious dimension of her verse must not be ignored. Nature, God, and poetry "cannot be reasoned apart into antagonistic principles" (*CW*, 6:272). The fusion of the three was evident in Barrett Browning's own life and work, and was present in her theory of (religious) poetry. Moreover, she understood the poet to have the religious function of directing the reader's mind back to God: "For every true poet, says a true poet,...has a [']religious passion in his soul'" (*BC*, 8:76). She consciously but respectfully reinterpreted traditional elements, such as the Genesis narrative and the Incarnation. She even went so far as to give the poet Aurora Leigh a Christ-like role in her desire to achieve a religious revaluation of the feminine, as well as the female poet. Given the growing interest in the religious in Victorian literature, I hope to have shed some light on the importance of Christian and theological themes in Elizabeth Barrett Browning, and to have demonstrated that there is material enough in her poetry for more fruitful research in this direction.

NOTES

1. Sandra Donaldson's excellent introduction in *Critical Essays on Elizabeth Barrett Browning*, ed. Sandra Donaldson (New York: G. K. Hall & Co., 1999), offers a thorough overview of Barrett Browning scholarship up to the present (1–14).
2. Alethea Hayter (*Mrs. Browning. A Poets Work and Its Setting* [London: Faber and Faber, 1962]), however, and more recent scholars such as Linda M. Lewis (*Elizabeth Barrett Browning's Spiritual Progress. Face to Face with God* [Columbia: University of Missouri Press, 1998]); Jerome Mazzaro ("Mapping Sublimity: Elizabeth Barrett Browning's *Sonnets from the Portuguese*," in *Critical Essays*, 291–305); and Cynthia Scheinberg (*Women's Poetry and Religion in Victorian England: Jewish Identity and Christian Culture* [Cambridge: Cambridge University Press, 2002]) have focused on the strong Judeo-Christian influence in Elizabeth Barrett Browning's life and work. According to Hayter, "Mrs Browning's religious faith...always pervaded her

opinion on every subject, but it was so little obtruded that her critics have made some wild guesses about it. Her French and Italian biographers... have attributed to her an entirely idiosyncratic religion. She was a pantheist, a demonist, an Essene, a Cabbalist, certainly a pagan of some sort... Some recent biographers... have felt that she *couldn't* really have believed in all that nonsense about the will of God and the sacredness of suffering, and have sought for some more piquant psychological explanation behind her piety" (*Mrs. Browning*, 27–28).

3. Elizabeth Barrett Browning, *The Book of the Poets*, in *The Complete Works of Elizabeth Barrett Browning*, ed. Charlotte Porter and Helen A. Clarke, 6 vols. (1900; reprint, New York: AMS Press, 1973), 6:296; see 6:240–311; hereafter *CW*. I owe this reference to Barbara Neri.

4. Scheinberg, *Women's Poetry*, 3.

5. Scheinberg stresses the importance of the complex relationships the Victorian female poets had "to their own religious traditions..." (3). She continues to draw attention to the effect the "alliance between Christian ideology and poetry" must have had on Christian women poets (ibid.).

6. In the correspondence Barrett Browning kept with the Reverend William Merry from 1843 to 1844 on predestination and salvation by works, she identifies herself quite clearly as a Congregationalist: "I am not a Baptist—but a Congregational Christian,—in the holding of my private opinions" (*The Brownings' Correspondence*, ed. Philip Kelley, Ronald Hudson, and Scott Lewis, 14 vols. [Winfield, Kansas: Wedgestone Press, 1984–98], 8:150; hereafter *BC*.

7. Congregationalism is a movement within the Calvinist tradition that came into prominence in English life during the seventeenth-century Civil War. Its system of ecclesiastical polity regards all legislative, disciplinary, and judicial functions to be in the power of the individual church, or local congregation of believers. It is called Independent because the congregation does not allow any interference from external authority whether it be legislative, episcopal, presbyterial, or judicial.

8. This is witnessed in several of her poems and letters, where Barrett Browning addresses her father as "High Priest," or "grand Signor" (Cf. *Letters of Elizabeth Barrett Browning*, to Mary Russell Mitford 1836–1854, ed. Meredith B. Raymond, and Mary Rose Sullivan, 3 vols. [Winfields Kansas: Armstrong Browning Library of Baylor University, Browning Institute, Wedgestone Press & Wellesley College 1983], 3:127, 129; hereafter *LMRM*). Furthermore, in her poetry she says the following: "For 'neath thy gentleness of praise, / My Father! Rose my early lays! / And when the lyre was scarce awake, / I lov'd its strings for *thy* lov'd sake; / Woo'd the kind Muses but the while / Thought only how to win thy smile—" (*To My Father on His Birthday* (1826), lines 33–38, in (*CW*, 1:100–01)). Cf. Angela Leighton, *Elizabeth Barrett Browning* (Bloomington: Indiana University Press, 1986), 23–54.

9. Hayter, *Mrs. Browning*, 28.

10. Margaret Forster, *Elizabeth Barrett Browning: A Biography* (London: Vintage, 1998), 49.

11. Peter Dally, *Elizabeth Barrett Browning. A Psychological Portrait* (London: Macmillan, 1989), 12.

12. Forster, *Elizabeth Barrett Browning*, 50.

13. Mr. Barrett was deeply impressed by the preaching of Edward Irving, the Scottish founder of the Catholic Apostolic Church. Mr. Irving's writings, full

of denunciations of the world, had been approved Hope End readings ever since 1823; see Forster, *Elizabeth Barrett Browning*, 49.

14. See Glennis Stephenson, *Elizabeth Barrett Browning and the Poetry of Love* (Ann Arbor: UMI Press, 1989), 16–17.

15. Ibid., 17.

16. Lewis, *Spiritual Progress*, 9.

17. Letters of Elizabeth Barrett Browing, ed. Frederic G. Kenyon, 2 vols. [New York: Macmillan, 1897].

18. Hayter, *Mrs. Browning*, 28.

19. Elizabeth Barrett Browning, *Diary by E. B. B.: The Unpublished Diary of Elizabeth Barrett Browning, 1831–32*, ed. Philip Kelley and Ronald Hudson. (Athens: Ohio University Press, 1969), 19.

20. Evidence of Barrett Browning's firm biblical knowledge can also be found in the many biblical references in her letters.

21. Cf. the letter Barrett Browning wrote to Miss Mitford on March 13, 1844, where she related how she had been exalted by her friend, the poet Mr. Horne "with all manners of devices, . . . & and with the aid of 'charming notes to fair friends';—& Hebrew roots & Plato enough to frighten away friends fair and brown" (*Letters of Elizabeth Barrett Browning to Mary Russell Mitford 1836–1854*, ed. Meredith B. Raymond and Mary Rose Sullivan, 3 vols. [Winfield, Kansas: Wedgestone Press, 1983], 2:395; hereafter *LMRM*).

22. Stephenson, *Poetry of Love*, 29.

23. Cf. Hayter who emphasizes Barrett Browning's extraordinary academic achievement in translating and commenting on *The Greek Christian Poets*. Hayter writes: "Byzantine studies were far more of a rarity in Mrs. Browning's day than now. . . . In these articles she digested a mass of difficult material, all unknown and inaccessible even to the cultivated public which she was addressing" (*Mrs. Browning*, 14–15).

24. Gregory of Nazianzus (329–89) was one of the Greek Fathers of the Eastern Church. His poems comprise autobiographical verses, epigrams, epitaphs, and epistles. Of these, the epitaphs were translated by Barrett Browning's friend Hugh Stuart Boyd (London, 1826). Some critics place the poems in the front rank of Gregory's compositions. After her mother's death, Barrett Browning found comfort in the "theological writings of Gregory of Nazianzen . . . and her bible" (Forster, *Elizabeth Barrett Browning*, 50).

25. Elizabeth Barrett Browning, *Notes on the Greek Christian Fathers*, around 1831, unpublished document 1 (Armstrong Browning Library, Baylor University, Waco, Texas).

26. God, in her earlier works, is seen as the judge: "the thick-bossed shield of God's judgement in the field" (*Rhyme of the Duchess May*, lines 423–24, in *CW*, 3:27). Compare these lines with Christ saying to Adam and Eve that he is the "Emmanuel," the God who is with humanity: "I AM HERE !" (*DE*, line 1758).

27. Stephenson, *Poetry of Love*, 89.

28. I am indebted to Corinne Davis for this insight.

29. Stephenson, *Poetry of Love*, 116.

30. Scheinberg, *Women's Poetry*, 71–72. Cf. Lewis who also stresses the identification between the poet Barrett Browning and "Eve's mythic and theological role . . . [and] the religious doctrines taught by Eve in *A Drama of Exile*" (*Spiritual Progress*, 49–50).

31. Cf. the preface to *A Drama of Exile*.

32. Alison Milbank, *Dante and the Victorians* (Manchester: Manchester University Press, 1998), 1.

33. The poet's task is also a bitter one, not a simple celebration of unfallen nature; the contrast the poet achieves in her art between the vision of beauty lost and the condition of brokenness she encounters in the world causes her great sadness. "[The poet's] voice trembles and pauses . . . and, after she has looked in the face of human Truth, which is begrimed with dust, and of human Love, which is pale, though steadfast, she goes out, as Peter did, from her place of pride, and weeps bitterly" (*CW*, 6:356).

34. Barrett Browning confessed that she was not sure whether to say " 'how beautiful' or 'how good.' " Thus, she decided to return back to "her Greeks" "who when they said 'how beautiful' *meant* 'how good' " (*BC*, 3:178).

35. Barrett Browning places the poet in the position assigned to the philosopher by Plato. In Plato's *Republic*, the philosophic nature loves "field of study which reveals to them something of that reality which is eternal and is not subject to that vicissitudes of generation and destruction" (Plato, *Republic*, translated by Robin Waterfield (Oxford: Oxford University Press, 1993, 485b). The philosopher sees what is "organized, permanent, and unchanging" (Plato, *Republic*, 500b–c). Thus, in terms of bringing "undistorted good" into the world, the philosopher is in the ideal position: she looks in each direction "towards that which is inherently moral, right, self-disciplined, and so on, and on the other hand towards what they're creating in the human realm" (Plato, *Republic*, 501b). I owe this reference to Férdia Stone-Davis.

36. The soul's "learning" of the forms in Plato is in fact a process of remembering, *anamnesis*: the movement of the soul as it comes to a right understanding of reality is elucidated in the Allegory of the Cave in the *Republic*. The understanding moves from shadows to images to things in themselves (514a–517c).

37. Dorothy Mermin, *Elizabeth Barrett Browning. The Origins of a New Poetry* (Chicago: The University of Chicago Press, 1989), 88.

38. See Lewis, *Spritiual Progress*, 50, 66.

39. Cf. the angelic chorus at the end of the *Drama*, singing, "[being] [e]xiled is not lost!" (*DE*, line 2258).

40. Barrett Browning possessed and read the Plato dialogues in their entirety; the one volume of her collection still existing in the Armstrong Browning Library, Waco, Texas, bears witness to this. In addition, we know from her work and from the remains of her library that she was also well read in the later Platonists.

References

Adams, James Eli. *Dandies and Desert Saints: Styles of Victorian Manhood*. Ithaca: Cornell University Press, 1995.

Aime-Martin, L. *The Education of the Mothers of Families; or, the Civilization of the Human Race by Women*. Translated by Edwin Lee. London: Adams, 1860.

Alderson, David. *Mansex Fine: Religion, Manliness, and Imperialism in Nineteenth-Century British Culture*. Manchester: Manchester University Press, 1998.

Altholz, Josef L. *Anatomy of a Controversy: The Debate over "Essays and Reviews."* Hants, England: Scholar Press, 1994.

———. "The Vatican Decrees Controversy, 1874–1875." *Catholic Historical Review* 57 (1971–72): 593–605.

Altick, Richard D. *Victorian People and Ideas*. New York: W. W. Norton, 1973.

Anderson, William. *Green Man: The Archetype of Our Oneness with the Earth*. London: Harper Collins, 1990. Reprint. Compassbooks, 2002.

Anon. *A Critical History of the Language and Literature of Ancient Greece* (1850). *Quarterly Review* 87 (1850): 434–68.

———. Review of William Mure. "Who Wrote Dickens?" *Macmillan's Magazine* 54 (June 1886): 112–15.

Armstrong, Isobel. "Swinburne: Agonistic Republican"; "Hopkins: Agonistic Reactionary." In *Victorian Poetry: Poetry, Poetics and Politics*. Edited by Isobel Armstrong. London: Routledge, 1993. 402–39.

Arnold, Matthew. "The Bishop and the Philosopher." In *The Complete Prose Works of Matthew Arnold*. Edited by R. H. Super. Vol. 3. Ann Arbor: The University of Michigan Press, 1973. 40–55.

———. "The Function of Criticism at the Present Time." In *The Complete Prose Works of Matthew Arnold*. Edited by R. H. Super. Vol. 3. Ann Arbor: The University of Michigan Press, 1973. 258–85.

———. *The Letters of Matthew Arnold*. Edited by Cecil Y. Lang. 4 vols. Charlottesville: The University Press of Virginia, 1996–2000.

———. "The Literary Influence of Academies." In *The Complete Prose Works of Matthew Arnold*. Edited by R. H. Super. Vol. 3. Ann Arbor: The University of Michigan Press, 1973. 232–57.

———. *The Poems of Matthew Arnold*. Edited by Kenneth Allott and Miriam Allott. 2nd ed. London: Longman, 1965.

Arnstein, Walter L. "The Murphy Riots: A Victorian Dilemma." *Victorian Studies* 19 (1975): 51–71.

———. *Protestant versus Catholic in Mid-Victorian England: Mr. Newdegate and the Nuns*. Columbia: University of Missouri Press, 1982.

Astell, Mary. *The Christian Religion, as Profess'd by a Daughter of the Church of England*. London: R. Wilkin, 1705.

———. *A Serious Proposal to The Ladies, for the Advancement of Their True and greatest Interest*. By a Lover of Her Sex. London: R. Wilkin, 1694.

Astell, Mary. *A Serious Proposal to The Ladies, Part II. Wherein a Method is Offer'd for the Improvement of Their Minds.* London: Richard Wilkin, 1697.

——. *Some Reflections Upon Marriage. With Additions.* 4th ed. 1730. New York: Source Book Press, 1970.

Auerbach, Eric. *Mimesis: The Representation of Reality in Western Literature.* New Jersey: Princeton University Press, 1953.

Bachelard, Gaston. *The Poetics of Space.* Translated by Maria Jolas. Boston: Beacon Press, 1969.

Badger, Kingsbury. " 'See the Christ Stand': Browning's Religion." In *Robert Browning: A Collection of Critical Essays.* Edited by Philip Drew. New York: Houghton Mifflin, 1966. 72–95.

Bailey, Suzanne. " 'Decomposing Texts': Browning's Poetics and Higher Critical Parody." *Religion and the Arts* 5, nos. 1–2 (2001): 63–80.

Ball, Patricia. *The Science of Aspects: The Changing Role of Fact in the Work of Coleridge, Ruskin and Hopkins.* London: Athlone Press, 1971.

Barthes, Roland. *A Lover's Discourse.* Translated by Richard Howard. New York: Hill and Wang, 1978.

Baumgarten, Murray. "Fictions of the City." In *The Cambridge Companion to Charles Dickens.* Edited by John O. Jordan. Cambridge: Cambridge University Press, 2001. 106–19.

Bayles, Martha. "Closing the Curtain on 'Perverse Modernism.' " *The Chronicle of Higher Education*, October 16, 2001, B14.

Beer, Gillian. *Darwin's Plots: Evolutionary Narrative in Darwin, George Eliot, and Nineteenth-Century Fiction.* London: Ark Paperbacks, 1985.

——. *Open Fields: Science in Cultural Encounter.* New York: Oxford University Press, 1996.

Bengough, J. W. "The Higher Criticism." In *Motley: Verses Grave and Gay.* Toronto: William Briggs, 1895. 163–66.

Benjamin, Andrew E., Geoffrey N. Cantor, and John R. R. Christie, ed. *The Figural and the Literal: Problems of Language in the History of Science and Philosophy, 1630–1800.* Manchester: Manchester University Press, 1987.

Berlin-Lieberman, Judith. *Robert Browning and Hebraism: A Study of the Poems of Browning Which are Based on Rabbinical Writings.* Jerusalem: [s.n.], 1934.

Besant, Annie. *Annie Besant: An Autobiography.* London: T. Fisher Unwin, 1893.

——. *Autobiographical Sketches.* London: Freethought, 1885.

——. *A World Without God: A Reply to Miss Frances Power Cobbe.* London: Freethought, 1885.

Best, G. F. A. "Popular Protestantism in Victorian Britain." In *Ideas and Institutions of Victorian Britain: Essays in Honour of George Kitson Clark.* Edited by Robert Robson. New York: Barnes, 1967. 115–42.

The Book of Common Prayer. Oxford: Oxford University Press, 1899.

Booth, Catherine. *The Boy's Own Text-Book.* Containing a Text from the Old and New Testaments for Every Morning and Evening in the Year. Selected by a Lady. London: J. F. Shaw, 1857.

——. "The Christs of the Nineteenth Century compared with the Christ of God." Lecture at Princes Hall, Piccadilly, 1887. *Popular Christianity.* 1–26.

——. "Conditions of Effectual Prayer." *Papers on Godliness.* 59–70.

——. *Female Ministry: Woman's Right to Preach the Gospel.* London: Morgan & Chase, 1870.

——. "The Holy Ghost." *Papers on Aggressive Christianity.* 1–13.

——. "Notes of Three Addresses on Household Gods." *Popular Christianity.* 174–80.

——. *Papers on Aggressive Christianity.* London: S. W. Partridge, 1881. [Individually paginated.]

——. *Papers on Godliness.* 1882. London: Salvation Army, 1890. [Individually paginated.]

——. *Popular Christianity.* London: Salvation Army Book Depot, 1887.

——. *The Salvation Army in Relation to the Church and State.* London: S. W. Partridge, 1883.

Braddon, Mary Elizabeth. *Lady Audley's Secret.* Oxford: Oxford University Press, 1987.

Bradstock, Andrew, Sean Gill, Anne Hogan, and Sue Morgan, eds. *Masculinity and Spirituality in Victorian Culture.* New York: St. Martin's Press, 2000.

Brecht, Bertolt. *Galileo.* Edited by Eric Bentley. New York: Grove Press, 1966.

Bronfen, Elizabeth. *Over Her Dead Body: Death, Femininity and the Aesthetic.* New York: Routledge, 1992.

Brontë, Anne. *The Tenant of Wildfell Hall.* Oxford World's Classics. New York: Oxford University Press, 1992.

Brontë, Charlotte. *Jane Eyre.* New York: W. W. Norton, 1987.

——. *Shirley.* Edited by Andrew and Judith Hook. 1849. New York: Penguin, 1985.

Brontë, Emily. *Wuthering Heights.* New York: W. W. Norton, 1990.

Brown, Daniel. *Hopkins' Idealism: Philosophy, Physics, Poetry.* Oxford: Clarendon Press, 1997.

The Brownings' Correspondence. Edited by Philip Kelley, Ronald Hudson and Scott Lewis. 14 vols. Winfield, Kansas: Wedgestone Press, 1984–98.

Browning, Elizabeth Barrett. *Aurora Leigh.* Edited by Margaret Reynolds. New York: W. W. Norton, 1996.

——. *The Complete Works of Elizabeth Barrett Browning.* Edited by Charlotte Porter and Helen A. Clarke. 6 vols. 1900. Reprint. New York: AMS reprint 1973.

——. *Diary by E. B. B.: The Unpublished Diary of Elizabeth Barrett Browning, 1831–32.* Edited by Philip Kelley and Ronald Hudson. Athens, Ohio: Ohio University Press, 1969.

——. *Letters of Elizabeth Barrett Browning.* Edited by Frederic G. Kenyon. 2 vols. New York: Macmillan, 1897, 1898.

——. *Letters of Elizabeth Barrett Browning to Mary Russell Mitford 1836–1854.* Edited by Meredith B. Raymond and Mary Rose Sullivan. 3 vols. Winfield, Kansas: Wedgestone Press, 1983.

Browning, Robert. *The Complete Works of Robert Browning with Variants & Annotations.* Edited by Susan Crowl and Roma A. King, Jr. 16 vols. Athens: Ohio University Press, 1969–98.

——. *The Poems of Robert Browning.* Edited by John Pettigrew and Thomas J. Collins. 2 vols. New Haven: Yale University Press, 1981.

——. *The Ring and the Book.* Edited by R. D. Altick. New Haven: Yale University Press, 1981.

Bruns, Gerald L. *Hermeneutics Ancient and Modern.* New Haven: Yale University Press, 1992.

Buckler, William E. "The Poetry of Swinburne: An Essay in Critical Reenforcement." In *The Victorian Imagination: Essays in Aesthetic Exploration.* Edited by William E. Buckler. New York: New York University Press, 1980. 227–59.

Buckler, William E. *Poetry and Truth in Robert Browning's The Ring and the Book*. New York: New York University Press, 1985.

Buel, Oliver Prince. *The Abraham Lincoln Myth, an Essay in Higher Criticism*. New York: Mascot Publishing, 1894.

Bullen, J. B., ed. *The Sun Is God: Painting, Literature, and Mythology in the Nineteenth Century*. Oxford: Clarendon Press, 1989.

Bump, Jerome. *Gerard Manley Hopkins*. Boston: Twayne, 1982.

——. "Hopkins' Imagery and Medievalist Poetics." *Victorian Poetry* 15 (1977): 99–119.

——. Review of *Gerard Manley Hopkins and Tractarian Poetry*, by Margaret Johnson. *English Literature in Transition* 41, no. 4 (1998): 232–36.

Buschkühl, Matthias. *Great Britain and the Holy See, 1746–1870*. Dublin: Irish Academic Press, 1982.

Butler, Josephine E. "Introduction." In *Woman's Work and Woman's Culture*. Edited by Josephine E. Butler. London: Macmillan, 1869. vii–lxiv.

——. "Woman's Place in Church Work." *Magazine of Christian Literature* 6 (April 1892): 30–32.

Butler, Samuel. *The Way of All Flesh*. New York: Penguin, 1986.

Butterfield, Herbert. *The Origins of History*. New York: Basic Books, Inc, 1981.

Cahan, David, ed. *From Natural Philosophy to the Sciences: Writing the History of Nineteenth-Century Science*. Chicago: The University of Chicago Press, 2003.

Caine, Barbara. *Victorian Feminists*. Oxford: Oxford University Press, 1992.

Cameron, Nigel M. de S. *Biblical Higher Criticism and the Defense of Infallibilism in 19th Century Britain*. Lewiston: The Edwin Mellen Press, 1987.

Carey, John. *The Violent Effigy: A Study of Dickens' Imagination*. London: Faber and Faber, 1973.

Carlyle, Thomas. *Sartor Resartus*. Edited by Rodger L. Tarr and Mark Engel. Berkeley: University of California Press, 2000.

Carmichael, James. *How Two Documents May Be Found in One: A Monograph in Connection with the Higher Criticism*. Montreal: Gazette Print, 1895.

Caroline Bowles Southey, 1786–1854: The Making of Woman Writer. Edited by Virginia Blain. Aldershot: Ashgate, 1998.

Carpenter, J. Estlin. *The Bible in the Nineteenth Century*. London: Longmans, Green, 1903.

Carpenter, Mary Wilson. *George Eliot and the Landscape of Time: Narrative Form and Protestant Apocalyptic History*. Chapel Hill: University of North Carolina Press, 1986.

——. "George Eliot and the School of the Prophets." In *George Eliot and the Landscape of Time: Narrative Form and Protestant Apocalyptic History*. Chapel Hill: University of North Carolina Press, 1986. 3–29.

Chadwick, Owen. *The Victorian Church*. 2 vols. New York: Oxford University Press, 1966.

Charles Dickens: The Critical Heritage. Edited by Philip Collins. New York: Barnes and Noble, 1971.

Cheskin, Amold. "Jochanan Hakkadosh: Rabbi Ben Browning." *Studies in Robert Browning and His Circle* 12 (1984): 134–47.

——. "Robert Browning's Climacteric Hebraic Connections with Emma Lazarus and Emily Harris." *Studies in Robert Browning and His Circle* 10 (1982): 9–22.

——. "'Tis Only the Coat of a Page to Borrow': Robert Browning's Hebraic Borrowings and Concealments for 'Jochanan Hakkadosh.'" *Browning Society Notes* 20 (1990): 31–38.

Clapperton, J. H. "Agnosticism and Women: A Reply." *The Nineteenth Century* 7 (May 1880): 840–44.

Clough, A. H. *The Poems of Arthur Hugh Clough*. Edited by E. L. Mulhauser. Oxford: Clarendon Press, 1974.

Cobbe, Frances Power. "Bishop Colenso." *The Christian Examiner* 83 (July 1867): 1–15.

——. *Broken Lights: An Inquiry into the Present Condition and Future Prospects of Religious Faith*. London: Trübner, 1864.

——. *Dawning Lights: An Inquiry Concerning the Secular Results of the New Reformation*. 1867. London: Williams and Norgate, 1882.

——. *Essay on Intuitive Morals, Being an Attempt to Popularise Ethical Science*. Part I: *Theory of Morals*. London: Longman, Brown, Green, and Longman, 1855.

——. *Life of Frances Power Cobbe, by Herself*. 2 vols. Boston: Houghton Mifflin, 1894.

——. "Notice, by the Editor." In *Sermons—Prayers. The Collected Works of Theodore Parker*. Edited by Frances Power Cobbe. Vol. 2. London: Trübner, 1863. ii–v.

——. "Preface." In *A Discourse on Matters Pertaining to Religion. The Collected Works of Theodore Parker*. Edited by Frances Power Cobbe. Vol. 1. London: Trübner, 1863. iv–xxxvi.

Cockshut, A. O. J. *Religious Controversies of the Nineteenth Century: Selected Documents*. London: Methuen, 1966.

Coleridge, Samuel Taylor. *Aids to Reflection. The Collected Works of Samuel Taylor Coleridge*. Edited by John Beer. Vol. 9. New Jersey: Princeton University Press, 1993.

——. *Biographia Literaria*. Edited by James Engell and Walter Jackson Bate. Vol. 1. New Jersey: Princeton University Press, 1983.

——. "Confessions of an Inquiring Spirit." In *The Collected Works of Samuel Taylor Coleridge*. Edited by H. L. Jackson and J. R. de J. Jackson. Vol. 12. New Jersey: Princeton University Press, 1995. 1111–71.

——. *The Statesman's Manual or The Bible the Best Guide to Political Skill and Foresight: A Lay Sermon*. In *Collected Works of Samuel Taylor Coleridge*. Edited by R. J. White. Vol. 6. 1816. Reprint. New Jersey: Princeton University Press, 1972.

Colley, Linda. *Britons: Forging the Nation, 1707–1837*. New Haven: Yale University Press, 1992.

The Compact Edition of the Oxford English Dictionary. 2 vols. Oxford: Oxford University Press, 1971.

Connor, Steven. "Conclusion: Myth and Meta-Myth in Max Müller and Walter Pater." In *The Sun is God: Painting, Literature, and Mythology in the Nineteenth Century*. Edited by J. B. Bullen. Oxford: Clarendon Press, 1989. 199–222.

Cook, Sir. Edward T. *The Life of Florence Nightingale*. 2 vols. London: Macmillan, 1913.

Cooper, Helen. *Elizabeth Barrett Browning, Woman and Artist*. Chapel Hill: University of North Carolina Press, 1988.

Cosslett, Tess. *The "Scientific Movement" and Victorian Literature*. New York: St. Martin's Press, 1982.

Cotsell, Michael. "*The Uncommercial Traveller* on the Commercial Road: Dickens's East End, Part Two." *Dickens Quarterly* 3, no. 3 (1986): 115–22.

Craik, Dinah. *Olive*. Oxford World's Classics. New York: Oxford University Press, 1996.

Crinkley, Richmond. *Walter Pater: Humanist*. Lexington: University Press of Kentucky, 1970.

Culler, Jonathan. "Comparative Literature and the Pieties." *Profession* (1986): 30–32.

Cunningham, Valentine. *Everywhere Spoken Against: Dissent in the Victorian Novel*. Oxford: Clarendon Press, 1975.

Dale, Peter Allan. *In Pursuit of a Scientific Culture: Science, Art, and Society in the Victorian Age*. Madison: The University of Wisconsin Press, 1989.

Dally, Peter. *Elizabeth Barrett Browning: A Psychological Portrait*. London: Macmillan, 1989.

Daly, Ann Carson. "Ever Old, Ever New: The Novelistic Heart of Newman." http://www.ewtn.com/library/HUMANITY/FR89406.TXT.

Darwin, Charles. *The Autobiography of Charles Darwin, 1809–1882*. Edited by Nora Barlow. New York: W. W. Norton, 1993.

———. *The Origin of Species*. New York: Penguin, 1958.

Davidoff, Leonore and Catherine Hall. *Family Fortunes: Men and Women of the English Middle Class, 1780–1850*. Chicago: University of Chicago Press, 1987.

Davis, Kris. "Browning's Caponsacchi: Stuck in the Gap." *Victorian Poetry* 25 (1987): 57–66.

Decrees of the First Vatican Council. Edited by Norman Tanner. August 16, 1999. http://abbey.apana.org.au/councils/ecum20.htm.

De Quincey, Thomas. "Homer and the *Homeridae*." Pts. 1 and 2. *Blackwood's Edinburgh Magazine* 50 (October 1841): 411–27; (November 1841): 618–31.

De Laura, David J. *Hebrew and Hellene in Victorian England*. Austin: University of Texas Press, 1969.

De l'Education des Meres de Familles, ou de la civilisation de genre humain par les Femme. By L. Aime-Martin. Review. *Westminster Review* 22 (January–April 1835): 504–10.

Derrida, Jacques. "Faith and Knowledge: the Two Sources of 'Religion' at the Limits of Reason Alone." In *Religion: Cultural Memory in the Present*. Edited by Jacques Derrida and Gianni Vattimo. California: Stanford University Press, 1998. 1–78.

———. "On a Newly Arisen Apocalyptic Tone in Philosophy." In *Raising the Tone of Philosophy: Late Essays by Immanuel Kant, Transformative Critique by Jacques Derrida*. Edited by Peter Fenves. Baltimore: Johns Hopkins University Press, 1993. 117–71.

———. "Tympan." In *Margins of Philosophy*. Translated by Alan Bass. Chicago: University of Chicago Press, 1982. ix–xxix.

DeVane, William C. *A Browning Handbook*. New York: Appleton-Century-Crofts, 1955.

Dickens, Charles. *David Copperfield*. Edited by Jerome H. Buckley. New York: W. W. Norton, 1990.

———. *Great Expectations*. New York: Penguin, 1996.

———. *The Letters of Charles Dickens*. Edited by Madeline House, Graham Storey, and Kathleen Tillotson. 12 vols. New York: Oxford University Press, 1965–2001.

———. *The Life of Our Lord*. New York: Simon and Schuster, 1934.

———. "Old Lamps for New Ones." *The Amusements of the People and Other Papers: Reports, Essays and Reviews, 1834–51*. Edited by Michael Slater. Columbus: Ohio State University Press, 1996. 242–48.

———. *The Oxford Illustrated Dickens*. 21 vols. Oxford: Oxford University Press, 1989.

——. *The Uncommercial Traveller and Other Papers, 1859–1870.* Edited by Michael Slater and John Drew. Columbus: Ohio State University Press, 2000.

Dictionary of Mining, Mineral, and Related Terms. U.S. Bureau of Mines. http://imcg.wr.usgs.gov/dmmrt/.

Dillard, Annie, "Living Like Weasels." *Teaching a Stone to Talk.* New York: Harpercollins, 1982. 11–16.

Dobson, James. Radio Interviews with Columbine murder witnesses, *Focus on the Family,* May 5 and 15, 1999.

Dodd, Philip, ed. *Walter Pater: An Imaginative Sense of Fact.* London: Frank Cass, 1981.

Donaldson, Sandra, ed. *Critical Essays on Elizabeth Barrett Browning.* New York: G. K. Hall & Co., 1999.

Dowling, Linda. *Language and Decadence in the Victorian fin de siecle.* New Jersey: Princeton University Press, 1986.

Duffy, Eamon. *Saints and Sinners: A History of the Popes.* New Haven: Yale University Press, 1997.

Eagleton, Terry. *After Theory.* New York: Basic Books, 2003.

Efrati, Carol. "A. E. Housman's Use of Biblical Narrative." In *A. E. Housman: A Reassessment.* Edited by Alan W. Holden and J. Roy Birch. New York: Macmillan, 2000. 188–209.

Eliot, George. *Adam Bede.* Oxford World's Classics. New York: Oxford University Press, 1996.

——. *The Mill on the Floss.* New York: W. W. Norton, 1994.

Eliot, T.S. *The Complete Poems and Plays, 1909–1950.* New York: Brace and Company, 1958.

——. "Tradition and the Individual Talent." In *Selected Prose of T. S. Eliot.* Edited by F. Kermode. New York: Harcourt, Brace, Jovanovich, 1975. 38.

Ellis, Ieuan. *Seven Against Christ: A Study of Essays and Reviews.* Leiden: E. J. Brill, 1980.

Encyclopaedia Britannica, 11th ed. (1910–11). s.v. Barthold Georg Niebuhr.

Engelhardt, Carol Marie. "The Paradigmatic Angel in the House: The Virgin Mary and Victorian Anglicans." In *Women of Faith in Victorian Culture: Reassessing the Angel in the House.* Edited by Anne Hogan and Andrew Bradstock. New York: St. Martin's Press, 1998. 159–71.

Essays and Reviews: The 1860 Text and Its Reading. Edited by Victor Shea and William Whitla. Charlottesville: University Press of Virginia, 2000.

Farrar, Frederic W. *History of Interpretation.* Bampton Lectures. New York: E. P. Dutton, 1886.

Faulkenberg, Marilyn. *Church, City and Labyrinth in Brontë, Dickens, Hardy and Butor.* New York: Peter Lang, 1993.

Fellows, Jay. *Tombs, Despoiled and Haunted: "Under-Textures" and "After-Thoughts" in Walter Pater.* Stanford: Stanford University Press, 1991.

Ferriera, M. Jamie. "The Grammar of the Heart." In *Discourse and Context: An Interdisciplinary Study of John Henry Newman.* Edited by Gerard McGill. Carbondale: Southern Illinois University Press, 1993. 129–43.

Fleishman, Avrom. *Figures of Autobiography: The Language of Self-Writing.* Berkeley: University of California Press, 1983.

Fiumara, Gemma Corradi. *The Other Side of Language: A Philosophy of Listening.* Translated by Charles Lambert. London: Routledge, 1990.

Forster, Margaret. *Elizabeth Barrett Browning: A Biography.* London: Vintage, 1998.

Foucault, Michel. *The Archaeology of Knowledge.* New York: Pantheon, 1972.

Foucault, Michel. *Discipline and Punish: The Birth of the Prison*. Translated by
    Alan Sheridan. New York: Vintage Books, 1979.
——. *The Foucault Reader*. Edited by Paul Rabinow. New York: Pantheon Books, 1984.
——. *The History of Sexuality. Volume 1: An Introduction*. Translated by Robert
    Hurley. New York: Vintage Books, 1990.
——. *The History of Sexuality. Volume 2: The Use of Pleasure*. Translated by Robert
    Hurley. New York: Vintage Books, 1985.
——. *The History of Sexuality. Volume 3: The Care of the Self*. Translated by Robert
    Hurley. New York: Vintage Books, 1988.
——. *The Order of Things*. New York: Vintage, 1994.
——. "What Is an Author?" *Bulletin de la Societe Francaise de Philosophie*. 1969.
    Reprint. In *The Critical Tradition: Classic Texts and Contemporary Trends*. Edited
    by David H. Richter. 2nd ed. Boston: Bedford/St. Martin's, 1998. 890–900.
Frank, Lawrence. "*Pictures from Italy:* Dickens, Rome, and the Eternal City of the
    Mind." *Il Confronto Letterario* (Padua, Italy) 14, no. 2 (1997): 239–55.
Freed, Mark M. "The Moral Irrelevance of Dogma: Mary Ward and Critical Theology
    in England." In *Women's Theology in Nineteenth-Century Britain: Transfiguring the
    Faith of Their Fathers*. Edited Julie Melnyk. New York: Garland, 1998. 133–47.
Frei, Hans W. *The Eclipse of Biblical Narrative: A Study in Eighteenth and Nineteenth
    Century Hermeneutics*. New Haven: Yale University Press, 1974.
Frye, Northrop. *Anatomy of Criticism: Four Essays*. New Jersey: Princeton University
    Press, 1957; New York: Athenaeum, 1969.
Gabler, Neal. "This Time the Scene Was Real." *New York Times*, September 16,
    2001, sec. 4.2.
Geldart, Martin. *A Son of Belial: Autobiographical Sketches*. London: Trubner & Co.,
    1882.
——. [Nitram Tradleg]. *A Son of Belial: Autobiographical Sketches*. 1882. Ann Arbor:
    UMI, 1990.
Gibbs, Nancy. "In Sorrow and Disbelief." *Time Magazine, Online*.
    May 2, 1999. http://www.time.com/time/archive/preview/from_newsfile/
    0,10987, 1101990503-23541,00.html.
Gibson, Mary Ellis, ed. *Critical Essays on Robert Browning*. New York: G. K. Hall, 1992.
Gill, Sean. "Ecce Homo: Representations of Christ as the Model of Masculinity in
    Victorian Art and Lives of Jesus." In *Masculinity and Spirituality in Victorian
    Culture*. Edited by Andrew Bradstock, Sean Gill, Anne Hogan, and Sue Morgan.
    London: Macmillan, 2000. 164–78.
Gilley, Sheridan. "Roman Catholicism." In *Nineteenth-Century English Religious
    Traditions: Retrospect and Prospect*. Edited by D. G. Paz. Westport, Connecticut:
    Greenwood Press, 1995. 33–56.
*The Girl's Own Text Book. Containing a Text from the Old and New Testaments for Every
    Morning and Evening in the Year*. Selected by a Lady. London: J. F. Shaw, 1858.
Gladstone, William. " 'Robert Elsmere' and the Battle of Belief." *The Nineteenth
    Century* 23 (May 1888): 766–88.
——. "The Vatican Decrees in Their Bearing on Civil Allegiance: A Political
    Expostulation." In *Newman and Gladstone: The Vatican Decrees*. Edited by Alvan
    S. Ryan. Notre Dame, Indiana: University of Notre Dame Press, 1962. 5–72.
Gleig, G. R. "The Great Problem: Can it be Solved?" *Blackwood's Edinburgh
    Magazine* 117 (January 1875): 132–44.
Graef, Hilda C. *Mary: A History of Doctrine and Devotion*. Vol. 2. New York: Sheed
    and Ward, 1965.
Hair, Donald. *Robert Browning's Language*. Toronto: University of Toronto Press, 1999.

Haley, Bruce. *The Healthy Body and Victorian Culture.* Cambridge, Massachusetts: Harvard University Press, 1978.

Hall, Donald E., ed. *Muscular Christianity: Embodying the Victorian Age.* New York: Cambridge University Press, 1994.

——. "Muscular Christianity: Reading and Writing the Male Social Body." In *Muscular Christianity: Embodying the Victorian Age.* Edited by Donald E. Hall. New York: Cambridge University Press, 1994. 3–13.

Hall, Michael. "What Do Victorian Churches Mean? Symbolism and Sacramentalism in Anglican Church Architecture, 1850–1870." *Journal of the Society of Architectural Historians* 59, no. 1 (2000): 78–95.

Hanson, Ellis. *Decadence and Catholicism.* Cambridge, Massachusetts: Harvard University Press, 1997.

Hardy, Thomas. *Far from the Madding Crowd.* New York: W. W. Norton, 1986.

——. *Jude the Obscure.* New York: Signet, 1961.

——. *Jude the Obscure.* New York: W. W. Norton, 1978.

Harris, Wilson. *Jonestown.* London: Faber and Faber, 1996.

Harrison, Antony H. *Victorian Poets and Romantic Poems: Intertextuality and Ideology.* Charlottesville: University Press of Virginia, 1990.

Hartman, Geoffrey H. *Saving the Text: Literature/Derrida/Philosophy.* Baltimore: Johns Hopkins University Press, 1981.

Hassett, Constance W. *The Elusive Self in the Poetry of Robert Browning.* Athens: Ohio University Press, 1982.

Havens, Raymond Dexter. *The Influence of Milton on English Poetry.* 1922. New York: Russell & Russell, 1961.

Hayter, Alethea. *Mrs. Browning. A Poet's Work and Its Setting.* London: Faber and Faber, 1962.

Helmstadter, Richard J. "Orthodox Nonconformity." In *Nineteenth-Century English Religious Traditions: Retrospect and Prospect.* Edited by D. G. Paz. Westport, Connecticut: Greenwood Press, 1995. 57–84.

Helsinger, Elizabeth K., Robin Lauterbach Sheets, and William Veeder, eds. *The Woman Question in Society and Literature in Britain and America, 1837–1883.* Social Issues. Vol. 2. Chicago: University of Chicago Press, 1983.

Hempton, David. *Religion and Political Culture in Britain and Ireland: From the Glorious Revolution to the Decline of Empire.* New York: Cambridge University Press, 1996.

Henderson, Heather. *The Victorian Self: Autobiography and Biblical Narrative.* Ithaca: Cornell University Press, 1989.

Herbert, Christopher. *Victorian Relativity: Radical Thought and Scientific Discovery.* Chicago: University Press of Chicago, 2001.

Higgins, Lesley. "But who is 'she'?: Female subjectivity in Pater's Writings," *Nineteenth-Century Prose* 24, no. 2 (1997): 37–65.

Hinchliff, Peter. *Frederick Temple: Archbishop of Canterbury.* Oxford: Clarendon Press, 1998.

——. *God and History: Aspects of British Theology, 1875–1914.* Oxford: Clarendon Press, 1992.

Hobhouse, Hermione. *Lost London: A Century of Demolition and Decay.* London: Macmillan, 1971.

Hogan, Anne and Andrew Bradstock, eds. *Women of Faith in Victorian Culture.* New York: St. Martin's Press, 1998.

Hollis, Hilda. "Advice Not Taken: Attacking Hopkins' Dragon Through Stanza Sixteen." *Victorian Poetry* 36 (1998): 47–57.

Hopkins, Gerard Manley. *The Correspondence of Gerard Manley Hopkins and Richard Watson Dixon.* Edited by Claude Colleer Abbott. 2nd ed. London: Oxford University Press, 1970.

Hopkins, Gerard Manley. *The Journals and Papers of Gerard Manley Hopkins.* Edited by Humphry House and Graham Storey. London: Oxford University Press, 1959.

——. *Further Letters of Gerard Manley Hopkins Including His Correspondence with Coventry Patmore.* Edited by Claude Colleer Abbott. 2nd ed. London: Oxford University Press, 1970.

——. *The Letters of Gerard Manley Hopkins to Robert Bridges.* Edited by Claude Colleer Abbott. 2nd imp. London: Oxford University Press, 1970.

——. *The Poetical Works of Gerard Manley Hopkins.* Edited by Norman H. MacKenzie. Oxford: Clarendon Press, 1990.

——. *The Sermons and Devotional Writings of Gerard Manley Hopkins.* Edited by Christopher Devlin. London: Oxford University Press, 1959.

Houghton, Walter. *The Victorian Frame of Mind, 1830–1870.* New Haven: Yale University Press, 1957.

House, Humphrey. *The Dickens World.* 2nd ed. London: Oxford University Press, 1965.

Hughes, Thomas. *The Manliness of Christ.* Philadelphia: Henry Altemus, n.d.

Huxley, Thomas. *Science and Culture.* New York: D. Appleton, 1888.

Inge, W. R. *Christian Mysticism.* 4th ed. London: Metheun, 1918.

Iser, Wolfgang. *Walter Pater: The Aesthetic Moment.* 1960. Translated by David Henry Wilson. Cambridge: Cambridge University Press, 1987.

Jackson, Arlene. "Agnes Wickfield and the Church Motif in *David Copperfield.*" *Dickens Studies Annual* 9 (1981): 53–65.

Jakobson, Roman and Grete Lübbe-Grothues. "The Language of Schizophrenia: Hölderlin's Speech and Poetry." In *Verbal Art, Verbal Sign, Verbal Time.* Translated by Susan Kitron. Edited by Krystyna Pomorska and Stephen Rudy. Minneapolis: University of Minnesota Press, 1985. 133–40.

Jameson, Fredric. *The Political Unconscious: Narrative as a Socially Symbolic Act.* Ithaca: Cornell University Press, 1981.

Jauss, Hans Robert. *Toward an Aesthetic of Reception.* Translated by T. Bahti. Minneapolis: University of Minnesota Press, 1982.

Jenkins, Ruth Y. *Reclaiming Myths of Power: Women Writers and the Victorian Spiritual Crisis.* Lewisburg, Pennsylvania: Bucknell University Press, 1995.

Jennings, Peter. Interview with Mrs. Schnerr, mother of surviving Columbine Massacre victim Val Schnerr, *ABC Evening News*, April 28, 1999.

"Jesuits." *The Encyclopaedia Britannica.* 9th ed.

Johnson, Margaret. *Gerard Manley Hopkins and Tractarian Poetry.* Aldershot: Ashgate, 1997.

Jowett, Benjamin. "Darwinism, and Faith in God." In *Sermons on Faith and Doctrine.* Edited by W. H. Fremantle. London: John Murray, 1901. 1–22.

——. *Dear Miss Nightingale: A Selection of Benjamin Jowett's Letters to Florence Nightingale, 1860–1893.* Edited by Vincent Quinn and John Prest. Oxford: Clarendon Press, 1987.

Joyce, G. H. "The Church." *The Catholic Encyclopedia.* 1908. On-line ed. 1999. August 6, 1999. http://www.newadvent.org/cathen/03744a.htm.

Keble, John. Keble's Lectures on Poetry. Translated by E. Francis. 2 vols. Oxford: Clarendon Press, 1912. 2: 481.

Keefe, Robert and Janice Keefe. *Walter Pater and the Gods of Disorder.* Athens: Ohio University Press, 1990.

Kent, John. "A Renovation of Images: Nineteenth-Century Protestant 'Lives of Jesus' and Roman Catholic Alleged Appearances of the Blessed Virgin Mary." In *The Critical Spirit and the Will to Believe: Essays in Nineteenth-Century Literature and Religion*. Edited by David Jasper and T. R. Wright. New York: St. Martin's Press, 1989. 37–51.

Ker, Ian. *John Henry Newman, A Biography*. Oxford: Oxford University Press, 1988.

Kermode, Frank. *The Sense of an Ending: Studies in the Theory of Fiction*. London: Oxford University Press, 1967.

Kingsley, Charles. *The Gospel of the Pentateuch: A Set of Parish Sermons; and David, Five Sermons*. London: Macmillan, 1881.

Kirch, K. "Vatican Council." *The Catholic Encyclopedia*. 1912. On-line ed. 1999. August 8, 1999. http://www.newadvent.org/cathen/15303a.htm.

Knoepflmacher, U. C. *Religious Humanism and the Victorian Novel: George Eliot, Walter Pater, and Samuel Butler*. New Jersey: Princeton University Press, 1965.

Kontje, Todd. *The German Bildungsroman: History of a National Genre*. Columbia, South Carolina: Camden House, 1993.

Kramer, Lawrence. *Music and Poetry: The Nineteenth Century and After*. Berkeley: University of California Press, 1984.

Krueger, Christine L. *The Reader's Repentance: Women Preachers, Women Writers, and Nineteenth-Century Social Discourse*. Chicago: The University of Chicago Press, 1992.

Lafourcade, Georges. *La Jeunesse de Swinburne*. 2 vols. Paris, 1928.

Landow, George P, ed. *Approaches to Victorian Autobiography*. Athens: Ohio University Press, 1979.

——. *Victorian Types Victorian Shadows: Biblical Typology in Victorian Literature, Art, and Thought*. Boston: Routledge, 1980.

——. *William Holman Hunt and Typological Symbolism*. New Haven: Yale University Press, 1979.

Lansbury, Bertha. "Agnosticism and Women." *The Nineteenth Century* 7 [April 1880]: 619–27.

Larkin, Philip. "Church Going." In *Collected Poems*. London: Marvell and Faber and Faber, 1988. 97.

Larson, Janet L. *Dickens and the Broken Scripture*. Athens: University of Georgia Press, 1985.

——. "Where Is the Woman in This Text? Frances Power Cobbe's Voices in *Broken Lights*." *Victorian Literature and Culture* 31 (2003): 99–129.

Leighton, Angela. *Elizabeth Barrett Browning*. Bloomington: Indiana University Press, 1986.

Lessing, Gotthold. *Gesammelte Werke*. 2 vols. Munich: Carl Hanser, 1959.

Leavis, F. R. and Q. D. Leavis. *Dickens: The Novelist*. London: Chatto & Windus, 1970.

Levine, George, ed. *Darwin and the Novelists: Patterns of Science in Victorian Fiction*. Chicago: The University of Chicago Press, 1991.

——. "Matthew Arnold's Science of Religion: The Uses of Imprecision." *Victorian Poetry* 26 (1988): 143–83.

——. *One Culture: Essays in Science and Literature*. Madison: The University of Wisconsin Press, 1987.

Lewis, Linda M. *Elizabeth Barrett Browning's Spiritual Progress. Face to Face with God*. Columbia: University of Missouri Press, 1998.

Lewis, Sarah. *Woman's Mission and Woman's Influence*. 1839. 10th ed. New York: International Book Co., n.d.

Lightman, Bernard ed. *Victorian Science in Context.* Chicago: The University Press of Chicago, 1997.

Lineham, Peter J. "The Protestant 'Sects.' " In *Nineteenth-Century English Religious Traditions: Retrospect and Prospect.* Edited by D. G. Paz. Westport, Connecticut: Greenwood Press, 1995. 143–70.

Litzinger, Boyd and Donald Smalley, eds. *Browning: The Critical Heritage.* New York: Barnes & Noble, 1970.

Louis, Margot K. *Swinburne and His Gods: The Roots and Growth of an Agnostic Poetry.* Montreal: McGill-Queen's University Press, 1990.

MacKay, Carol Hanbery. "The Multiple Deconversions of Annie Wood Besant." In *Creative Negativity: Four Victorian Exemplars of the Female Quest.* Edited by Carol Hanbery MacKay. Stanford: Stanford University Press, 2001. 96–134.

Maitland, Brownlow. "False Coin in Sacred Hermeneutics." *Blackwood's Edinburgh Magazine* 132 (November 1882): 559–73.

Mandler, Peter. " 'The Wand of Fancy': The Historical Imagination of the Victorian Tourist." In *Material Memories.* Edited by Marius Kwint, Christopher Breward, and Jeremy Asynsley. New York: Berg, 1999. 125–41.

Manning, Henry Edward. "Archbishop Manning on the Temporal Power." *The Temporal Power of the Pope in Its Political Aspect.* 1866. *Anti-Catholicism in Victorian England.* Edited by E. R. Norman. New York: Barnes, 1968. 186–93.

Marcus, Steven. *Dickens: From Pickwick to Dombey.* New York: Basic Books, 1965.

Mariani, Paul L. *A Commentary on the Complete Poems of Gerard Manley Hopkins.* Ithaca: Cornell University Press, 1970.

——. "The New Aestheticism: A Reading of 'Andromeda.' " In *A Usable Past: Essays on Modern and Contemporary Poetry.* Amherst: University of Massachusetts Press, 1984. 107–22.

Marsh, Joss Lutz. "Imagining Victorian London: An Entertainment and Itinerary (Chas. Dickens, Guide)." *Stanford Humanities Review* 3, no. 1 (1993): 67–97.

——. *Word Crimes: Blasphemy, Culture, and Literature in Nineteenth-Century England.* Chicago: The University of Chicago Press, 1998.

Martin, Robert Bernard. *Gerard Manley Hopkins: A Very Private Life.* New York: Putnam's, 1991.

Maurice, Frederick Denison. *Claims of the Bible and Science.* London: Macmillan, 1863.

Maynard, John. "Speaker, Listener, and Overhearer: The Reader in the Dramatic Poem." *Browning Institute Studies* 15 (1987): 105–12.

——. *Victorian Discourses on Sexuality and Religion.* New York: Cambridge University Press, 1993.

Mazza, Ernico. *The Celebration of the Eucharist: The Origin of the Rite and the Development of Its Interpretation.* Trans. Matthew J. O'Connell. Collegeville, Minnesota: The Liturgical Press, 1999. 236.

Mazzaro, Jerome. "Mapping Sublimity: Elizabeth Barrett Browning's *Sonnets from the Portuguese.*" In *Critical Essays on Elizabeth Barrett Browning.* Edited by Sandra Donaldson. New York: G. K. Hall & Co., 1999. 291–305.

McCloskey, John C. "The Apostolate of Personal Influence in the Work of Cardinal Newman." http://www.catholicity.com/cathedral/mccloskey/newman.html.

McGann, Jerome J. *The Beauty of Inflections: Literary Investigations in Historical Method and Theory.* Oxford: Clarendon Press, 1985.

——. *Swinburne: An Experiment in Criticism*. Chicago: University of Chicago Press, 1972.

McKee, Alexander. *The Golden Wreck: The True Story of a Great Maritime Disaster*. London: Souvenir Press, 1961.

McKnight, Natalie. "Dickens's Philosophy of Fathering." *Dickens Quarterly* 18, no. 3 (2001): 129–38.

——. *Idiots, Madmen, and Other Prisoners in Dickens*. New York: St. Martins' Press, 1993.

Mermin, Dorothy. "Browning and the Primitive." In *Critical Essays on Robert Browning*. Edited by Mary Ellis Gibson. New York: G. K. Hall, 1992. 202–25.

——. *Elizabeth Barrett Browning. The Origins of a New Poetry*. Chicago: The University of Chicago Press, 1989.

——. *Godiva's Ride: Women of Letters in England, 1830–1880*. Bloomington: Indiana University Press, 1993.

Milbank, Alison. *Dante and the Victorians*. Manchester: Manchester University Press, 1998.

Miller, J. Hillis. *Charles Dickens: The World of His Novels*. Bloomington: Indiana University Press, 1958.

——. *The Disappearance of God: Five Nineteenth-Century Writers*. Cambridge, Massachusetts: Harvard University Press, 1981.

——. "The Fiction of Realism: *Sketches by Boz, Oliver Twist*, and Cruikshank's Illustrations." In *Dickens Centennial Essays*. Edited by Ada Nisbet and Blake Nevius. Berkeley: University of California Press, 1971. 85–153.

——. "Foreword." In Fellows, Jay. *Tombs, Despoiled and Haunted: "Under-Textures" and "After-Thoughts" in Walter Pater*. Stanford: Stanford University Press, 1991. xi–xix.

Milroy, James. *The Language of Gerard Manley Hopkins*. London: Andre Deutsch, 1977.

Milton, John. *Paradise Lost*. Edited by Scott Elledge. Norton Critical Edition. 2nd ed. New York: W. W. Norton, 1993.

Moberly, George. *Sermons on the Beatitude*. 3rd ed. Oxford: James Parker, 1870.

Monsman, Gerald C. "Introduction: On Reading Pater." In *Walter Pater: An Imaginative Sense of Fact*. Edited by Philip Dodd. London: Frank Cass, 1981. 1–11.

——. "Old Mortality at Oxford." *Studies in Philology* 67 (1970): 359–89.

——. "Pater, Hopkins, and Fichte's Ideal Student." *South Atlantic Quarterly* 70 (1971): 365–76.

Morgan, Thaïs E. "Is There an Intertext in This Text? Literary and Interdisciplinary Approaches to Intertextuality." *The American Journal of Semiotics* 3 (1985): 1–40.

——. "Victorian Sage Discourse and the Feminine: *An Introduction*." In *Victorian Sages and Cultural Discourse: Renegotiating Gender and Power*. Edited by Thaïs E. Morgan. New Brunswick: Rutgers University Press, 1990. 1–18.

——. "Violence, Creativity, and the Feminine: Poetics and Gender Politics in Swinburne and Hopkins." In *Gender and Discourse in Victorian Literature and Art*. Edited by Antony H. Harrison and Beverly Taylor. DeKalb: Northern Illinois University Press, 1992. 84–107.

Müller, Max. *Chips from a German Workshop. Vol. I: Essays on the Science of Religion*. New York: Charles Scribner's Sons, 1887.

——. *Chips from a German Workshop. Vol. II: Essays on Mythology, Traditions, and Customs*. New York: Charles Scribner's Sons, 1890.

Müller, Max. *Introduction to the Science of Religion: Four Lectures delivered at the Royal Institution in February and March 1870*. Varanasi: Bharata Manisha, 1972.

——. *Natural Religion: The Gifford Lectures, 1888*. London: Longmans, Green and Co., 1889.

Mumford, Louis. *The City in History: Its Origins, Its Transformations, Its Prospects*. New York: Harcourt, 1961.

Must We Burn Our Bibles? A Few Honest Words About the "Essays and Reviews"; Addressed to Honest People, by an Honest Man. Bristol: J. Wright, 1861.

Najarian, James. Rev. "Of *Decadence and Catholicism*, by Ellis Hanson." *Journal of Pre-Raphaelite Studies* 8 (1999): 106–10.

Newman, Francis W. *Discourse Against Hero-Making in Religion*. London: Trubner, 1864.

Newman, John Henry Cardinal. *Apologia pro Vita Sua*. Edited by Philip Hughes. Garden City, New York: Doubleday Image Books, 1956.

——. *Apologia Pro Vita Sua*. Edited by David J. DeLaura. New York: W. W. Norton, 1968.

——. *Callista, a Tale of the Third Century*. Edited by Alan G. Hill. Notre Dame: University of Notre Dame Press, 2000.

——. *Discussions and Arguments on Various Subjects*. New ed. London: Longmans Green & Co, 1891.

——. *Essay in Aid of a Grammar of Assent*. Notre Dame: University of Notre Dame Press, 1979.

——. *Historical Sketches*. Vol. II. Westminster, Maryland: Christian Classics, Inc, 1970.

——. "Ignorance of Evil." In *Parochial and Plain Sermons*. London: Longman, Green, 1891; San Francisco: Ignatius Press, 1997. 1714–21.

——. "A Legend of St. Gundleus." In *The Lives of the English Saints, Written by Various Hands at the Suggestion of John Henry Newman, Afterwards Cardinal*. Introduction by Arthur Wollaston Hutton. Vol. 3. London: Freemantle & Co., 1901. 5–12.

——. *Letters and Diaries of John Henry Newman*. Edited by Charles Stephen Dessain. Vol. 19. New York: Thomas Nelson, 1973.

——. *Loss and Gain*. Edited by Alan G. Hill. The World's Classics. Oxford: Oxford University Press, 1986.

——. *The Philosophical Notebooks*. Edited by Edward Sillem. Vol. 2. New York: Humanities Press, 1970.

——. *Plain and Parochial Sermons*. 8 vols. London: Rivington, 1875.

——. "Poetry, with Reference to Aristotle's *Poetics*." In *Essays and Sketches*. Vol. I. New York: Longmans Green & Co, 1948. 58–81.

——. *Sermons Preached on Various Occasions*. London: Burns & Lambert, 1862.

Nicholls, David. *Deity and Domination: Images of God and the State in the Nineteenth and Twentieth Centuries*. 1989. London: Routledge, 1994.

Nightingale, Florence. *Cassandra*. 1860. Old Westbury, New York: Feminist Press, 1979.

——. *"Cassandra" and Other Selections from "Suggestions for Thought."* 1860. Edited by Mary Poovey. New York: New York University Press, 1992.

Nimmo, Duncan. "Learning against Religion; Learning as Religion: Mark Pattison and the 'Victorian Crisis of Faith.'" In *Religion and Humanism*. Edited by Keith Robbins. Oxford: Basil Blackwell, 1981. 311–24.

Nixon, Jude V. *Gerard Manley Hopkins and His Contemporaries: Liddon, Newman, Darwin, and Pater*. New York: Garland, 1994.

——. " 'Kill[ing] Our Souls with Literalism': Reading *Essays and Reviews*." *Religion and the Arts* 5, nos. 1–2 (2001): 34–64.

——. " 'Return Alphias': The Carlyle/Forster Unpublished Letters and Re-tailoring the Sage." *Carlyle Studies Annual* 18 (1998): 83–122.

Norman, E. R. "Introduction." In *Anti-Catholicism in Victorian England*. New York: Barnes, 1968. 13–104.

Nuttall, A. D. *Dead From the Waist Down: Scholars and Scholarship in Literature and Popular Imagination*. New Haven: Yale University Press, 2003.

Ormond, Leonee. "Dickens and Painting: Contemporary Art." *Dickensian* 80, no. 1 (1984): 2–25.

Overholser, Renée Value. *Hopkins's Conversions: The Case of A. C. Swinburne*. Ann Arbor, Michigan: University Microfilms, 1996.

Palazzo, Lynda. *Christina Rossetti's Feminist Theology*. New York: Palgrave, 2002.

Pals, Daniel L. *The Victorian "Lives" of Jesus*. San Antonio: Trinity University Press, 1982.

Parker, David. "Our Pew at Church." *Dickensian* 88, no. 1 (1992): 40–42.

Pater, Walter. "The Aesthetic Life." bMS Eng 1150 (7). Houghton Library, Harvard University.

——. "Art and Religion." bMS Eng 1150 (11). Houghton Library, Harvard University.

——. "Coleridge's Writings." *Westminster Review* 85 (January 1866): 48–60.

——. "Corot." bMS Eng 1150 (25). Houghton Library, Harvard University.

——. "English Literature." bMS Eng 1150 (13). Houghton Library, Harvard University.

——. "The History of Philosophy." bMS Eng 1150 (3). Houghton Library, Harvard University.

——. *Marius the Epicurean*. London: Macmillan, 1910.

——. *Miscellaneous Studies*. London: Macmillan, 1910.

——. "Moral Philosophy." bMS Eng 1150 (17). Houghton Library, Harvard University.

——. *Plato and Platonism*. London: Macmillan, 1910.

——. "Plato's Ethics." bMS Eng 1150 (1). Houghton Library, Harvard University.

——. *The Renaissance: Studies in Art and Poetry*. Edited by Donald L. Hill. Berkeley: University of California Press, 1980.

——. "Thistle." bMS Eng 1150 (31). Houghton Library, Harvard University.

Paz, D. G. "Introduction." In *Nineteenth-Century English Religious Traditions: Retrospect and Prospect*. Westport, Connecticut: Greenwood Press, 1995. ix–xiv.

——. *Popular Anti-Catholicism in Mid-Victorian England*. California: Stanford University Press, 1992.

Pelikan, Jaroslav. "The Woman Clothed with the Sun"; "The Great Exception, Immaculately Conceived." In *Mary Through the Centuries: Her Place in the History of Culture*. New Haven: Yale University Press, 1996. 177–200.

Peterson, Linda H. *Traditions of Victorian Women's Autobiography: The Poetics and Politics of Life Writing*. Charlottesville: University Press of Virginia, 1999.

Pettit, Alexander. "Place, Time, and Parody in *The Ring and the Book*." *Victorian Poetry* 31 (1993): 95–106.

Phillips, Gary A. and Danna Nolan Fewell. "Ethics, Bible, Reading As If." *Semeia* 77 (1997): 1–22.

Plato. *Republic*. Translated by Robin Waterfield. Oxford: Oxford University Press, 1993.

Plotkin, Cary. *The Tenth Muse: Victorian Philology and the Genesis of the Poetic Language of Gerard Manley Hopkins*. Carbondale: Southern Illinois University Press, 1989.

Poland, Lynn M. *Literary Criticism and Biblical Hermeneutics: A Critique of Formalist Approaches*. Chico, California: Scholars Press, 1985.

Polhemus, Robert. "Comic and Erotic Faith Meet Faith in the Child: Charles Dickens's *The Old Curiosity Shop* ('That Old Cupiosity Shape')." In *Critical Reconstructions: The Relationship of Fiction and Life*. Edited by Robert M. Polhemus and Roger B. Henkle. Stanford: Stanford University Press, 1994. 71–89.

Pollock, Griselda. *Avant-Garde Gambits 1888–1893: Gender and the Colour of Art History*. London: Thames and Hudson, 1992.

Pope, Barbara Corrado. "Immaculate and Powerful: The Marian Revival in the Nineteenth Century." In *Immaculate and Powerful: The Female in Sacred Image and Social Reality*. Edited by Clarissa W. Atkinson, Constance H. Buchanan, and Margaret R. Miles. Boston: Beacon Press, 1985. 173–200.

Pope, Norris. *Dickens and Charity*. New York: Columbia University Press, 1978.

Prickett, Stephen. "Purging Christianity of Its Semitic Origins: Kingsley, Arnold and the Bible." In *Rethinking Victorian Culture*. Edited by Juliet John and Alice Jenkins. New York: St. Martin's Press, 2000. 63–79.

Pusey, Edward B. *Lectures on Types and Prophecies of the Old Testament*. MS. Pusey House, Oxford.

——. *Nine Sermons Preached Before the University of Oxford and Printed Chiefly between 1843–1855*, by the Rev. E. B. Pusey, D. D., Regius Professor of Hebrew and Canon of Christ Church. Oxford: James Parker and Co., 1879.

Qualls, Barry V. *The Secular Pilgrims of Victorian Fiction*. Cambridge: Cambridge University Press, 1982.

Quinn, Dermot. *Patronage and Piety: The Politics of English Roman Catholicism, 1850–1900*. Stanford: Stanford University Press, 1993.

Rabinow, Saul. "Introduction." In *The Foucault Reader*. Edited by Paul Rabinow. New York: Pantheon Books, 1984. 3–30.

Raymond, William O. *The Infinite Moment and Other Essays in Robert Browning*. Toronto: University of Toronto Press, 1965.

Ricoeur, Paul. "Philosophical Hermeneutics and Theological Hermeneutics." *Studies in Religion* 5, no. 1 (1975): 14–33.

Riede, David G. *Swinburne: A Study of Romantic Mythmaking*. Charlottesville: University Press of Virginia, 1978.

"Ritualism: *Hansard's Parliamentary Debates*." In *Religion in Victorian Britain*. Edited by Gerald Parson. Vol. 3. Manchester: Manchester University Press, 1988. 301–08.

Roberts, Gerald. "'England's Fame's Fond Lover'—The Toryism of Gerard Manly [*sic*] Hopkins." *Studies: An Irish Quarterly Review* 69 (1980): 129–36.

Rogerson, John. *Old Testament Criticism in the Nineteenth Century*. London: SPCK, 1984.

Rooksby, Rikky. *A. C. Swinburne: A Poet's Life*. Aldershot: Scholar Press, 1997.

Rosenberg, John, ed. "Introduction." In *Swinburne: Selected Poetry and Prose*. New York: Random, 1968. vi–xxxiv.

Rowell, Geoffrey. *Hell and the Victorians*. Oxford: Clarendon Press, 1974.

Rozmovits, Linda. *Shakespeare and the Politics of Culture in Late Victorian England*. Baltimore: The Johns Hopkins University Press, 1998.

Rudman, Harry W. *Italian Nationalism and English Letters: Figures of the Risorgimento and Victorian Men of Letters*. New York: Columbia University Press, 1940.

Ruskin, John. *Praeterita*. New York: Oxford University Press, 1989.

Ryals, Clyde de L. *The Life of Robert Browning: A Critical Biography*. Oxford: Blackwell, 1993.

Said, Edward W. *The World, the Text, and the Critic*. Cambridge, Massachusetts: Harvard University Press, 1983.

Sanders, Andrew. *Charles Dickens: Resurrectionist*. New York: St. Martin's Press, 1982.

Scheinberg, Cynthia. "Victorian Poetry and Religious Diversity." In *The Cambridge Companion to Victorian Poetry*. Edited by Joseph Bristow. New York: Cambridge University Press, 2000. 159–79.

——. *Women's Poetry and Religion in Victorian England: Jewish Identity and Christian Culture*. New York: Cambridge University Press, 2002.

Schneider, Elisabeth W. *The Dragon in the Gate: Studies in the Poetry of G. M. Hopkins*. Berkeley: University of California Press, 1968.

Schleiermacher, Friedrich. *Luke: A Critical Study*. [1825] Edited by Terrence N. Tice. Translated by Connop Thirlwall. Lewiston, Maine: Edwin Mellen Press, 1993.

Schweickart, Patrocinio P. "Reading Ourselves: Toward a Feminist Theory of Reading." In *Gender and Reading: Essays on Readers, Texts, and Contexts*. Edited by Elizabeth A. Flynn and Patrocinio P. Schweickart. Baltimore: The Johns Hopkins University Press, 1986. 31–62.

Schweik, Robert C. "Swinburne, Hopkins, and the Roots of Modernism." *University of Hartford Studies in Literature* 11 (1979): 157–72.

Scott, Robert. "The Jabbberwock, Traced to Its True Source, by Thomas Chatterton." *Macmillan's Magazine* 25 (February 1872): 337–38.

Shaffer, Elinor S. *"Kubla Khan" and the Fall of Jerusalem: The Mythological School in Biblical Criticism and Secular Literature 1770–1880*. Cambridge: Cambridge University Press, 1975.

Shewan, Alexander. *Homeric Games at an Ancient St Andrews: An Epyllium Edited From a Comparatively Modern Papyrus and Shattered by Means of the Higher Criticism*. Edinburgh: J. Thin, 1911.

Shires, Linda. "Fantasy, Nonsense, Parody, and the Status of the Real: The Example of Carroll." *Victorian Poetry* 26 (1988): 267–83.

Singleton, John. "The Virgin Mary and Religious Conflict in Victorian Britain." *JEH* 43 (1992): 16–34.

Slinn, E. Warwick. *Browning and the Fictions of Identity*. Totowa: Barnes & Noble, 1982.

Small, Ian. "Pater's Criticism: Some Distinctions." In *Walter Pater: An Imaginative Sense of Fact*. Edited by Philip Dodd. London: Frank Cass, 1981. 31–38.

Smith, William Hawley. *The New Hamlet: Intermixed and Interwoven with a Revised Version of Romeo and Juliet*. Chicago: Rand, McNally and Co., 1902.

Smith, William Henry. "M. Ernest Renan." *Blackwood's Edinburgh Magazine* 90 (November 1861): 626–39.

Solmi, Arrigo. *The Making of Modern Italy*. Port Washington, New York: Kennikat Press, 1970.

Stead, W. T. *Life of Mrs. Booth: The Founder of the Salvation Army*. New York: Fleming H. Revell, 1900.

Stein, Richard. "Street Figures: Victorian Urban Iconography." In *Victorian Literature and the Victorian Visual Imagination*. Edited by Carol T. Christ and John O. Jordan. Berkeley: University of California Press, 1995. 233–63.

Steiner, George. "Homer and the Scholars." In *Homer: A Collection of Critical Essays*. Edited by George Steiner and Robert Fagles. Englewood Cliffs, New Jersey: Prentice Hall, 1962. 1–18.

Stephenson, Glennis. *Elizabeth Barrett Browning and the Poetry of Love*. Ann Arbor: UMI Press, 1989.

Stevens, Wallace. *The Palm at the End of the Mind*. Edited by Holly Stevens. New York: Random House, Vintage, 1967.

Street, Sean. *The Wreck of the Deutschland*. London: Souvenir Press, 1992.

Stuart, T. McK. *Divine Inspiration vs. the Documentary Theory of the Higher Criticism*. Cincinnati: Jennings and Graham; New York: Eaton and Mains, 1904.

Sulloway, Alison G. *Gerard Manley Hopkins and the Victorian Temper*. New York: Columbia University Press, 1972.

Sussman, Herbert. *Victorian Masculinities: Manhood and Masculine Poetics in Early Victorian Literature and Art*. Cambridge: Cambridge University Press, 1995.

Swinburne, Algernon Charles. *The Collected Poems of Algernon Charles Swinburne*. 6 vols. London: Chatto and Windus, 1905.

——. *The Swinburne Letters*. Edited by Cecil Y. Lang. 6 vols. New Haven: Yale University Press, 1959.

Syllabus of Pius IX. 1862. August 15, 1999. http://listserv.american.edu/catholic/church/papal/piusix/p9syll.html.

Taylor, Dennis. "The Need for a Religious Literary Criticism." In *Seeing Into the Life of Things: Essays on Literature and Religious Experience*. Edited by John L. Mahoney. New York: Fordham University Press, 1998. 3–30.

Tennyson, George B. *Victorian Devotional Poetry: The Tractarian Mode*. Cambridge, Massachusetts: Harvard University Press, 1981.

Thackeray, William Makepeace. *The Letters and Private Papers of William Makepeace Thackeray*. Edited by Gordon N. Ray. Vol. 3. London: Oxford University Press, 1946.

Tierney, John J. "Melchisedech." In *The Catholic Encyclopedia*. 1911. On-line edition. 1999. August 6, 1999. http://www.newadvent.org/cathen/10156b.htm.

Tucker, Herbert F. *Browning's Beginnings: The Art of Disclosure*. Minneapolis: University of Minnesota Press, 1980.

——., ed. *A Companion to Victorian Literature and Culture*. Oxford: Blackwell, 1999.

——. "Dramatic Monologue and the Overhearing of Lyric." In *Lyric Poetry: Beyond New Criticism*. Edited by Chaviva Hošek and Patricia Parker. Ithaca: Cornell University Press, 1985. 226–43.

Turner, Frank M. *Contesting Cultural Authority: Essays in Victorian Intellectual Life*. New York: Cambridge University Press, 1993.

Tyndall, John. *Fragments of Science*. 2 vols. New York: P. F. Collier, 1900.

——. *Heat Considered as a Mode of Motion*. New York: D. Appleton, 1863.

Vance, Norman. *The Sinews of the Spirit: The Ideal of Christian Manliness in Victorian Literature and Religious Thought*. Cambridge: Cambridge University Press, 1985.

Vassall-Phillips, O. R. *After Fifty Years*. New York: Benziger Brothers, 1928.

Vattimo, Gianni. "The Trace of the Trace." In *Religion: Cultural Memory in the Present*. Edited by Jacques Derrida and Gianni Vattimo. California: Stanford University Press, 1998. 79–94.

Viswanathan, Gauri. *Outside the Fold: Conversion, Modernity, and Belief.* New Jersey: Princeton University Press, 1998.

Vlock, Deborah. *Dickens, Novel Reading, and the Victorian Popular Theatre.* Cambridge: Cambridge University Press, 1998.

Vlock-Keyes, Deborah. "Music and Dramatic Voice in Robert Browning and Robert Schumann." *Victorian Poetry* 29 (1991): 227–39.

"*Voyages Extraordinaries:* Dicken's 'Travelling Essays' and The Uncommercial Traveller," Parts 1, 2. *Dickens Quarterly* 13, nos. 2, 3 (June–September 1996): 76–96, 127–50.

Walder, Dennis. *Dickens and Religion.* London: George Allen and Unwin, 1981.

Walkowitz, Judith R. *City of Dreadful Delight: Narratives of Sexual Danger in Late-Victorian London.* Chicago: University of Chicago Press, 1992.

Ward, David. "Distorted Religion: Dickens, Dissent, and Bleak House." *Dickens Studies Annual* 29 (2000): 195–232.

Ward, Mary. "The New Reformation: A Dialogue." *The Nineteenth Century* 25 (1889): 454–80.

———. *Robert Elsmere.* Edited by Clyde De L. Ryals. 1888. Lincoln: University of Nebraska Press, 1967.

———. *Robert Elsmere.* Edited by Rosemary Ashton. 1888. Oxford World's Classics. New York: Oxford University Press, 1987.

———. *A Writer's Recollections.* 2 vols. New York: Harper Brothers, 1918.

Warner, Marina. *Alone of All Her Sex: The Myth and the Cult of the Virgin Mary.* New York: Knopf, 1976.

Webster's International Dictionary of the English Language. 2nd ed.

Welsh, Alexander. *The City of Dickens.* Cambridge, Massachusetts: Harvard University Press, 1986.

Wheeler, Michael. *Death and the Future Life in Victorian Literature and Theology.* New York: Cambridge University Press, 1990.

———. *Ruskin's God.* New York: Cambridge University Press, 1999.

White, Hayden. *Tropics of Discourse: Essays in Cultural Criticism.* Baltimore: The Johns Hopkins University Press, 1978.

White, Norman. *Hopkins: A Literary Biography.* Oxford: Clarendon Press, 1992.

Willey, Basil. "How 'Robert Elsmere' Struck Some Contemporaries." *Essays and Studies* 10 (1957): 53–68.

———. *More Nineteenth Century Studies.* New York: Columbia University Press, 1956.

Wilson, David Sloan. *Darwin's Cathedral: Evolution, Religion, and the Nature of Society.* Chicago: The University of Chicago Press, 2002.

Wolfreys, Julian. *Writing London: The Trace of the Urban Text from Blake to Dickens.* New York: St. Martin's Press, 1998.

Wollstonecraft, Mary. *A Vindication of the Rights of Woman.* Edited by Carol H. Poston. 2nd ed. 1892. New York: W. W. Norton, 1988.

"Women and Scepticism." [Anon.] *Fraser's Magazine* 68 (December 1863): 679–98.

Yetman, Michael G. "Giuseppe Caponsacchi: 'A Very Reputable Priest'?" *Baylor Browning Interests* 21 (1970): 5–24.

Zaniello, Tom. *Hopkins in the Age of Darwin.* Iowa City: University of Iowa Press, 1988.

Zemka, Sue. *Victorian Testaments: The Bible, Christology, and Literary Authority in Early-Nineteenth-Century British Culture.* California: Stanford University Press, 1997.

INDEX

Adam and Eve, 19, 88, 240, 241, 243–9
aestheticism, 189, 190–1, 195, 196,
    199–200, 202, 203, 242
agnosticism, 108–10
Aime-Martin, M.
    De l'Education des Meres de familles, 94
à Kempis, Thomas
    Imitation of Christ, The, 3, 4
Altholz, Josef L., 74
Ambrose, Isaac, 4
Anglicanism, 1, 2, 132, 178, 189
Anglo-Catholicism, 189
see also Puseyism; High-Church;
    Tractarianism; The Oxford Movement
apocalypse, 14, 27, 56, 138, 144, 149–50,
    152, 169, 189, 191
Aquinas, Thomas, 162
    Summa, 162–3
Armenianism, 237
Arnold, Matthew, 3, 4, 55, 81, 85, 105, 191
    "The Bishop and the Philosopher,"
        73–4
    "The Function of Criticism," 74, 99
    "The Literary Influence of Academies," 74
Arnold, Thomas, 78, 91, 94, 104
Athanasius, St., 180
Auerbach, Eric, 55, 63, 72
Austen, Jane, 179–80
autobiography, 4

Bachelaid, Gaston, 214
Bagehot, Walter, 217
Bailey, Suzanne, 14, 17, 117–29
Balliol College, 31–2, 53, 76, 80, 132
Barrett Browning, Elizabeth, 18–19, 75,
    235–52
    Literary Essays
    Basil, St., 180
    The Book of the Poets, 240
    The Greek Christian Poets, 240, 241–2,
        243, 251
    Thought on Thoughts, A, 240, 241
    Poetry
    Aurora Leigh, 7, 18, 237, 240

A Drama of Exile, 18–19, 237, 239,
    240–1, 243–9
Isobel's Child, 236
The Romaunt of Margret, 236
The Seraphim, and Other Poems, 19,
    236, 239
Sonnets from the Portuguese, 239
Baumgarten, Murray, 205–6
Bengough, J. W., 96, 117–18
    "The Higher Criticism," 90
Besant, Annie, 91
The Bible, 2, 5, 6, 7, 9, 10, 13, 29, 33, 56,
    58, 59, 61, 62, 63, 66, 68, 70–3, 83,
    85, 86, 89, 91, 92, 94, 99, 100, 106,
    107, 118–19, 182
    The Old Testament, 16, 34, 36, 40, 62,
        72, 100: Amos, 5; Chronicles, 2;
        Daniel, 2, 57, 88; Exodus, 2, 181;
        Genesis, 2, 58, 62–3, 240, 245, 246,
        249; Isaiah, 5, 58; Job, 2; Jonah, 2,
        3; Kings, 2, 37; Leviticus, 6;
        Proverbs, 159; Psalms, 2, 64; Ruth, 9;
        Samuel, 2
    The New Testament, 30, 40, 62, 220,
        238: Acts, 28, 36; I Corinthians, 37,
        163; Hebrews, 37; John, 29, 37, 41;
        Matthew, 4, 239; Revelation, 2;
        I Timothy, 103
The Bible Society, 10
Bildungsroman, 4
Bismarck, Otto von, 138–9, 150
Blair, Hugh, 29
Bloom, Harold, 29
Booth, Catherine, 85, 95, 96, 98, 99, 105
    "The Christs of the Nineteenth Century,"
        95–6
    "Conditions of Effectual Prayer," 96
    *Female Ministry: Woman's Right to Preach
        the Gospel*, 96
    "The Holy Ghost," 96
    "Notes of Three Addresses on Household
        Gods," 96
    Papers on Aggressive Christianity, 96
    Papers on Godliness, 96, 102

Booth, Catherine—*continued*
  Popular Christianity, 95
  *The Salvation Army in Relation to the
    Church and State*, 102
The Boy's Own Text Book, 88
Bradstock, Andrew, 13
Brecht, Bertolt
  Galileo 1, 51, 63
Broad Church, 31, 80, 94, 96, 98, 104
Brontë, Anne, 4
  Tenant of Wildfell Hall, 14
Brontë, Charlotte, 4, 13, 85, 91
  Jane Eyre, 1–2, 4
  Shirley, 5–6, 7, 15, 17, 103–5
Brontë, Emily, 4
  Wuthering Heights, 7
Browning, Robert, 3, 16, 17, 117–29,
    157–73
  "Christmas-Eve," 118, 120
  "A Death in the Desert," 120, 125
  "Development," 122–3
  "Easter-Day," 119, 120
  "Fifine at the Fair," 120
  "Fra Lippo Lippi," 74
  "Gold Hair," 120
  "The Heretic's Tragedy," 120
  "Jochanan Hakkadosh," 14, 125–6
  "Parleyings with Christopher Smart," 120
  The Ring and the Book, 15, 17–18, 120,
    157–73
Buchanan, Robert, 160
Buel, Oliver Prince
  The Abraham Lincoln Myth, 117, 120–1
Bump, Jerome, 16, 27–47
Bunsen, Baron von, 40, 42, 57–9, 78
Bunyan, John, 4, 10
  Life and Holy War, 5, 7, 10
  The Pilgrim's Progress, 1, 3, 4, 5, 7, 8,
    10, 19
Butler, Bishop Joseph, 56, 77
Butler, Josephine, 89, 91
Butler, Samuel
  The Way of all Flesh, 64–5, 79
Butor, Michael, 226
Byron, George Gordon Lord, 137

Calvinism, 62, 89, 236, 237, 250
Cameron, Nigel, 68, 70
Carey, John, 212, 227
Carlyle, Thomas, 4, 56, 71, 230
  Sartor Resartus, 53, 63, 65, 68–9, 79, 80
Carmichael, James
  How two Documents may be Found in One,
    121
Carpenter, Mary Wilson, 5, 14, 57

Chadwick, Owen, 67
Chrysostom, St., 180
Clapperton, J. H., 109–10
Clark, Kitson, 3
Clough, A. H., 13, 119, 137
Cobbe, Frances Power, 85, 90, 91, 107–8
  Broken Lights, 17, 83, 84–5, 96–7, 98, 99
  Dawning Lights, 17, 97–8
Cockshut, A. O. J., 64
Cole, Natalie Bell, 18, 205–34
Colenso, J. W.
  The Pentateuch Critically Examined, 73
Coleridge, Samuel Taylor, 34, 44, 61, 62,
    71, 74, 181, 190
  Aids to Reflection, 59, 66
  "Confessions of an Inquiring Spirit," 59
  The Stateman's Manual, 32–3
Colley, Linda, 1, 10, 131
Collins, Philip, 207
Congregationalism, 236, 237, 250
Cotsell, Michael, 206, 211
Craik, Dinah
  Olive, 7, 15
Culler, Jonathan, 11, 19
Cunningham, Valentine, 6

Dante, 2, 9, 53, 204, 224
Darwin, Charles, 6–7, 39, 59, 62, 71–3,
    75–6, 195
  The Origin of Species, 16, 51, 52, 64–5,
    75, 76, 79, 80, 89
Davidoff, Leonore, 208
deconstruction, 12
Defoe, Daniel
  The History of the Devil, 1
Denison, Archbishop, 42–3
De Quincey, Thomas, 122
Derrida, Jacques
  "Apocalyptic Tone," 152
  "Faith and Knowledge," 10
  "Tympan," 157
Dickens, Charles, 18, 177, 178, 205–34
  Bleak House, 216, 218, 219
  Christmas Stories, 223
  "City of the Absent," 211
  "City of London Churches," 207, 221,
    222, 223–6
  David Copperfield, 4, 206, 216–18, 219
  Dombey and Son, 211–15, 217, 227
  Great Expectations, 3, 221, 222, 223
  Hard Times, 223
  Life of Our Lord, 4, 206, 209, 211–15,
    227
  Little Doritt, 4, 216, 220
  Martin Chuzzlewit, 207

Master Humphrey's Clock, 219–20
Mystery of Edwin Drood, The, 220, 221, 224–5
Nicholas Nickleby, 223
Old Curiosity Shop, 209–10, 211, 215, 217, 218
Oliver Twist, 208–9
"On an Amateur Beat," 218–19
Our Mutual Friend, 210, 220, 223–4
Pickwick Papers, 212
"Shipwreck," 207, 226–8
Sketches by Boz, 222
Sunday under Three Heads, 208, 221
The Uncommercial Traveler, 18, 206, 211, 221, 222, 228
"Wapping Workhouse," 222
Dowling, Linda, 124
Drew, John, 206, 227
Duns Scotus, 36, 44
Dupras, Joe, 17–18, 157–73

Eagleton, Terry, 11, 74
Eisenman, Peter, 206
Eliot, George, 4, 12, 13, 125, 177, 178
  Adam Bede, 5, 6
  Middlemarch, 2, 4, 7, 21
  The Mill on the Floss, 2–3, 4–5, 15
  Romola, 4, 15, 20
Eliot, T. S.
  The Four Quartets, 69
  "Tradition and the Individual Talent," 38
Ellis, Ieuan, 52
Englishness, 1, 2
Essays and Reviews, 2, 14, 15, 16–17, 18, 31, 32, 40, 51–81, 84, 85, 90, 91, 206
eucharist, 34, 35, 36, 37–8, 41–3, 45, 48
evangelicalism, 4, 8, 31, 33, 100

Ferriera, M. Jamie, 176
Feuerbach, Ludwig, 4
FitzGerald, Edward
  The Rubáiyát of Omar Khayyám, 14–15
Foxe's Book of Martyrs, 7, 10
Foucault, Michel, 16, 192, 193, 217
  The Archaeology of Knowledge, 54, 73
  "Nietzsche, Genealogy, History," 192
  "What is an Author?" 90–1
Frye, Northrop, 13, 56
Fun
  "Old Boy," 123

Gaskell, Elizabeth, 4, 12, 13, 178
  Ruth, 15
Geldart, Martin
  Son of Belial, A, 31–2, 53, 76, 80

Gibson, Mary Ellis, 118
Gill, Sean, 228
The Girls' Own Text Book, 88–9
Gladstone, W. E., 53, 85, 105–6, 107, 132, 137, 145, 149
  Expostulation, 138
Gleig, G. R., 119, 124
Goodwin, C. W., 14
  "On the Mosaic Cosmogony," 62–5
Gregory of Nazianus, 238

Hall, Catherine, 208
Hall, Donald, 85
Hardy, Thomas, 13, 22, 177, 178
  Far From the Madding Crowd, 7–8, 9
  Jude the Obscure, 8–9, 32
Harris, Wilson
  Jonestown, 69
Hecht, Anthony
  "More Light," 176
Helmholtz, Hermann von, 56
Helmstadter, Richard, 1
Hemans, Felicia, 137
Hempton, David, 7–8, 221
Herbert, Christopher, 69, 74
Higgins, Lesley, 18, 189–204
High-Church, 9, 43, 132, 207, 222, 225
higher criticism, 4, 16, 51–81, 85, 91, 96, 103, 117–29, 181–3
Hillis-Miller, J., 8, 12, 14, 33–4, 197, 206–7, 221
Hinchliff, Peter, 55, 75–6
Hogan, Anne, 13
Holloway, John, 28
Homer, 53, 63, 72, 77, 78, 118, 119, 122, 128
homosexuality, 15, 151
Hooker, Richard, 2
  Ecclesiastical Polity, 36
Hopkins, Gerard Manley, 4, 15, 16, 17, 27–49, 131–53
  "Ad Mariam," 133, 134–5
  "Andromeda," 139
  "God's Grandeur," 43, 44
  "Hurrahing in Harvest," 30, 37, 38, 43, 44
  "Moonrise," 139
  "Penmaen Pool," 139
  "Rosa Mystica," 133, 135
  "The Starlight Night," 44, 63
  "The Woodlark," 139
  "The Wreck of the Deutschland," 135, 138–9, 140–5
Hopkins, Manley
  Hawaii, 39

House, Humphry, 207, 215
Hughes, Rev. Stephen, 227–8
Hughes, Thomas,
  The Manliness of Christ, 84, 110
  Tom Brown, 65, 84, 208
Hunt, Holman
  The Light of the World, 4, 15

The Incarnation, 42, 59, 133, 243, 248, 249
The Irish Question, 1, 73
Iser, Wolfgang, 194

Jackson, Arlene, 217
Jameson, Fredric, 54
Jauss, Hans Robert, 46
Jenkins, Ruth Y., 5, 13
Joule, James Precott, 56
Jowett, Benjamin, 14, 17, 31, 32, 52, 85,
    89, 99, 100–1, 191
  "Darwinism, and Faith in God," 80
  "On the Interpretation of Scripture," 54,
    55, 67–73
Joyce, G. H., 144
Judaism, 9, 14, 23, 58–9, 62–4, 78, 125–6,
  160, 201

Kant, Immanuel, 197
Keble, John, 9
  The Christian Year, 3, 10, 22, 32,
    38, 41
  Lectures on Poetry, 34–5
Kermode, Frank, 13–14
Kingsley, Charles, 13
  Yeast, 103
Knoepflmacher, U. C., 195, 198
Krueger, Christine, L., 12

Lacan, Jacques, 166
Landow, George
  Elegant Jeremiahs, 12
  Victorian Types Victorian Shadows, 12,
    30–1
  *William Holman Hunt and Typological
    Symbolism*, 15
Lansbury, Bertha, 108–9, 110
Larkin, Philip
  "Church Going," 205
Larson, Janet, 16–17, 18, 83–116, 206,
  210, 213
Leavis, F. R., 3
Leavis, Q. D., 3
Lessing, G. E., 200
  The Education of the Human Race, 56
Lewis, C. S.
  Surprised by Joy, 179

Lewis, Sarah
  Woman's Mission, 17, 85, 92–5
Liddon, Henry Parry, 32, 57
Lincoln, Abraham, 117, 120
Lineham, Peter, 14
Locke, John
  "The Reasonableness of Christianity," 66
Lutheranism, 62

Maitland, Brownlow, 123, 124
Mandler, Peter, 223
Manning, Archbishop Henry Edward, 132,
  136, 137
Marcus, Stephen, 15, 217
Marsh, Joss, 13, 206
Martineau, Harriet, 91
Mary, 15, 132, 133–5
Maurice, F. D., 84
Maynard, John, 13, 158
McKnight, Natalie, 214
Mermin, Dorothy, 1, 19, 53
metalepsis, 29–30
Methodism, 5, 89
Millais, John Everett
  Christ in the House of His Parents, 15, 206
Millbank, Alison, 240
Mill, John Stuart, 4
Milton, John, 7, 8, 139, 140
  "Lycidas," 162
  Paradise Lost, 4, 19, 76, 103
miracles, 60, 101, 169
Moberly, George, 52, 54, 55
Monophysite, 177
Montaigne, 197, 204
Morgan, Thaïs, E., 12, 14
Max Müller, Friedrich, 15, 16, 27–49, 199
  Chips from a German Workshop, 39–40,
    41, 52
  "Comparative Mythology," 39
  Introduction to the Science of Religion, 198
  Natural Religion, 44–5
  The Science of Language, 39
mythology, 39, 41, 43–4, 56, 63, 76,
  120–1, 134

Neri, St. Philip, 185
Newman, Francis, 85
  Discourse on Hero-Making, 97
Newman, John Henry Cardinal, 4, 18, 32,
  35, 38, 41, 55, 65, 77, 78, 103, 145,
  146, 149, 175–87, 195, 196–7, 200
  Apologia Pro Vita Sua, 9, 60, 75, 77, 175,
    177, 181, 182, 185
  Callista, 177–8, 184
  Discussions and Arguments, 183

Doctrine of Development, 197
"Dream of Gerontius," 22, 185
An Essay in Aid of a Grammar of Assent, 181, 197
"Ignorance of Evil," 175, 184, 186
Loss and Gain, 178–9
"Moses the Type of Christ," 30
Oxford University Sermons, 176, 184, 186
"Tract LXXIII," 92
Nietzsche, Frederich, 18, 56, 192
Nightingale, Florence, 13, 80, 85, 91, 98, 99, 101, 102–3
Cassandra, 17, 90, 100, 102, 106, 107
Suggestions for Thought, 17, 83, 90, 99–102
Nixon, Jude, V., 1–24, 51–81, 84, 150
Nuttall, A. D., 2

Old Mortality, 132
Oliphant, Margaret, 215–16
Overholser, Renée V., 15, 17, 131–53
The Oxford Movement, 31, 32, 33, 51, 53, 77, 78, 103

Palazzo, Lynda, 12
Papist, 1, 14
parables, 72–3
Pater, Walter, 4, 16, 189–204
"The Aesthetic Life," 18, 190, 191, 199–200, 201
"Art and Religion," 18, 190, 191–2, 195, 196, 200, 201
"Coleridge's Writings," 190, 193, 197, 198
"English Literature," 192
Gaston de Latour, 194, 195, 196, 198, 200
"The History of Philosophy," 18, 190, 192, 195–6
Marius the Epicurean, 189, 193, 194, 195, 198, 199, 200
Miscellaneous Studies, 190, 192, 194, 198, 199, 201
"Moral Philosophy," 18, 190, 193–4, 199
Plato and Platonism, 192, 198
The Renaissance, 189, 199
"Thistle," 18, 190, 200
"Writings of Cardinal Newman," 197
Patmore, Coventry, 13, 88, 89
Pattison, Mark, 21
"The Present State of Theology in Germany," 65
"Tendencies of Religious Thought in England," 65–7, 86–8, 90, 95
Pelagians, 236–7

Pirandello, Luigi
Six Characters in Search of an Author, 121
Plato, 101, 237, 242, 249, 252
Polhemus, Robert, 206–7, 209–10
Poor Richard's Almanac, 5
Powell, Baden, 14, 52, 56, 62
"On the Study of the Evidences of Christianity," 59–60
Pre-Raphaelites, 15, 28–9
Prickett, Stephen, 52
Protestantism, 1, 7, 10, 31, 45, 60, 62, 131, 179
Punch, 123–4
Pusey, E. B., 16, 27–49
"The Holy Eucharist a Comfort to the Penitent," 41–3
Lectures on Types and Prophecies of the Old Testament, 32–3, 34, 35–7, 38
Nine Sermons, 42
Puseyism, 31, 68, 104
see also Anglo-Catholicism; Tractarianism; The Oxford Movement

Qually, Barry V., 19

religious doubt, 61, 64–5, 66, 77, 86
see also agnosticism; skepticism
Renan, Ernest, 119, 124
Vie de Jesus, 84, 95, 97, 98
Ricoeur, Paul, 55–6, 59
Risorgimento, 132, 139, 150
ritualism, 32
Roman Catholicism, 1, 15, 17, 30, 31, 33, 34, 41, 42, 45, 131–53, 178–87, 202, 207
Romanticism, 71, 176, 206, 208, 215, 237
Rossetti, Christina, 3, 12
Rossetti, Dante Gabriel, 2
Rossetti, William, 29
Rozmovits, Linda, 53
Ruskin, John, 4, 13, 71

sacrament, 38, 178, 209, 226–7, 231
sage, 23
Saint *see under individual names*
Scheinberg, Cynthia, 3, 8, 14–15, 240
Schneider, Elizabeth W., 140
science, 21, 51–2, 59, 60, 61, 62, 63, 64, 79, 80, 182
Scott, Sir Walter, 102
Seeley, J. R.
Ecce Homo, 84, 98
Shaffer, Elinor S., 53
Shakespeare, William, 117, 121

skepticism, 92, 194, 195, 196
see also agnosticism; religious doubt
slavery, 70, 78, 107–8
Small, Ian, 201
Smith, William Henry, 17, 124
Southey, Caroline Bowles
   The Birth-Day, 8
Spinoza, Benedict de, 71, 73, 81, 125
Stanley, A. P., 54, 70
   Life of Arnold, 104
   Sinai and Palestine, 101
Steiner, George, 118
Stein, Richard, 219
Stephens, Frederic
   The Germ, 28–9
Stephenson, Glennis, 238
Strauss, D. F., 4, 95, 119, 125
   Das Leben Jesu, 118
Stuart, Rev. T. McK
   The Documentary Theory, 121
Swinburne, Algernon Charles, 4, 17, 131–53
   "Dolores," 134, 135
   "Hymn of Man," 139–40, 142
   "Hymn to Proserpine," 134
   Order on the Proclamation of the French Republic, 141, 142
   "Song of Italy, A," 141
   Songs Before Sunrise, 134, 139, 140, 141, 144
   Songs of Two Nations, 134
symbol, 32–3, 242
see also typology

Taylor, Dennis, 11
Taylor, Jeremy
   Holy Living and Dying, 1, 2, 5
Temple, Frederick, 52, 54–5, 60
   "The Education of the World," 14, 56–7, 84

Tennyson, Alfred Lord, 3
Tennyson, George, 13, 33, 35
Tractarianism, 9, 31, 33, 34, 35, 40, 41, 42, 44, 65, 79
Tracts for the Times, 7, 10, 66
Tucker, Herbert, 117, 158
Turner, Frank, 1, 3, 7
Tyndall, John, 62, 63
typology, 29–31, 33, 38, 40, 44
see also symbol

Ultramontane, 132
Unitarianism, 9, 18, 91, 206, 209
Ussher, Bishop James, 182

Vatican Council I, 132, 135–6, 137–40
Vattimo, Gianni, 5, 6, 16
Viswanathan, Gauri, 1, 13, 14

Walder, Dennis, 18, 206
Ward, Mary (Mrs. Humphry), 85
   Robert Elsmere, 9–10, 17, 65, 92, 105–6, 119
Watterman Ward, Bernadette, 18, 175–87
Welsh, Alexander, 224
Wheeler, Michael, 13
White, Hayden, 15
Willey, Basil, 67–8
Williams, Roland, 14, 42, 56, 60
   "Bunsen Biblical Researches," 40, 57–9
Wilson, David Sloan, 6
Wilson, Henry Bristow, 89, 111
   "The National Church," 6–62
Wolfreys, Julian, 215, 217
Wordsworth, William, 34
Wörn, Alexandra M. B., 18–19, 235–52

Zemka, Sue, 4, 53, 54, 57, 70, 74, 206, 211, 227